THE CAPTIVE

THE
CAPTIVE

Marcel Proust

TRANSLATED
FROM THE FRENCH BY
C. K. Scott Moncrieff

Vintage Books
A DIVISION OF RANDOM HOUSE
NEW YORK

TO
LUCY LUNN

CONTENTS

Part I

THE CAPTIVE

PART I

CHAPTER ONE

LIFE WITH ALBERTINE

AT daybreak, my face still turned to the wall, and before I had seen above the big inner curtains what tone the first streaks of light assumed, I could already tell what sort of day it was. The first sounds from the street had told me, according to whether they came to my ears dulled and distorted by the moisture of the atmosphere or quivering like arrows in the resonant and empty area of a spacious, crisply frozen, pure morning; as soon as I heard the rumble of the first tramcar, I could tell whether it was sodden with rain or setting forth into the blue. And perhaps these sounds had themselves been forestalled by some swifter and more pervasive emanation which, stealing into my slumber, diffused in it a melancholy that seemed to presage snow, or gave utterance (through the lips of a little person who occasionally reappeared there) to so many hymns to the glory of the sun that, having first of all begun to smile in my sleep, having prepared my eyes, behind their shut lids, to be dazzled, I awoke finally amid deafening strains of music. It was, moreover, principally from my bedroom that I took in the life of the outer world during this period. I know that Bloch reported that, when he called to see me in the evenings, he could hear the sound of conversation; as my mother was at Combray and he never found anybody in my room, he concluded that I was talking to myself. When, much later, he learned that Albertine had been staying with me at the time, and realised that I had concealed her presence from all my friends, he declared that he saw at last the reason why, during that episode in my life, I had always refused to go out of doors. He was wrong. His mistake was, however, quite pardonable, for the truth, even if it is inevitable, is not always conceivable as a whole. People who learn some accurate detail of another person's life at once deduce consequences which are not accurate, and see in the newly discovered fact an explanation of things that have no connexion with it whatsoever.

When I reflect now that my mistress had come, on our return from Balbec, to live in Paris under the same roof as myself, that she had abandoned the idea of going on a cruise, that she was installed in a bedroom within twenty paces of my own, at the end of the corridor, in my father's tapestried study, and that late every night, before leaving me, she used to slide her tongue between my lips like a portion of daily bread, a nourishing food that had the almost sacred character of all flesh upon which the sufferings that we have endured on its account have come in time to confer a sort of spiritual grace, what I at once call to mind in comparison is not the night that Captain de Borodino allowed me to spend in barracks, a favour which cured what was after all only a passing distemper, but the night on which my father sent Mamma to sleep in the little bed by the side of my own. So it is that life, if it is once again to deliver us from an anguish that has seemed inevitable, does so in conditions that are different, so diametrically opposed at times that it is almost an open sacrilege to assert the identity of the grace bestowed upon us.

When Albertine had heard from Françoise that, in the darkness of my still curtained room, I was not asleep, she had no scruple about making a noise as she took her bath, in her own dressing-room. Then, frequently, instead of waiting until later in the day, I would repair to a bathroom adjoining hers, which had a certain charm of its own. Time was, when a stage manager would spend hundreds of thousands of francs to begem with real emeralds the throne upon which a great actress would play the part of an empress. The Russian ballet has taught us that simple arrangements of light will create, if trained upon the right spot, jewels as gorgeous and more varied. This decoration, itself immaterial, is not so graceful, however, as that which, at eight o'clock in the morning, the sun substitutes for what we were accustomed to see when we did not arise before noon. The windows of our respective bathrooms, so that their occupants might not be visible from without, were not of clear glass but clouded with an artificial and old-fashioned kind of frost. All of a sudden, the sun would colour this drapery of glass, gild it, and discovering in myself an earlier young man whom habit had long concealed, would intoxicate me with memories, as though I were out in the open country gazing at a hedge of golden leaves in which even a bird was not lacking. For I could hear Albertine ceaselessly humming:

> For melancholy
> Is but folly,
> And he who heeds it is a fool.

I loved her so well that I could spare a joyous smile for her bad taste in music. This song had, as it happened, during the past summer, delighted Mme. Bontemps, who presently heard people say that it was silly, with the result that, instead of asking Albertine to sing it, when she had a party, she would substitute:

> A song of farewell rises from troubled springs,

which in its turn became 'an old jingle of Massenet's, the child is always dinning into our ears.'

A cloud passed, blotting out the sun; I saw extinguished and replaced by a grey monochrome the modest, screening foliage of the glass.

The partition that divided our two dressing-rooms (Albertine's, identical with my own, was a bathroom which Mamma, who had another at the other end of the flat, had never used for fear of disturbing my rest) was so slender that we could talk to each other as we washed in double privacy, carrying on a conversation that was interrupted only by the sound of the water, in that intimacy which, in hotels, is so often permitted by the smallness and proximity of the rooms, but which, in private houses in Paris, is so rare.

On other mornings, I would remain in bed, drowsing for as long as I chose, for orders had been given that no one was to enter my room until I had rung the bell, an act which, owing to the awkward position in which the electric bulb had been hung above my bed, took such a time that often, tired of feeling for it and glad to be left alone, I would lie back for some moments and almost fall asleep again. It was not that I was wholly indifferent to Albertine's presence in the house. Her separation from her girl friends had the effect of sparing my heart any fresh anguish. She kept it in a state of repose, in a semi-immobility which would help it to recover. But after all, this calm which my mistress was procuring for me was a release from suffering rather than a positive joy. Not that it did not permit me to taste many joys, from which too keen a grief had debarred me, but these joys, so far from my owing them to Albertine, in whom for that matter I could no longer see any beauty and who was beginning to bore me, with whom I was now clearly conscious that I was not in love, I tasted on the contrary when Albertine was not with me. And so, to begin the morning, I did not send for her at once, especially if it was a fine day. For some moments, knowing that he would make me happier than Albertine, I remained closeted with the little person inside me, hymning the rising sun, of whom I have already spoken. Of those elements which compose our personality, it is not the most obvious that are most essential. In myself, when ill health has succeeded in uprooting them one after another, there will still remain two or three, endowed with a hardier constitution than the rest, notably a certain philosopher who is happy only when he has discovered in two works of art, in two sensations, a common element. But the last of all, I have sometimes asked myself whether it would not be this little mannikin, very similar to another whom the optician at Combray used to set up in his shop window to forecast the weather, and who, doffing his hood when the sun shone, would put it on again if it was going to rain. This little mannikin, I know his egoism; I may be suffering from a choking fit which the mere threat of rain would calm; he pays no heed, and, at the first drops so impatiently awaited, losing his gaiety, sullenly pulls down his hood. Conversely, I dare say that in my last agony, when all my other 'selves' are dead, if a ray of sunshine steals into the room, while I am drawing my last breath, the little fellow of the barometer will feel a great relief, and will throw back his hood to sing: "Ah! Fine weather at last!"

I rang for Françoise. I opened the *Figaro*. I scanned its columns and made sure that it did not contain an article, or so-called article, which I had sent to the editor, and which was no more than a slightly revised version of the page that had recently come to light, written long ago in Dr. Percepied's carriage, as I gazed at the spires of Martinville. Then I read Mamma's letter. She felt it to be odd, in fact shocking, that a girl should be staying in the house alone with me. On the first day, at the moment of leaving Balbec, when she saw how wretched I was, and was distressed by the prospect of leaving me by myself, my mother had perhaps been glad when she heard that Albertine was travelling with us, and saw that, side by side with our own boxes (those boxes among which I had passed a night in tears in the Balbec hotel), there had been hoisted into the 'Twister' Albertine's boxes also, narrow and black, which had seemed to me to have the appearance of coffins, and as to which I knew not whether they were bringing to my house life or death. But I had never even asked myself the question, being all overjoyed, in the radiant morning, after the fear of having to remain at Balbec, that I was taking Albertine with me. But to this proposal, if at the start my mother had not been hostile (speaking kindly to my friend like a mother whose son has been seriously wounded and who is grateful to the young mistress who is nursing him with loving care), she had acquired hostility now that it had been too completely realised, and the girl was prolonging her sojourn in our house, and moreover in the absence of my parents. I cannot, however, say that my mother ever made this hostility apparent. As in the past, when she had ceased to dare to reproach me with my nervous instability, my laziness, now she felt a hesitation—which I perhaps did not altogether perceive at the moment or refused to perceive—to run the risk, by offering any criticism of the girl to whom I had told her that I intended to make an offer of marriage, of bringing a shadow into my life, making me in time to come less devoted to my wife, of sowing perhaps for a season when she herself would no longer be there, the seeds of remorse at having grieved her by marrying Albertine. Mamma preferred to seem to be approving a choice which she felt herself powerless to make me reconsider. But people who came in contact with her at this time have since told me that in addition to her grief at having lost her mother she had an air of constant preoccupation. This mental strife, this inward debate, had the effect of overheating my mother's brow, and she was always opening the windows to let in the fresh air. But she did not succeed in coming to any decision, for fear of influencing me in the wrong direction and so spoiling what she believed to be my happiness. She could not even bring herself to forbid me to keep Albertine for the time being in our house. She did not wish to appear more strict than Mme. Bontemps, who was the person principally concerned, and who saw no harm in the arrangement, which greatly surprised my mother. All the same, she regretted that she had been obliged to leave us together, by departing at that very time for Combray where she might have to remain (and did in fact remain) for months on end, during which my great-aunt required her incessant attention by day and night. Everything was made easy for her down there, thanks to the kindness, the devotion of Legrandin who, gladly undertaking any trouble that was required, kept putting off his return to Paris from week to week, not that he knew my aunt at all well, but simply, first of all, because she had been his mother's friend, and also because he knew that the invalid, condemned to die, valued his attentions and could not get on without him. Snobbishness is a serious malady of the spirit, but one that is localised and does not taint it as a whole. I, on the other hand, unlike Mamma, was extremely glad of her absence at Combray, but for which I should have been afraid (being unable to warn Albertine not to mention it) of her learning of the girl's friendship with Mlle. Vinteuil. This would have been to my mother an insurmountable obstacle, not merely to a marriage as to which she had, for that matter, begged me to say nothing definite as yet to Albertine, and the thought of which was becoming more and more intolerable to myself, but even to the latter's being allowed to stay for any length of time in the house. Apart from so grave a reason, which in this case did not apply, Mamma, under the dual influence of my grandmother's liberating and edifying example, according to whom, in her admiration of George Sand, virtue consisted in nobility of heart, and of my own corruption, was now indulgent towards women whose conduct she would have condemned in the past, or even now, had they been any of her own middle-class friends in Paris or at Combray, but whose lofty natures I extolled to her and to whom she pardoned much because of their affection for myself. But when all is said, and apart from any question of propriety, I doubt whether Albertine could have put up with Mamma who had acquired from Combray, from my aunt Léonie, from all her kindred, habits of punctuality and order of which my mistress had not the remotest conception.

She would never think of shutting a door and, on the other hand, would no more hesitate to enter a room if the door stood open than would a dog or a cat. Her somewhat disturbing charm was, in fact, that of taking the place in the household not so much of a girl as of a domestic animal which comes into a room, goes out, is to be found wherever one does not expect to find it and (in her case) would—bringing me a profound sense of repose—come and lie down on my bed by my side, make a place for herself from which she never stirred, without being in my way as a person would have been. She ended, however, by conforming to my hours of sleep, and not only never attempted to enter my room but would take care not to make a sound until I had rung my bell. It was Françoise who impressed these rules of conduct upon her.

She was one of those Combray servants, conscious of their master's place in the world, and that the least that they can do is to see that he is treated with all the respect to which they consider him entitled. When a stranger on leaving after a visit gave Françoise a gratuity to be shared with the kitchenmaid, he had barely slipped his coin into her hand before Françoise, with an equal display of speed, discretion and energy, had passed the word to the kitchenmaid who came forward to thank him, not in a whisper, but openly and aloud, as Françoise had told her that she must do. The parish priest of Combray was no genius, but he also knew what was due him. Under his instruction, the daughter of some

Protestant cousins of Mme. Sazerat had been received into the Church, and her family had been most grateful to him: it was a question of her marriage to a young nobleman of Méséglise. The young man's relatives wrote to inquire about her in a somewhat arrogant letter, in which they expressed their dislike of her Protestant origin. The Combray priest replied in such a tone that the Méséglise nobleman, crushed and prostrate, wrote a very different letter in which he begged as the most precious favour the award of the girl's hand in marriage.

Françoise deserved no special credit for making Albertine respect my slumbers. She was imbued with tradition. From her studied silence, or the peremptory response that she made to a proposal to enter my room, or to send in some message to me, which Albertine had expressed in all innocence, the latter realised with astonishment that she was now living in an alien world, where strange customs prevailed, governed by rules of conduct which one must never dream of infringing. She had already had a foreboding of this at Balbec, but, in Paris, made no attempt to resist, and would wait patiently every morning for the sound of my bell before venturing to make any noise.

The training that Françoise gave her was of value also to our old servant herself, for it gradually stilled the lamentations which, ever since our return from Balbec, she had not ceased to utter. For, just as we were boarding the tram, she remembered that she had forgotten to say good-bye to the housekeeper of the Hotel, a whiskered dame who looked after the bedroom floors, barely knew Françoise by sight, but had been comparatively civil to her. Françoise positively insisted upon getting out of the tram, going back to the Hotel, saying good-bye properly to the housekeeper, and not leaving for Paris until the following day. Common sense, coupled with my sudden horror of Balbec, restrained me from granting her this concession, but my refusal had infected her with a feverish distemper which the change of air had not sufficed to cure and which lingered on in Paris. For, according to Françoise's code, as it is illustrated in the carvings of Saint-André-des-Champs, to wish for the death of an enemy, even to inflict it is not forbidden, but it is a horrible sin not to do what is expected of you, not to return a civility, to refrain, like a regular churl, from saying good-bye to the housekeeper before leaving a hotel. Throughout the journey, the continually recurring memory of her not having taken leave of this woman had dyed Françoise's cheeks with a scarlet flush that was quite alarming. And if she refused to taste bite or sup until we reached Paris, it was perhaps because this memory heaped a 'regular load' upon her stomach (every class of society has a pathology of its own) even more than with the intention of punishing us.

Among the reasons which led Mamma to write me a daily letter, and a letter which never failed to include some quotation from Mme. de Sévigné, there was the memory of my grandmother. Mamma would write to me: "Mme. Sazerat gave us one of those little luncheons of which she possesses the secret and which, as your poor grandmother would have said, quoting Mme. de Sévigné, deprive us of solitude without affording us company." In one of my own earlier letters I was so inept as to write to Mamma: "By those quotations, your mother would recognise you at once." Which brought me, three days later, the reproof: "My poor boy, if it was only to speak to me of *my mother,* your reference to Mme. de Sévigné was most inappropriate. She would have answered you as she answered Mme. de Grignan: 'So she was nothing to you? I had supposed that you were related.'"

By this time, I could hear my mistress leaving or returning to her room. I rang the bell, for it was time now for Andrée to arrive with the chauffeur, Morel's friend, lent me by the Verdurins, to take Albertine out. I had spoken to the last-named of the remote possibility of our marriage; but I had never made her any formal promise; she herself, from discretion, when I said to her: "I can't tell, but it might perhaps be possible," had shaken her head with a melancholy sigh, as much as to say: "Oh, no, never," in other words: "I am too poor." And so, while I continued to say: "It is quite indefinite," when speaking of future projects, at the moment I was doing everything in my power to amuse her, to make life pleasant to her, with perhaps the unconscious design of thereby making her wish to marry me. She herself laughed at my lavish generosity. "Andrée's mother would be in a fine state if she saw me turn into a rich lady like herself, what she calls a lady who has her own 'horses, carriages, pictures.' What? Did I never tell you that she says that. Oh, she's a character! What surprises me is that she seems to think pictures just as important as horses and carriages." We shall see in due course that, notwithstanding the foolish ways of speaking that she had not outgrown, Albertine had developed to an astonishing extent, which left me unmoved, the intellectual superiority of a woman friend having always interested me so little that if I have ever complimented any of my friends upon her own, it was purely out of politeness. Alone, the curious genius of Céleste might perhaps appeal to me. In spite of myself, I would continue to smile for some moments, when, for instance, having discovered that Françoise was not in my room, she accosted me with: "Heavenly deity reclining on a bed!" "But why, Céleste," I would say, "why deity?" "Oh, if you suppose that you have anything in common with the mortals who make their pilgrimage on our vile earth, you are greatly mistaken!" "But why 'reclining' on a bed, can't you see that I'm lying in bed?" "You never lie. Who ever saw anybody lie like that? You have just alighted there. With your white pyjamas, and the way you twist your neck, you look for all the world like a dove."

Albertine, even in the discussion of the most trivial matters, expressed herself very differently from the little girl that she had been only a few years earlier at Balbec. She went so far as to declare, with regard to a political incident of which she disapproved: "I consider that ominous." And I am not sure that it was not about this time that she learned to say, when she meant that she felt a book to be written in a bad style: "It is interesting, but really, it might have been written *by a pig.*"

The rule that she must not enter my room until I had rung amused her greatly. As she had adopted our family habit of quotation, and in following it drew upon the plays in which she had acted at her convent and for which I had expressed admiration, she always compared me to Assuérus:

> And death is the reward of whoso dares
> To venture in his presence unawares. . . .
> None is exempt; nor is there any whom
> Or rank or sex can save from such a doom;
> Even I myself . . .
> Like all the rest, I by this law am bound;
> And, to address him, I must first be found
> By him, or he must call me to his side.

Physically, too, she had altered. Her blue, almond-shaped eyes, grown longer, had not kept their form; they were indeed of the same colour, but seemed to have passed into a liquid state. So much so that, when she shut them it was as though a pair of curtains had been drawn to shut out a view of the sea. It was no doubt this one of her features that I remembered most vividly each night after we had parted. For, on the contrary, every morning the ripple of her hair continued to give me the same surprise, as though it were some novelty that I had never seen before. And yet, above the smiling eyes of a girl, what could be more beautiful than that clustering coronet of black violets? The smile offers greater friendship; but the little gleaming tips of blossoming hair, more akin to the flesh, of which they seem to be a transposition into tiny waves, are more provocative of desire.

As soon as she entered my room, she sprang upon my bed and sometimes would expatiate upon my type of intellect, would vow in a transport of sincerity that she would sooner die than leave me: this was on mornings when I had shaved before sending for her. She was one of those women who can never distinguish the cause of their sensations. The pleasure that they derive from a smooth cheek they explain to themselves by the moral qualities of the man who seems to offer them a possibility of future happiness, which is capable, however, of diminishing and becoming less necessary the longer he refrains from shaving.

I inquired where she was thinking of going.

"I believe Andrée wants to take me to the Buttes-Chaumont; I have never been there."

Of course it was impossible for me to discern among so many other words whether beneath these a falsehood lay concealed. Besides, I could trust Andrée to tell me of all the places that she visited with Albertine.

At Balbec, when I felt that I was utterly tired of Albertine, I had made up my mind to say, untruthfully, to Andrée: "My little Andrée, if only I had met you again sooner! It is you that I would have loved. But now my heart is pledged in another quarter. All the same, we can see a great deal of each other, for my love for another is causing me great anxiety, and you will help me to find consolation." And lo, these identical lying words had become true within the space of three weeks. Perhaps, Andrée had believed in Paris that it was indeed a lie and that I was in love with her, as she would doubtless have believed at Balbec. For the truth is so variable for each of us, that other people have difficulty in recognising themselves in it. And as I knew that she would tell me everything that she and Albertine had done, I had asked her, and she had agreed to come and call for Albertine almost every day. In this way I might without anxiety remain at home.

Also, Andrée's privileged position as one of the girls of the little band gave me confidence that she would obtain everything that I might require from Albertine. Truly, I could have said to her now in all sincerity that she would be capable of setting my mind at rest.

At the same time, my choice of Andrée (who happened to be staying in Paris, having given up her plan of returning to Balbec) as guide and companion to my mistress was prompted by what Albertine had told me of the affection that her friend had felt for me at Balbec, at a time when, on the contrary, I had supposed that I was boring her; indeed, if I had known this at the time, it is perhaps with Andrée that I would have fallen in love.

"What, you never knew," said Albertine, "but we were always joking about it. Do you mean to say you never noticed how she used to copy all your ways of talking and arguing? When she had just been with you, it was too obvious. She had no need to tell us whether she had seen you. As soon as she joined us, we could tell at once. We used to look at one another, and laugh. She was like a coalheaver who tries to pretend that he isn't one. He is black all over. A miller has no need to say that he is a miller, you can see the flour all over his clothes; and the mark of the sacks he has carried on his shoulder. Andrée was just the same, she would knit her eyebrows the way you do, and stretch out her long neck, and I don't know what all. When I take up a book that has been in your room, even if I'm reading it out of doors, I can tell at once that it belongs to you because it still reeks of your beastly fumigations. It's only a trifle, still it's rather a nice trifle, don't you know. Whenever anybody spoke nicely about you, seemed to think a lot of you, Andrée was in ecstasies."

Notwithstanding all this, in case there might have been some secret plan made behind my back, I advised her to give up the Buttes-Chaumont for that day and to go instead to Saint-Cloud or somewhere else.

It was certainly not, as I was well aware, because I was the least bit in love with Albertine. Love is nothing more perhaps than the stimulation of those eddies which, in the wake of an emotion, stir the soul. Certain such eddies had indeed stirred my soul through and through when Albertine spoke to me at Balbec about Mlle. Vinteuil, but these were now stilled. I was no longer in love with Albertine, for I no longer felt anything of the suffering, now healed, which I had felt in the tram at Balbec, upon learning how Albertine had spent her girlhood, with visits perhaps to Montjouvain. All this, I had too long taken for granted, was healed. But, now and again, certain expressions used by Albertine made me suppose— why, I cannot say—that she must in the course of her life, short as it had been, have received declarations of affection, and have received them with

pleasure, that is to say with sensuality. Thus, she would say, in any connexion: "Is that true? Is it really true?" Certainly, if she had said, like an
Odette: "Is it really true, that thumping lie?" I should not have been
disturbed, for the absurdity of the formula would have explained itself
as a stupid inanity of feminine wit. But her questioning air: "Is that
true?" gave on the one hand the strange impression of a creature incapable of judging things by herself, who appeals to you for your testimony, as though she were not endowed with the same faculties as yourself
(if you said to her: "Why, we've been out for a whole hour," or "It is
raining," she would ask: "Is that true?"). Unfortunately, on the other
hand, this want of facility in judging external phenomena for herself
could not be the real origin of her "Is that true? Is it really true?" It
seemed rather that these words had been, from the dawn of her precocious
adolescence, replies to: "You know, I never saw anybody as pretty as
you." "You know I am madly in love with you, I am most terribly excited."
—affirmations that were answered, with a coquettishly consenting modesty, by these repetitions of: "Is that true? Is it really true?" which
no longer served Albertine, when in my company, save to reply by a question to some such affirmation as: "You have been asleep for more than
an hour." "Is that true?"

Without feeling that I was the least bit in the world in love with
Albertine, without including in the list of my pleasures the moments
that we spent together, I was still preoccupied with the way in which she
disposed of her time; had I not, indeed, fled from Balbec in order to make
certain that she could no longer meet this or that person with whom I was
so afraid of her misbehaving, simply as a joke (a joke at my expense, perhaps), that I had adroitly planned to sever, at one and the same time,
by my departure, all her dangerous entanglements? And Albertine was
so entirely passive, had so complete a faculty of forgetting things and
submitting to pressure, that these relations had indeed been severed and
I myself relieved of my haunting dread. But that dread is capable of assuming as many forms as the undefined evil that is its cause. So long
as my jealousy was not reincarnate in fresh people, I had enjoyed after the
passing of my anguish an interval of calm. But with a chronic malady,
the slightest pretext serves to revive it, as also with the vice of the person
who is the cause of our jealousy the slightest opportunity may serve her
to practise it anew (after a lull of chastity) with different people. I had
managed to separate Albertine from her accomplices, and, by so doing, to
exorcise my hallucinations; even if it was possible to make her forget
people, to cut short her attachments, her sensual inclination was, itself
also, chronic and was perhaps only waiting for an opportunity to afford
itself an outlet. Now Paris provided just as many opportunities as Balbec.

In any town whatsoever, she had no need to seek, for the evil existed not
in Albertine alone, but in others to whom any opportunity for enjoyment is good. A glance from one, understood at once by the other, brings
the two famished souls in contact. And it is easy for a clever woman to
appear not to have seen, then five minutes later to join the person who
has read her glance and is waiting for her in a side street, and, in a few

words, to make an appointment. Who will ever know? And it was so simple for Albertine to tell me, in order that she might continue these practices, that she was anxious to see again some place on the outskirts of Paris that she had liked. And so it was enough that she should return later than usual, that her expedition should have taken an unaccountable time, although it was perfectly easy perhaps to account for it without introducing any sensual reason, for my malady to break out afresh, attached this time to mental pictures which were not of Balbec, and which I would set to work, as with their predecessors, to destroy, as though the destruction of an ephemeral cause could put an end to a congenital malady. I did not take into account the fact that in these acts of destruction, in which I had as an accomplice, in Albertine, her faculty of changing, her ability to forget, almost to hate the recent object of her love, I was sometimes causing a profound grief to one or other of those persons unknown with whom in turn she had taken her pleasure, and that this grief I was causing them in vain, for they would be abandoned, replaced, and, parallel to the path strewn with all the derelicts of her light-hearted infidelities, there would open for me another, pitiless path broken only by an occasional brief respite; so that my suffering could end only with Albertine's life or with my own. Even in the first days after our return to Paris, not satisfied by the information that Andrée and the chauffeur had given me as to their expeditions with my mistress, I had felt the neighbourhood of Paris to be as tormenting as that of Balbec, and had gone off for a few days in the country with Albertine. But everywhere my uncertainty as to what she might be doing was the same; the possibility that it was something wrong as abundant, vigilance even more difficult, with the result that I returned with her to Paris. In leaving Balbec, I had imagined that I was leaving Gomorrah, plucking Albertine from it; in reality, alas, Gomorrah was dispersed to all the ends of the earth. And partly out of jealousy, partly out of ignorance of such joys (a case which is rare indeed), I had arranged unawares this game of hide and seek in which Albertine was always to escape me.

I questioned her point-blank: "Oh, by the way, Albertine, am I dreaming, or did you tell me that you knew Gilberte Swann?" "Yes; that is to say, she used to talk to me at our classes, because she had a set of the French history notes, in fact she was very nice about it, and let me borrow them, and I gave them back the next time I saw her." "Is she the kind of woman that I object to?" "Oh, not at all, quite the opposite." But, rather than indulge in this sort of criminal investigation, I would often devote to imagining Albertine's excursion the energy that I did not employ in sharing it, and would speak to my mistress with that ardour which remains intact in our unfulfilled designs. I expressed so keen a longing to see once again some window in the Sainte-Chapelle, so keen a regret that I was not able to go there with her alone, that she said to me lovingly: "Why, my dear boy, since you seem so keen about it, make a little effort, come with us. We can start as late as you like, whenever you're ready. And if you'd rather be alone with me, I have only to send Andrée home, she can come another time." But these very entreaties to me to go out added to the calm which allowed me to yield to my desire to remain indoors.

It did not occur to me that the apathy that was indicated by my dele-gating thus to Andrée or the chauffeur the task of soothing my agitation by leaving them to keep watch over Albertine, was paralysing in me, ren-dering inert all those imaginative impulses of the mind, all those inspira-tions of the will, which enable us to guess, to forestall, what some one else is about to do; indeed the world of possibilities has always been more open to me than that of real events. This helps us to understand the human heart, but we are apt to be taken in by individuals. My jealousy was born of mental images, a form of self torment not based upon probability. Now there may occur in the lives of men and of nations (and there was to occur, one day, in my own life) a moment when we need to have within us a superintendent of police, a clear-sighted diplomat, a master-detective, who instead of pondering over the concealed possibilities that extend to all the points of the compass, reasons accurately, says to himself: "If Germany announces this, it means that she intends to do something else, not just 'something' in the abstract but precisely this or that or the other, which she may perhaps have begun already to do." "If So-and-So has fled, it is not in the direction a or b or d, but to the point c, and the place to which we must direct our search for him is c." Alas, this faculty which was not highly developed in me, I allowed to grow slack, to lose its power, to vanish, by acquiring the habit of growing calm the moment that other people were engaged in keeping watch on my behalf.

As for the reason for my reluctance to leave the house, I should not have liked to explain it to Albertine. I told her that the doctor had ordered me to stay in bed. This was not true. And if it had been true, his prescription would have been powerless to prevent me from accompanying my mistress. I asked her to excuse me from going out with herself and Andrée. I shall mention only one of my reasons, which was dictated by prudence. When-ever I went out with Albertine, if she left my side for a moment, I became anxious, began to imagine that she had spoken to, or simply cast a glance at somebody. If she was not in the best of tempers, I thought that I was causing her to miss or to postpone some appointment. Reality is never more than an allurement to an unknown element in quest of which we can never progress very far. It is better not to know, to think as little as pos-sible, not to feed our jealousy with the slightest concrete detail. Unfortu-nately, even when we eliminate the outward life, incidents are created by the inward life also; though I held aloof from Albertine's expeditions, the random course of my solitary reflexions furnished me at times with those tiny fragments of the truth which attract to themselves, like a magnet, an inkling of the unknown, which, from that moment, becomes painful. Even if we live in a hermetically sealed compartment, associations of ideas, memories continue to act upon us. But these internal shocks did not occur immediately; no sooner had Albertine started on her drive than I was re-vivified, were it only for a few moments, by the stimulating virtues of solitude.

I took my share of the pleasures of the new day; the arbitrary desire—the capricious and purely spontaneous inclination to taste them would not have sufficed to place them within my reach, had not the peculiar state of the weather not merely reminded me of their images in the past but affirmed their reality in the present, immediately accessible to all men whom a contingent and consequently negligible circumstance did not compel to remain at home. On certain fine days the weather was so cold, one was in such full communication with the street that it seemed as though a breach had been made in the outer walls of the house, and, whenever a tramcar passed, the sound of its bell throbbed like that of a silver knife striking a wall of glass. But it was most of all in myself that I heard, with intoxication, a new sound rendered by the hidden violin. Its strings are tightened or relaxed by mere changes of temperature, of light, in the world outside. In our person, an instrument which the uniformity of habit has rendered silent, song is born of these digressions, these variations, the source of all music: the change of climate on certain days makes us pass at once from one note to another. We recapture the forgotten air the mathematical inevitability of which we might have deduced, and which for the first few moments we sing without recognising it. By themselves these modifications (which, albeit coming from without, were internal) refashioned for me the world outside. Communicating doors, long barred, opened themselves in my brain. The life of certain towns, the gaiety of certain expeditions resumed their place in my consciousness. All athrob in harmony with the vibrating string, I would have sacrificed my dull life in the past, and all my life to come, erased with the india-rubber of habit, for one of these special, unique moments.

If I had not gone out with Albertine on her long drive, my mind would stray all the farther afield, and, because I had refused to savour with my senses this particular morning, I enjoyed in imagination all the similar mornings, past or possible, or more precisely a certain type of morning of which all those of the same kind were but the intermittent apparition which I had at once recognised; for the keen air blew the book open of its own accord at the right page, and I found clearly set out before my eyes, so that I might follow it from my bed, the Gospel for the day. This ideal morning filled my mind full of a permanent reality, identical with all similar mornings, and infected me with a cheerfulness which my physical ill-health did not diminish: for, inasmuch as our sense of well-being is caused not so much by our sound health as by the unemployed surplus of our strength, we can attain to it, just as much as by increasing our strength, by diminishing our activity. The activity with which I was overflowing and which I kept constantly charged as I lay in bed, made me spring from side to side, with a leaping heart, like a machine which, prevented from moving in space, rotates on its own axis.

Françoise came in to light the fire, and to make it draw, threw upon it a handful of twigs, the scent of which, forgotten for a year past, traced round the fireplace a magic circle within which, perceiving myself poring over a book, now at Combray, now at Doncières, I was as joyful, while remaining in my bedroom in Paris, as if I had been on the point of starting for a walk along the Méséglise way, or of going to join Saint-Loup and his friends on the training-ground. It often happens that the pleasure which everyone takes in turning over the keepsakes that his memory has collected is keenest in those whom the tyranny of bodily ill-health and the daily hope of recovery prevent, on the one hand, from going out to seek in nature scenes that resemble those memories, and, on the other hand, leave so convinced that they will shortly be able to do so that they can remain gazing at them in a state of desire, of appetite, and not regard them merely as memories, as pictures. But, even if they were never to be anything more than memories to me, even if I, as I recalled them, saw merely pictures, immediately they recreated in me, of me as a whole, by virtue of an identical sensation, the boy, the youth who had first seen them. There had been not merely a change in the weather outside, or, inside the room, the introduction of a fresh scent, there had been in myself a difference of age, the substitution of another person. The scent, in the frosty air, of the twigs of brushwood, was like a fragment of the past, an invisible floe broken off from the ice of an old winter that stole into my room, often variegated moreover with this perfume or that light, as though with a sequence of different years, in which I found myself plunged, over-whelmed, even before I had identified them, by the eagerness of hopes long since abandoned. The sun's rays fell upon my bed and passed through the transparent shell of my attenuated body, warmed me, made me as hot as a sheet of scorching crystal. Whereupon, a famished convalescent who has already begun to batten upon all the dishes that are still for-bidden him, I asked myself whether marriage with Albertine would not spoil my life, as well by making me assume the burden, too heavy for my shoulders, of consecrating myself to another person, as by forcing me to live in absence from myself because of her continual presence and depriv-ing me, forever, of the delights of solitude.

And not of these alone. Even when we ask of the day nothing but desires, there are some—those that are excited not by things but by people—whose character it is to be unlike any other. If, on rising from my bed, I went to the window and drew the curtain aside for a moment, it was not merely, as a pianist for a moment turns back the lid of his instrument, to ascertain whether, on the balcony and in the street, the sunlight was tuned to exactly the same pitch as in my memory, it was also to catch a glimpse of some laundress carrying her linen-basket, a bread-seller in her blue apron, a dairymaid in her tucker and sleeves of white linen, carrying the yoke from which her jugs of milk are suspended, some haughty golden-haired miss escorted by her governess, a composite image, in short, which the differences of outline, numerically perhaps insignificant, were enough to make as different from any other as, in a phrase of music, the difference between two notes, an image but for the vision of which I should have impoverished my day of the objects which it might have to offer to my desires of happiness. But, if the surfeit of joy, brought me by the spectacle of women whom it was impossible to imagine a priori, made more desirable, more deserving of exploration, the street, the town, the world, it set me longing, for that very reason, to recover my health, to go out of doors and, without Albertine, to be a free man. How often, at the moment when the unknown woman who was to haunt my dreams passed beneath the window, now on foot, now at the full speed of her motor-car, was I made wretched that my body could not follow my gaze which kept pace with her, and falling upon her as though shot from the embrasure of my window by an arquebus, arrest the flight of the face that held out for me the offer of a happiness which, cloistered thus, I should never know.

Of Albertine, on the other hand, I had nothing more to learn. Every day, she seemed to me less attractive. Only, the desire that she aroused in other people, when, upon hearing of it, I began to suffer afresh and was impelled to challenge their possession of her, raised her in my sight to a lofty pinnacle. Pain, she was capable of causing me; joy, never. Pain alone kept my tedious attachment alive. As soon as my pain vanished, and with it the need to soothe it, requiring all my attention, like some agonising distraction, I felt that she meant absolutely nothing to me, that I must mean absolutely nothing to her. It made me wretched that this state should persist, and, at certain moments, I longed to hear of something terrible that she had done, something that would be capable of keeping us at armslength until I was cured, so that we might then be able to be reconciled, to refashion in a different and more flexible form the chain that bound us.

In the meantime, I was employing a thousand circumstances, a thousand pleasures to procure for her in my society the illusion of that happiness which I did not feel myself capable of giving her. I should have liked, as soon as I was cured, to set off for Venice, but how was I to manage it, if I married Albertine, I, who was so jealous of her that even in Paris whenever I decided to stir from my room it was to go out with her? Even when I stayed in the house all the afternoon, my thoughts accompanied her on her drive, traced a remote, blue horizon, created round the centre that was myself a fluctuating zone of vague uncertainty. "How completely," I said to myself, "would Albertine spare me the anguish of separation if, in the course of one of these drives, seeing that I no longer say anything to her about marriage, she decided not to come back, and went off to her aunt's, without my having to bid her good-bye!" My heart, now that its scar had begun to heal, was ceasing to adhere to the heart of my mistress; I could by imagination shift her, separate her from myself without pain. No doubt, failing myself, some other man would be her husband, and in her freedom she would meet perhaps with those adventures which filled me with horror. But the day was so fine, I was so certain that she would return in the evening, that even if the idea of possible misbehaviour did enter my mind, I could, by an exercise of free will, imprison it in a part of my brain in which it had no more importance than would have had in my real life the vices of an imaginary person; bringing into play the supple hinges of my thought, I had, with an energy which I felt in my head to be at once physical and mental, as it were a muscular movement and a spiritual impulse, broken away from the state of perpetual preoccupation in which I had until then been confined, and was beginning to move in a free atmosphere, in which the idea of sacrificing everything in order to prevent Albertine from marrying some one else and to put an obstacle in the way of her fondness for women seemed as unreasonable to my own mind as to that of a person who had never known her.

However, jealousy is one of those intermittent maladies, the cause of which is capricious, imperative, always identical in the same patient, some-times entirely different in another. There are asthmatic persons who can soothe their crises only by opening the windows, inhaling the full blast of the wind, the pure air of the mountains, others by taking refuge in the heart of the city, in a room heavy with smoke. Rare indeed is the jealous man whose jealousy does not allow certain concessions. One will consent to infidelity, provided that he is told of it, another provided that it is con-cealed from him, wherein they appear to be equally absurd, since if the latter is more literally deceived inasmuch as the truth is not disclosed to him, the other demands in that truth the food, the extension, the renewal of his sufferings.

What is more, these two parallel manias of jealousy extend often beyond words, whether they implore or reject confidences. We see a jealous lover who is jealous only of the women with whom his mistress has relations in his absence, but allows her to give herself to another man, if it is done with his authorisation, near at hand, and, if not actually before his eyes, under his roof. This case is not at all uncommon among elderly men who are in love with young women. Such a man feels the difficulty of winning her favour, sometimes his inability to satisfy her, and, rather than be be-trayed, prefers to admit to his house, to an adjoining room, some man whom he considers incapable of giving her bad advice, but not incapable of giving her pleasure. With another man it is just the opposite; never allowing his mistress to go out by herself for a single minute in a town that he knows, he keeps her in a state of bondage, but allows her to go for a month to a place which he does not know, where he cannot form any mental picture of what she may be doing. I had with regard to Albertine both these sorts of sedative mania. I should not have been jealous if she had enjoyed her pleasures in my company, with my encouragement, pleas-ures over the whole of which I could have kept watch, thus avoiding any fear of falsehood; I might perhaps not have been jealous either if she had removed to a place so unfamiliar and remote that I could not imagine nor find any possibility, feel any temptation to know the manner of her life. In either alternative, my uncertainty would have been killed by a knowl-edge or an ignorance equally complete.

The decline of day plunging me back by an act of memory in a cool atmosphere of long ago, I breathed it with the same delight with which Orpheus inhaled the subtle air, unknown upon this earth, of the Elysian Fields.

But already the day was ending and I was overpowered by the desolation of the evening. Looking mechanically at the clock to see how many hours must elapse before Albertine's return, I saw that I had still time to dress and go downstairs to ask my landlady, Mme. de Guermantes, for par-ticulars of various becoming garments which I was anxious to procure for my mistress. Sometimes I met the Duchess in the courtyard, going out for a walk, even if the weather was bad, in a close-fitting hat and furs. I knew quite well that, to many people of intelligence, she was merely a lady like any other, the name Duchesse de Guermantes signifying nothing, now that there are no longer any sovereign Duchies or Principalities, but

I had adopted a different point of view in my method of enjoying people and places. All the castles of the territories of which she was Duchess, Princess, Viscountess, this lady in furs defying the weather seemed to me to be carrying them on her person, as a figure carved over the lintel of a church door holds in his hand the cathedral that he has built or the city that he has defended. But these castles, these forests, my mind's eye alone could discern them in the left hand of the lady in furs, whom the King called cousin. My bodily eyes distinguished in it only, on days when the sky was threatening, an umbrella with which the Duchess was not afraid to arm herself. "One can never be certain, it is wiser, I may find myself miles from home, with a cabman demanding a fare *beyond my means.*" The words 'too dear' and 'beyond my means' kept recurring all the time in the Duchess's conversation, as did also: 'I am too poor'—without its being possible to decide whether she spoke thus because she thought it amusing to say that she was poor, being so rich, or because she thought it smart, being so aristocratic, in spite of her affectation of peasant ways, not to attach to riches the importance that people give them who are merely rich and nothing else, and who look down upon the poor. Perhaps it was, rather, a habit contracted at a time in her life when, already rich, but not rich enough to satisfy her needs, considering the expense of keeping up all those properties, she felt a certain shortage of money which she did not wish to appear to be concealing. The things about which we most often jest are generally, on the contrary, the things that embarrass us, but we do not wish to appear to be embarrassed by them, and feel perhaps a secret hope of the further advantage that the person to whom we are talking, hearing us treat the matter as a joke, will conclude that it is not true.

But upon most evenings, at this hour, I could count upon finding the Duchess at home, and I was glad of this, for it was more convenient for me to ask her in detail for the information that Albertine required. And down I went almost without thinking how extraordinary it was that I should be calling upon that mysterious Mme. de Guermantes of my boyhood, simply in order to make use of her for a practical purpose, as one makes use of the telephone, a supernatural instrument before whose miracles we used to stand amazed, and which we now employ without giving it a thought, to summon our tailor or to order ices for a party.

Albertine delighted in any sort of finery. I could not deny myself the pleasure of giving her some new trifle every day. And whenever she had spoken to me with rapture of a scarf, a stole, a sunshade which, from the window or as they passed one another in the courtyard, her eyes that so quickly distinguished anything smart, had seen round the throat, over the shoulders, in the hand of Mme. de Guermantes, knowing how the girl's naturally fastidious taste (refined still further by the lessons in elegance of attire which Elstir's conversation had been to her) would not be at all satisfied by any mere substitute, even of a pretty thing, such as fills its place in the eyes of the common herd, but differs from it entirely, I went in secret to make the Duchess explain to me where, how, from what model the article had been created that had taken Albertine's fancy, how I should set about to obtain one exactly similar, in what the creator's secret, the charm (what Albertine called the '*chic*,' the 'style') of his manner, the precise name—the beauty of the material being of importance also—and quality of the stuffs that I was to insist upon their using.

When I mentioned to Albertine, on our return from Balbec, that the Duchesse de Guermantes lived opposite to us, in the same mansion, she had assumed, on hearing the proud title and great name, that air more than indifferent, hostile, contemptuous, which is the sign of an impotent desire in proud and passionate natures. Splendid as Albertine's nature might be, the fine qualities which it contained were free to develop only amid those hindrances which are our personal tastes, or that lamentation for those of our tastes which we have been obliged to relinquish—in Albertine's case snobbishness—which is called antipathy. Albertine's antipathy to people in society occupied, for that matter, but a very small part in her nature, and appealed to me as an aspect of the revolutionary spirit—that is to say an embittered love of the nobility—engraved upon the opposite side of the French character to that which displays the aristocratic manner of Mme. de Guermantes. To this aristocratic manner Albertine, in view of the impossibility of her acquiring it, would perhaps not have given a thought, but remembering that Elstir had spoken to her of the Duchess as the best dressed woman in Paris, her republican contempt for a Duchess gave place in my mistress to a keen interest in a fashionable woman. She was always asking me to tell her about Mme. de Guermantes, and was glad that I should go to the Duchess to obtain advice as to her own attire. No doubt I might have got this from Mme. Swann and indeed I did once write to her with this intention. But Mme. de Guermantes seemed to me to carry to an even higher pitch the art of dressing. If, on going down for a moment to call upon her, after making sure that she had not gone out and leaving word that I was to be told as soon as Albertine returned, I found the Duchess swathed in the mist of a garment of grey crépe de chine, I accepted this aspect of her which I felt to be due to complex causes and to be quite inevitable, I let myself be overpowered by the atmosphere which it exhaled, like that of certain late afternoons cushioned in pearly grey by a vaporous fog; if, on the other hand, her indoor gown was Chinese with red and yellow flames, I gazed at it as at a glowing sunset; these garments were not a casual decoration alterable at her pleasure, but a definite and poetical reality like that of the weather, or the light peculiar to a certain hour of the day.

Of all the outdoor and indoor gowns that Mme. de Guermantes wore, those which seemed most to respond to a definite intention, to be endowed with a special significance, were the garments made by Fortuny from old Venetian models. Is it their historical character, is it rather the fact that each one of them is unique that gives them so special a significance that the pose of the woman who is wearing one while she waits for you to appear or while she talks to you assumes an exceptional importance, as though the costume had been the fruit of a long deliberation and your conversation was detached from the current of everyday life like a scene in a novel? In the novels of Balzac, we see his heroines purposely put on one or another dress on the day on which they are expecting some particular visitor. The dresses of to-day have less character, always excepting the creations of Fortuny. There is no room for vagueness in the novelist's description, since the gown does really exist, and the merest sketch of it is as naturally preordained as a copy of a work of art. Before putting on one or another of them, the woman has had to make a choice between two garments, not more or less alike but each one profoundly individual, and answering to its name. But the dress did not prevent me from thinking of the woman.

Indeed, Mme. de Guermantes seemed to me at this time more attractive than in the days when I was still in love with her. Expecting less of her (whom I no longer went to visit for her own sake), it was almost with the ease and comfort of a man in a room by himself, with his feet on the fender, that I listened to her as though I were reading a book written in the speech of long ago. My mind was sufficiently detached to enjoy in what she said that pure charm of the French language which we no longer find either in the speech or in the literature of the present day. I listened to her conversation as to a folk song deliciously and purely French, I realised that I would have allowed her to belittle Maeterlinck (whom for that matter she now admired, from a feminine weakness of intellect, influenced by those literary fashions whose rays spread slowly), as I realised that Mérimée had belittled Baudelaire, Stendhal Balzac, Paul-Louis Courier Victor Hugo, Meilhac Mallarmé. I realised that the critic had a far more restricted outlook than his victim, but also a purer vocabulary. That of Mme. de Guermantes, almost as much as that of Saint-Loup's mother, was purified to an enchanting degree. It is not in the bloodless formulas of the writers of to-day, who say: *au fait* (for ' in reality'), *singulièrement* (for 'in particular'), *étonné* (for 'struck with amazement'), and the like, that we recapture the old speech and the true pronunciation of words, but in conversing with a Mme. de Guermantes or a Françoise; I had learned from the latter, when I was five years old, that one did not say 'the Tarn' but 'the Tar'; not 'Béarn' but 'Béar.' The effect of which was that at twenty, when I began to go into society, I had no need to be taught there that one ought not to say, like Mme. Bontemps: 'Madame de Béarn.'

It would be untrue to pretend that of this territorial and semi-peasant quality which survived in her the Duchess was not fully conscious, indeed she displayed a certain affectation in emphasising it. But, on her part, this was not so much the false simplicity of a great lady aping the country-woman or the pride of a Duchess bent upon snubbing the rich ladies who express contempt for the peasants whom they do not know as the almost artistic preference of a woman who knows the charm of what belongs to her, and is not going to spoil it with a coat of modern varnish. In the same way, everybody will remember at Dives a Norman innkeeper, landlord of the Guillaume le Conquérant, who carefully refrained—which is very rare —from giving his hostelry the modern comforts of an hotel, and, albeit a millionaire, retained the speech, the blouse of a Norman peasant and allowed you to enter his kitchen and watch him prepare with his own hands, as in a farmhouse, a dinner which was nevertheless infinitely better and even more expensive than are the dinners in the most luxurious hotels.

All the local sap that survives in the old noble families is not enough, there must also be born of them a person of sufficient intelligence not to despise it, not to conceal it beneath the varnish of society. Mme. de Guermantes, unfortunately clever and Parisian, who, when I first knew her, retained nothing of her native soil but its accent, had at least, when she wished to describe her life as a girl, found for her speech one of those compromises (between what would have seemed too spontaneously provincial on the one hand or artificially literary on the other), one of those compromises which form the attraction of George Sand's *La Petite Fadette* or of certain legends preserved by Chateaubriand in his *Mémoires d'Outre-Tombe*. My chief pleasure was in hearing her tell some anecdote which brought peasants into the picture with herself. The historic names, the old customs gave to these blendings of the castle with the village a distinctly attractive savour. Having remained in contact with the lands over which it once ruled, a certain class of the nobility has remained regional, with the result that the simplest remark unrolls before our eyes a political and physical map of the whole history of France.

If there was no affectation, no desire to fabricate a special language, then this manner of pronouncing words was a regular museum of French history displayed in conversation. 'My great-uncle Fitt-jam' was not at all surprising, for we know that the Fitz-James family are proud to boast that they are French nobles, and do not like to hear their name pronounced in the English fashion. One must, incidentally, admire the touching docility of the people who had previously supposed themselves obliged to pronounce certain names phonetically, and who, all of a sudden, after hearing the Duchesse de Guermantes pronounce them otherwise, adopted the pronunciation which they could never have guessed. Thus the Duchess, who had had a great-grandfather in the suite of the Comte de Chambord, liked to tease her husband for having turned Orleanist by proclaiming: "We old Frochedorf people. . . ." The visitor, who had always imagined that he was correct in saying 'Frohsdorf,' at once turned his coat, and ever afterwards might be heard saying 'Frochedorf.'

On one occasion when I asked Mme. de Guermantes who a young blood was whom she had introduced to me as her nephew but whose name I had failed to catch, I was none the wiser when from the back of her throat the Duchess uttered in a very loud but quite inarticulate voice: *"C'est l'* . . . *i Eon . . . l . . . b . . . frère à Robert.* He makes out that he has the same shape of skull as the ancient Gauls." Then I realised that she had said: *"C'est le petit Léon,"* and that this was the Prince de Léon, who was indeed Robert de Saint-Loup's brother-in-law. "I know nothing about his skull," she went on, "but the way he dresses, and I must say he does dress quite well, is not at all in the style of those parts. Once when I was staying at Josselin, with the Rohans, we all went over to one of the pilgrimages, where there were peasants from every part of Brittany. A great hulking fellow from one of the Léon villages stood gaping open-mouthed at Robert's brother-in-law in his beige breeches! 'What are you staring at me like that for?' said Léon. 'I bet you don't know who I am?' The peasant admitted that he did not. 'Very well,' said Léon, 'I'm your Prince.' 'Oh!' said the peasant, taking off his cap and apologising. 'I thought you were an *Englische.*' "

And if, taking this opportunity, I led Mme. de Guermantes on to talk about the Rohans (with whom her own family had frequently intermarried), her conversation would become impregnated with a hint of the wistful charm of the Pardons, and (as that true poet Pampille would say) with "the harsh savour of pancakes of black grain fried over a fire of rushes."

Of the Marquis du Lau (whose tragic decline we all know, when, himself deaf, he used to be taken to call on Mme. H . . . who was blind), she would recall the less tragic years when, after the day's sport, at Guermantes, he would change into slippers before taking tea with the Prince of Wales, to whom he would not admit himself inferior, and with whom, as we see, he stood upon no ceremony. She described all this so picturesquely that she seemed to invest him with the plumed musketeer bonnet of the somewhat vainglorious gentlemen of the Périgord.

But even in the mere classification of different people, her care to distinguish and indicate their native provinces was in Mme. de Guermantes, when she was her natural self, a great charm which a Parisian-born woman could never have acquired, and those simple names Anjou, Poitou, the Périgord, filled her conversation with pictorial landscapes.

To revert to the pronunciation and vocabulary of Mme. de Guermantes, it is in this aspect that the nobility shews itself truly conservative, with everything that the word implies at once somewhat puerile and somewhat perilous, stubborn in its resistance to evolution but interesting also to an artist. I was anxious to know the original spelling of the name Jean. I learned it when I received a letter from a nephew of Mme. de Villeparisis who signs himself—as he was christened, as he figures in Gotha—Jehan de Villeparisis, with the same handsome, superfluous, heraldic h that we admire, illuminated in vermilion or ultramarine in a Book of Hours or in a window.

Unfortunately, I never had time to prolong these visits indefinitely, for I was anxious, if possible, not to return home after my mistress. But it was only in driblets that I was able to obtain from Mme. de Guermantes that information as to her garments which was of use in helping me to order garments similar in style, so far as it was possible for a young girl to wear them, for Albertine. "For instance, Madame, that evening when you dined with Mme. de Saint-Euverte, and then went on to the Princesse de Guermantes, you had a dress that was all red, with red shoes, you were marvellous, you reminded me of a sort of great blood-red blossom, a blazing ruby—now, what was that dress? Is it the sort of thing that a girl can wear?"

The Duchess, imparting to her tired features the radiant expression that the Princesse des Laumes used to assume when Swann, in years past, paid her compliments, looked, with tears of merriment in her eyes, quizzingly, questioningly and delightedly at M. de Bréauté who was always there at that hour and who set beaming from behind his monocle a smile that seemed to pardon this outburst of intellectual trash for the sake of the physical excitement of youth which seemed to him to lie beneath it. The Duchess appeared to be saying: "What is the matter with him? He must be mad." Then turning to me with a coaxing air: "I wasn't aware that I looked like a blazing ruby or a blood-red blossom, but I do remember, as it happens, that I had on a red dress: it was red satin, which was being worn that season. Yes, a girl can wear that sort of thing at a pinch, but you told me that your friend never went out in the evening. That is a full evening dress, not a thing that she can put on to pay calls."

What is extraordinary is that of the evening in question, which after all was not so very remote, Mme. de Guermantes should remember nothing but what she had been wearing, and should have forgotten a certain incident which nevertheless, as we shall see presently, ought to have mattered to her greatly. It seems that among men and women of action (and people in society are men and women of action on a minute, a microscopic scale, but are nevertheless men and women of action), the mind, overcharged by the need of attending to what is going to happen in an hour's time, confides only a very few things to the memory. As often as not, for instance, it was not with the object of putting his questioner in the wrong and making himself appear not to have been mistaken that M. de Norpois, when you reminded him of the prophecies he had uttered with regard to an alliance with Germany of which nothing had ever come, would say: "You must be mistaken, I have no recollection of it whatever, it is not like me, for in that sort of conversation I am always most laconic, and I would never have predicted the success of one of those *coups d'éclat* which are often nothing more than *coups de tête* and almost always degenerate into *coups de force*. It is beyond question that in the remote future a Franco-German *rapprochement* might come into being and would be highly profitable to both countries, nor would France have the worse of the bargain, I dare say, but I have never spoken of it because the fruit is not yet ripe, and if you wish to know my opinion, in asking our late enemies to join with us in solemn wedlock, I consider that we should be setting out to meet a severe rebuff, and that the attempt could end only in disaster." In saying this M. de Norpois was not being untruthful, he had simply forgotten. We quickly forget what we have not deeply considered, what has been dictated to us by the spirit of imitation, by the passions of our neighbours. These change, and with them our memory undergoes alteration. Even more than diplomats, politicians are unable to remember the point of view which they adopted at a certain moment, and some of their palinodes are due less to a surfeit of ambition than to a shortage of memory. As for people in society, there are very few things that they remember.

Mme. de Guermantes assured me that, at the party to which she had gone in a red gown, she did not remember Mme. de Chaussepierre's being present, and that I must be mistaken. And yet, heaven knows, the Chaussepierres had been present enough in the minds of both Duke and Duchess since then. For the following reason. M. de Guermantes had been the senior vice-president of the Jockey, when the president died. Certain members of the club who were not popular in society and whose sole pleasure was to blackball the men who did not invite them to their houses started a campaign against the Duc de Guermantes who, certain of being elected, and relatively indifferent to the presidency which was a small matter for a man in his social position, paid no attention. It was urged against him that the Duchess was a Dreyfusard (the Dreyfus case had long been concluded, but twenty years later people were still talking about it, and so far only two years had elapsed), and entertained the Rothschilds, that so much consideration had been shewn of late to certain great international magnates like the Duc de Guermantes, who was half German. The campaign found its ground well prepared, clubs being always jealous of men who are in the public eye, and detesting great fortunes.

Chaussepierre's own fortune was no mere pittance, but nobody could take offence at it; he never spent a penny, the couple lived in a modest apartment, the wife went about dressed in black serge. A passionate music-lover, she did indeed give little afternoon parties to which many more singers were invited than to the Guermantes. But no one ever mentioned these parties, no refreshments were served, the husband did not put in an appearance even, and everything went off quite quietly in the obscurity of the Rue de la Chaise. At the Opera, Mme. de Chaussepierre passed unnoticed, always among people whose names recalled the most 'die-hard' element of the intimate circle of Charles X, but people quite obsolete, who went nowhere. On the day of the election, to the general surprise, obscurity triumphed over renown: Chaussepierre, the second vice-president, was elected president of the Jockey, and the Duc de Guermantes was left sitting —that is to say, in the senior vice-president's chair. Of course, being president of the Jockey means little or nothing to Princes of the highest rank such as the Guermantes. But not to be it when it is your turn, to see preferred to you a Chaussepierre to whose wife Oriane, two years earlier, had not merely refused to bow but had taken offence that an unknown scarecrow like that should bow to her, this the Duke did find hard to endure. He pretended to be superior to this rebuff, asserting moreover that it was his long-standing friendship with Swann that was at the root of it. Actually his anger never cooled.

One curious thing was that nobody had ever before heard the Duc de Guermantes make use of the quite commonplace expression 'out and out,' but ever since the Jockey election, whenever anybody referred to the Dreyfus case, pat would come 'out and out.' "Dreyfus case, Dreyfus case, that's soon said, and it's a misuse of the term. It is not a question of religion, it's *out and out* a political matter." Five years might go by without your hearing him say 'out and out' again, if during that time nobody mentioned the Dreyfus case, but if, at the end of five years, the name Dreyfus cropped up, 'out and out' would at once follow automatically. The Duke could not, anyhow, bear to hear any mention of the case, "which has been responsible," he would say, "for so many disasters" albeit he was really conscious of one and one only; his own failure to become president of the Jockey. And so on the afternoon in question, when I reminded Madame de Guermantes of the red gown that she had worn at her cousin's party, M. de Bréauté was none too well received when, determined to say something, by an association of ideas which remained obscure and which he did not illuminate, he began, twisting his tongue about between his pursed lips: "Talking of the Dreyfus case—" (why in the world of the Dreyfus case, we were talking simply of a red dress, and certainly poor Bréauté, whose only desire was to make himself agreeable, can have had no malicious intention). But the mere name of Dreyfus made the Duc de Guermantes knit his Jupiterian brows. "I was told," Bréauté went on, "a jolly good thing, damned clever, 'pon my word, that was said by our friend Cartier" (we must warn the reader that this Cartier, Mme. de Villefranche's brother, was in no way related to the jeweller of that name) "not that I'm in the least surprised, for he's got plenty of brains to spare." "Oh!" broke in Oriane, "he can spare me his brains. I hardly like to tell you how much your friend Cartier has always bored me, and I have never been able to understand the boundless charm that Charles de La Trémoïlle and his wife seem to find in the creature, for I meet him there every time that I go to their house." "My dear Dutt-yess," replied Bréauté, who was unable to pronounce the soft *c*, "I think you are very hard upon Cartier. It is true that he has perhaps made himself rather too mutt-y-at home at the La Trémoïlles', but after all he does provide Tyarles with a sort of—what shall I say?—a sort of *fidus Achates*, which has become a very rare bird indeed in these days. Anyhow, this is the story as it was told to me. Cartier appears to have said that if M. Zola had gone out of his way to stand his trial and to be convicted, it was in order to enjoy the only sensation he had never yet tried, that of being in prison." "And so he ran away before they could arrest him," Oriane broke in. "Your story doesn't hold water. Besides, even if it was plausible, I think his remark absolutely idiotic. If that's what you call being witty!" "Good grate-ious, my dear Oriane," replied Bréauté who, finding himself contradicted, was beginning to lose confidence, "it's not my remark, I'm telling you it as it was told to me, take it for what's it worth. Anyhow, it earned M. Cartier a first rate blowing up from that excellent fellow La Trémoïlle who, and quite rightly, does not like people to discuss what one might call, so to speak, current events, in his drawing-room, and was all the more annoyed because Mme. Alphonse Rothschild was present. Cartier had to listen to a positive jobation from La Trémoïlle." "I should think so," said the Duke, in the worst of tempers, "the Alphonse Rothschilds, even if they have the tact never to speak of that abominable affair, are Dreyfusards at heart, like all the Jews. Indeed that is an argument *ad hominem*" (the Duke was a trifle vague in his use of the expression *ad hominem*) "which is not sufficiently made use of to prove the dishonesty of the Jews. If a Frenchman robs or murders somebody, I do not consider myself bound, because he is a Frenchman like myself, to find him innocent. But the Jews will never admit that one of their fellow-countrymen is a traitor, although they know it perfectly well, and never think of the terrible repercussions" (the Duke was thinking, naturally, of that accursed defeat by Chaussepierre) "which the crime of one of their people can bring even to . . . Come, Oriane, you're not going to pretend that it ain't damning to the Jews that they all support a traitor. You're not going to tell me that it ain't because they're Jews."

"Of course not," retorted Oriane (feeling, with a trace of irritation, a certain desire to hold her own against Jupiter Tonans and also to set 'intellect' above the Dreyfus case). "Perhaps it is just because they are Jews and know their own race that they realise that a person can be a Jew and not necessarily a traitor and anti-French, as M. Drumont seems to maintain. Certainly, if he'd been a Christian, the Jews wouldn't have taken any interest in him, but they did so because they knew quite well that if he hadn't been a Jew people wouldn't have been so ready to think him a traitor *a priori*, as my nephew Robert would say." "Women never understand a thing about politics," exclaimed the Duke, fastening his gaze upon the Duchess. "That shocking crime is not simply a Jewish cause, but *out and out* an affair of vast national importance which may lead to the most appalling consequences for France, which ought to have driven out all the Jews, whereas I am sorry to say that the measures taken up to the present have been directed (in an ignoble fashion, which will have to be overruled) not against them but against the most eminent of their adversaries, against men of the highest rank, who have been flung into the gutter, to the ruin of our unhappy country."

I felt that the conversation had taken a wrong turning and reverted hurriedly to the topic of clothes.

"Do you remember, Madame," I said, "the first time that you were friendly with me?" "The first time that I was friendly with him," she repeated, turning with a smile to M. de Bréauté, the tip of whose nose grew more pointed, his smile more tender out of politeness to Mme. de Guermantes, while his voice, like a knife on the grindstone, emitted various vague and rusty sounds. "You were wearing a yellow gown with big black flowers." "But, my dear boy, that's the same thing, those are evening dresses." "And your hat with the cornflowers that I liked so much! Still, those are all things of the past. I should like to order for the girl I mentioned to you a fur cloak like the one you had on yesterday morning. Would it be possible for me to see it?" "Of course; Hannibal has to be going in a moment. You shall come to my room and my maid will shew you anything you want to look at. Only, my dear boy, though I shall be delighted to lend you anything, I must warn you that if you have things from Callot's or Doucet's or Paquin's copied by some small dressmaker, the result is never the same." "But I never dreamed of going to a small dressmaker, I know quite well it wouldn't be the same thing, but I should be interested to hear you explain why." "You know quite well I can never explain anything, I am a perfect fool, I talk like a peasant. It is a question of handiwork, of style; as far as furs go, I can at least give you a line to my furrier, so that he shan't rob you. But you realise that even then it will cost you eight or nine thousand francs." "And that indoor gown that you were wearing the other evening, with such a curious smell, dark, fluffy, speckled, streaked with gold like a butterfly's wing?" "Ah! That is one of Fortuny's. Your young lady can quite well wear that in the house. I have heaps of them; you shall see them presently, in fact I can give you one or two if you like. But I should like you to see one that my cousin Talleyrand has. I must write to her for the loan of it." "But you had such charming shoes as well, are they Fortuny's too?" "No, I know the ones you mean, they are made of some gilded kid we came across in London, when I was shopping with Consuelo Manchester. It was amazing. I could never make out how they did it, it was just like a golden skin, simply that with a tiny diamond in front. The poor Duchess of Manchester is dead, but if it's any help to you I can write and ask Lady Warwick or the Duchess of Marlborough to try and get me some more. I wonder, now, if I haven't a piece of the stuff left. You might be able to have a pair made here. I shall look for it this evening, and let you know."

As I endeavoured as far as possible to leave the Duchess before Albertine had returned, it often happened that I met in the courtyard as I came away from her door M. de Charlus and Morel on their way to take tea at Jupien's, a supreme favour for the Baron. I did not encounter them every day but they went there every day. Here we may perhaps remark that the regularity of a habit is generally in proportion to its absurdity. The sensational things, we do as a rule only by fits and starts. But the senseless life, in which the maniac deprives himself of all pleasure and inflicts the greatest discomforts upon himself, is the type that alters least. Every ten years, if we had the curiosity to inquire, we should find the poor wretch still asleep at the hours when he might be living his life, going out at the hours when there is nothing to do but let oneself be murdered in the streets, sipping iced drinks when he is hot, still trying desperately to cure a cold. A slight impulse of energy, for a single day, would be sufficient to change these habits for good and all. But the fact is that this sort of life is almost always the appanage of a person devoid of energy. Vices are another aspect of these monotonous existences which the exercise of will power would suffice to render less painful. These two aspects might be observed simultaneously when M. de Charlus came every day with Morel to take tea at Jupien's. A single outburst had marred this daily custom. The tailor's niece having said one day to Morel: "That's all right then, come to-morrow and I'll stand you a tea," the Baron had quite justifiably considered this expression very vulgar on the lips of a person whom he regarded as almost a prospective daughter-in-law, but as he enjoyed being offensive and became carried away by his own anger, instead of simply saying to Morel that he begged him to give her a lesson in polite manners, the whole of their homeward walk was a succession of violent scenes. In the most insolent, the most arrogant tone: "So your 'touch' which, I can see, is not necessarily allied to 'tact,' has hindered the normal development of your sense of smell, since you could allow that fetid expression 'stand a tea'—at fifteen centimes, I suppose—to waft its stench of sewage to my regal nostrils? When you have come to the end of a violin solo, have you ever seen yourself in my house rewarded with a fart, instead of frenzied applause, or a silence more eloquent still, since it is due to exhaustion from the effort to restrain, not what your young woman lavishes upon you, but the sob that you have brought to my lips?"

When a public official has had similar reproaches heaped upon him by his chief, he invariably loses his post next day. Nothing, on the contrary, could have been more painful to M. de Charlus than to dismiss Morel, and, fearing indeed that he had gone a little too far, he began to sing the girl's praises in detailed terms, with an abundance of good taste mingled with impertinence. "She is charming; as you are a musician, I suppose that she seduced you by her voice, which is very beautiful in the high notes, where she seems to await the accompaniment of your B sharp. Her lower register appeals to me less, and that must bear some relation to the triple rise of her strange and slender throat, which when it seems to have come to an end begins again; but these are trivial details, it is her outline that I admire. And as she is a dressmaker and must be handy with her scissors, you must make her give me a charming silhouette of herself cut out in paper."

Charlie had paid but little attention to this eulogy, the charms which it extolled in his betrothed having completely escaped his notice. But he said, in reply to M. de Charlus: "That's all right, my boy, I shall tell her off properly, and she won't talk like that again." If Morel addressed M. de Charlus thus as his 'boy,' it was not that the good-looking violinist was unaware that his own years numbered barely a third of the Baron's. Nor did he use the expression as Jupien would have done, but with that simplicity which in certain relations postulates that a suppression of the difference in age has tacitly preceded affection. A feigned affection on Morel's part. In others, a sincere affection. Thus, about this time M. de Charlus received a letter worded as follows: "My dear Palamède, when am I going to see thee again? I am longing terribly for thee and always thinking of thee. PIERRE." M. de Charlus racked his brains to discover which of his relatives it could be that took the liberty of addressing him so familiarly, and must consequently know him intimately, although he failed to recognise the handwriting. All the Princes to whom the Almanach de Gotha accords a few lines passed in procession for days on end through his mind. And then, all of a sudden, an address written on the back of the letter enlightened him: the writer was the page at a gambling club to which M. de Charlus sometimes went. This page had not felt that he was being discourteous in writing in this tone to M. de Charlus, for whom on the contrary he felt the deepest respect. But he thought that it would not be civil not to address in the second person singular a gentleman who had many times kissed one, and thereby—he imagined in his simplicity—bestowed his affection. M. de Charlus was really delighted by this familiarity. He even brought M. de Vaugoubert away from an afternoon party in order to shew him the letter. And yet, heaven knows that M. de Charlus did not care to go about with M. de Vaugoubert. For the latter, his monocle in his eye, kept gazing in all directions at every passing youth. What was worse, emancipating himself when he was with M. de Charlus, he employed a form of speech which the Baron detested. He gave feminine endings to all the masculine words and, being intensely stupid, imagined this pleasantry to be extremely witty, and was continually in fits of laughter. As at the same time he attached enormous importance to his position in the diplomatic service, these deplorable outbursts of merriment in the street were perpetually interrupted by the shock caused him by the simultaneous appearance of somebody in society, or, worse still, of a civil servant. "That little telegraph messenger," he said, nudging the disgusted Baron with his elbow, "I used to know her, but she's turned respectable, the wretch! Oh, that messenger from the Galeries Lafayette, what a dream! Good God, there's the head of the Commercial Department. I hope he didn't notice anything. He's quite capable of mentioning it to the Minister, who would put me on the retired list, all the more as, it appears, he's so himself." M. de Charlus was speechless with rage. At length, to bring this infuriating walk to an end, he decided to produce the letter and give it to the Ambassador to read, but warned him not to be discreet, for he liked to pretend that Charlie was jealous, in order to be able to make people think that he was enamoured. "And," he added with an indescribable air of benevolence, "we ought always to try to cause as little trouble as possible." Before we come back to Jupien's shop, the author would like to say how deeply he would regret it should any reader be offended by his portrayal of such unusual characters. On the one hand (and this is the less important aspect of the matter), it may be felt that the aristocracy is, in these pages, disproportionately accused of degeneracy in comparison with the other classes of society. Were this true, it would be in no way surprising. The oldest families end by displaying, in a red and bulbous nose, or a deformed chin, characteristic signs in which everyone admires 'blood.' But among these persistent and perpetually developing features, there are others that are not visible, to wit tendencies and tastes. It would be a more serious objection, were there any foundation for it, to say that all this is alien to us, and that we ought to extract truth from the poetry that is close at hand. Art extracted from the most familiar reality does indeed exist and its domain is perhaps the largest of any. But it is no less true that a strong interest, not to say beauty, may be found in actions inspired by a cast of mind so remote from anything that we feel, from anything that we believe, that we cannot ever succeed in understanding them, that they are displayed before our eyes like a spectacle without rhyme or reason. What could be more poetic than Xerxes, son of Darius, ordering the sea to be scourged with rods for having engulfed his fleet?

We may be certain that Morel, relying on the influence which his personal attractions give him over the girl, communicated to her, as coming from himself, the Baron's criticism, for the expression 'stand you a tea' disappeared as completely from the tailor's shop as disappears from a drawing-room some intimate friend who used to call daily, and with whom, for one reason or another, we have quarrelled, or whom we are trying to keep out of sight and meet only outside the house. M. de Charlus was satisfied by the cessation of 'stand you a tea.' He saw in it a proof of his own ascendancy over Morel and the removal of its one little blemish from the girl's perfection. In short, like everyone of his kind, while genuinely fond of Morel and of the girl who was all but engaged to him, an ardent advocate of their marriage, he thoroughly enjoyed his power to create at his pleasure more or less inoffensive little scenes, aloof from and above which he himself remained as Olympian as his brother.

Morel had told M. de Charlus that he was in love with Jupien's niece, and wished to marry her, and the Baron liked to accompany his young friend upon visits in which he played the part of father-in-law to be, indulgent and discreet. Nothing pleased him better.

My personal opinion is that 'stand you a tea' had originated with Morel himself, and that in the blindness of her love the young seamstress had adopted an expression from her beloved which clashed horribly with her own pretty way of speaking. This way of speaking, the charming manners that went with it, the patronage of M. de Charlus brought it about that many customers for whom she had worked received her as a friend, invited her to dinner, introduced her to their friends, though the girl accepted their invitations only with the Baron's permission and on the evenings that suited him. "A young seamstress received in society?" the reader will exclaim, "how improbable!" If you come to think of it, it was no less improbable that at one time Albertine should have come to see me at midnight, and that she should now be living in my house. And yet this might perhaps have been improbable of anyone else, but not of Albertine, a fatherless and motherless orphan, leading so uncontrolled a life that at first I had taken her, at Balbec, for the mistress of a bicyclist, a girl whose next of kin was Mme. Bontemps who in the old days, at Mme. Swann's, had admired nothing about her niece but her bad manners and who now shut her eyes, especially if by doing so she might be able to get rid of her by securing for her a wealthy marriage from which a little of the wealth would trickle into the aunt's pocket (in the highest society, a mother who is very well-born and quite penniless, when she has succeeded in finding a rich bride for her son, allows the young couple to support her, accepts presents of furs, a motor-car, money from a daughter-in-law whom she does not like but whom she introduces to her friends).

The day may come when dressmakers—nor should I find it at all shocking—will move in society. Jupien's niece being an exception affords us no base for calculation, for one swallow does not make a summer. In any case, if the very modest advancement of Jupien's niece did scandalise some people, Morel was not among them, for, in certain respects, his stupidity was so intense that not only did he label 'rather a fool' this girl a thousand times cleverer than himself, and foolish only perhaps in her love for himself, but he actually took to be adventuresses, dressmakers' assistants in disguise playing at being ladies, the persons of rank and position who invited her to their houses and whose invitations she accepted without a trace of vanity. Naturally these were not Guermantes, nor even people who knew the Guermantes, but rich and smart women of the middle-class, broad-minded enough to feel that it is no disgrace to invite a dressmaker to your house and at the same time servile enough to derive some satisfaction from patronising a girl whom His Highness the Baron de Charlus was in the habit—without any suggestion, of course, of impropriety—of visiting daily.

Nothing could have pleased the Baron more than the idea of this marriage, for he felt that in this way Morel would not be taken from him. It appears that Jupien's niece had been, when scarcely more than a child, 'in trouble.' And M. de Charlus, while he sang her praises to Morel, would have had no hesitation in revealing this secret to his friend, who would be furious, and thus sowing the seeds of discord. For M. de Charlus, although terribly malicious, resembled a great many good people who sing the praises of some man or woman, as a proof of their own generosity, but would avoid like poison the soothing words, so rarely uttered, that would be capable of putting an end to strife. Notwithstanding this, the Baron refrained from making any insinuation, and for two reasons. "If I tell him," he said to himself, "that his ladylove is not spotless, his vanity will be hurt, he will be angry with me. Besides, how am I to know that he is not in love with her? If I say nothing, this fire of straw will burn itself out before long, I shall be able to control their relations as I choose, he will love her only to the extent that I shall allow. If I tell him of his young lady's past transgression, who knows that my Charlie is not still sufficiently enamoured of her to become jealous. Then I shall by my own doing be converting a harmless and easily controlled flirtation into a serious passion, which is a difficult thing to manage." For these reasons, M. de Charlus preserved a silence which had only the outward appearance of discretion, but was in another respect meritorious, since it is almost impossible for men of his sort to hold their tongues.

Anyhow, the girl herself was charming, and M. de Charlus, who found that she satisfied all the aesthetic interest that he was capable of feeling in women, would have liked to have hundreds of photographs of her. Not such a fool as Morel, he was delighted to hear the names of the ladies who invited her to their houses, and whom his social instinct was able to place, but he took care (as he wished to retain his power) not to mention this to Charlie who, a regular idiot in this respect, continued to believe that, apart from the 'violin class' and the Verdurins, there existed only the Guermantes, and the few almost royal houses enumerated by the Baron, all the rest being but 'dregs' or 'scum.' Charlie interpreted these expressions of M. de Charlus literally.

Among the reasons which made M. de Charlus look forward to the marriage of the young couple was this, that Jupien's niece would then be in a sense an extension of Morel's personality, and so of the Baron's power over and knowledge of him. As for 'betraying' in the conjugal sense the violinist's future wife, it would never for a moment have occurred to M. de Charlus to feel the slightest scruple about that. But to have a 'young couple' to manage, to feel himself the redoubtable and all-powerful protector of Morel's wife, who if she regarded the Baron as a god would thereby prove that Morel had inculcated this idea into her, and would thus contain in herself something of Morel, added a new variety to the form of M. de Charlus's domination and brought to light in his 'creature,' Morel, a creature the more, that is to say gave the Baron something different, new, curious, to love in him. Perhaps even this domination would be stronger now than it had ever been. For whereas Morel by himself, naked so to speak, often resisted the Baron whom he felt certain of reconquering, once he was married, the thought of his home, his house, his future would alarm him more quickly, he would offer to M. de Charlus's desires a wider surface, an easier hold. All this, and even, failing anything else, on evenings when he was bored, the prospect of stirring up trouble between husband and wife (the Baron had never objected to battle-pictures) was pleasing to him. Less pleasing, however, than the thought of the state of dependence upon himself in which the young people would live. M. de Charlus's love for Morel acquired a delicious novelty when he said to himself: "His wife too will be mine just as much as he is, they will always take care not to annoy me, they will obey my caprices, and thus she will be a sign (which hitherto I have failed to observe) of what I had almost forgotten, what is so very dear to my heart, that to all the world, to everyone who sees that I protect them, house them, to myself, Morel is mine." This testimony in the eyes of the world and in his own pleased M. de Charlus more than anything. For the possession of what we love is an even greater joy than love itself. Very often those people who conceal this possession from the world do so only from the fear that the beloved object may be taken from them. And their happiness is diminished by this prudent reticence.

The reader may remember that Morel had once told the Baron that his great ambition was to seduce some young girl, and this girl in particular, that to succeed in his enterprise he would promise to marry her, and, the outrage accomplished, would 'cut his hook'; but this confession, what with the declarations of love for Jupien's niece which Morel had come and poured out to him, M. de Charlus had forgotten. What was more, Morel had quite possibly forgotten it himself. There was perhaps a real gap between Morel's nature—as he had cynically admitted, perhaps even artfully exaggerated it—and the moment at which it would regain control of him. As he became better acquainted with the girl, she had appealed to him, he began to like her. He knew himself so little that he doubtless imagined that he was in love with her, perhaps indeed that he would be in love with her always. To be sure his initial desire, his criminal intention remained, but glossed over by so many layers of sentiment that there is nothing to shew that the violinist would not have been sincere in saying that this vicious desire was not the true motive of his action. There was, moreover, a brief period during which, without his actually admitting it to himself, this marriage appeared to him to be necessary. Morel was suffering at the time from violent cramp in the hand, and found himself obliged to contemplate the possibility of his having to give up the violin. As, in everything but his art, he was astonishingly lazy, the question who was to maintain him loomed before him, and he preferred that it should be Jupien's niece rather than M. de Charlus, this arrangement offering him greater freedom and also a wider choice of several kinds of women, ranging from the apprentices, perpetually changing, whom he would make Jupien's niece debauch for him, to the rich and beautiful ladies to whom he would prostitute her. That his future wife might refuse to lend herself to these arrangements, that she could be so perverse never entered Morel's calculations for a moment. However, they passed into the background, their place being taken by pure love, now that his cramp had ceased. His violin would suffice, together with his allowance from M. de Charlus, whose claims upon him would certainly be reduced once he, Morel, was married to the girl. Marriage was the urgent thing, because of his love, and in the interest of his freedom. He made a formal offer of marriage to Jupien, who consulted his niece. This was wholly unnecessary. The girl's passion for the violinist streamed round about her, like her hair when she let it down, like the joy in her beaming eyes. In Morel, almost everything that was agreeable or advantageous to him awakened moral emotions and words to correspond, sometimes even melting him to tears. It was therefore sincerely—if such a word can be applied to him—that he addressed Jupien's niece in speeches as steeped in sentimentality (sentimental too are the speeches that so many young noblemen who look forward to a life of complete idleness address to some charming daughter of a middle-class millionaire) as had been steeped in unredeemed vileness the speech he had made to M. de Charlus about the seduction and deflowering of a virgin. Only there was another side to this virtuous enthusiasm for a person who afforded him pleasure and the solemn engagement that he made with her. As soon as the person ceased to afford him pleasure, or indeed if, for example, the obligation to fulfil the promise that he had made caused him displeasure, she at once became the object of an antipathy which he justified in his own eyes and which, after some neurasthenic disturbance, enabled him to prove to himself, as soon as the balance of his nervous system was restored, that he was, even looking at the matter from a purely virtuous point of view, released from any obligation. Thus, towards the end of his stay at Balbec, he had managed somehow to lose all his money and, not daring to mention the matter to M. de Charlus, looked about for some one to whom he might appeal. He had learned from his father (who at the same time had forbidden him ever to become a 'sponger') that in such circumstances the correct thing is to write to the person whom you intend to ask for a loan, "that you have to speak to him on business," to "ask him for a business appointment." This magic formula had so enchanted Morel that he would, I believe, have been glad to lose his money, simply to have the pleasure of asking for an appointment 'on business.' In the course of his life he had found that the formula had not quite the virtue that he supposed. He had discovered that certain people, to whom otherwise he would never have written at all, did not reply within five minutes of receiving his letter asking to speak to them 'on business.' If the afternoon went by without his receiving an answer, it never occurred to him that, to put the best interpretation on the matter, it was quite possible that the gentleman addressed had not yet come home, or had had other letters to write, if indeed he had not gone away from home altogether, fallen ill, or something of that sort. If by an extraordinary stroke of fortune Morel was given an appointment for the following morning, he would accost his intended creditor with: "I was quite surprised not to get an answer, I was wondering if there was anything wrong with you, I'm glad to see you're quite well," and so forth. Well then, at Balbec, and without telling me that he wished to talk 'business' to him, he had asked me to introduce him to that very Bloch to whom he had made himself so unpleasant a week earlier in the train. Bloch had not hesitated to lend him—or rather to secure a loan for him, from M. Nissim Bernard, of five thousand francs. From that moment Morel had worshipped Bloch. He asked himself with tears in his eyes how he could shew his indebtedness to a person who had saved his life. Finally, I under-took to ask on his behalf for a thousand francs monthly from M. de Charlus, a sum which he would at once forward to Bloch who would thus find him-self repaid within quite a short time. The first month, Morel, still under the impression of Bloch's generosity, sent him the thousand francs immedi-ately, but after this he doubtless found that a different application of the remaining four thousand francs might be more satisfactory to himself, for he began to say all sorts of unpleasant things about Bloch. The mere sight of Bloch was enough to fill his mind with dark thoughts, and Bloch him-self having forgotten the exact amount that he had lent Morel, and hav-ing asked him for 3,500 francs instead of 4,000 which would have left the violinist 500 francs to the good, the latter took the line that, in view of so preposterous a fraud, not only would he not pay another centime but his creditor might think himself very fortunate if Morel did not bring an action against him for slander. As he said this his eyes blazed. He did not content himself with asserting that Bloch and M. Nissim Bernard had no cause for complaint against him, but was soon saying that they might consider themselves lucky that he made no complaint against them. Finally, M. Nissim Bernard having apparently stated that Thibaut played as well as Morel, the last-named decided that he ought to take the matter into court, such a remark being calculated to damage him in his profession, then, as there was no longer any justice in France, especially against the Jews (anti-semitism being in Morel the natural effect of a loan of 5,000 francs from an Israelite), took to never going out without a loaded re-volver. A similar nervous reaction, in the wake of keen affection, was soon to occur in Morel with regard to the tailor's niece. It is true that M. de Charlus may have been unconsciously responsible, to some extent, for this change, for he was in the habit of saying, without meaning what he said for an instant, and merely to tease them, that, once they were married, he would never set eyes on them again but would leave them to fly upon their own wings. This idea was, in itself, quite insufficient to detach Morel from the girl; but, lurking in his mind, it was ready when the time came to combine with other analogous ideas, capable, once the compound was formed, of becoming a powerful disruptive agent.

It was not very often, however, that I was fated to meet M. de Charlus and Morel. Often they had already passed into Jupien's shop when I came away from the Duchess, for the pleasure that I found in her society was such that I was led to forget not merely the anxious expectation that pre-ceded Albertine's return, but even the hour of that return.

I shall set apart from the other days on which I lingered at Mme. de Guermantes's, one that was distinguished by a trivial incident the cruel sig-nificance of which entirely escaped me and did not enter my mind until long afterwards. On this particular afternoon, Mme. de Guermantes had given me, knowing that I was fond of them, some branches of syringa which had been sent to her from the South. When I left the Duchess and went upstairs to our flat, Albertine had already returned, and on the stair-case I ran into Andrée who seemed to be distressed by the powerful fra-grance of the flowers that I was bringing home.

"What, are you back already?" I said. "Only this moment, but Albertine had letters to write, so she sent me away." "You don't think she's up to any mischief?" "Not at all, she's writing to her aunt, I think, but you know how she dislikes strong scents, she won't be particularly pleased to see those syringas." "How stupid of me! I shall tell Françoise to put them out on the service stair." "Do you imagine Albertine won't notice the scent of them on you? Next to tuberoses they've the strongest scent of any flower, I always think; anyhow, I believe Françoise has gone out shopping." "But in that case, as I haven't got my latchkey, how am I to get in?" "Oh, you've only got to ring the bell. Albertine will let you in. Besides, Françoise may have come back by this time."

I said good-bye to Andrée. I had no sooner pressed the bell than Albertine came to open the door, which required some doing, as Françoise had gone out and Albertine did not know where to turn on the light. At length she was able to let me in, but the scent of the syringas put her to flight. I took them to the kitchen, with the result that my mistress, leaving her letter unfinished (why, I did not understand), had time to go to my room, from which she called to me, and to lay herself down on my bed. Even then, at the actual moment, I saw nothing in all this that was not perfectly natural, at the most a little confused, but in any case unimportant. She had nearly been caught out with Andrée and had snatched a brief respite for herself by turning out the lights, going to my room so that I should not see the disordered state of her own bed, and pretending to be busy writing a letter. But we shall see all this later on, a situation the truth of which I never ascertained. In general, and apart from this isolated incident, everything was quite normal when I returned from my visit to the Duchess. Since Albertine never knew whether I might not wish to go out with her before dinner, I usually found in the hall her hat, cloak and umbrella, which she had left lying there in case they should be needed. As soon as, on opening the door, I caught sight of them, the atmosphere of the house became breathable once more. I felt that, instead of a rarefied air, it was happiness that filled it. I was rescued from my melancholy, the sight of these trifles gave me possession of Albertine, I ran to greet her.

On the days when I did not go down to Mme. de Guermantes, to pass the time somehow, during the hour that preceded the return of my mistress, I would take up an album of Elstir's work, one of Bergotte's books, Vinteuil's sonata.

Then, just as those works of art which seem to address themselves to the eye or ear alone require that, if we are to enjoy them, our awakened intelligence shall collaborate closely with those organs, I would unconsciously evoke from myself the dreams that Albertine had inspired in me long ago, before I knew her, dreams that had been stifled by the routine of everyday life. I cast them into the composer's phrase or the painter's image as into a crucible, or used them to enrich the book that I was reading. And no doubt the book appeared all the more vivid in consequence. But Albertine herself profited just as much by being thus transported out of one of the two worlds to which we have access, and in which we can place alternately the same object, by escaping thus from the crushing weight of matter to play freely in the fluid space of mind. I found myself suddenly and for the instant capable of feeling an ardent desire for this irritating girl. She had at that moment the appearance of a work by Elstir or Bergotte, I felt a momentary enthusiasm for her, seeing her in the perspective of imagination and art.

Presently some one came to tell me that she had returned; though there was a standing order that her name was not to be mentioned if I was not alone, if for instance I had in the room with me Bloch, whom I would compel to remain with me a little longer so that there should be no risk of his meeting my mistress in the hall. For I concealed the fact that she was staying in the house, and even that I ever saw her there, so afraid was I that one of my friends might fall in love with her, and wait for her outside, or that in a momentary encounter in the passage or the hall she might make a signal and fix an appointment. Then I heard the rustle of Albertine's petticoats on her way to her own room, for out of discretion and also no doubt in that spirit in which, when we used to go to dinner at la Raspelière, she took care that I should have no cause for jealousy, she did not come to my room, knowing that I was not alone. But it was not only for this reason, as I suddenly realised. I remembered; I had known a different Albertine, then all at once she had changed into another, the Albertine of to-day. And for this change I could hold no one responsible but myself. The admissions that she would have made to me, easily at first, then deliberately, when we were simply friends, had ceased to flow from her as soon as she had suspected that I was in love with her, or, without perhaps naming Love, had divined the existence in me of an inquisitorial sentiment that desires to know, is pained by the knowledge, and seeks to learn yet more. Ever since that day, she had concealed everything from me. She kept away from my room if she thought that my companion was (rarely as this happened) not male but female, she whose eyes used at one time to sparkle so brightly whenever I mentioned a girl: "You must try and get her to come here. I should like to meet her." "But she has what you call a bad style." "Of course, that makes it all the more fun." At that moment, I might perhaps have learned all that there was to know. And indeed when in the little Casino she had withdrawn her breast from Andrée's, I believe that this was due not to my presence but to that of Cottard, who was capable, she doubtless thought, of giving her a bad reputation. And yet, even then, she had already begun to 'set,' the confiding speeches no longer issued from her lips, her gestures became reserved. After this, she had stripped herself of everything that could stir my emotions. To those parts of her life of which I knew nothing she ascribed a character the inoffensiveness of which my ignorance made itself her accomplice in accentuating. And now, the transformation was completed, she went straight to her room if I was not alone, not merely from fear of disturbing me, but in order to shew me that she did not care who was with me. There was one thing alone which she would never again do for me, which she would have done only in the days when it would have left me cold, which she would then have done without hesitation for that very reason, namely make me a detailed admission. I should always be obliged, like a judge, to draw indefinite conclusions from imprudences of speech that were perhaps not really inexplicable without postulating criminality. And always she would feel that I was jealous, and judging her.

As I listened to Albertine's footsteps with the consoling pleasure of thinking that she would not be going out again that evening, I thought how wonderful it was that for this girl, whom at one time I had supposed that I could never possibly succeed in knowing, the act of returning home every day was nothing else than that of entering my home. The pleasure, a blend of mystery and sensuality, which I had felt, fugitive and fragmentary, at Balbec, on the night when she had come to sleep at the hotel, was completed, stabilised, filled my dwelling, hitherto void, with a permanent store of domestic, almost conjugal bliss (radiating even into the passages) upon which all my senses, either actively, or, when I was alone, in imagination as I waited for her to return, quietly battened. When I had heard the door of Albertine's room shut behind her, if I had a friend with me, I made haste to get rid of him, not leaving him until I was quite sure that he was on the staircase, down which I might even escort him for a few steps. He warned me that I would catch cold, informing me that our house was indeed icy, a cave of the winds, and that he would not live in it if he was paid to do so. This cold weather was a source of complaint because it had just begun, and people were not yet accustomed to it, but for that very reason it released in me a joy accompanied by an unconscious memory of the first evenings of winter when, in past years, returning from the country, in order to reestablish contact with the forgotten delights of Paris, I used to go to a café-concert. And so it was with a song on my lips that, after bidding my friend good-bye, I climbed the stair again and entered the flat. Summer had flown, carrying the birds with it. But other musicians, invisible, internal, had taken their place. And the icy blast against which Bloch had inveighed, which was whistling delightfully through the ill fitting doors of our apartment was (as the fine days of summer by the woodland birds) passionately greeted with snatches, irrepressibly hummed, from Fragson, Mayol or Paulus. In the passage, Albertine was coming towards me. "I say, while I'm taking off my things, I shall send you Andrée, she's looked in for a minute to say how d'ye do." And still swathed in the big grey veil, falling from her chinchilla toque, which I had given her at Balbec, she turned from me and went back to her room, as though she had guessed that Andrée, whom I had charged with the duty of watching over her, would presently, by relating their day's adventures in full detail, mentioning their meeting with some person of their acquaintance, impart a certain clarity of outline to the vague regions in which that excursion had been made which had taken the whole day and which I had been incapable of imagining. Andrée's defects had become more evident; she was no longer as pleasant a companion as when I first knew her. One noticed now, on the surface, a sort of bitter uneasiness, ready to gather like a swell on the sea, merely if I happened to mention something that gave pleasure to Albertine and myself. This did not prevent Andrée from being kinder to me, liking me better—and I have had frequent proof of this—than other more sociable people. But the slightest look of happiness on a person's face, if it was not caused by herself, gave a shock to her nerves, as unpleasant as that given by a banging door. She could allow the pains in which she had no part, but not the pleasures; if she saw that I was unwell, she was distressed, was sorry for me, would have stayed to nurse me. But if I displayed a satisfaction as trifling as that of stretching myself with a blissful expression as I shut a book, saying: "Ah! I have spent a really happy afternoon with this entertaining book," these words, which would have given pleasure to my mother, to Albertine, to Saint-Loup, provoked in Andrée a sort of disapprobation, perhaps simply a sort of nervous irritation. My satisfactions caused her an annoyance which she was unable to conceal. These defects were supplemented by others of a more serious nature; one day when I mentioned that young man so learned in matters of racing and golf, so uneducated in all other respects, Andrée said with a sneer: "You know that his father is a swindler, he only just missed being prosecuted. They're swaggering now more than ever, but I tell everybody about it. I should love them to bring an action for slander against me. I should be wonderful in the witness-box!" Her eyes sparkled. Well, I discovered that the father had done nothing wrong, and that Andrée knew this as well as anybody. But she had thought that the son looked down upon her, had sought for something that would embarrass him, put him to shame, had invented a long story of evidence which she imagined herself called upon to give in court, and, by dint of repeating the details to herself, was perhaps no longer aware that they were not true. And so, in her present state (and even without her fleeting, foolish hatreds), I should not have wished to see her, were it merely on account of that malicious susceptibility which clasped with a harsh and frigid girdle her warmer and better nature. But the information which she alone could give me about my mistress was of too great interest for me to be able to neglect so rare an opportunity of acquiring it. Andrée came into my room, shutting the door behind her; they had met a girl they knew, whom Albertine had never mentioned to me. "What did they talk about?" "I can't tell you; I took the opportunity, as Albertine wasn't alone, to go and buy some worsted." "Buy some worsted?" "Yes, it was Albertine asked me to get it." "All the more reason not to have gone, it was perhaps a plot to get you out of the way." "But she asked me to go for it before we met her friend." "Ah!" I replied, drawing breath again. At once my suspicion revived; she might, for all I knew, have made an appointment beforehand with her friend and have provided herself with an excuse to be left alone when the time came. Besides, could I be certain that it was not my former hypothesis (according to which Andrée did not always tell me the truth) that was correct? Andrée was perhaps in the plot with Albertine. Love, I used to say to myself, at Balbec, is what we feel for a person whose actions seem rather to arouse our jealousy; we feel that if she were to tell us everything, we might perhaps easily be cured of our love for her. However skilfully jealousy is concealed by him who suffers from it, it is at once detected by her who has inspired it, and who when the time comes is no less skilful. She seeks to lead us off the trail of what might make us unhappy, and succeeds, for, to the man who is not forewarned, how should a casual utterance reveal the falsehoods that lie beneath it? We do not distinguish this utterance from the rest; spoken in terror, it is received without attention. Later on, when we are by ourselves, we shall return to this speech, it will seem to us not altogether adequate to the facts of the case. But do we remember it correctly? It seems as though there arose spontaneously in us, with regard to it and to the accuracy of our memory, an uncertainty of the sort with which, in certain nervous disorders, we can never remember whether we have bolted the door, no better after the fiftieth time than after the first, it would seem that we can repeat the action indefinitely without its ever being accompanied by a precise and liberating memory. At any rate, we can shut the door again, for the fifty-first time. Whereas the disturbing speech exists in the past in an imperfect hearing of it which it does not lie in our power to repeat. Then we concentrate our attention upon other speeches which conceal nothing and the sole remedy which we do not seek is to be ignorant of everything, so as to have no desire for further knowledge.

As soon as jealousy is discovered, it is regarded by her who is its object as a challenge which authorises deception. Moreover, in our endeavour to learn something, it is we who have taken the initiative in lying and deceit. Andrée, Aimé may promise us that they will say nothing, but will they keep their promise? Bloch could promise nothing because he knew nothing, and Albertine has only to talk to any of the three in order to learn, with the help of what Saint-Loup would have called cross-references, that we are lying to her when we pretend to be indifferent to her actions and morally incapable of having her watched. And so, replacing in this way my habitual boundless uncertainty as to what Albertine might be doing, an uncertainty too indeterminate not to remain painless, which was to jealousy what is to grief that beginning of forgetfulness in which relief is born of vagueness, the little fragment of response which Andrée had brought me at once began to raise fresh questions; the only result of my exploration of one sector of the great zone that extended round me had been to banish further from me that unknowable thing which, when we seek to form a definite idea of it, another person's life invariably is to us. I continued to question Andrée, while Albertine, from discretion and in order to leave me free (was she conscious of this?) to question the other, prolonged her toilet in her own room. "I think that Albertine's uncle and aunt both like me," I stupidly said to Andrée, forgetting her peculiar nature.

At once I saw her gelatinous features change. Like a syrup that has turned, her face seemed permanently clouded. Her mouth became bitter. Nothing remained in Andrée of that juvenile gaiety which, like all the little band and notwithstanding her feeble health, she had displayed in the year of my first visit to Balbec and which now (it is true that Andrée was now several years older) was so speedily eclipsed in her. But I was to make it reappear involuntarily before Andrée left me that evening to go home to dinner. "Somebody was singing your praises to me to-day in the most glowing language," I said to her. Immediately a ray of joy beamed from her eyes, she looked as though she really loved me. She avoided my gaze but smiled at the empty air with a pair of eyes that suddenly became quite round. "Who was it?" she asked, with an artless, avid interest. I told her, and, whoever it was, she was delighted.

Then the time came for us to part, and she left me. Albertine came to my room; she had undressed, and was wearing one of the charming crêpe de chine wrappers, or one of the Japanese gowns which I had asked Mme. de Guermantes to describe to me, and for some of which supplementary details had been furnished me by Mme. Swann, in a letter that began: "After your long eclipse, I felt as I read your letter about my tea-gowns that I was receiving a message from the other world."

Albertine had on her feet a pair of black shoes studded with brilliants which Françoise indignantly called 'pattens,' modelled upon the shoes which, from the drawing-room window, she had seen Mme. de Guermantes wearing in the evening, just as a little later Albertine took to wearing slippers, some of gilded kid, others of chinchilla, the sight of which was pleasant to me because they were all of them signs (which other shoes would not have been) that she was living under my roof. She had also certain things which had not come to her from me, including a fine gold ring. I admired upon it the outspread wings of an eagle. "It was my aunt gave me it," she explained. "She can be quite nice sometimes after all. It makes me feel terribly old, because she gave it to me on my twentieth birthday."

Albertine took a far keener interest in all these pretty things than the Duchess, because, like every obstacle in the way of possession (in my own case the ill health which made travel so difficult and so desirable), poverty, more generous than opulence, gives to women what is better than the garments that they cannot afford to buy, the desire for those garments which is the genuine, detailed, profound knowledge of them. She, because she had never been able to afford these things, I, because in ordering them for her I was seeking to give her pleasure, we were both of us like students who already know all about the pictures which they are longing to go to Dresden or Vienna to see. Whereas rich women, amid the multitude of their hats and gowns, are like those tourists to whom the visit to a gallery, being preceded by no desire, gives merely a sensation of bewilderment, boredom and exhaustion.

A particular toque, a particular sable cloak, a particular Doucet wrapper, its sleeves lined with pink, assumed for Albertine, who had observed them, coveted them and, thanks to the exclusiveness and minute nicety that are elements of desire, had at once isolated them from everything else in a void against which the lining or the scarf stood out to perfection, and learned them by heart in every detail—and for myself who had gone to Mme. de Guermantes in quest of an explanation of what constituted the peculiar merit, the superiority, the smartness of the garment and the inimitable style of the great designer—an importance, a charm which they certainly did not possess for the Duchess, surfeited before she had even acquired an appetite and would not, indeed, have possessed for myself had I beheld them a few years earlier while accompanying some lady of fashion on one of her wearisome tours of the dressmakers' shops.

To be sure, a lady of fashion was what Albertine was gradually becoming.

For, even if each of the things that I ordered for her was the prettiest of its kind, with all the refinements that had been added to it by Mme. de Guermantes or Mme. Swann, she was beginning to possess these things in abundance. But no matter, so long as she admired them from the first, and each of them separately.

When we have been smitten by one painter, then by another, we may end by feeling for the whole gallery an admiration that is not frigid, for it is made up of successive enthusiasms, each one exclusive in its day, which finally have joined forces and become reconciled in one whole.

She was not, for that matter, frivolous, read a great deal when she was by herself, and used to read aloud when she was with me. She had become extremely intelligent. She would say, though she was quite wrong in saying: "I am appalled when I think that but for you I should still be quite ignorant. Don't contradict. You have opened up a world of ideas to me which I never suspected, and whatever I may have become I owe entirely to you."

It will be remembered that she had spoken in similar terms of my influence over Andrée. Had either of them a sentimental regard for me? And, in themselves, what were Albertine and Andrée? To learn the answer, I should have to immobilise you, to cease to live in that perpetual expectation, ending always in a different presentment of you, I should have to cease to love you, in order to fix you, to cease to know your interminable and ever disconcerting arrival, oh girls, oh recurrent ray in the swirl wherein we throb with emotion upon seeing you reappear while barely recognising you, in the dizzy velocity of light. That velocity, we should perhaps remain unaware of it and everything would seem to us motionless, did not a sexual attraction set us in pursuit of you, drops of gold always different, and always passing our expectation! On each occasion a girl so little resembles what she was the time before (shattering in fragments as soon as we catch sight of her the memory that we had retained of her and the desire that we were proposing to gratify), that the stability of nature which we ascribe to her is purely fictitious and a convenience of speech. We have been told that some pretty girl is tender, loving, full of the most delicate sentiments. Our imagination accepts this assurance, and when we behold for the first time, within the woven girdle of her golden hair, the rosy disc of her face, we are almost afraid that this too virtuous sister may chill our ardour by her very virtue, that she can never be to us the lover for whom we have been longing. What secrets, at least, we confide in her from the first moment, on the strength of that nobility of heart, what plans we discuss together. But a few days later, we regret that we were so confiding, for the rose-leaf girl, at our second meeting, addresses us in the language of a lascivious Fury. As for the successive portraits which after a pulsation lasting for some days the renewal of the rosy light presents to us, it is not even certain that a momentum external to these girls has not modified their aspect, and this might well have happened with my band of girls at Balbec.

People extol to us the gentleness, the purity of a virgin. But afterwards they feel that something more seasoned would please us better, and recommend her to shew more boldness. In herself was she one more than the other? Perhaps not, but capable of yielding to any number of different possibilities in the headlong current of life. With another girl, whose whole attraction lay in something implacable (which we counted upon subduing to our own will), as, for instance, with the terrible jumping girl at Balbec who grazed in her spring the bald pates of startled old gentlemen, what a disappointment when, in the fresh aspect of her, just as we were addressing her in affectionate speeches stimulated by our memory of all her cruelty to other people, we heard her, as her first move in the game, tell us that she was shy, that she could never say anything intelligent to anyone at a first introduction, so frightened was she, and that it was only after a fortnight or so that she would be able to talk to us at her ease. The steel had turned to cotton, there was nothing left for us to attempt to break, since she herself had lost all her consistency. Of her own accord, but by our fault perhaps, for the tender words which we had addressed to Severity had perhaps, even without any deliberate calculation on her part, suggested to her that she ought to be gentle.

Distressing as the change may have been to us, it was not altogether maladroit, for our gratitude for all her gentleness would exact more from us perhaps than our delight at overcoming her cruelty. I do not say that a day will not come when, even to these luminous maidens, we shall not assign sharply differentiated characters, but that will be because they have ceased to interest us, because their entry upon the scene will no longer be to our heart the apparition which it expected in a different form and which leaves it overwhelmed every time by fresh incarnations. Their immobility will spring from our indifference to them, which will hand them over to the judgment of our mind. This will not, for that matter, be expressed in any more categorical terms, for after it has decided that some defect which was prominent in one is fortunately absent from the other, it will see that this defect had as its counterpart some priceless merit. So that the false judgment of our intellect, which comes into play only when we have ceased to take any interest, will define permanent characters of girls, which will enlighten us no more than the surprising faces that used to appear every day when, in the dizzy speed of our expectation, our friends presented themselves daily, weekly, too different to allow us, as they never halted in their passage, to classify them, to award degrees of merit. As for our sentiments, we have spoken of them too often to repeat again now that as often as not love is nothing more than the association of the face of a girl (whom otherwise we should soon have found intolerable) with the heartbeats inseparable from an endless, vain expectation, and from some trick that she has played upon us. All this is true not merely of imaginative young men brought into contact with changeable girls. At the stage that our narrative has now reached, it appears, as I have since heard, that Jupien's niece had altered her opinion of Morel and M. de Charlus. My motorist, reinforcing the love that she felt for Morel, had extolled to her, as existing in the violinist, boundless refinements of delicacy in which she was all too ready to believe. And at the same time Morel never ceased to complain to her of the despotic treatment that he received from M. de

Charlus, which she ascribed to malevolence, never imagining that it could be due to love. She was moreover bound to acknowledge that M. de Charlus was tyrannically present at all their meetings. In corroboration of all this, she had heard women in society speak of the Baron's terrible spite. Now, quite recently, her judgment had been completely reversed. She had discovered in Morel (without ceasing for that reason to love him) depths of malevolence and perfidy, compensated it was true by frequent kindness and genuine feeling, and in M. de Charlus an unimaginable and immense generosity blended with asperities of which she knew nothing. And so she had been unable to arrive at any more definite judgment of what, each in himself, the violinist and his protector really were, than I was able to form of Andrée, whom nevertheless I saw every day, or of Albertine who was living with me. On the evenings when the latter did not read aloud to me, she would play to me or begin a game of draughts, or a conversation, either of which I would interrupt with kisses. The simplicity of our relations made them soothing. The very emptiness of her life gave Albertine a sort of eagerness to comply with the only requests that I made of her. Behind this girl, as behind the purple light that used to filter beneath the curtains of my room at Balbec, while outside the concert blared, were shining the blue-green undulations of the sea. Was she not, after all (she in whose heart of hearts there was now regularly installed an idea of myself so familiar that, next to her aunt, I was perhaps the person whom she distinguished least from herself), the girl whom I had seen the first time at Balbec, in her flat polo-cap, with her insistent laughing eyes, a stranger still, exiguous as a silhouette projected against the waves? These effigies preserved intact in our memory, when we recapture them, we are astonished at their unlikeness to the person whom we know, and we begin to realise what a task of remodelling is performed every day by habit. In the charm that Albertine had in Paris, by my fireside, there still survived the desire that had been aroused in me by that insolent and blossoming parade along the beach, and just as Rachel retained in Saint-Loup's eyes, even after he had made her abandon it, the prestige of her life on the stage, so in this Albertine cloistered in my house, far from Balbec, from which I had hurried her away, there persisted the emotion, the social confusion, the uneasy vanity, the roving desires of life by the seaside. She was so effectively caged that on certain evenings I did not even ask her to leave her room for mine, her to whom at one time all the world gave chase, whom I had found it so hard to overtake as she sped past on her bicycle, whom the lift-boy himself was unable to capture for me, leaving me with scarcely a hope of her coming, although I sat up waiting for her all the night. Had not Albertine been—out there in front of the Hotel—like a great actress of the blazing beach, arousing jealousy when she advanced upon that natural stage, not speaking to anyone, thrusting past its regular frequenters, dominating the girls, her friends, and was not this so greatly coveted actress the same who, withdrawn by me from the stage, shut up in my house, was out of reach now of the desires of all the rest, who might hereafter seek for her in vain, sitting now in my room, now in her own, and engaged in tracing or cutting out some pattern?

No doubt, in the first days at Balbec, Albertine seemed to be on a parallel plane to that upon which I was living, but one that had drawn closer (after my visit to Elstir) and had finally become merged in it, as my relations with her, at Balbec, in Paris, then at Balbec again, grew more intimate. Besides, between the two pictures of Balbec, at my first visit and at my second, pictures composed of the same villas from which the same girls walked down to the same sea, what a difference! In Albertine's friends at the time of my second visit, whom I knew so well, whose good and bad qualities were so clearly engraved on their features, how was I to recapture those fresh, mysterious strangers who at first could not, without making my heart throb, thrust open the door of their bungalow over the grinding sand and set the tamarisks shivering as they came down the path! Their huge eyes had, in the interval, been absorbed into their faces, doubtless because they had ceased to be children, but also because those ravishing strangers, those ravishing actresses of the romantic first year, as to whom I had gone ceaselessly in quest of information, no longer held any mystery for me. They had become obedient to my caprices, a mere grove of budding girls, from among whom I was quite distinctly proud of having plucked, and carried off from them all, their fairest rose.

Between the two Balbec scenes, so different one from the other, there was the interval of several years in Paris, the long expanse of which was dotted with all the visits that Albertine had paid me. I saw her in successive years of my life occupying, with regard to myself, different positions, which made me feel the beauty of the interposed gaps, that long extent of time in which I never set eyes on her and against the diaphanous background of which the rosy person that I saw before me was modelled with mysterious shadows and in bold relief. This was due also to the superimposition not merely of the successive images which Albertine had been for me, but also of the great qualities of brain and heart, the defects of character, all alike unsuspected by me, which Albertine, in a germination, a multiplication of herself, a carnal efflorescence in sombre colours, had added to a nature that formerly could scarcely have been said to exist, but was now deep beyond plumbing. For other people, even those of whom we have so often dreamed that they have become nothing more than a picture, a figure by Benozzo Gozzoli standing out upon a background of verdure, as to whom we were prepared to believe that the only variations depended upon the point of view from which we looked at them, their distance from us, the effect of light and shade, these people, while they change in relation to ourselves, change also in themselves, and there had been an enrichment, a solidification and an increase of volume in the figure once so simply outlined against the sea. Moreover, it was not only the sea at the close of day that came to life for me in Albertine, but sometimes the drowsy murmur of the sea upon the shore on moonlit nights.

Sometimes, indeed, when I rose to fetch a book from my father's study, and had given my mistress permission to lie down while I was out of the room, she was so tired after her long outing in the morning and afternoon in the open air that, even if I had been away for a moment only, when I returned I found Albertine asleep and did not rouse her.

Stretched out at full length upon my bed, in an attitude so natural that no art could have designed it, she reminded me of a long blossoming stem that had been laid there, and so indeed she was: the faculty of dreaming which I possessed only in her absence I recovered at such moments in her presence, as though by falling asleep she had become a plant. In this way her sleep did to a certain extent make love possible. When she was present, I spoke to her, but I was too far absent from myself to be able to think. When she was asleep, I no longer needed to talk to her, I knew that she was no longer looking at me, I had no longer any need to live upon my own outer surface.

By shutting her eyes, by losing consciousness, Albertine had stripped off, one after another, the different human characters with which she had deceived me ever since the day when I had first made her acquaintance. She was animated now only by the unconscious life of vegetation, of trees, a life more different from my own, more alien, and yet one that belonged more to me. Her personality did not escape at every moment, as when we were talking, by the channels of her unacknowledged thoughts and of her gaze. She had called back into herself everything of her that lay outside, had taken refuge, enclosed, reabsorbed, in her body. In keeping her before my eyes, in my hands, I had that impression of possessing her altogether, which I never had when she was awake. Her life was submitted to me, exhaled towards me its gentle breath.

I listened to this murmuring, mysterious emanation, soft as a breeze from the sea, fairylike as that moonlight which was her sleep. So long as it lasted, I was free to think about her and at the same time to look at her, and, when her sleep grew deeper, to touch, to kiss her. What I felt then was love in the presence of something as pure, as immaterial in its feelings, as mysterious, as if I had been in the presence of those inanimate creatures which are the beauties of nature. And indeed, as soon as her sleep became at all heavy, she ceased to be merely the plant that she had been; her sleep, on the margin of which I remained musing, with a fresh delight of which I never tired, but could have gone on enjoying indefinitely, was to me an undiscovered country. Her sleep brought within my reach something as calm, as sensually delicious as those nights of full moon on the bay of Balbec, turned quiet as a lake over which the branches barely stir, where stretched out upon the sand one could listen for hours on end to the waves breaking and receding.

When I entered the room, I remained standing in the doorway, not venturing to make a sound, and hearing none but that of her breath rising to expire upon her lips at regular intervals, like the reflux of the sea, but drowsier and more gentle. And at the moment when my ear absorbed that divine sound, I felt that there was, condensed in it, the whole person, the whole life of the charming captive, outstretched there before my eyes. Carriages went rattling past in the street, her features remained as motionless, as pure, her breath as light, reduced to the simplest expulsion of the necessary quantity of air. Then, seeing that her sleep would not be disturbed, I advanced cautiously, sat down upon the chair that stood by the bedside, then upon the bed itself.

I have spent charming evenings talking, playing games with Albertine, but never any so pleasant as when I was watching her sleep. Granted that she might have, as she chatted with me, or played cards, that spontaneity which no actress could have imitated, it was a spontaneity carried to the second degree that was offered me by her sleep. Her hair, falling all along her rosy face, was spread out beside her on the bed, and here and there a separate straight tress gave the same effect of perspective as those moon-lit trees, lank and pale, which one sees standing erect and stiff in the backgrounds of Elstir's Raphaelesque pictures. If Albertine's lips were closed, her eyelids, on the other hand, seen from the point at which I was standing, seemed so loosely joined that I might almost have questioned whether she really was asleep. At the same time those drooping lids introduced into her face that perfect continuity, unbroken by any intrusion of eyes. There are people whose faces assume a quite unusual beauty and majesty the moment they cease to look out of their eyes.

I measured with my own Albertine outstretched at my feet. Now and then a slight, unaccountable tremor ran through her body, as the leaves of a tree are shaken for a few moments by a sudden breath of wind. She would touch her hair, then, not having arranged it to her liking, would raise her hand to it again with motions so consecutive, so deliberate, that I was convinced that she was about to wake. Not at all, she grew calm again in the sleep from which she had not emerged. After this she lay without moving. She had laid her hand on her bosom with a sinking of the arm so artlessly childlike that I was obliged, as I gazed at her, to suppress the smile that is provoked in us by the solemnity, the innocence and the charm of little children.

I, who was acquainted with many Albertines in one person, seemed now to see many more again, reposing by my side. Her eyebrows, arched as I had never seen them, enclosed the globes of her eyelids like a halcyon's downy nest. Races, atavisms, vices reposed upon her face. Whenever she moved her head, she created a fresh woman, often one whose existence I had never suspected. I seemed to possess not one, but innumerable girls. Her breathing, as it became gradually deeper, was now regularly stirring her bosom and, through it, her folded hands, her pearls, displaced in a different way by the same movement, like the boats, the anchor chains that are set swaying by the movement of the tide. Then, feeling that the tide of her sleep was full, that I should not ground upon reefs of conscious-ness covered now by the high water of profound slumber, deliberately, I crept without a sound upon the bed, lay down by her side, clasped her waist in one arm, placed my lips upon her cheek and heart, then upon every part of her body in turn laid my free hand, which also was raised, like the pearls, by Albertine's breathing; I myself was gently rocked by its regular motion: I had embarked upon the tide of Albertine's sleep. Sometimes it made me taste a pleasure that was less pure. For this I had no need to make any movement, I allowed my leg to dangle against hers, like an oar which one allows to trail in the water, imparting to it now and again a gentle oscillation like the intermittent flap given to its wing by a bird asleep in the air. I chose, in gazing at her, this aspect of her face which no one ever saw and which was so pleasing.

It is I suppose comprehensible that the letters which we receive from a person are more or less similar and combine to trace an image of the writer so different from the person whom we know as to constitute a second personality. But how much stranger is it that a woman should be conjoined, like Rosita and Doodica, with another woman whose different beauty makes us infer another character, and that in order to behold one we must look at her in profile, the other in full face. The sound of her breathing as it grew louder might give the illusion of the breathless ecstasy of pleasure and, when mine was at its climax, I could kiss her without having interrupted her sleep. I felt at such moments that I had been possessing her more completely, like an unconscious and unresisting object of dumb nature. I was not affected by the words that she muttered occasionally in her sleep, their meaning escaped me, and besides, whoever the unknown person to whom they referred, it was upon my hand, upon my cheek that her hand, as an occasional tremor recalled it to life, stiffened for an instant. I relished her sleep with a disinterested, soothing love, just as I would remain for hours listening to the unfurling of the waves.

Perhaps it is laid down that people must be capable of making us suffer intensely before, in the hours of respite, they can procure for us the same soothing calm as Nature. I had not to answer her as when we were engaged in conversation, and even if I could have remained silent, as for that matter I did when it was she that was talking, still while listening to her voice I did not penetrate so far into herself. As I continued to hear, to gather from moment to moment the murmur, soothing as a barely perceptible breeze, of her breath, it was a whole physiological existence that was spread out before me, for me; as I used to remain for hours lying on the beach, in the moonlight, so long could I have remained there gazing at her, listening to her.

Sometimes one would have said that the sea was becoming rough, that the storm was making itself felt even inside the bay, and like the bay I lay listening to the gathering roar of her breath. Sometimes, when she was too warm, she would take off, already half asleep, her kimono which she flung over my armchair. While she was asleep I would tell myself that all her correspondence was in the inner pocket of this kimono, into which she always thrust her letters. A signature, a written appointment would have sufficed to prove a lie or to dispel a suspicion. When I could see that Albertine was sound asleep, leaving the foot of the bed where I had been standing motionless in contemplation of her, I took a step forward, seized by a burning curiosity, feeling that the secret of this other life lay offering itself to me, flaccid and defenceless, in that armchair. Perhaps I took this step forward also because to stand perfectly still and watch her sleeping became tiring after a while. And so, on tiptoe, constantly turning round to make sure that Albertine was not waking, I made my way to the armchair. There I stopped short, stood for a long time gazing at the kimono, as I had stood for a long time gazing at Albertine. But (and here perhaps I was wrong) never once did I touch the kimono, put my hand in the pocket, examine the letters. In the end, realising that I would never make up my mind, I started back, on tiptoe, returned to Albertine's bedside and began again to watch her sleeping, her who would tell me nothing, whereas I could see lying across an arm of the chair that kimono which would have told me much. And just as people pay a hundred francs a day for a room at the Hotel at Balbec in order to breathe the sea air, I felt it to be quite natural that I should spend more than that upon her since I had her breath upon my cheek, between her lips which I parted with my own, through which her life flowed against my tongue.

But this pleasure of seeing her sleep, which was as precious as that of feeling her live, was cut short by another pleasure, that of seeing her wake. It was, carried to a more profound and more mysterious degree, the same pleasure that I felt in having her under my roof. It was gratifying, of course, in the afternoon, when she alighted from the carriage, that it should be to my address that she was returning. It was even more so to me that when from the underworld of sleep she climbed the last steps of the stair of dreams, it was in my room that she was reborn to consciousness and life, that she asked herself for an instant: "Where am I?" and, seeing all the things in the room round about her, the lamp whose light scarcely made her blink her eyes, was able to assure herself that she was at home, as soon as she realised that she was waking in my home. In that first delicious moment of uncertainty, it seemed to me that once again I took a more complete possession of her since, whereas after an outing it was to her own room that she returned, it was now my room that, as soon as Albertine should have recognised it, was about to enclose, to contain her, without any sign of misgiving in the eyes of my mistress, which remained as calm as if she had never slept at all.

The uncertainty of awakening revealed by her silence was not at all revealed in her eyes. As soon as she was able to speak she said: "My ———" or "My dearest———" followed by my Christian name, which, if we give the narrator the same name as the author of this book, would be 'My Marcel,' or 'My dearest Marcel.' After this I would never allow my relatives, by calling me 'dearest,' to rob of their priceless uniqueness the delicious words that Albertine uttered to me. As she uttered them, she pursed her lips in a little pout which she herself transformed into a kiss. As quickly as, earlier in the evening, she had fallen asleep, so quickly had she awoken.

No more than my own progression in time, no more than the act of gazing at a girl seated opposite to me beneath the lamp, which shed upon her a different light from that of the sun when I used to behold her striding along the seashore, was this material enrichment, this autonomous progress of Albertine the determining cause of the difference between my present view of her and my original impression of her at Balbec. A longer term of years might have separated the two images without effecting so complete a change; it had come to pass, essential and sudden, when I learned that my mistress had been virtually brought up by Mlle. Vinteuil's friend. If at one time I had been carried away by excitement when I thought that I saw a trace of mystery in Albertine's eyes, now I was happy only at the moments when from those eyes, from her cheeks even, as mirroring as her eyes, so gentle now but quickly turning sullen, I succeeded in expelling every trace of mystery.

The image for which I sought, upon which I reposed, against which I would have liked to lean and die, was no longer that of Albertine leading a hidden life, it was that of an Albertine as familiar to me as possible (and for this reason my love could not be lasting unless it was unhappy, for in its nature it did not satisfy my need of mystery), an Albertine who did not reflect a distant world, but desired nothing else—there were moments when this did indeed appear to be the case—than to be with me, a person like myself, an Albertine the embodiment of what belonged to me and not of the unknown. When it is in this way, from an hour of anguish caused by another person, when it is from uncertainty whether we shall be able to keep her or she will escape, that love is born, such love bears the mark of the revolution that has created it, it recalls very little of what we had previously seen when we thought of the person in question. And my first impressions at the sight of Albertine, against a background of sea, might to some small extent persist in my love of her: actually, these earlier impressions occupy but a tiny place in a love of this sort; in its strength, in its agony, in its need of comfort and its return to a calm and soothing memory with which we would prefer to abide and to learn nothing more of her whom we love, even if there be something horrible that we ought to know—would prefer still more to consult only these earlier memories —such a love is composed of very different material!

Sometimes I put out the light before she came in. It was in the darkness, barely guided by the glow of a smouldering log, that she lay down by my side. My hands, my cheeks alone identified her without my eyes beholding her, my eyes that often were afraid of finding her altered. With the result that by virtue of this unseeing love she may have felt herself bathed in a warmer affection than usual. On other evenings, I undressed, I lay down, and, with Albertine perched on the side of my bed, we resumed our game or our conversation interrupted by kisses; and, in the desire that alone makes us take an interest in the existence and character of another person, we remain so true to our own nature (even if, at the same time, we abandon successively the different people whom we have loved in turn), that on one occasion, catching sight of myself in the glass at the moment when I was kissing Albertine and calling her my little girl, the sorrowful, passionate expression on my own face, similar to the expression it had assumed long ago with Gilberte whom I no longer remembered, and would perhaps assume one day with another girl, if I was fated ever to forget Albertine, made me think that over and above any personal considerations (instinct requiring that we consider the person of the moment as the only true person) I was performing the duties of an ardent and painful devotion dedicated as an oblation to the youth and beauty of Woman. And yet with this desire, honouring youth with an *ex voto*, with my memories also of Balbec, there was blended, in the need that I felt of keeping Albertine in this way every evening by my side, something that had hitherto been unknown, at least in my amorous existence, if it was not entirely novel in my life.

It was a soothing power the like of which I had not known since the evenings at Combray long ago when my mother, stooping over my bed,

brought me repose in a kiss. To be sure, I should have been greatly astonished at that time, had anyone told me that I was not wholly virtuous,
and more astonished still to be told that I would ever seek to deprive some
one else of a pleasure. I must have known myself very slightly, for my
pleasure in having Albertine to live with me was much less a positive pleasure than that of having withdrawn from the world, where everyone was
free to enjoy her in turn, the blossoming damsel who, if she did not bring
me any great joy, was at least withholding joy from others. Ambition,
fame would have left me unmoved. Even more was I incapable of feeling
hatred. And yet to me to love in a carnal sense was at any rate to enjoy
a triumph over countless rivals. I can never repeat it often enough; it was
first and foremost a sedative.

For all that I might, before Albertine returned, have doubted her loyalty,
have imagined her in the room at Montjouvain, once she was in her dressing-gown and seated facing my chair, or (if, as was more frequent, I had
remained in bed) at the foot of my bed, I would deposit my doubts in her,
hand them over for her to relieve me of them, with the abnegation of a
worshipper uttering his prayer. All the evening she might have been there,
huddled in a provoking ball upon my bed, playing with me, like a great
cat; her little pink nose, the tip of which she made even tinier with a
coquettish glance which gave it that sharpness which we see in certain
people who are inclined to be stout, might have given her a fiery and rebellious air; she might have allowed a tress of her long, dark hair to fall
over a cheek of rosy wax and, half shutting her eyes, unfolding her arms,
have seemed to be saying to me: "Do with me what you please!"; when,
as the time came for her to leave me, she drew nearer to say good night,
it was a meekness that had become almost a part of my family life that
I kissed on either side of her firm throat which now never seemed to me
brown or freckled enough, as though these solid qualities had been in
keeping with some loyal generosity in Albertine.

When it was Albertine's turn to bid me good night, kissing me on either
side of my throat, her hair caressed me like a wing of softly bristling
feathers. Incomparable as were those two kisses of peace, Albertine slipped
into my mouth, making me the gift of her tongue, like a gift of the Holy
Spirit, conveyed to me a viaticum, left me with a provision of tranquillity
almost as precious as when my mother in the evening at Combray used to
lay her lips upon my brow.

"Are you coming with us to-morrow, you naughty man?" she asked before leaving me. "Where are you going?" "That will depend on the weather
and on yourself. But have you written anything to-day, my little darling?
No? Then it was hardly worth your while, not coming with us. Tell me,
by the way, when I came in, you knew my step, you guessed at once who
it was?" "Of course. Could I possibly be mistaken, couldn't I tell my little
sparrow's hop among a thousand? She must let me take her shoes off, before she goes to bed, it will be such a pleasure to me. You are so nice and
pink in all that white lace."

Such was my answer; among the sensual expressions, we may recognise
others that were peculiar to my grandmother and mother for, little by

little, I was beginning to resemble all my relatives, my father who—in a very different fashion from myself, no doubt, for if things do repeat themselves, it is with great variations—took so keen an interest in the weather; and not my father only, I was becoming more and more like my aunt Léonie. Otherwise, Albertine could not but have been a reason for my going out of doors, so as not to leave her by herself, beyond my control. My aunt Léonie, wrapped up in her religious observances, with whom I could have sworn that I had not a single point in common, I so passionately keen on pleasure, apparently worlds apart from that maniac who had never known any pleasure in her life and lay mumbling her rosary all day long, I who suffered from my inability to embark upon a literary career whereas she had been the one person in the family who could never understand that reading was anything more than an amusing pastime, which made reading, even at the paschal season, lawful upon Sunday, when every serious occupation is forbidden, in order that the day may be hallowed by prayer alone. Now, albeit every day I found an excuse in some particular indisposition which made me so often remain in bed, a person (not Albertine, not any person that I loved, but a person with more power over me than any beloved) had migrated into me, despotic to the extent of silencing at times my jealous suspicions or at least of preventing me from going to find out whether they had any foundation, and this was my aunt Léonie. It was quite enough that I should bear an exaggerated resemblance to my father, to the extent of not being satisfied like him with consulting the barometer, but becoming an animated barometer myself; it was quite enough that I should allow myself to be ordered by my aunt Léonie to stay at home and watch the weather, from my bedroom window or even from my bed; yet here I was talking now to Albertine, at one moment as the child that I had been at Combray used to talk to my mother, at another as my grandmother used to talk to me.

When we have passed a certain age, the soul of the child that we were and the souls of the dead from whom we spring come and bestow upon us in handfuls their treasures and their calamities, asking to be allowed to cooperate in the new sentiments which we are feeling and in which, obliterating their former image, we recast them in an original creation. Thus my whole past from my earliest years, and earlier still the past of my parents and relatives, blended with my impure love for Albertine the charm of an affection at once filial and maternal. We have to give hospitality, at a certain stage in our life, to all our relatives who have journeyed so far and gathered round us.

Before Albertine obeyed and allowed me to take off her shoes, I opened her chemise. Her two little upstanding breasts were so round that they seemed not so much to be an integral part of her body as to have ripened there like fruit; and her belly (concealing the place where a man's is marred as though by an iron clamp left sticking in a statue that has been taken down from its niche) was closed, at the junction of her thighs, by two valves of a curve as hushed, as reposeful, as cloistral as that of the horizon after the sun has set. She took off her shoes, and lay down by my side.

O mighty attitudes of Man and Woman, in which there seeks to be re-united, in the innocence of the world's first age and with the humility of clay, what creation has cloven apart, in which Eve is astonished and sub-missive before the Man by whose side she has awoken, as he himself, alone still, before God Who has fashioned him. Albertine folded her arms behind her dark hair, her swelling hip, her leg falling with the inflexion of a swan's neck that stretches upwards and then curves over towards its starting point. It was only when she was lying right on her side that one saw a certain aspect of her face (so good and handsome when one looked at it from in front) which I could not endure, hook-nosed as in some of Leonardo's caricatures, seeming to indicate the shiftiness, the greed for profit, the cunning of a spy whose presence in my house would have filled me with horror and whom that profile seemed to unmask. At once I took Albertine's face in my hands and altered its position.

"Be a good boy, promise me that if you don't come out to-morrow you will work," said my mistress as she slipped into her chemise. "Yes, but don't put on your dressing-gown yet." Sometimes I ended by falling asleep by her side. The room had grown cold, more wood was wanted. I tried to find the bell above my head, but failed to do so, after fingering all the copper rods in turn save those between which it hung, and said to Alber-tine who had sprung from the bed so that Françoise should not find us lying side by side: "No, come back for a moment, I can't find the bell."

Comforting moments, gay, innocent to all appearance, and yet moments in which there accumulates in us the never suspected possibility of disaster, which makes the amorous life the most precarious of all, that in which the incalculable rain of sulphur and brimstone falls after the most radiant moments, after which, without having the courage to derive its lesson from our mishap, we set to work immediately to rebuild upon the slopes of the crater from which nothing but catastrophe can emerge. I was as careless as everyone who imagines that his happiness will endure.

It is precisely because this comfort has been necessary to bring grief to birth—and will return moreover at intervals to calm it—that men can be sincere with each other, and even with themselves, when they pride themselves upon a woman's kindness to them, although, taking things all in all, at the heart of their intimacy there lurks continually in a secret fashion, unavowed to the rest of the world, or revealed unintentionally by questions, inquiries, a painful uncertainty. But as this could not have come to birth without the preliminary comfort, as even afterwards the intermittent comfort is necessary to make suffering endurable and to pre-vent ruptures, their concealment of the secret hell that life can be when shared with the woman in question, carried to the pitch of an ostentatious display of an intimacy which, they pretend, is precious, expresses a genuine point of view, a universal process of cause and effect, one of the modes in which the production of grief is rendered possible.

It no longer surprised me that Albertine should be in the house, and would not be going out to-morrow save with myself or in the custody of Andrée. These habits of a life shared in common, this broad outline which defined my existence and within which nobody might penetrate but Albertine, also (in the future plan, of which I was still unaware, of my life to come, like the plan traced by an architect for monumental structures which will not be erected until long afterwards) the remoter lines, parallel to the others but vaster, that sketched in me, like a lonely hermitage, the somewhat rigid and monotonous formula of my future loves, had in reality been traced that night at Balbec when, in the little tram, after Albertine had revealed to me who it was that had brought her up, I had decided at any cost to remove her from certain influences and to prevent her from straying out of my sight for some days to come. Day after day had gone by, these habits had become mechanical, but, like those primitive rites the meaning of which historians seek to discover, I might (but would not) have said to anybody who asked me what I meant by this life of seclusion which I carried so far as not to go any more to the theatre, that its origin was the anxiety of a certain evening, and my need to prove to myself, during the days that followed, that the girl whose unfortunate childhood I had learned should not find it possible, if she wished, to expose herself to similar temptations. I no longer thought, save very rarely, of these possibilities, but they were nevertheless to remain vaguely present in my consciousness. The fact that I was destroying—or trying to destroy—them day by day was doubtless the reason why it comforted me to kiss those cheeks which were no more beautiful than many others; beneath any carnal attraction which is at all profound, there is the permanent possibility of danger.

I had promised Albertine that, if I did not go out with her, I would settle down to work, but in the morning, just as if, taking advantage of our being asleep, the house had miraculously flown, I awoke in different weather beneath another clime. We do not begin to work at the moment of landing in a strange country to the conditions of which we have to adapt ourself. But each day was for me a different country. Even my laziness itself, beneath the novel forms that it had assumed, how was I to recognise it?

Sometimes, on days when the weather was, according to everyone, past praying for, the mere act of staying in the house, situated in the midst of a steady and continuous rain, had all the gliding charm, the soothing silence, the interest of a sea voyage; at another time, on a bright day, to lie still in bed was to let the lights and shadows play around me as round a tree-trunk.

Or yet again, in the first strokes of the bell of a neighbouring convent, rare as the early morning worshippers, barely whitening the dark sky with their fluttering snowfall, melted and scattered by the warm breeze, I had discerned one of those tempestuous, disordered, delightful days, when the roofs soaked by an occasional shower and dried by a breath of wind or a ray of sunshine let fall a cooing eavesdrop, and, as they wait for the wind to resume its turn, preen in the momentary sunlight that has burnished them their pigeon's-breast of slates, one of those days filled with so many changes of weather, atmospheric incidents, storms, that the idle man does not feel that he has wasted them, because he has been taking an interest in the activity which, in default of himself, the atmosphere, acting in a sense in his stead, has displayed; days similar to those times of revolution or war which do not seem empty to the schoolboy who has played truant from his classroom, because by loitering outside the Law Courts or by reading the newspapers, he has the illusion of finding, in the events that have occurred, failing the lesson which he has not learned, an intellectual profit and an excuse for his idleness; days to which we may compare those on which there occurs in our life some exceptional crisis from which the man who has never done anything imagines that he is going to acquire, if it comes to a happy issue, laborious habits; for instance, the morning on which he sets out for a duel which is to be fought under particularly dangerous conditions; then he is suddenly made aware, at the moment when it is perhaps about to be taken from him, of the value of a life of which he might have made use to begin some important work, or merely to enjoy pleasures, and of which he has failed to make any use at all. "If I can only not be killed," he says to himself, "how I shall settle down to work this very minute, and how I shall enjoy myself too."

Life has in fact suddenly acquired, in his eyes, a higher value, because he puts into life everything that it seems to him capable of giving, instead of the little that he normally makes it give. He sees it in the light of his desire, not as his experience has taught him that he was apt to make it, that is to say so tawdry! It has, at that moment, become filled with work, travel, mountain-climbing, all the pleasant things which, he tells himself, the fatal issue of the duel may render impossible, whereas they were already impossible before there was any question of a duel, owing to the bad habits which, even had there been no duel, would have persisted. He returns home without even a scratch, but he continues to find the same obstacles to pleasures, excursions, travel, to everything of which he had feared for a moment to be for ever deprived by death; to deprive him of them life has been sufficient. As for work—exceptional circumstances having the effect of intensifying what previously existed in the man, labour in the laborious, laziness in the lazy—he takes a holiday.

I followed his example, and did as I had always done since my first resolution to become a writer, which I had made long ago, but which seemed to me to date from yesterday, because I had regarded each intervening day as non-existent. I treated this day in a similar fashion, allowing its showers of rain and bursts of sunshine to pass without doing anything, and vowing that I would begin to work on the morrow. But then I was no longer the same man beneath a cloudless sky; the golden note of the bells did not contain merely (as honey contains) light, but the sensation of light and also the sickly savour of preserved fruits (because at Combray it had often loitered like a wasp over our cleared dinner-table). On this day of dazzling sunshine, to remain until nightfall with my eyes shut was a thing permitted, customary, healthgiving, pleasant, seasonable, like keeping the outside shutters closed against the heat.

It was in such weather as this that at the beginning of my second visit to Balbec I used to hear the violins of the orchestra amid the bluish flow of the rising tide. How much more fully did I possess Albertine to-day.

There were days when the sound of a bell striking the hour bore upon the sphere of its resonance a plate so cool, so richly loaded with moisture or with light that it was like a transcription for the blind, or if you prefer a musical interpretation of the charm of rain or of the charm of the sun. So much so that, at that moment, as I lay in bed, with my eyes shut, I said to myself that everything is capable of transposition and that a universe which was merely audible might be as full of variety as the other. Travelling lazily upstream from day to day, as in a boat, and seeing appear before my eyes an endlessly changing succession of enchanted memories, which I did not select, which a moment earlier had been invisible, and which my mind presented to me one after another, without my being free to choose them, I pursued idly over that continuous expanse my stroll in the sunshine.

Those morning concerts at Balbec were not remote in time. And yet, at that comparatively recent moment, I had given but little thought to Albertine. Indeed, on the very first mornings after my arrival, I had not known that she was at Balbec. From whom then had I learned it? Oh, yes, from Aimé. It was a fine sunny day like this. He was glad to see me again. But he does not like Albertine. Not everybody can be in love with her. Yes, it was he who told me that she was at Balbec. But how did he know? Ah! he had met her, had thought that she had a bad style. At that moment, as I regarded Aimé's story from another aspect than that in which he had told me it, my thoughts, which hitherto had been sailing blissfully over these untroubled waters, exploded suddenly, as though they had struck an invisible and perilous mine, treacherously moored at this point in my memory. He had told me that he had met her, that he had thought her style bad. What had he meant by a bad style? I had understood him to mean a vulgar manner, because, to contradict him in advance, I had declared that she was most refined. But no, perhaps he had meant the style of Gomorrah. She was with another girl, perhaps their arms were round one another's waist, they were staring at other women, they were indeed displaying a 'style' which I had never seen Albertine adopt in my presence. Who was the other girl, where had Aimé met her, this odious Albertine?

I tried to recall exactly what Aimé had said to me, in order to see whether it could be made to refer to what I imagined, or he had meant nothing more than common manners. But in vain might I ask the question, the person who put it and the person who might supply the recollection were, alas, one and the same person, myself, who was momentarily duplicated but without adding anything to my stature. Question as I might, it was myself who answered, I learned nothing fresh. I no longer gave a thought to Mlle. Vinteuil. Born of a novel suspicion, the fit of jealousy from which I was suffering was novel also, or rather it was only the prolongation, the extension of that suspicion, it had the same theatre, which was no longer Montjouvain, but the road upon which Aimé had met Albertine, and for its object the various friends one or other of whom might be she who had been with Albertine that day. It was perhaps a certain Elisabeth, or else perhaps those two girls whom Albertine had watched in the mirror at the Casino, while appearing not to notice them. She had doubtless been having relations with them, and also with Esther, Bloch's cousin. Such relations, had they been revealed to me by a third person, would have been enough almost to kill me, but as it was myself that was imagining them, I took care to add sufficient uncertainty to deaden the pain.

We succeed in absorbing daily, under the guise of suspicions, in enormous doses, this same idea that we are being betrayed, a quite minute quantity of which might prove fatal, if injected by the needle of a stabbing word. It is no doubt for that reason, and by a survival of the instinct of self-preservation, that the same jealous man does not hesitate to form the most terrible suspicions upon a basis of innocuous details, provided that, whenever any proof is brought to him, he may decline to accept its evidence. Anyhow, love is an incurable malady, like those diathetic states in which rheumatism affords the sufferer a brief respite only to be replaced by epileptiform headaches. Was my jealous suspicion calmed, I then felt a grudge against Albertine for not having been gentle with me, perhaps for having made fun of me to Andrée. I thought with alarm of the idea that she must have formed if Andrée had repeated all our conversations; the future loomed black and menacing. This mood of depression left me only if a fresh jealous suspicion drove me upon another quest or if, on the other hand, Albertine's display of affection made the actual state of my fortunes seem to me immaterial. Whoever this girl might be, I should have to write to Aimé, to try to see him, and then I should check his statement by talking to Albertine, hearing her confession. In the meantime, convinced that it must be Bloch's cousin, I asked Bloch himself, who had not the remotest idea of my purpose, simply to let me see her photograph, or, better still, to arrange if possible for me to meet her.

How many persons, cities, roads does not jealousy make us eager thus to know? It is a thirst for knowledge thanks to which, with regard to various isolated points, we end by acquiring every possible notion in turn except those that we require. We can never tell whether a suspicion will not arise, for, all of a sudden, we recall a sentence that was not clear, an alibi that cannot have been given us without a purpose. And yet, we have not seen the person again, but there is such a thing as a posthumous jealousy, that is born only after we have left her, a jealousy of the doorstep. Perhaps the habit that I had formed of nursing in my bosom several simultaneous desires, a desire for a young girl of good family such as I used to see pass beneath my window escorted by her governess, and especially of the girl whom Saint-Loup had mentioned to me, the one who frequented houses of ill fame, a desire for handsome lady's-maids, and especially for the maid of Mme. Putbus, a desire to go to the country in early spring, to see once again hawthorns, apple trees in blossom, storms at sea, a desire for Venice, a desire to settle down to work, a desire to live like other people —perhaps the habit of storing up, without assuaging any of them, all these desires, contenting myself with the promise, made to myself, that I would not forget to satisfy them one day, perhaps this habit, so many years old already, of perpetual postponement, of what M. de Charlus used to castigate under the name of procrastination, had become so prevalent in me that it assumed control of my jealous suspicions also and, while it made me take a mental note that I would not fail, some day, to have an explanation from Albertine with regard to the girl, possibly the girls (this part of the story was confused, rubbed out, that is to say obliterated, in my memory) with whom Aimé had met her, made me also postpone this explanation. In any case, I would not mention it this evening to my mistress for fear of making her think me jealous and so offending her.

And yet when, on the following day, Bloch had sent me the photograph of his cousin Esther, I made haste to forward it to Aimé. And at the same moment I remembered that Albertine had that morning refused me a pleasure which might indeed have tired her. Was that in order to reserve it for some one else? This afternoon, perhaps? For whom?

Thus it is that jealousy is endless, for even if the beloved object, by dying for instance, can no longer provoke it by her actions, it so happens that posthumous memories, of later origin than any event, take shape suddenly in our minds as though they were events also, memories which hitherto we have never properly explored, which had seemed to us unimportant, and to which our own meditation upon them has been sufficient, without any external action, to give a new and terrible meaning. We have no need of her company, it is enough to be alone in our room, thinking, for fresh betrayals of us by our mistress to come to light, even though she be dead. And so we ought not to fear in love, as in everyday life, the future alone, but even the past which often we do not succeed in realising until the future has come and gone; and we are not speaking only of the past which we discover long afterwards, but of the past which we have long kept stored up in ourselves and learn suddenly how to interpret.

No matter, I was very glad, now that afternoon was turning to evening, that the hour was not far off when I should be able to appeal to Albertine's company for the consolation of which I stood in need. Unfortunately, the evening that followed was one of those on which this consolation was not afforded me, on which the kiss that Albertine would give me when she left me for the night, very different from her ordinary kiss, would no more soothe me than my mother's kiss had soothed me long ago, on days when she was vexed with me and I dared not send for her, but at the same time knew that I should not be able to sleep. Such evenings were now those on which Albertine had formed for the morrow some plan of which she did not wish me to know. Had she confided in me, I would have employed, to assure its successful execution, an ardour which none but Albertine could have inspired in me. But she told me nothing, nor had she any need to tell me anything; as soon as she came in, before she had even crossed the threshold of my room, as she was still wearing her hat or toque, I had already detected the unknown, restive, desperate, indomitable desire. Now, these were often the evenings when I had awaited her return with the most loving thoughts, and looked forward to throwing my arms round her neck with the warmest affection.

Alas, those misunderstandings that I had often had with my parents, whom I found cold or cross at the moment when I was running to embrace them, overflowing with love, are nothing in comparison with these that occur between lovers! The anguish then is far less superficial, far harder to endure, it has its abode in a deeper stratum of the heart.

This evening, however, Albertine was obliged to mention the plan that she had in her mind; I gathered at once that she wished to go next day to pay a call on Mme. Verdurin, a call to which in itself I would have had no objection. But evidently her object was to meet some one there, to prepare some future pleasure. Otherwise she would not have attached so much importance to this call. That is to say, she would not have kept on assuring me that it was of no importance. I had in the course of my life developed in the opposite direction to those races which make use of phonetic writing only after regarding the letters of the alphabet as a set of symbols; I, who for so many years had sought for the real life and thought of other people only in the direct statements with which they furnished me of their own free will, failing these had come to attach importance, on the contrary, only to the evidence that is not a rational and analytical expression of the truth; the words themselves did not enlighten me unless they could be interpreted in the same way as a sudden rush of blood to the cheeks of a person who is embarrassed, or, what is even more telling, a sudden silence.

Some subsidiary word (such as that used by M. de Cambremer when he understood that I was 'literary,' and, not having spoken to me before, as he was describing a visit that he had paid to the Verdurins, turned to me with: "*Why*, Boreli was there!") bursting into flames at the unintended, sometimes perilous contact of two ideas which the speaker has not expressed, but which, by applying the appropriate methods of analysis or electrolysis I was able to extract from it, told me more than a long speech.

Albertine sometimes allowed to appear in her conversation one or other of these precious amalgams which I made haste to 'treat' so as to transform them into lucid ideas. It is by the way one of the most terrible calamities for the lover that if particular details—which only experiment, espionage, of all the possible realisations, would ever make him know— are so difficult to discover, the truth on the other hand is easy to penetrate or merely to feel by instinct.

Often I had seen her, at Balbec, fasten upon some girls who came past us a sharp and lingering stare, like a physical contact, after which, if I knew the girls, she would say to me: "Suppose we asked them to join us? I should so love to be rude to them." And now, for some time past, doubtless since she had succeeded in reading my character, no request to me to invite anyone, not a word, never even a sidelong glance from her eyes, which had become objectless and mute, and as revealing, with the vague and vacant expression of the rest of her face, as had been their magnetic swerve before. Now it was impossible for me to reproach her, or to ply her with questions about things which she would have declared to be so petty, so trivial, things that I had stored up in my mind simply for the pleasure of making mountains out of molehills. It is hard enough to say: "Why did you stare at that girl who went past?" but a great deal harder to say: "Why did you not stare at her?" And yet I knew quite well, or at least I should have known, if I had not chosen to believe Albertine's assertions rather than all the trivialities contained in a glance, proved by it and by some contradiction or other in her speech, a contradiction which often I did not perceive until long after I had left her, which kept me on tenterhooks all the night long, which I never dared mention to her again, but which nevertheless continued to honour my memory from time to time with its periodical visits.

Often, in the case of these furtive or sidelong glances on the beach at Balbec or in the streets of Paris, I might ask myself whether the person who provoked them was not merely at the moment when she passed an object of desire but was an old acquaintance, or else some girl who had simply been mentioned to her, and of whom, when I heard about it, I was astonished that anybody could have spoken to her, so utterly unlike was she to anyone that Albertine could possibly wish to know. But the Gomorrah of to-day is a dissected puzzle made up of fragments which are picked up in the places where we least expected to find them. Thus I once saw at Rivebelle a big dinner-party of ten women, all of whom I happened to know—at least by name—women as unlike one another as possible, perfectly united nevertheless, so much so that I never saw a party so homogeneous, albeit so composite.

To return to the girls whom we passed in the street, never did Albertine gaze at an old person, man or woman, with such fixity, or on the other hand with such reserve, and as though she saw nothing. The cuckolded husbands who know nothing know everything all the same. But it requires more accurate and abundant evidence to create a scene of jealousy. Besides, if jealousy helps us to discover a certain tendency to falsehood in the woman whom we love, it multiplies this tendency an hundredfold when the woman has discovered that we are jealous. She lies (to an extent to which she has never lied to us before), whether from pity, or from fear, or because she instinctively withdraws by a methodical flight from our investigations. Certainly there are love affairs in which from the start a light woman has posed as virtue incarnate in the eyes of the man who is in love with her. But how many others consist of two diametrically opposite periods? In the first, the woman speaks almost spontaneously, with slight modifications, of her zest for sensual pleasure, of the gay life which it has made her lead, things all of which she will deny later on, with the last breath in her body, to the same man—when she has felt that he is jealous of and spying upon her. He begins to think with regret of the days of those first confidences, the memory of which torments him nevertheless. If the woman continued to make them, she would furnish him almost unaided with the secret of her conduct which he has been vainly pursuing day after day. And besides, what a surrender that would mean, what trust, what friendship. If she cannot live without betraying him, at least she would be betraying him as a friend, telling him of her pleasures, associating him with them. And he thinks with regret of the sort of life which the early stages of their love seemed to promise, which the sequel has rendered impossible, making of that love a thing exquisitely painful, which will render a final parting, according to circumstances, either inevitable or impossible.

Sometimes the script from which I deciphered Albertine's falsehoods, without being ideographic needed simply to be read backwards; so this evening she had flung at me in a careless tone the message, intended to pass almost unheeded: "It is possible that I may go to-morrow to the Verdurins', I don't in the least know whether I shall go, I don't really want to." A childish anagram of the admission: "I shall go to-morrow to the Verdurins', it is absolutely certain, for I attach the utmost importance to the visit." This apparent hesitation indicated a resolute decision and was intended to diminish the importance of the visit while warning me of it. Albertine always adopted a tone of uncertainty in speaking of her irrevocable decisions. Mine was no less irrevocable. I took steps to arrange that this visit to Mme. Verdurin should not take place. Jealousy is often only an uneasy need to be tyrannical, applied to matters of love. I had doubtless inherited from my father this abrupt, arbitrary desire to threaten the people whom I loved best in the hopes with which they were lulling themselves with a security that I determined to expose to them as false; when I saw that Albertine had planned without my knowledge, behind my back, an expedition which I would have done everything in the world to make easier and more pleasant for her, had she taken me into her confidence, I said carelessly, so as to make her tremble, that I intended to go out the next day myself.

I set to work to suggest to Albertine other expeditions in directions which would have made this visit to the Verdurins impossible, in words stamped with a feigned indifference beneath which I strove to conceal my excitement. But she had detected it. It encountered in her the electric shock of a contrary will which violently repulsed it; I could see the sparks flash from her eyes. Of what use, though, was it to pay attention to what her eyes were saying at that moment? How had I failed to observe long ago that Albertine's eyes belonged to the class which even in a quite ordinary person seem to be composed of a number of fragments, because of all the places which the person wishes to visit—and to conceal her desire to visit—that day. Those eyes which their falsehood keeps ever immobile and passive, but dynamic, measurable in the yards or miles to be traversed before they reach the determined, the implacably determined meeting-place, eyes that are not so much smiling at the pleasure which tempts them as they are shadowed with melancholy and discouragement because there may be a difficulty in their getting to the meeting-place. Even when you hold them in your hands, these people are fugitives. To understand the emotions which they arouse, and which other people, even better looking, do not arouse, we must take into account that they are not immobile but in motion, and add to their person a sign corresponding to what in physics is the sign that indicates velocity. If you upset their plans for the day, they confess to you the pleasure that they had hidden from you: "I did so want to go to tea at five o'clock with So-and-So, my dearest friend." Very well, if, six months later, you come to know the person in question, you will learn that the girl whose plans you upset, who, caught in the trap, in order that you might set her free, confessed to you that she was in the habit of taking tea like this with a dear friend, every day at the hour at which you did not see her,— has never once been inside this person's house, that they have never taken tea together, and that the girl used to explain that her whole time was take up by none other than yourself. And so the person with whom she confessed that she had gone to tea, with whom she begged you to allow her to go to tea, that person, the excuse that necessity made her plead, was not the real person, there was somebody, something else! Something else, what? Some one, who?

Alas, the kaleidoscopic eyes starting off into the distance and shadowed with melancholy might enable us perhaps to measure distance, but do not indicate direction. The boundless field of possibilities extends before us, and if by any chance the reality presented itself to our gaze, it would be so far beyond the bounds of possibility that, dashing suddenly against the boundary wall, we should fall over backwards. It is not even essential that we should have proof of her movement and flight, it is enough that we should guess them. She had promised us a letter, we were calm, we were no longer in love. The letter has not come; no messenger appears with it; what can have happened? anxiety is born afresh, and love. It is such people more than any others who inspire love in us, for our destruction. For every fresh anxiety that we feel on their account strips them in our eyes of some of their personality. We were resigned to suffering, thinking that we loved outside ourselves, and we perceive that our love is a function of our sorrow, that our love perhaps is our sorrow, and that its object is, to a very small extent only, the girl with the raven tresses. But, when all is said, it is these people more than any others who inspire love.

Generally speaking, love has not as its object a human body, except when an emotion, the fear of losing it, the uncertainty of finding it again have been infused into it. This sort of anxiety has a great affinity for bodies. It adds to them a quality which surpasses beauty even; which is one of the reasons why we see men who are indifferent to the most beautiful women fall passionately in love with others who appear to us ugly. To these people, these fugitives, their own nature, our anxiety fastens wings. And even when they are in our company the look in their eyes seems to warn us that they are about to take flight. The proof of this beauty, surpassing the beauty added by the wings, is that very often the same person is, in our eyes, alternately wingless and winged. Afraid of losing her, we forget all the others. Sure of keeping her, we compare her with those others whom at once we prefer to her. And as these emotions and these certainties may vary from week to week, a person may one week see sacrificed to her everything that gave us pleasure, in the following week be sacrificed herself, and so for weeks and months on end. All of which would be incomprehensible did we not know from the experience, which every man shares, of having at least once in a lifetime ceased to love, forgotten a woman, for how very little a person counts in herself when she is no longer—or is not yet—permeable by our emotions. And, be it understood, what we say of fugitives is equally true of those in prison, the captive women, we suppose that we are never to possess them. And so men detest procuresses, for these facilitate the flight, enhance the temptation, but if on the other hand they are in love with a cloistered woman, they willingly have recourse to a procuress to make her emerge from her prison and bring her to them. In so far as relations with women whom we abduct are less permanent than others, the reason is that the fear of not succeeding in procuring them or the dread of seeing them escape is the whole of our love for them and that once they have been carried off from their husbands, torn from their footlights, cured of the temptation to leave us, dissociated in short from our emotion whatever it may be, they are only themselves, that is to say almost nothing, and, so long desired, are soon forsaken by the very man who was so afraid of their forsaking him.

How, I have asked, did I not guess this? But had I not guessed it from the first day at Balbec? Had I not detected in Albertine one of those girls beneath whose envelope of flesh more hidden persons are stirring, than in . . . I do not say a pack of cards still in its box, a cathedral or a theatre before we enter it, but the whole, vast, ever changing crowd? Not only all these persons, but the desire, the voluptuous memory, the desperate quest of all these persons. At Balbec I had not been troubled because I had never even supposed that one day I should be following a trail, even a false trail. No matter! This had given Albertine, in my eyes, the plenitude of a person/filled to the brim by the superimposition of all these persons, and desires and voluptuous memories of persons. And now that she had one day let fall the words 'Mlle. Vinteuil,' I would have wished not to tear off her garments so as to see her body but through her body to see and read that memorandum block of her memories and her future, passionate engagements.

How suddenly do the things that are probably the most insignificant assume an extraordinary value when a person whom we love (or who has lacked only this duplicity to make us love her) conceals them from us! In itself, suffering does not of necessity inspire in us sentiments of love or hatred towards the person who causes it: a surgeon can hurt our body without arousing any personal emotion. But a woman who has continued for some time to assure us that we are everything in the world to her, without being herself everything in the world to us, a woman whom we enjoy seeing, kissing, taking upon our knee, we are astonished if we merely feel from a sudden resistance that we are not free to dispose of her life. Disappointment may then revive in us the forgotten memory of an old anguish, which we know, all the same, to have been provoked not by this woman but by others whose betrayals are milestones in our past life; if it comes to that, how have we the courage to wish to live, how can we move a finger to preserve ourselves from death, in a world in which love is provoked only by falsehood, and consists merely in our need to see our sufferings appeased by the person who has made us suffer? To restore us from the collapse which follows our discovery of her falsehood and her resistance, there is the drastic remedy of endeavouring to act against her will, with the help of people whom we feel to be more closely involved than we are in her life, upon her who is resisting us and lying to us, to play the cheat in turn, to make ourselves loathed. But the suffering caused by such a love is of the sort which must inevitably lead the sufferer to seek in a change of posture an illusory comfort.

These means of action are not wanting, alas! And the horror of the kind of love which uneasiness alone has engendered lies in the fact that we turn over and over incessantly in our cage the most trivial utterances; not to mention that rarely do the people for whom we feel this love appeal to us physically in a complex fashion, since it is not our deliberate preference, but the chance of a minute of anguish, a minute indefinitely prolonged by our weakness of character, which repeats its experiments every evening until it yields to sedatives, that chooses for us.

No doubt my love for Albertine was not the most barren of those to which, through feebleness of will, a man may descend, for it was not entirely platonic; she did give me carnal satisfaction and, besides, she was intelligent. But all this was a superfluity. What occupied my mind was not the intelligent remark that she might have made, but some chance utterance that had aroused in me a doubt as to her actions; I tried to remember whether she had said this or that, in what tone, at what moment, in response to what speech of mine, to reconstruct the whole scene of her dialogue with me, to recall at what moment she had expressed a desire to call upon the Verdurins, what words of mine had brought that look of vexation to her face. The most important matter might have been in question, without my giving myself so much trouble to establish the truth, to restore the proper atmosphere and colour. No doubt, after these anxieties have intensified to a degree which we find insupportable, we do sometimes manage to soothe them altogether for an evening. The party to which the mistress whom we love is engaged to go, the true nature of which our mind has been toiling for days to discover, we are invited to it also, our mistress has neither looks nor words for anyone but ourselves, we take her home and then we enjoy, all our anxieties dispelled, a repose as complete, as healing, as that which we enjoy at times in the profound sleep that comes after a long walk. And no doubt such repose deserves that we should pay a high price for it. But would it not have been more simple not to purchase for ourselves, deliberately, the preceding anxiety, and at a higher price still? Besides, we know all too well that however profound these momentary relaxations may be, anxiety will still be the stronger. Sometimes indeed it is revived by the words that were intended to bring us repose. But as a rule, all that we do is to change our anxiety. One of the words of the sentence that was meant to calm us sets our suspicions running upon another trail. The demands of our jealousy and the blindness of our credulity are greater than the woman whom we love could ever suppose.

When, of her own accord, she swears to us that some man is nothing more to her than a friend, she appalls us by informing us—a thing we never suspected—that he has been her friend. While she is telling us, in proof of her sincerity, how they took tea together, that very afternoon, at each word that she utters the invisible, the unsuspected takes shape before our eyes. She admits that he has asked her to be his mistress, and we suffer agonies at the thought that she can have listened to his overtures. She refused them, she says. But presently, when we recall what she told us, we shall ask ourselves whether her story is really true, for there is wanting, between the different things that she said to us, that logical and necessary connexion which, more than the facts related, is a sign of the truth. Besides, there was that terrible note of scorn in her: "I said to him no, absolutely," which is to be found in every class of society, when a woman is lying. We must nevertheless thank her for having refused, encourage her by our kindness to repeat these cruel confidences in the future. At the most, we may remark: "But if he had already made advances to you, why did you accept his invitation to tea?" "So that he should not be angry with me and say that I hadn't been nice to him." And we dare not reply that by refusing she would perhaps have been nicer to us.

Albertine alarmed me further when she said that I was quite right to say, out of regard for her reputation, that I was not her lover, since "for that matter," she went on, "it's perfectly true that you aren't." I was not her lover perhaps in the full sense of the word, but then, was I to suppose that all the things that we did together she did also with all the other men whose mistress she swore to me that she had never been? The desire to know at all costs what Albertine was thinking, whom she was seeing, with whom she was in love, how strange it was that I should be sacrificing everything to this need, since I had felt the same need to know, in the case of Gilberte, names, facts, which now left me quite indifferent. I was perfectly well aware that in themselves Albertine's actions were of no greater interest. It is curious that a first love, if by the frail state in which it leaves our heart it opens the way to our subsequent loves, does not at least provide us, in view of the identity of symptoms and sufferings, with the means of curing them.

After all, is there any need to know a fact? Are we not aware beforehand, in a general fashion, of the mendacity and even the discretion of those women who have something to conceal? Is there any possibility of error? They make a virtue of their silence, when we would give anything to make them speak. And we feel certain that they have assured their accomplice: "I never tell anything. It won't be through me that anybody will hear about it, I never tell anything." A man may give his fortune, his life for a person, and yet know quite well that in ten years' time, more or less, he would refuse her the fortune, prefer to keep his life. For then the person would be detached from him, alone, that is to say null and void. What attaches us to people are those thousand roots, those innumerable threads which are our memories of last night, our hopes for to-morrow morning, those continuous trammels of habit from which we can never free ourselves. Just as there are misers who hoard money from generosity, so we are spendthrifts who spend from avarice, and it is not so much to a person that we sacrifice our life as to all that the person has been able to attach to herself of our hours, our days, of the things compared with which the life not yet lived, the relatively future life, seems to us more remote, more detached, less practical, less our own. What we require is to disentangle ourselves from those trammels which are so much more important than the person, but they have the effect of creating in us temporary obligations towards her, obligations which mean that we dare not leave her for fear of being misjudged by her, whereas later on we would so dare for, detached from us, she would no longer be ourselves, and because in reality we create for ourselves obligations (even if, by an apparent contradiction, they should lead to suicide) towards ourselves alone.

If I was not in love with Albertine (and of this I could not be sure) then there was nothing extraordinary in the place that she occupied in my life: we live only with what we do not love, with what we have brought to live with us only to kill the intolerable love, whether it be of a woman, of a place, or again of a woman embodying a place. Indeed we should be sorely afraid to begin to love again if a further separation were to occur. I had not yet reached this stage with Albertine. Her falsehoods, her admissions, left me to complete the task of elucidating the truth: her innumerable falsehoods because she was not content with merely lying, like everyone who imagines that he or she is loved, but was by nature, quite apart from this, a liar, and so inconsistent moreover that, even if she told me the truth every time, told me what, for instance, she thought of other people, she would say each time something different; her admissions, because, being so rare, so quickly cut short, they left between them, in so far as they concerned the past, huge intervals quite blank over the whole expanse of which I was obliged to retrace—and for that first of all to learn—her life.

As for the present, so far as I could interpret the sibylline utterances of Françoise, it was not only in particular details, it was as a whole that Albertine was lying to me, and 'one fine day' I would see what Françoise made a pretence of knowing, what she refused to tell me, what I dared not ask her. It was no doubt with the same jealousy that she had felt in the past with regard to Eulalie that Françoise would speak of the most improbable things, so vague that one could at the most suppose them to convey the highly improbable insinuation that the poor captive (who was a lover of women) preferred marriage with somebody who did not appear altogether to be myself. If this were so, how, notwithstanding her power of radiotelepathy, could Françoise have come to hear of it? Certainly, Albertine's statements could give me no definite enlightenment, for they were as different day by day as the colours of a spinning-top that has almost come to a standstill. However, it seemed that it was hatred, more than anything else, that impelled Françoise to speak. Not a day went by but she said to me, and I in my mother's absence endured such speeches as:

"To be sure, you yourself are kind, and I shall never forget the debt of gratitude that I owe to you" (this probably so that I might establish fresh claims upon her gratitude) "but the house has become a plague-spot now that kindness has set up knavery in it, now that cleverness is protecting the stupidest person that ever was seen, now that refinement, good manners, wit, dignity in everything allow to lay down the law and rule the roost and put me to shame, who have been forty years in the ᶠamily,—vice, everything that is most vulgar and abject."

What Françoise resented most about Albertine was having to take orders from somebody who was not one of ourselves, and also the strain of the additional housework which was affecting the health of our old servant, who would not, for all that, accept any help in the house, not being a 'good for nothing.' This in itself would have accounted for her nervous exhaustion, for her furious hatred. Certainly, she would have liked to see Albertine-Esther banished from the house. This was Françoise's dearest wish. And, by consoling her, its fulfilment alone would have given our old servant some repose. But to my mind there was more in it than this. So violent a hatred could have originated only in an overstrained body. And, more even than of consideration, Françoise was in need of sleep.

Albertine went to take off her things and, so as to lose no time in finding out what I wanted to know, I attempted to telephone to Andrée; I took hold of the receiver, invoked the implacable deities, but succeeded only in arousing their fury which expressed itself in the single word 'Engaged!' Andrée was indeed engaged in talking to some one else. As I waited for her to finish her conversation, I asked myself how it was—now that so many of our painters are seeking to revive the feminine portraits of the eighteenth century, in which the cleverly devised setting is a pretext for portraying expressions of expectation, spleen, interest, distraction— how it was that none of our modern Bouchers or Fragonards had yet painted, instead of 'The Letter' or 'The Harpsichord,' this scene which might be entitled 'At the Telephone,' in which there would come spontaneously to the lips of the listener a smile all the more genuine in that it is conscious of being unobserved. At length, Andrée was at the other end: "You are coming to call for Albertine to-morrow?" I asked, and as I uttered Albertine's name, thought of the envy I had felt for Swann when he said to me on the day of the Princesse de Guermantes's party: "Come and see Odette," and I had thought how, when all was said, there must be something in a Christian name which, in the eyes of the whole world including Odette herself, had on Swann's lips alone this entirely possessive sense.

Must not such an act of possession—summed up in a single word— over the whole existence of another person (I had felt whenever I was in love) be pleasant indeed! But, as a matter of fact, when we are in a position to utter it, either we no longer care, or else habit has not dulled the force of affection, but has changed its pleasure into pain. Falsehood is a very small matter, we live in the midst of it without doing anything but smile at it, we practise it without meaning to do any harm to anyone, but our jealousy is wounded by it, and sees more than the falsehood conceals (often our mistress refuses to spend the evening with us and goes to the theatre simply so that we shall not notice that she is not looking well). How blind it often remains to what the truth is concealing! But it can extract nothing, for those women who swear that they are not lying would refuse, on the scaffold, to confess their true character. I knew that I alone was in a position to say 'Albertine' in that tone to Andrée. And yet, to Albertine, to Andrée, and to myself, I felt that

I was nothing. And I realised the impossibility against which love is powerless.

We imagine that love has as its object a person whom we can see lying down before our eyes, enclosed in a human body. Alas, it is the extension of that person to all the points in space and time which the person has occupied and will occupy. If we do not possess its contact with this or that place, this or that hour, we do not possess it. But we cannot touch all these points. If only they were indicated to us, we might perhaps contrive to reach out to them. But we grope for them without finding them. Hence mistrust, jealousy, persecutions. We waste precious time upon absurd clues and pass by the truth without suspecting it.

But already one of the irascible deities, whose servants speed with the agility of lightning, was annoyed, not because I was speaking, but because I was saying nothing. "Come along, I've been holding the line for you all this time; I shall cut you off." However, she did nothing of the sort but, as she evoked Andrée's presence, enveloped it, like the great poet that a telephone girl always is, in the atmosphere peculiar to the home, the district, the very life itself of Albertine's friend. "Is that you?" asked Andrée, whose voice was projected towards me with an instantaneous speed by the goddess whose privilege it is to make sound more swift than light. "Listen," I replied; "go wherever you like, anywhere, except to Mme. Verdurin's. Whatever happens, you simply must keep Albertine away from there to-morrow." "Why, that's where she promised to go to-morrow." "Ah!"

But I was obliged to break off the conversation for a moment and to make menacing gestures, for if Françoise continued—as though it had been something as unpleasant as vaccination or as dangerous as the aeroplane—to refuse to learn to telephone, whereby she would have spared us the trouble of conversations which she might intercept without any harm, on the other hand she would at once come into the room whenever I was engaged in a conversation so private that I was particularly anxious to keep it from her ears. When she had left the room, not without lingering to take away various things that had been lying there since the previous day and might perfectly well have been left there for an hour longer, and to place in the grate a log that was quite unnecessary in view of my burning fever at the intruder's presence and my fear of finding myself 'cut off' by the operator: "I beg your pardon," I said to Andrée, "I was interrupted. Is it absolutely certain that she has to go to the Verdurins' to-morrow?" "Absolutely, but I can tell her that you don't like it." "No, not at all, but it is possible that I may come with you." "Ah!" said Andrée, in a tone of extreme annoyance and as though alarmed by my audacity, which was all the more encouraged by her opposition. "Then I shall say good night, and please forgive me for disturbing you for nothing." "Not at all," said Andrée, and (since nowadays, the telephone having come into general use, a decorative ritual of polite speeches has grown up round it, as round the tea-tables of the past) added: "It has been a great pleasure to hear your voice."

I might have said the same, and with greater truth than Andrée, for

I had been deeply touched by the sound of her voice, having never before noticed that it was so different from the voices of other people. Then I recalled other voices still, women's voices especially, some of them rendered slow by the precision of a question and by mental concentration, others made breathless, even silenced at moments, by the lyrical flow of what the speakers were relating; I recalled one by one the voices of all the girls whom I had known at Balbec, then Gilberte's voice, then my grandmother's, then that of Mme. de Guermantes, I found them all unlike, moulded in a language peculiar to each of the speakers, each playing upon a different instrument, and I said to myself how meagre must be the concert performed in paradise by the three or four angel musicians of the old painters, when I saw mount to the Throne of God, by tens, by hundreds, by thousands, the harmonious and multisonant salutation of all the Voices. I did not leave the telephone without thanking, in a few propitiatory words, her who reigns over the swiftness of sounds for having kindly employed on behalf of my humble words a power which made them a hundred times more rapid than thunder, by my thanksgiving received no other response than that of being cut off.

When Albertine returned to my room, she was wearing a garment of black satin which had the effect of making her seem paler, of turning her into the pallid, ardent Parisian, etiolated by want of fresh air, by the atmosphere of crowds and perhaps by vicious habits, whose eyes seemed more restless because they were not brightened by any colour in her cheeks. "Guess," I said to her, "to whom I've just been talking on the telephone. Andrée!" "Andrée?" exclaimed Albertine in a harsh tone of astonishment and emotion, which so simple a piece of intelligence seemed hardly to require. "I hope she remembered to tell you that we met Mme. Verdurin the other day." "Mme. Verdurin? I don't remember," I replied, as though I were thinking of something else, so as to appear indifferent to this meeting and not to betray Andrée who had told me where Albertine was going on the morrow.

But how could I tell that Andrée was not herself betraying me, and would not tell Albertine to-morrow that I had asked her to prevent her at all costs from going to the Verdurins', and had not already revealed to her that I had many times made similar appeals. She had assured me that she had never repeated anything, but the value of this assertion was counterbalanced in my mind by the impression that for some time past Albertine's face had ceased to shew that confidence which she had for so long reposed in me.

What is remarkable is that, a few days before this dispute with Albertine, I had already had a dispute with her, but in Andrée's presence. Now Andrée, while she gave Albertine good advice, had always appeared to be insinuating bad. "Come, don't talk like that, hold your tongue," she said, as though she were at the acme of happiness. Her face assumed the dry raspberry hue of those pious housekeepers who made us dismiss each of our servants in turn. While I was heaping reproaches upon Albertine which I ought never to have uttered, Andrée looked as though she were sucking a lump of barley sugar with keen enjoyment. At length she was unable to restrain an affectionate laugh. "Come, Titine, with me. You know, I'm your dear little sister." I was not merely exasperated by this rather sickly exhibition, I asked myself whether Andrée really felt the affection for Albertine that she pretended to feel. Seeing that Albertine, who knew Andrée far better than I did, had always shrugged her shoulders when I asked her whether she was quite certain of Andrée's affection, and had always answered that nobody in the world cared for her more, I was still convinced that Andrée's affection was sincere. Possibly, in her wealthy but provincial family, one might find an equivalent of some of the shops in the Cathedral square, where certain sweetmeats are declared to be 'the best quality.' But I do know that, for my own part, even if I had invariably come to the opposite conclusion, I had so strong an impression that Andrée was trying to rap Albertine's knuckles that my mistress at once regained my affection and my anger subsided.

Suffering, when we are in love, ceases now and then for a moment, but only to recur in a different form. We weep to see her whom we love no longer respond to us with those outbursts of sympathy, the amorous advances of former days, we suffer more keenly still when, having lost them with us, she recovers them for the benefit of others; then, from this suffering, we are distracted by a new and still more piercing grief, the suspicion that she was lying to us about how she spent the previous evening, when she doubtless played us false; this suspicion in turn is dispelled, the kindness that our mistress is shewing us soothes us, but then a word that we had forgotten comes back to our mind; some one has told us that she was ardent in moments of pleasure, whereas we have always found her calm; we try to picture to ourselves what can have been these frenzies with other people, we feel how very little we are to her, we observe an air of boredom, longing, melancholy, while we are talking, we observe like a black sky the unpretentious clothes which she puts on when she is with us, keeping for other people the garments with which she used to flatter us at first. If on the contrary she is affectionate, what joy for a moment; but when we see that little tongue outstretched as though in invitation, we think of those people to whom that invitation has so often been addressed, and that perhaps even here at home, even although Albertine was not thinking of them, it has remained, by force of long habit, an automatic signal. Then the feeling that we are bored with each other returns. But suddenly this pain is reduced to nothing when we think of the unknown evil element in her life, of the places impossible to identify where she has been, where she still goes perhaps at the hours when we are not with her, if indeed she is not planning to live there altogether, those places in which she is parted from us, does not belong to us, is happier than when she is with us. Such are the revolving searchlights of jealousy.

Jealousy is moreover a demon that cannot be exorcised, but always returns to assume a fresh incarnation. Even if we could succeed in exterminating them all, in keeping for ever her whom we love, the Spirit of Evil would then adopt another form, more pathetic still, despair at having obtained fidelity only by force, despair at not being loved.

Between Albertine and myself there was often the obstacle of a silence based no doubt upon grievances which she kept to herself, because she supposed them to be irremediable. Charming as Albertine was on some evenings, she no longer shewed those spontaneous impulses which I remembered at Balbec when she used to say: "How good you are to me all the same!" and her whole heart seemed to spring towards me without the reservation of any of those grievances which she now felt and kept to herself because she supposed them no doubt to be irremediable, impossible to forget, unconfessed, but which set up nevertheless between her and myself the significant prudence of her speech or the interval of an impassable silence.

"And may one be allowed to know why you telephoned to Andrée?" "To ask whether she had any objection to my joining you to-morrow, so that I may pay the Verdurins the call I promised them at la Raspelière." "Just as you like. But I warn you, there is an appalling mist this evening, and it's sure to last over to-morrow. I mention it, because I shouldn't like you to make yourself ill. Personally, you can imagine I would far rather you came with us. However," she added with a thoughtful air: "I'm not at all sure that I shall go to the Verdurins'. They've been so kind to me that I ought, really. . . . Next to yourself, they have been nicer to me than anybody, but there are some things about them that I don't quite like. I simply must go to the Bon Marché and the Trois-Quartiers and get a white scarf to wear with this dress which is really too black."

Allow Albertine to go by herself into a big shop crowded with people perpetually rubbing against one, furnished with so many doors that a woman can always say that when she came out she could not find the carriage which was waiting farther along the street; I was quite determined never to consent to such a thing, but the thought of it made me extremely unhappy. And yet I did not take into account that I ought long ago to have ceased to see Albertine, for she had entered, in my life, upon that lamentable period in which a person disseminated over space and time is no longer a woman, but a series of events upon which we can throw no light, a series of insoluble problems, a sea which we absurdly attempt, Xerxes-like, to scourge, in order to punish it for what it has engulfed. Once this period has begun, we are perforce vanquished. Happy are they who understand this in time not to prolong unduly a futile, exhausting struggle, hemmed in on every side by the limits of the imagination, a struggle in which jealousy plays so sorry a part that the same man who once upon a time, if the eyes of the woman who was always by his side rested for an instant upon another man, imagined an intrigue, suffered endless torments, resigns himself in time to allowing her to go out by herself, sometimes with the man whom he knows to be her lover, preferring to the unknown this torture which at least he does know! It is a question of the rhythm to be adopted, which afterwards one follows from force of habit. Neurotics who could never stay away from a dinner-party will afterwards take rest cures which never seem to them to last long enough; women who recently were still of easy virtue live for and by acts of penitence. Jealous lovers who, in order to keep a watch upon her whom they loved, cut short their own hours of sleep, deprived themselves of rest, feeling that her own personal desires, the world, so vast and so secret, time, are stronger than they, allow her to go out without them, then to travel, and finally separate from her. Jealousy thus perishes for want of nourishment and has survived so long only by clamouring incessantly for fresh food. I was still a long way from this state.

I was now at liberty to go out with Albertine as often as I chose. As there had recently sprung up all round Paris a number of aerodromes, which are to aeroplanes what harbours are to ships, and as ever since the day when, on the way to la Raspelière, that almost mythological encounter with an airman, at whose passage overhead my horse had shied, had been to me like a symbol of liberty, I often chose to end our day's excursion—with the ready approval of Albertine, a passionate lover of every form of sport—at one of these aerodromes. We went there, she and I, attracted by that incessant stir of departure and arrival which gives so much charm to a stroll along the pier, or merely upon the beach, to those who love the sea, and to loitering about an 'aviation centre' to those who love the sky. At any moment, amid the repose of the machines that lay inert and as though at anchor, we would see one, laboriously pushed by a number of mechanics, as a boat is pushed down over the sand at the bidding of a tourist who wishes to go for an hour upon the sea. Then the engine was started, the machine ran along the ground, gathered speed, until finally, all of a sudden, at right angles, it rose slowly, in the awkward, as it were paralysed ecstasy of a horizontal speed suddenly transformed into a majestic, vertical ascent. Albertine could not contain her joy, and demanded explanations of the mechanics who, now that the machine was in the air, were strolling back to the sheds. The passenger, meanwhile, was covering mile after mile; the huge skiff, upon which our eyes remained fixed, was nothing more now in the azure than a barely visible spot, which, however, would gradually recover its solidity, size, volume, when, as the time allowed for the excursion drew to an end, the moment came for landing. And we watched with envy, Albertine and I, as he sprang to earth, the passenger who had gone up like that to enjoy at large in those solitary expanses the calm and limpidity of evening. Then, whether from the aerodrome or from some museum, some church that we had been visiting, we would return home together for dinner. And yet, I did not return home calmed, as I used to be at Balbec by less frequent excursions which I rejoiced to see extend over a whole afternoon, used afterwards to contemplate standing out like clustering flowers from the rest of Albertine's life, as against an empty sky, before which we muse pleasantly, without thinking. Albertine's time did not belong to me then in such ample quantities as to-day. And yet, it had seemed to me then to be much more my own, because I took into account only—my love rejoicing in them as in the bestowal of a favour—the hours that she spent with me; now—my jealousy searching anxiously among them for the possibility of a betrayal—only those hours that she spent apart from me.

Well, on the morrow she was looking forward to some such hours. I must choose, either to cease from suffering, or to cease from loving. For, just as in the beginning it is formed by desire, so afterwards love is kept in existence only by painful anxiety. I felt that part of Albertine's life was escaping me. Love, in the painful anxiety as in the blissful desire, is the insistence upon a whole. It is born, it survives only if some part remains for it to conquer. We love only what we do not wholly possess. Albertine was lying when she told me that she probably would not go to the Verdurins', as I was lying when I said that I wished to go there. She was seeking merely to dissuade me from accompanying her, and I, by my abrupt announcement of this plan, which I had no intention of putting into practice, to touch what I felt to be her most sensitive spot, to track down the desire that she was concealing and to force her to admit that my company on the morrow would prevent her from gratifying it. She had virtually made this admission by ceasing at once to wish to go to see the Verdurins.

"If you don't want to go to the Verdurins'," I told her, "there is a splendid charity show at the Trocadéro." She listened to my urging her to attend it with a sorrowful air. I began to be harsh with her as at Balbec, at the time of my first jealousy. Her face reflected a disappointment, and I employed, to reproach my mistress, the same arguments that had been so often advanced against myself by my parents when I was little, and had appeared unintelligent and cruel to my misunderstood childhood. "No, for all your melancholy air," I said to Albertine, "I cannot feel any pity for you; I should feel sorry for you if you were ill, if you were in trouble, if you had suffered some bereavement; not that you would mind that in the least, I dare say, since you pour out false sentiment over every trifle. Anyhow, I have no opinion of the feelings of people who pretend to be so fond of us and are quite incapable of doing us the slightest service, and whose minds wander so that they forget to deliver the letter we have entrusted to them, on which our whole future depends."

These words—a great part of what we say being no more than a recitation from memory—I had heard spoken, all of them, by my mother, who was ever ready to explain to me that we ought not to confuse true feeling, what (she said) the Germans, whose language she greatly admired notwithstanding my father's horror of their nation, called *Empfindung,* and affectation or *Empfindelei.* She had gone so far, once when I was in tears, as to tell me that Nero probably suffered from his nerves and was none the better for that. Indeed, like those plants which bifurcate as they grow, side by side with the sensitive boy which was all that I had been, there was now a man of the opposite sort, full of common sense, of severity towards the morbid sensibility of others, a man resembling what my parents had been to me. No doubt, as each of us is obliged to continue in himself the life of his forebears, the balanced, cynical man who did not exist in me at the start had joined forces with the sensitive one, and it was natural that I should become in my turn what my parents had been to me.

What is more, at the moment when this new personality took shape in me, he found his language ready made in the memory of the speeches, ironical and scolding, that had been addressed to me, that I must now address to other people, and which came so naturally to my lips, whether I evoked them by mimicry and association of memories, or because the delicate and mysterious enchantments of the reproductive power had traced in me unawares, as upon the leaf of a plant, the same intonations, the same gestures, the same attitudes as had been adopted by the people from whom I sprang. For sometimes, as I was playing the wise counsellor in conversation with Albertine, I seemed to be listening to my grandmother; had it not, moreover, occurred to my mother (so many obscure unconscious currents inflected everything in me down to the tiniest movements of my fingers even, to follow the same cycles as those of my parents) to imagine that it was my father at the door, so similar was my knock to his.

On the other hand the coupling of contrary elements is the law of life, the principle of fertilisation, and, as we shall see, the cause of many disasters. As a general rule, we detest what resembles ourself, and our own faults when observed in another person infuriate us. How much the more does a man who has passed the age at which we instinctively display them, a man who, for instance, has gone through the most burning moments with an icy countenance, execrate those same faults, if it is another man, younger or simpler or stupider, that is displaying them. There are sensitive people to whom merely to see in other people's eyes the tears which they themselves have repressed is infuriating. It is because the similarity is too great that, in spite of family affection, and sometimes all the more the greater the affection is, families are divided.

Possibly in myself, and in many others, the second man that I had become was simply another aspect of the former man, excitable and sensitive in his own affairs, a sage mentor to other people. Perhaps it was so also with my parents according to whether they were regarded in relation to myself or in themselves. In the case of my grandmother and mother it was as clear as daylight that their severity towards myself was deliberate on their part and indeed cost them a serious effort, but perhaps in my father himself his coldness was but an external aspect of his sensibility. For it was perhaps the human truth of this twofold aspect: the side of private life, the side of social relations, that was expressed in a sentence which seemed to me at the time as false in its matter as it was commonplace in form, when some one remarked, speaking of my father: "Beneath his icy chill, he conceals an extraordinary sensibility; what is really wrong with him is that he is ashamed of his own feelings."

Did it not, after all, conceal incessant secret storms, that calm (interspersed if need be with sententious reflexions, irony at the maladroit exhibitions of sensibility) which was his, but which now I too was affecting in my relations with everybody and never laid aside in certain circumstances of my relations with Albertine?

I really believe that I came near that day to making up my mind to break with her and to start for Venice. What bound me afresh in my chains had to do with Normandy, not that she shewed any inclination to go to that region where I had been jealous of her (for it was my good fortune that her plans never impinged upon the painful spots in my memory), but because when I had said to her: "It is just as though I were to speak to you of your aunt's friend who lived at Infreville," she replied angrily, delighted—like everyone in a discussion, who is anxious to muster as many arguments as possible on his side—to shew me that I was in the wrong and herself in the right: "But my aunt never knew anybody at Infreville, and I have never been near the place."

She had forgotten the lie that she had told me one afternoon about the susceptible lady with whom she simply must take tea, even if by going to visit this lady she were to forfeit my friendship and shorten her own life. I did not remind her of her lie. But it appalled me. And once again I postponed our rupture to another day. A person has no need of sincerity, nor even of skill in lying, in order to be loved. I here give the name of love to a mutual torment. I saw nothing reprehensible this evening in speaking to her as my grandmother—that mirror of perfection—used to speak to me, nor, when I told her that I would escort her to the Verdurins', in having adopted my father's abrupt manner, who would never inform us of any decision except in the manner calculated to cause us the maximum of agitation, out of all proportion to the decision itself. So that it was easy for him to call us absurd for appearing so distressed by so small a matter, our distress corresponding in reality to the emotion that he had aroused in us. Since—like the inflexible wisdom of my grandmother—these arbitrary moods of my father had been passed on to myself to complete the sensitive nature to which they had so long remained alien, and, throughout my whole childhood, had caused so much suffering, that sensitive nature informed them very exactly as to the points at which they must take careful aim: there is no better informer than a reformed thief, or a subject of the nation we are fighting. In certain untruthful families, a brother who has come to call upon his brother without any apparent reason and asks him, quite casually, on the doorstep, as he is going away, for some information to which he does not even appear to listen, indicates thereby to his brother that this information was the main object of his visit, for the brother is quite familiar with that air of detachment, those words uttered as though in parentheses and at the last moment, having frequently had recourse to them himself. Well, there are also pathological families, kindred sensibilities, fraternal temperaments, initiated into that mute language which enables people in the family circle to make themselves understood without speaking. And who can be more nerve-wracking than a neurotic? Besides, my conduct, in these cases, may have had a more general, a more profound cause. I mean that in those brief but inevitable moments, when we detest some one whom we love—moments which last sometimes for a whole lifetime in the case of people whom we do not love —we do not wish to appear good, so as not to be pitied, but at once as wicked and as happy as possible so that our happiness may be truly hateful and may ulcerate the soul of the occasional or permanent enemy. To how many people have I not untruthfully slandered myself, simply in order that my 'successes' might seem to them immoral and make them all the more angry! The proper thing to do would be to take the opposite course, to shew without arrogance that we have generous feelings, instead of taking such pains to hide them. And it would be easy if we were able never to hate, to love all the time. For then we should be so glad to say only the things that can make other people happy, melt their hearts, make them love us.

To be sure, I felt some remorse at being so irritating to Albertine, and said to myself: "If I did not love her, she would be more grateful to me, for I should not be nasty to her; but no, it would be the same in the end, for I should also be less nice." And I might, in order to justify myself, have told her that I loved her. But the confession of that love, apart from the fact that it could not have told Albertine anything new, would perhaps have made her colder to myself than the harshness and deceit for which love was the sole excuse. To be harsh and deceitful to the person whom we love is so natural! If the interest that we shew in other people does not prevent us from being kind to them and complying with their wishes, then our interest is not sincere. A stranger leaves us indifferent, and indifference does not prompt us to unkind actions.

The evening passed. Before Albertine went to bed, there was no time to lose if we wished to make peace, to renew our embraces. Neither of us had yet taken the initiative. Feeling that, anyhow, she was angry with me already, I took advantage of her anger to mention Esther Lévy. "Bloch tells me" (this was untrue) "that you are a great friend of his cousin Esther." "I shouldn't know her if I saw her," said Albertine with a vague air. "I have seen her photograph," I continued angrily. I did not look at Albertine as I said this, so that I did not see her expression, which would have been her sole reply, for she said nothing.

It was no longer the peace of my mother's kiss at Combray that I felt when I was with Albertine on these evenings, but, on the contrary, the anguish of those on which my mother scarcely bade me good night, or even did not come up at all to my room, whether because she was vexed with me or was kept downstairs by guests. This anguish—not merely its transposition in terms of love—no, this anguish itself which had at one time been specialised in love, which had been allocated to love alone when the division, the distribution of the passions took effect, seemed now to be extending again to them all, become indivisible again as in my childhood, as though all my sentiments which trembled at the thought of my not being able to keep Albertine by my bedside, at once as a mistress, a sister, a daughter; as a mother too, of whose regular good-night kiss I was beginning again to feel the childish need, had begun to coalesce, to unify in the premature evening of my life which seemed fated to be as short as a day in winter. But if I felt the anguish of my childhood, the change of person that made me feel it, the difference of the sentiment that it inspired in me, the very transformation in my character, made it impossible for me to demand the soothing of that anguish from Albertine as in the old days from my mother.

I could no longer say: "I am unhappy." I confined myself, with death at my heart, to speaking of unimportant things which afforded me no progress towards a happy solution. I waded knee-deep in painful platitudes. And with that intellectual egoism which, if only some insignificant fact has a bearing upon our love, makes us pay great respect to the person who has discovered it, as fortuitously perhaps as the fortune-teller who has foretold some trivial event which has afterwards come to pass, I came near to regarding Françoise as more inspired than Bergotte and Elstir because she had said to me at Balbec: "That girl will only land you in trouble."

Every minute brought me nearer to Albertine's good night, which at length she said. But this evening her kiss, from which she herself was absent, and which did not encounter myself, left me so anxious that, with a throbbing heart, I watched her make her way to the door, thinking: "If I am to find a pretext for calling her back, keeping her here, making peace with her, I must make haste; only a few steps and she will be out of the room, only two, now one, she is turning the handle; she is opening the door, it is too late, she has shut it behind her!" Perhaps it was not too late, all the same. As in the old days at Combray when my mother had left me without soothing me with her kiss, I wanted to dart in pursuit of Albertine, I felt that there would be no peace for me until I had seen her again, that this next meeting was to be something immense which no such meeting had ever yet been, and that—if I did not succeed by my own efforts in ridding myself of this melancholy—I might perhaps acquire the shameful habit of going to beg from Albertine. I sprang out of bed when she was already in her room, I paced up and down the corridor, hoping that she would come out of her room and call me; I stood without breathing outside her door for fear of failing to hear some faint summons, I returned for a moment to my own room to see whether my mistress had not by some lucky chance forgotten her handkerchief, her bag, something which I might have appeared to be afraid of her wanting during the night, and which would have given me an excuse for going to her room. No, there was nothing. I returned to my station outside her door, but the crack beneath it no longer shewed any light. Albertine had put out the light, she was in bed, I remained there motionless, hoping for some lucky accident but none occurred; and long afterwards, frozen, I returned to bestow myself between my own sheets and cried all night long.

But there were certain evenings also when I had recourse to a ruse which won me Albertine's kiss. Knowing how quickly sleep came to her as soon as she lay down (she knew it also, for, instinctively, before lying down, she would take off her slippers, which I had given her, and her ring which she placed by the bedside, as she did in her own room when she went to bed), knowing how heavy her sleep was, how affectionate her awakening, I would plead the excuse of going to look for something and make her lie down upon my bed. When I returned to the room she was asleep and I saw before me the other woman that she became whenever one saw her full face. But she very soon changed her identity, for I lay down by her side and recaptured her profile. I could place my hand in her hand, on her shoulder, on her cheek. Albertine continued to sleep.

I might take her head, turn it round, press it to my lips, encircle my neck in her arms, she continued to sleep like a watch that does not stop, like an animal that goes on living whatever position you assign to it, like a climbing plant, a convulvulus which continues to thrust out its tendrils whatever support you give it. Only her breathing was altered by every touch of my fingers, as though she had been an instrument on which I was playing and from which I extracted modulations by drawing from first one, then another of its strings different notes. My jealousy grew calm, for I felt that Albertine had become a creature that breathes, that is nothing else besides, as was indicated by that regular breathing in which is expressed that pure physiological function which, wholly fluid, has not the solidity either of speech or of silence; and, in its ignorance of all evil, her breath, drawn (it seemed) rather from a hollowed reed than from a human being, was truly paradisal, was the pure song of the angels to me who, at these moments, felt Albertine to be withdrawn from everything, not only materially but morally. And yet in that breathing, I said to myself of a sudden that perhaps many names of people borne on the stream of memory must be playing. Sometimes indeed to that music the human voice was added. Albertine uttered a few words. How I longed to catch their meaning! It happened that the name of a person of whom we had been speaking and who had aroused my jealousy came to her lips, but without making me unhappy, for the memory that it brought with it seemed to be only that of the conversations that she had had with me upon the subject. This evening, however, when with her eyes still shut she was half awake, she said, addressing myself: "Andrée." I concealed my emotion. "You are dreaming, I am not Andrée," I said to her, smiling. She smiled also. "Of course not, I wanted to ask you what Andrée was saying to you." "I should have supposed that you were used to lying like this by her side." "Oh no, never," she said. Only, before making this reply, she had hidden her face for a moment in her hands. So her silences were merely screens, her surface affection merely kept beneath the surface a thousand memories which would have rent my heart, her life was full of those incidents the derisive account, the comic history of which form our daily gossip at the expense of other people, people who do not matter, but which, so long as a person remains lost in the dark forest of our heart, seem to us so precious a revelation of her life that, for the privilege of exploring that subterranean world, we would gladly sacrifice our own. Then her sleep appeared to me a marvellous and magic world in which at certain moments there rises from the depths of the barely translucent element the confession of a secret which we shall not understand. But as a rule, when Albertine was asleep, she seemed to have recovered her innocence. In the attitude which I had imposed upon her, but which in her sleep she had speedily made her own, she looked as though she were trusting herself to me! Her face had lost any expression of cunning or vulgarity, and between herself and me, towards whom she was raising her arm, upon whom her hand was resting, there seemed to be an absolute surrender, an indissoluble attachment. Her sleep moreover did not separate her from me and allowed her to retain her consciousness of our affection; its effect was rather to abolish everything else; I embraced her, told her that I was going to take a turn outside, she half-opened her eyes, said to me with an air of astonishment— indeed the hour was late: "But where are you off to, my darling ——" calling me by my Christian name, and at once fell asleep again. Her sleep was only a sort of obliteration of the rest of her life, a continuous silence over which from time to time would pass in their flight words of intimate affection. By putting these words together, you would have arrived at the unalloyed conversation, the secret intimacy of a pure love. This calm slumber delighted me, as a mother is delighted, reckoning it among his virtues, by the sound sleep of her child. And her sleep was indeed that of a child. Her waking also, and so natural, so loving, before she even knew where she was, that I sometimes asked myself with terror whether she had been in the habit, before coming to live with me, of not sleeping by herself but of finding, when she opened her eyes, some one lying by her side. But her childish charm was more striking. Like a mother again, I marvelled that she should always awake in so good a humour. After a few moments she recovered consciousness, uttered charming words, unconnected with one another, mere bird-pipings. By a sort of 'general post' her throat, which as a rule passed unnoticed, now almost startlingly beautiful, had acquired the immense importance which her eyes, by being closed in sleep, had forfeited, her eyes, my regular informants to which I could no longer address myself after the lids had closed over them. Just as the closed lids impart an innocent, grave beauty to the face by suppressing all that the eyes express only too plainly, there was in the words, not devoid of meaning, but interrupted by moments of silence, which Albertine uttered as she awoke, a pure beauty that is not at every moment polluted, as is conversation, by habits of speech, commonplaces, traces of blemish. Anyhow, when I had decided to wake Albertine, I had been able to do so without fear, I knew that her awakening would bear no relation to the evening that we had passed together, but would emerge from her sleep as morning emerges from night. As soon as she had begun to open her eyes with a smile, she had offered me her lips, and before she had even uttered a word, I had tasted their fresh savour, as soothing as that of a garden still silent before the break of day.

On the morrow of that evening when Albertine had told me that she would perhaps be going, then that she would not be going to see the Verdurins, I awoke early, and, while I was still half asleep, my joy informed me that there was, interpolated in the winter, a day of spring. Outside, popular themes skilfully transposed for various instruments, from the horn of the mender of porcelain, or the trumpet of the chair weaver, to the flute of the goat driver who seemed, on a fine morning, to be a Sicilian goatherd, were lightly orchestrating the matutinal air, with an 'Overture for a Public Holiday.' Our hearing, that delicious sense, brings us the company of the street, every line of which it traces for us, sketches all the figures that pass along it, shewing us their colours. The iron shutters of the baker's shop, of the dairy, which had been lowered last night over every possibility of feminine bliss, were rising now like the canvas of a ship which is setting sail and about to proceed, crossing the transparent sea, over a vision of young female assistants. This sound of the iron curtain being raised would perhaps have been my sole pleasure in a different part of the town. In this quarter a hundred other sounds contributed to my joy, of which I would not have lost a single one by remaining too long asleep. It is the magic charm of the old aristocratic quarters that they are at the same time plebeian. Just as, sometimes, cathedrals used to have them within a stone's throw of their porches (which have even preserved the name, like the porch of Rouen styled the Booksellers', because these latter used to expose their merchandise in the open air against its walls), so various minor trades, but peripatetic, used to pass in front of the noble Hôtel de Guermantes, and made one think at times of the ecclesiastical France of long ago. For the appeal which they launched at the little houses on either side had, with rare exceptions, nothing of a song. It differed from song as much as the declamation—barely coloured by imperceptible modulations—of *Boris Godounov* and *Pelléas*; but on the other hand recalled the psalmody of a priest chanting his office of which these street scenes are but the good-humoured, secular, and yet half liturgical counterpart. Never had I so delighted in them as since Albertine had come to live with me; they seemed to me a joyous signal of her awakening, and by interesting me in the life of the world outside made me all the more conscious of the soothing virtue of a beloved presence, as constant as I could wish. Several of the foodstuffs cried in the street, which personally I detested, were greatly to Albertine's liking, so much so that Françoise used to send her young footman out to buy them, slightly humiliated perhaps at finding himself mingled with the plebeian crowd. Very distinct in this peaceful quarter (where the noise was no longer a cause of lamentation to Françoise and had become a source of pleasure to myself), there came to me, each with its different modulation, recitatives declaimed by those humble folk as they would be in the music—so entirely popular —of *Boris*, where an initial intonation is barely altered by the inflexion of one note which rests upon another, the music of the crowd which is more a language than a music. It was *"ah! le bigorneau, deux sous le bigorneau,"* which brought people running to the cornets in which were sold those horrid little shellfish, which, if Albertine had not been there, would have disgusted me, just as the snails disgusted me which I heard cried for sale at the same hour. Here again it was of the barely lyrical declamation of Moussorgsky that the vendor reminded me, but not of it alone. For after having almost 'spoken': *"Les escargots, ils sont frais, ils sont beaux,"* it was with the vague melancholy of Maeterlinck, transposed into music by Debussy, that the snail vendor, in one of those pathetic finales in which the composer of *Pelléas* shews his kinship with Rameau: "If vanquished I must be, is it for thee to be my vanquisher?" added with a singsong melancholy: *"On les vend six sous la douzaine. . . ."*

I have always found it difficult to understand why these perfectly simple words were sighed in a tone so far from appropriate, mysterious, like the secret which makes everyone look sad in the old palace to which Mélisande has not succeeded in bringing joy, and profound as one of the thoughts of the aged Arkel who seeks to utter, in the simplest words, the whole lore of wisdom and destiny. The very notes upon which rises with an increasing sweetness the voice of the old King of Allemonde or that of Go-land, to say: "We know not what is happening here, it may seem strange, maybe nought that happens is in vain," or else: "No cause here for alarm, 'twas a poor little mysterious creature, like all the world," were those which served the snail vendor to resume, in an endless cadenza: *"On les vend six sous la douzaine. . . ."* But this metaphysical lamentation had not time to expire upon the shore of the infinite, it was interrupted by a shrill trumpet. This time, it was no question of victuals, the words of the libretto were: *"Tond les chiens, coupe les chats, les queues et les oreilles."*

It was true that the fantasy, the spirit of each vendor or vendress frequently introduced variations into the words of all these chants that I used to hear from my bed. And yet a ritual suspension interposing a silence in the middle of a word, especially when it was repeated a second time, constantly reminded me of some old church. In his little cart drawn by a she-ass which he stopped in front of each house before entering the court-yard, the old-clothes man, brandishing a whip, intoned: *"Habits, marchand d'habits, ha . . . bits"* with the same pause between the final syllables as if he had been intoning in plain chant: *"Per omnia saecula saeculo . . . rum"* or *"requiescat in pa . . . ce"* albeit he had no reason to believe in the immortality of his clothes, nor did he offer them as cerements for the supreme repose in peace. And similarly, as the motives were beginning, even at this early hour, to become confused, a vegetable woman, pushing her little hand-cart, was using for her litany the Gregorian division:

> *A la tendresse, à la verduresse,*
> *Artichauts tendres et beaux,*
> *Arti . . . chauts.*

although she had probably never heard of the antiphonal, or of the seven tones that symbolise four the sciences of the quadrivium and three those of the trivium.

Drawing from a penny whistle, from a bagpipe, airs of his own southern country whose sunlight harmonised well with these fine days, a man in a blouse, wielding a bull's pizzle in his hand and wearing a basque béret on his head, stopped before each house in turn. It was the goatherd with two dogs driving before him his string of goats. As he came from a distance, he arrived fairly late in our quarter; and the women came running out with bowls to receive the milk that was to give strength to their little ones. But with the Pyrenean airs of this good shepherd was now blended the bell of the grinder, who cried: *"Couteaux, ciseaux, rasoirs."* With him the saw-setter was unable to compete, for, lacking an instrument, he had to be content with calling: *"Avez-vous des scies à repasser, v'là le repasseur,"* while in a gayer mood the tinker, after enumerating the pots, pans and everything else that he repaired, intoned the refrain:

> *Tam, tam, tam,*
> *C'est moi qui rétame*
> *Même le macadam,*
> *C'est moi qui mets des fonds partout,*
> *Qui bouche tous les trous, trou, trou;*

and young Italians carrying big iron boxes painted red, upon which the numbers—winning and losing—were marked, and springing their rattles, gave the invitation: *"Amusez-vous, mesdames, v'là le plaisir."*

Françoise brought in the *Figaro*. A glance was sufficient to shew me that my article had not yet appeared. She told me that Albertine had asked whether she might come to my room and sent word that she had quite given up the idea of calling upon the Verdurins, and had decided to go, as I had advised her, to the 'special' matinée at the Trocadéro—what nowadays would be called, though with considerably less significance, a 'gala' matinée—after a short ride which she had promised to take with Andrée. Now that I knew that she had renounced her desire, possibly evil, to go and see Mme. Verdurin, I said with a laugh: "Tell her to come in," and told myself that she might go where she chose and that it was all the same to me. I knew that by the end of the afternoon, when dusk began to fall, I should probably be a different man, moping, attaching to every one of Albertine's movements an importance that they did not possess at this morning hour when the weather was so fine. For my indifference was accompanied by a clear notion of its cause, but was in no way modified by it. "Françoise assured me that you were awake and that I should not be disturbing you," said Albertine as she entered the room. And since next to making me catch cold by opening the window at the wrong moment, what Albertine most dreaded was to come into my room when I was asleep: "I hope I have not done anything wrong," she went on. "I was afraid you would say to me: What insolent mortal comes here to meet his doom?" and she laughed that laugh which I always found so disturbing. I replied in the same vein of pleasantry: "Was it for you this stern decree was made?"—and, lest she should ever venture to break it, added: "Although I should be furious if you did wake me." "I know, I know, don't be frightened," said Albertine. And, to relieve the situation, I went on, still enacting the scene from *Esther* with her, while in the street below the cries continued, drowned by our conversation: "I find in you alone a certain grace That charms me and of which I never tire" (and to myself I thought: "yes, she does tire me very often"). And remembering what she had said to me overnight, as I thanked her extravagantly for having given up the Verdurins, so that another time she would obey me similarly with regard to something else, I said: "Albertine, you distrust me who love you and you place your trust in other people who do not love you" (as though it were not natural to distrust the people who love us and who alone have an interest in lying to us in order to find out things, to hinder us), and added these lying words: "You don't really believe that I love you, which is amusing. As a matter of fact, I don't *adore* you." She lied in her turn when she told me that she trusted nobody but myself and then became sincere when she assured me that she knew very well that I loved her. But this affirmation did not seem to imply that she did not believe me to be a liar and a spy. And she seemed to pardon me as though she had seen these defects to be the agonising consequence of a strong passion or as though she herself had felt herself to be less good. "I beg of you, my dearest girl, no more of that *haute voltige* you were practising the other day. Just think, Albertine, if you were to meet with an accident!" Of course I did not wish her any harm. But what a pleasure it would be if, with her horses, she should take it into her head to ride off somewhere, wherever she chose, and never to return again to my house. How it would simplify everything, that she should go and live happily somewhere else, I did not even wish to know where. "Oh! I know you wouldn't survive me for more than a day; you would commit suicide."

So we exchanged lying speeches. But a truth more profound than that which we would utter were we sincere may sometimes be expressed and announced by another channel than that of sincerity. "You don't mind all that noise outside," she asked me; "I love it. But you're such a light sleeper anyhow." I was on the contrary an extremely heavy sleeper (as I have already said, but I am obliged to repeat it in view of what follows), especially when I did not begin to sleep until the morning. As this kind of sleep is—on an average—four times as refreshing, it seems to the awakened sleeper to have lasted four times as long, when it has really been four times as short. A splendid, sixteenfold error in multiplication which gives so much beauty to our awakening and makes life begin again on a different scale, like those great changes of rhythm which, in music, mean that in an andante a quaver has the same duration as a minim in a prestissimo, and which are unknown in our waking state. There life is almost always the same, whence the disappointments of travel. It may seem indeed that our dreams are composed of the coarsest stuff of life, but that stuff is treated, kneaded so thoroughly, with a protraction due to the fact that none of the temporal limitations of the waking state is there to prevent it from spinning itself out to heights so vast that we fail to recognise it. On the mornings after this good fortune had befallen me, after the sponge of sleep had obliterated from my brain the signs of everyday occupations that are traced upon it as upon a blackboard, I was obliged to bring my memory back to life; by the exercise of our will we can recapture what the amnesia of sleep or of a stroke has made us forget, what gradually returns to us as our eyes open or our paralysis disappears. I had lived through so many hours in a few minutes that, wishing to address Françoise, for whom I had rung, in language that corresponded to the facts of real life and was regulated by the clock, I was obliged to exert all my power of internal repression in order not to say: "Well, Françoise, here we are at five o'clock in the evening and I haven't set eyes on you since yesterday afternoon." And seeking to dispel my dreams, giving them the lie and lying to myself as well, I said boldly, compelling myself with all my might to silence, the direct opposite: "Françoise, it must be at least ten!" I did not even say ten o'clock in the morning, but simply ten, so that this incredible hour might appear to be uttered in a more natural tone. And yet to say these words, instead of those that continued to run in the mind of the half-awakened sleeper that I still was, demanded the same effort of equilibrium that a man requires when he jumps out of a moving train and runs for some yards along the platform, if he is to avoid falling. He runs for a moment because the environment that he has just left was one animated by great velocity, and utterly unlike the inert soil upon which his feet find it difficult to keep their balance.

Because the dream world is not the waking world, it does not follow that the waking world is less genuine, far from it. In the world of sleep, our perceptions are so overcharged, each of them increased by a counterpart which doubles its bulk and blinds it to no purpose, that we are not able even to distinguish what is happening in the bewilderment of awakening; was it Françoise that had come to me, or I that, tired of waiting, went to her? Silence at that moment was the only way not to reveal anything, as at the moment when we are brought before a magistrate cognisant of all the charges against us, when we have not been informed of them ourselves. Was it Françoise that had come, was it I that had summoned her? Was it not, indeed, Françoise that had been asleep and I that had just awoken her; nay more, was not Françoise enclosed in my breast, for the distinction between persons and their reaction upon one another barely exists in that murky obscurity in which reality is as little translucent as in the body of a porcupine, and our all but non-existent perception may perhaps furnish an idea of the perception of certain animals. Besides, in the limpid state of unreason that precedes these heavy slumbers, if fragments of wisdom float there luminously, if the names of Taine and George Eliot are not unknown, the waking life does still retain the superiority, inasmuch as it is possible to continue it every morning, whereas it is not possible to continue the dream life every night. But are there perhaps other worlds more real than the waking world? Even if we have seen transformed by every revolution in the arts, and still more, at the same time, by the degree of proficiency and culture that distinguishes an artist from an ignorant fool.

And often an extra hour of sleep is a paralytic stroke after which we must recover the use of our limbs, learn to speak. Our will would not be adequate for this task. We have slept too long, we no longer exist. Our waking is barely felt, mechanically and without consciousness, as a water pipe might feel the turning off of a tap. A life more inanimate than that of the jellyfish follows, in which we could equally well believe that we had been drawn up from the depths of the sea or released from prison, were we but capable of thinking anything at all. But then from the highest heaven the goddess Mnemotechnia bends down and holds out to us in the formula 'the habit of ringing for our coffee' the hope of resurrection. However, the instantaneous gift of memory is not always so simple. Often we have before us, in those first minutes in which we allow ourself to slip into the waking state, a truth composed of different realities among which we imagine that we can choose, as among a pack of cards.

It is Friday morning and we have just returned from our walk, or else it is teatime by the sea. The idea of sleep and that we are lying in bed and in our nightshirt is often the last that occurs to us.

Our resurrection is not effected at once; we think that we have rung the bell, we have not done so, we utter senseless remarks. Movement alone restores our thought, and when we have actually pressed the electric button we are able to say slowly but distinctly: "It must be at least ten o'clock, Françoise, bring me my coffee." Oh, the miracle! Françoise could have had no suspicion of the sea of unreality in which I was still wholly immersed and through which I had had the energy to make my strange question pass. Her answer was: "It is ten past ten." Which made my remark appear quite reasonable, and enabled me not to let her perceive the fantastic conversations by which I had been interminably beguiled, on days when it was not a mountain of non-existence that had crushed all life out of me. By strength of will, I had reinstated myself in life. I was still enjoying the last shreds of sleep, that is to say of the only inventiveness, the only novelty that exists in story-telling, since none of our narrations in the waking state, even though they be adorned with literary graces, admit those mysterious differences from which beauty derives. It is easy to speak of the beauty created by opium. But to a man who is accustomed to sleeping only with the aid of drugs, an unexpected hour of natural sleep will reveal the vast, matutinal expanse of a country as mysterious and more refreshing. By varying the hour, the place at which we go to sleep, by wooing sleep in an artificial manner, or on the contrary by returning for once to natural sleep —the strangest kind of all to whoever is in the habit of putting himself to sleep with soporifics—we succeed in producing a thousand times as many varieties of sleep as a gardener could produce of carnations or roses. Gardeners produce flowers that are delicious dreams, and others too that are like nightmares. When I fell asleep in a certain way I used to wake up shivering, thinking that I had caught the measles, or, what was far more painful, that my grandmother (to whom I never gave a thought now) was hurt because I had laughed at her that day when, at Balbec, in the belief that she was about to die, she had wished me to have a photograph of herself. At once, albeit I was awake, I felt that I must go and explain to her that she had misunderstood me. But, already, my bodily warmth was returning. The diagnosis of measles was set aside, and my grandmother became so remote that she no longer made my heart throb. Sometimes over these different kinds of sleep there fell a sudden darkness. I was afraid to continue my walk along an entirely unlighted avenue, where I could hear prowling footsteps. Suddenly a dispute broke out between a policeman and one of those women whom one often saw driving hackney carriages, and mistook at a distance for young men. Upon her box among the shadows I could not see her, but she spoke, and in her voice I could read the perfections of her face and the youthfulness of her body. I strode towards her, in the darkness, to get into her carriage before she drove off. It was a long way. Fortunately, her dispute with the policeman continued. I overtook the carriage which was still drawn up. This part of the avenue was lighted by street lamps. The driver became visible. She was indeed a woman, but old and corpulent, with white hair tumbling beneath her hat, and a red birthmark on her face. I walked past her, thinking: Is this what happens to the youth of women? Those whom we have met in the past, if suddenly we desire to see them again, have they become old? Is the young woman whom we desire like a character on the stage, when, unable to secure the actress who created the part, the management is obliged to entrust it to a new star? But then it is no longer the same.

With this a feeling of melancholy invaded me. We have thus in our sleep a number of Pities, like the 'Pietà' of the Renaissance, but not, like them, wrought in marble, being, rather, unsubstantial. They have their purpose, however, which is to make us remember a certain outlook upon things, more tender, more human, which we are too apt to forget in the common sense, frigid, sometimes full of hostility, of the waking state. Thus I was reminded of the vow that I had made at Balbec that I would always treat Françoise with compassion. And for the whole of that morning at least I would manage to compel myself not to be irritated by Françoise's quarrels with the butler, to be gentle with Françoise to whom the others shewed so little kindness. For that morning only, and I would have to try to frame a code that was a little more permanent; for, just as nations are not governed for any length of time by a policy of pure sentiment, so men are not governed by the memory of their dreams. Already this dream was beginning to fade away. In attempting to recall it in order to portray it I made it fade all the faster. My eyelids were no longer so firmly sealed over my eyes. If I tried to reconstruct my dream, they opened completely. At every moment we must choose between health and sanity on the one hand, and spiritual pleasures on the other. I have always taken the cowardly part of choosing the former. Moreover, the perilous power that I was renouncing was even more perilous than we suppose. Pities, dreams, do not fly away unaccompanied. When we alter thus the conditions in which we go to sleep, it is not our dreams alone that fade, but, for days on end, for years it may be, the faculty not merely of dreaming but of going to sleep. Sleep is divine but by no means stable; the slightest shock makes it volatile. A lover of habits, they retain it every night, being more fixed than itself, in the place set apart for it, they preserve it from all injury, but if we displace it, if it is no longer subordinated, it melts away like a vapour. It is like youth and love, never to be recaptured.

In these various forms of sleep, as likewise in music, it was the lengthening or shortening of the interval that created beauty. I enjoyed this beauty, but, on the other hand, I had lost in my sleep, however brief, a good number of the cries which render perceptible to us the peripatetic life of the tradesmen, the victuallers of Paris. And so, as a habit (without, alas, foreseeing the drama in which these late awakenings and the Draconian, Medo-Persian laws of a Racinian Assuérus were presently to involve me) I made an effort to awaken early so as to lose none of these cries.

And, more than the pleasure of knowing how fond Albertine was of them and of being out of doors myself without leaving my bed, I heard in them as it were the symbol of the atmosphere of the world outside, of the dangerous stirring life through the veins of which I did not allow her to move save under my tutelage, from which I withdrew her at the hour of my choosing to make her return home to my side. And so it was with the most perfect sincerity that I was able to say in answer to Albertine: "On the contrary, they give me pleasure because I know that you like them." "*A la barque, les huitres, à la barque.*" "Oh, oysters! I've been simply longing for some!" Fortunately Albertine, partly from inconsistency, partly from docility, quickly forgot the things for which she had been longing, and before I had time to tell her that she would find better oysters at Prunier's, she wanted in succession all the things that she heard cried by the fish hawker: "*A la crevette, à la bonne crevette, j'ai de la raie toute en vie, toute en vie.*" "*Merlans à frire, à frire.*" "*Il arrive le maquereau, maquereau frais, maquereau nouveau.*" "*Voilà le maquereau, mesdames, il est beau le maquereau.*" "*A la moule fraîche et bonne, à la moule!*" In spite of myself, the warning: "*Il arrive le maquereau*" made me shudder. But as this warning could not, I felt, apply to our chauffeur, I thought only of the fish of that name, which I detested, and my uneasiness did not last. "Ah! Mussels," said Albertine, "I should so like some mussels." "My darling! They were all very well at Balbec, here they're not worth eating; besides, I implore you, remember what Cottard told you about mussels." But my remark was all the more ill-chosen in that the vegetable woman who came next announced a thing that Cottard had forbidden even more strictly:

> *A la romaine, à la romaine!*
> *On ne le vend pas, on la promène.*

Albertine consented, however, to sacrifice her lettuces, on the condition that I would promise to buy for her in a few days' time from the woman who cried: "*J'ai de la belle asperge d'Argenteuil, j'ai de la belle asperge.*" A mysterious voice, from which one would have expected some stranger utterance, insinuated: "*Tonneaux, tonneaux!*" We were obliged to remain under the disappointment that nothing more was being offered us than barrels, for the word was almost entirely drowned by the appeal: "*Vitri, vitri-er, carreaux cassés, voilà le vitrier, vitri-er,*" a Gregorian division which reminded me less, however, of the liturgy than did the appeal of the rag vendor, reproducing unconsciously one of those abrupt interruptions of sound, in the middle of a prayer, which are common enough in the ritual of the church: "*Praeceptis salutaribus moniti et divina institutione formati audemus dicere,*" says the priest, ending sharply upon '*dicere*.' Without irreverence, as the populace of the middle ages used to perform plays and farces within the consecrated ground of the church, it is of that '*dicere*' that this rag vendor makes one think when, after drawling the other words, he utters the final syllable with a sharpness befitting the accentuation laid down by the great Pope of the seventh century: "*Chiffons, ferrailles à vendre*" (all this chanted slowly, as are the two syllables that follow, whereas the last concludes more briskly than '*dicere*') "*peaux d'la-pins.*" "*La Valence, la belle Valence, la fraîche orange.*" The humble leeks even: "*Voilà d'beaux poireaux,*" the onions: "*Huit sous mon oignon,*" sounded for me as if it were an echo of the rolling waves in which, left to herself, Albertine might have perished, and thus assumed the sweetness of a "*Suave mari magno.*" "*Voilà des carrottes à deux ronds la botte.*" "Oh!" exclaimed Albertine, "cabbages, carrots, oranges. All the things I want to eat. Do make Françoise go out and buy some. She shall cook us a dish of creamed carrots. Besides, it will be so nice to eat all these things together. It will be all the sounds that we hear, transformed into a good dinner. . . . Oh, please, ask Françoise to give us instead a ray with black butter. It is so good!" "My dear child, of course I will, but don't wait; if you do, you'll be asking for all the things on the vegetable-barrows." "Very well, I'm off, but I never want anything again for our dinners except what we've heard cried in the street. It is such fun. And to think that we shall have to wait two whole months before we hear: '*Haricots verts et tendres, haricots, v'là l'haricot vert.*' How true that is: tender haricots; you know I like them as soft as soft, dripping with vinegar sauce, you wouldn't think you were eating, they melt in the mouth like drops of dew. Oh dear, it's the same with the little hearts of cream cheese, such a long time to wait: '*Bon fromage à la cré, à la cré, bon fromage.*' And the water-grapes from Fontainebleau: '*J'ai du bon chasselas.*' " And I thought with dismay of all the time that I should have to spend with her before the water-grapes were in season. "Listen, I said that I wanted only the things that we had heard cried, but of course I make exceptions. And so it's by no means impossible that I may look in at Rebattet's and order an ice for the two of us. You will tell me that it's not the season for them, but I do so want one!" I was disturbed by this plan of going to Rebattet's, rendered more certain and more suspicious in my eyes by the words 'it's by no means impossible.' It was the day on which the Verdurins were at home, and, ever since Swann had informed them that Rebattet's was the best place, it was there that they ordered their ices and pastry. "I have no objection to an ice, my darling Albertine, but let me order it for you, I don't know myself whether it will be from Poiré-Blanche's, or Rebattet's, or the Ritz, anyhow I shall see." "Then you're going out?" she said with an air of distrust. She always maintained that she would be delighted if I went out more often, but if anything that I said could make her suppose that I would not be staying indoors, her uneasy air made me think that the joy that she would feel in seeing me go out every day was perhaps not altogether sincere. "I may perhaps go out, perhaps not, you know quite well that I never make plans beforehand. In any case ices are not a thing that is cried, that people hawk in the streets, why do you want one?" And then she replied in words which shewed me what a fund of intelligence and latent taste had developed in her since Balbec, in words akin to those which, she pretended, were due entirely to my influence, to living continually in my company, words which, however, I should never have uttered, as though I had been in some way forbidden by some unknown authority ever to decorate my conversation with literary forms. Perhaps the future was not destined to be the same for Albertine as for myself. I had almost a presentiment of this when I saw her eagerness to employ in speech images so 'written,' which seemed to me to be reserved for another, more sacred use, of which I was still ignorant. She said to me (and I was, in spite of everything, deeply touched, for I thought to myself: Certainly I would not speak as she does, and yet, all the same, but for me she would not be speaking like this, she has come profoundly under my influence, she cannot therefore help loving me, she is my handiwork): "What I like about these foodstuffs that are cried is that a thing which we hear like a rhapsody changes its nature when it comes to our table and addresses itself to my palate. As for ices (for I hope that you won't order me one that isn't cast in one of those old-fashioned moulds which have every architectural shape imaginable), whenever I take one, temples, churches, obelisks, rocks, it is like an illustrated geography-book which I look at first of all and then convert its raspberry or vanilla monuments into coolness in my throat." I thought that this was a little too well expressed, but she felt that I thought that it was well expressed, and went on, pausing for a moment when she had brought off her comparison to laugh that beautiful laugh of hers which was so painful to me because it was so voluptuous. "Oh dear, at the Ritz I'm afraid you'll find Vendôme Columns of ice, chocolate ice or raspberry, and then you will need a lot of them so that they may look like votive pillars or pylons erected along an avenue to the glory of Coolness. They make raspberry obelisks too, which will rise up here and there in the burning desert of my thirst, and I shall make their pink granite crumble and melt deep down in my throat which they will refresh better than any oasis" (and here the deep laugh broke out, whether from satisfaction at talking so well, or in derision of herself for using such hackneyed images, or, alas, from a physical pleasure at feeling inside herself something so good, so cool, which was tantamount to a sensual satisfaction). "Those mountains of ice at the Ritz sometimes suggest Monte Rosa, and indeed, if it is a lemon ice, I do not object to its not having a monumental shape, its being irregular, abrupt, like one of Elstir's mountains. It ought not to be too white then, but slightly yellowish, with that look of dull, dirty snow that Elstir's mountains have. The ice need not be at all big, only half an ice if you like, those lemon ices are still mountains, reduced to a tiny scale, but our imagination restores their dimensions, like those little Japanese dwarf trees which, one knows quite well, are still cedars, oaks, manchineels; so much so that if I arranged a few of them beside a little trickle of water in my room I should have a vast forest stretching down to a river, in which children would be lost. In the same way, at the foot of my yellowish lemon ice, I can see quite clearly postilions, travellers, post chaises over which my tongue sets to work to roll down freezing avalanches that will swallow them up" (the cruel delight with which she said this excited my jealousy); "just as," she went on, "I set my lips to work to destroy, pillar after pillar, those Venetian churches of a porphyry that is made with strawberries, and send what I spare of them crashing down upon the worshippers. Yes, all those monuments will pass from their stony state into my inside which throbs already with their melting coolness. But, you know, even without ices, nothing is so exciting or makes one so thirsty as the advertisements of mineral springs. At Montjouvain, at Mlle. Vinteuil's, there was no good confectioner who made ices in the neighbourhood, but we used to make our own tour of France in the garden by drinking a different sparkling water every day, like Vichy water which, as soon as you pour it out, sends up from the bottom of the glass a white cloud which fades and dissolves if you don't drink it at once." But to hear her speak of Montjouvain was too painful, I cut her short. "I am boring you, good-bye, my dear boy." What a change from Balbec, where I would defy Elstir himself to have been able to divine in Albertine this wealth of poetry, a poetry less strange, less personal than that of Céleste Albaret, for instance. Albertine would never have thought of the things that Céleste used to say to me, but love, even when it seems to be nearing its end, is partial. I preferred the illustrated geography-book of her ices, the somewhat facile charm of which seemed to me a reason for loving Albertine and a proof that I had an influence over her, that she was in love with me.

As soon as Albertine had gone out, I felt how tiring it was to me, this perpetual presence, insatiable of movement and life, which disturbed my sleep with its movements, made me live in a perpetual chill by that habit of leaving doors open, forced me—in order to find pretexts that would justify me in not accompanying her, without, however, appearing too unwell, and at the same time to see that she was not unaccompanied—to display every day greater ingenuity than Scheherezade. Unfortunately, if by a similar ingenuity the Persian story-teller postponed her own death, I was hastening mine. There are thus in life certain situations which are not all created, as was this, by amorous jealousy and a precarious state of health which does not permit us to share the life of a young and active person, situations in which nevertheless the problem of whether to continue a life shared with that person or to return to the separate existence of the past sets itself almost in medical terms; to which of the two sorts of repose ought we to sacrifice ourselves (by continuing the daily strain, or by returning to the agonies of separation) to that of the head or of the heart?

In any event, I was very glad that Andrée was to accompany Albertine to the Trocadéro, for certain recent and for that matter entirely trivial incidents had brought it about that while I had still, of course, the same confidence in the chauffeur's honesty, his vigilance, or at least the perspicacity of his vigilance did not seem to be quite what it had once been. It so happened that, only a short while since, I had sent Albertine alone in his charge to Versailles, and she told me that she had taken her luncheon at the Réservoirs; as the chauffeur had mentioned the restaurant Vatel, the day on which I noticed this contradiction, I found an excuse to go downstairs and speak to him (it was still the same man, whose acquaintance we had made at Balbec) while Albertine was dressing. "You told me that you had had your luncheon at the Vatel. Mlle. Albertine mentions the Réservoirs. What is the meaning of that?" The driver replied: "Oh, I said that I had had my luncheon at the Vatel, but I cannot tell where Mademoiselle took hers. She left me as soon as we reached Versailles to take a horse cab, which she prefers when it is not a question of time." Already I was furious at the thought that she had been alone; still, it was only during the time that she spent at her luncheon. "You might surely," I suggested mildly (for I did not wish to appear to be keeping Albertine actually under surveillance, which would have been humiliating to myself, and doubly so, for it would have shewn that she concealed her activities from me), "have had your luncheon, I do not say at her table, but in the same restaurant?" "But all she told me was to meet her at six o'clock at the Place d'Armes. I had no orders to call for her after luncheon." "Ah!" I said, making an effort to conceal my dismay. And I returned upstairs. And so it was for more than seven hours on end that Albertine had been alone, left to her own devices. I might assure myself, it is true, that the cab had not been merely an expedient whereby to escape from the chauffeur's supervision. In town, Albertine preferred driving in a cab, saying that one had a better view, that the air was more pleasant. Nevertheless, she had spent seven hours, as to which I should never know anything. And I dared not think of the manner in which she must have employed them. I felt that the driver had been extremely clumsy, but my confidence in him was now absolute. For if he had been to the slightest extent in league with Albertine, he would never have acknowledged that he had left her unguarded from eleven o'clock in the morning to six in the afternoon. There could be but one other explanation, and it was absurd, of the chauffeur's admission. This was that some quarrel between Albertine and himself had prompted him, by making a minor disclosure to me, to shew my mistress that he was not the sort of man who could be hushed, and that if, after this first gentle warning, she did not do exactly as he told her, he would take the law into his own hands. But this explanation was absurd; I should have had first of all to assume a non-existent quarrel between him and Albertine, and then to label as a consummate blackmailer this good-looking motorist who had always shewn himself so affable and obliging. Only two days later, as it happened, I saw that he was more capable than I had for a moment supposed in my frenzy of suspicion of exercising over Albertine a discreet and far-seeing vigilance. For, having managed to take him aside and talk to him of what he had told me about Versailles, I said to him in a careless, friendly tone: "That drive to Versailles that you told me about the other day was everything that it should be, you behaved perfectly as you always do. But, if I may give you just a little hint, I have so much responsibility now that Mme. Bontemps has placed her niece under my charge, I am so afraid of accidents, I reproach myself so for not going with her, that I prefer that it should be yourself, you who are so safe, so wonderfully skilful, to whom no accident can ever happen, that shall take Mlle. Albertine everywhere. Then I need fear nothing." The charming apostolic motorist smiled a subtle smile, his hand resting upon the consecration-cross of his wheel. Then he uttered these words which (banishing all the anxiety from my heart where its place was at once filled by joy) made me want to fling my arms round his neck: "Don't be afraid," he said to me. "Nothing can happen to her, for, when my wheel is not guiding her, my eye follows her everywhere. At Versailles, I went quietly along and visited the town with her, as you might say. From the Réser-voirs she went to the Château, from the Château to the Trianons, and I following her all the time without appearing to see her, and the astonishing thing is that she never saw me. Oh, if she had seen me, the fat would have been in the fire. It was only natural, as I had the whole day before me with nothing to do that I should visit the castle too. All the more as Mademoiselle certainly hasn't failed to notice that I've read a bit myself and take an interest in all those old curiosities" (this was true, indeed I should have been surprised if I had learned that he was a friend of Morel, so far more refined was his taste than the violinist's). "Anyhow, she didn't see me." "She must have met some of her own friends, of course, for she knows a great many ladies at Versailles." "No, she was alone all the time." "Then people must have stared at her, a girl of such striking appearance, all by herself." "Why, of course they stared at her, but she knew nothing about it; she went all the time with her eyes glued to her guide-book, or gazing up at the pictures." The chauffeur's story seemed to me all the more accurate in that it was indeed a 'card' with a picture of the Château, and another of the Trianons, that Albertine had sent me on the day of her visit. The care with which the obliging chauffeur had followed every step of her course touched me deeply. How was I to suppose that this correction—in the form of a generous amplification—of his account given two days earlier was due to the fact that in those two days Albertine, alarmed that the chauffeur should have spoken to me, had surrendered, and made her peace with him. This suspicion never even occurred to me. It is beyond question that this version of the driver's story, as it rid me of all fear that Albertine might have deceived me, quite naturally cooled me towards my mistress and made me take less interest in the day that she had spent at Versailles. I think, however, that the chauffeur's explanations, which, by absolving Albertine, made her even more tedious than before, would not perhaps have been sufficient to calm me so quickly. Two little pimples which for some days past my mistress had had upon her brow were perhaps even more effective in modifying the sentiments of my heart. Finally these were diverted farther still from her (so far that I was conscious of her existence only when I set eyes upon her) by the strange confidence volunteered me by Gilberte's maid, whom I happened to meet. I learned that, when I used to go every day to see Gilberte, she was in love with a young man of whom she saw a great deal more than of myself. I had had an inkling of this for a moment at the time, indeed I had questioned this very maid. But, as she knew that I was in love with Gilberte, she had denied, sworn that never had Mlle. Swann set eyes on the young man. Now, however, knowing that my love had long since died, that for years past I had left all her letters unanswered—and also perhaps because she was no longer in Gilberte's service—of her own accord she gave me a full account of the amorous episode of which I had known nothing. This seemed to her quite natural. I supposed, remembering her oaths at the time, that she had not been aware of what was going on. Far from it, it was she herself who used to go, at Mme. Swann's orders, to inform the young man whenever the object of my love was alone. The object then of my love. . . . But I asked myself whether my love of those days was as dead as I thought, for this story pained me. As I do not believe that jealousy can revive a dead love, I supposed that my painful impression was due, in part at least, to the injury to my self-esteem, for a number of people whom I did not like and who at that time and even a little later—their attitude has since altered—affected a contemptuous attitude towards myself, knew perfectly well, while I was in love with Gilberte, that I was her dupe. And this made me ask myself retrospectively whether in my love for Gilberte there had not been an element of self-love, since it so pained me now to discover that all the hours of affectionate intercourse, which had made me so happy, were known to be nothing more than a deliberate hoodwinking of me by my mistress, by people whom I did not like. In any case, love or self-love, Gilberte was almost dead in me but not entirely, and the result of this annoyance was to prevent me from worrying myself beyond measure about

Albertine, who occupied so small a place in my heart. Nevertheless, to return to her (after so long a parenthesis) and to her expedition to Versailles, the postcards of Versailles (is it possible, then, to have one's heart caught in a noose like this by two simultaneous and interwoven jealousies, each inspired by a different person?) gave me a slightly disagreeable impression whenever, as I tidied my papers, my eye fell upon them. And I thought that if the driver had not been such a worthy fellow, the harmony of his second narrative with Albertine's 'cards' would not have amounted to much, for what are the first things that people send you from Versailles but the Château and the Trianons, unless that is to say the card has been chosen by some person of refined taste who adores a certain statue, or by some idiot who selects as a 'view' of Versailles the station of the horse tramway or the goods depot. Even then I am wrong in saying an idiot, such postcards not having always been bought by a person of that sort at random, for their interest as coming from Versailles. For two whole years men of intelligence, artists, used to find Siena, Venice, Granada a 'bore,' and would say of the humblest omnibus, of every railway-carriage: "There you have true beauty." Then this fancy passed like the rest. Indeed, I cannot be certain that people did not revert to the 'sacrilege of destroying the noble relics of the past.' Anyhow, a first class railway carriage ceased to be regarded as *a priori* more beautiful than St. Mark's at Venice. People continued to say: "Here you have real life, the return to the past is artificial," but without drawing any definite conclusion. To make quite certain, without forfeiting any of my confidence in the chauffeur, in order that Albertine might not be able to send him away without his venturing to refuse for fear of her taking him for a spy, I never allowed her to go out after this without the reinforcement of Andrée, whereas for some time past I had found the chauffeur sufficient. I had even allowed her then (a thing I would never dare do now) to stay away for three whole days by herself with the chauffeur and to go almost as far as Balbec, so great was her longing to travel at high speed in an open car. Three days during which my mind had been quite at rest, although the rain of postcards that she had showered upon me did not reach me, owing to the appalling state of the Breton postal system (good in summer, but disorganised, no doubt, in winter), until a week after the return of Albertine and the chauffeur, in such health and vigour that on the very morning of their return they resumed, as though nothing had happened, their daily outings. I was delighted that Albertine should be going this afternoon to the Trocadéro, to this 'special' matinée, but still more reassured that she would have a companion there in the shape of Andrée.

Dismissing these reflexions, now that Albertine had gone out, I went and took my stand for a moment at the window. There was at first a silence, amid which the whistle of the tripe vendor and the horn of the tramcar made the air ring in different octaves, like a blind piano-tuner. Then gradually the interwoven motives became distinct, and others were combined with them. There was also a new whistle, the call of a vendor the nature of whose wares I have never discovered, a whistle that was itself exactly like the scream of the tramway, and, as it was not carried out of earshot by its own velocity, one thought of a single car, not endowed with motion, or broken down, immobilised, screaming at short intervals like a dying animal. And I felt that, should I ever have to leave this aristocratic quarter—unless it were to move to one that was entirely plebeian—the streets and boulevards of central Paris (where the fruit, fish and other trades, stabilised in huge stores, rendered superfluous the cries of the street hawkers, who for that matter would not have been able to make themselves heard) would seem to me very dreary, quite uninhabitable, stripped, drained of all these litanies of the small trades and peripatetic victuals, deprived of the orchestra that returned every morning to charm me. On the pavement a woman with no pretence to fashion (or else obedient to an ugly fashion) came past, too brightly dressed in a sack overcoat of goatskin; but no, it was not a woman, it was a chauffeur who, enveloped in his ponyskin, was proceeding on foot to his garage. Escaped from the big hotels, their winged messengers, of variegated hue, were speeding towards the termini, bent over their handlebars, to meet the arrivals by the morning trains. The throb of a violin was due at one time to the passing of a motor-car, at another to my not having put enough water in my electric kettle. In the middle of the symphony there rang out an old-fashioned 'air'; replacing the sweet seller, who generally accompanied her song with a rattle, the toy seller, to whose pipe was attached a jumping jack which he sent flying in all directions, paraded similar puppets for sale, and without heeding the ritual declamation of Gregory the Great, the reformed declamation of Palestrina or the lyrical declamation of the modern composers, entoned at the top of his voice, a belated adherent of pure melody: *"Allons les papas, allons les mamans, contentez vos petits enfants, c'est moi qui les fais, c'est moi qui les vends, et c'est moi qui boulotte l'argent. Tra la la la. Tra la la la laire, tra la la la la la la. Allons les petits!"* Some Italian boys in felt bérets made no attempt to compete with this lively aria, and it was without a word that they offered their little statuettes. Soon, however, a young fifer compelled the toy merchant to move on and to chant more inaudibly, though in brisk time: *"Allons les papas, allons les mamans."* This young fifer, was he one of the dragoons whom I used to hear in the mornings at Doncières? No, for what followed was: *"Voilà le réparateur de faïence et de porcelaine. Je répare le verre, le marbre, le cristal, l'os, l'ivoire et objets d'antiquité. Voilà le réparateur."* In a butcher's shop, between an aureole of sunshine on the left and a whole ox suspended from a hook on the right, an assistant, very tall and slender, with fair hair and a throat that escaped above his sky-blue collar, was displaying a lightning speed and a religious conscientiousness in putting on one side the most exquisite fillets of beef, on the other the coarsest parts of the rump, placed them upon glittering scales surmounted by a cross, from which hung down a number of beautiful chains, and—albeit he did nothing afterwards but arrange in the window a display of kidneys, steaks, ribs—was really far more suggestive of a handsome angel who, on the day of the Last Judgment, will prepare for God, according to their quality, the separation of the good and the evil and the weighing of souls. And once again the thin crawling music of the fife rose in the air, herald no longer of the destruction that Françoise used to dread whenever a regiment of cavalry filed past, but of 'repairs' promised by an 'antiquary,' simpleton or rogue, who, in either case highly eclectic, instead of specialising, applied his art to the most diverse materials. The young bread carriers hastened to stuff into their baskets the long rolls ordered for some luncheon party, while the milk girls attached the bottles of milk to their yokes. The sense of longing with which my eyes followed these young damsels, ought I to consider it quite justified? Would it not have been different if I had been able to detain for a few moments at close quarters one of those whom from the height of my window I saw only inside her shop or in motion. To estimate the loss that I suffered by my seclusion, that is to say the wealth that the day held in store for me, I should have had to intercept in the long unrolling of the animated frieze some girl carrying her linen or her milk, make her pass for a moment, like a silhouette from some mobile scheme of decoration, from the wings to the stage, within the proscenium of my bedroom door, and keep her there under my eye, not without eliciting some information about her which would enable me to find her again some day, like the inscribed ring which ornithologists or ichthyologists attach before setting them free to the legs or bellies of the birds or fishes whose migrations they are anxious to trace.

And so I asked Françoise, since I had a message that I wished taken, to be good enough to send up to my room, should any of them call, one or other of those girls who were always coming to take away the dirty or bring back the clean linen, or with bread, or bottles of milk, and whom she herself used often to send on errands. In doing so I was like Elstir, who, obliged to remain closeted in his studio, on certain days in spring when the knowledge that the woods were full of violets gave him a hunger to gaze at them, used to send his porter's wife out to buy him a bunch; then it was not the table upon which he had posed the little vegetable model, but the whole carpet of the underwoods where he had seen in other years, in their thousands, the serpentine stems, bowed beneath the weight of their blue beaks, that Elstir would fancy that he had before his eyes, like an imaginary zone defined in his studio by the limpid odour of the sweet, familiar flower.

Of a laundry girl, on a Sunday, there was not the slightest prospect. As for the girl who brought the bread, as ill luck would have it, she had rung the bell when Françoise was not about, had left her rolls in their basket on the landing, and had made off. The fruit girl would not call until much later. Once I had gone to order a cheese at the dairy, and, among the various young assistants, had remarked one girl, extravagantly fair, tall in stature though still little more than a child, who, among the other errand girls, seemed to be dreaming, in a distinctly haughty attitude. I had seen her in the distance only, and for so brief an instant that I could not have described her appearance, except to say that she must have grown too fast and that her head supported a fleece that gave the impression far less of capillary details than of a sculptor's conventional rendering of the separate channels of parallel drifts of snow upon a glacier. This was all that I had been able to make out, apart from a nose sharply outlined (a rare thing in a child) upon a thin face which recalled the beaks of baby vultures. Be-

sides, this clustering of her comrades round about her had not been the
only thing that prevented me from seeing her distinctly, there was also
my uncertainty whether the sentiments which I might, at first sight and
subsequently, inspire in her would be those of injured pride, or of irony,
or of a scorn which she would express later on to her friends. These alternative suppositions which I had formed, in an instant, with regard to her,
had condensed round about her the troubled atmosphere in which she disappeared, like a goddess in the cloud that is shaken by thunder. For moral
uncertainty is a greater obstacle to an exact visual perception than any
defect of vision would be. In this too skinny young person, who moreover
attracted undue attention, the excess of what another person would perhaps have called her charms was precisely what was calculated to repel me,
but had nevertheless had the effect of preventing me from perceiving even,
far more from remembering anything about the other young dairymaids,
whom the hooked nose of this one and her gaze—how unattractive it was!
—pensive, personal, with an air of passing judgment, had plunged in perpetual night, as a white streak of lightning darkens the landscape on either
side of it. And so, of my call to order a cheese, at the dairy, I had remembered (if we can say 'remember' in speaking of a face so carelessly observed that we adapt to the nullity of the face ten different noses in succession), I had remembered only this girl who had not attracted me. This
is sufficient to engender love. And yet I should have forgotten the extravagantly fair girl and should never have wished to see her again, had not
Françoise told me that, child as she was, she had all her wits about her and
would shortly be leaving her employer, since she had been going too fast
and owed money among the neighbours. It has been said that beauty is a
promise of happiness. Inversely, the possibility of pleasure may be a beginning of beauty.

I began to read Mamma's letter. Beneath her quotations from Madame
de Sévigné: "If my thoughts are not entirely black at Combray, they are
at least dark grey, I think of you at every moment; I long for you; your
health, your affairs, your absence, what sort of cloud do you suppose they
make in my sky?" I felt that my mother was vexed to find Albertine's stay
in the house prolonged, and my intention of marriage, although not yet
announced to my mistress, confirmed. She did not express her annoyance
more directly because she was afraid that I might leave her letters lying
about. Even then, veiled as her letters were, she reproached me with not
informing her immediately, after each of them, that I had received it:
"You remember how Mme. de Sévigné said: 'When we are far apart, we
no longer laugh at letters which begin with *I have received yours*.'"
Without referring to what distressed her most, she said that she was annoyed by my lavish expenditure: "Where on earth does all your money
go? It is distressing enough that, like Charles de Sévigné, you do not know
what you want and are 'two or three people at once,' but do try at least
not to be like him in spending money so that I may never have to say of
you: 'he has discovered how to spend and have nothing to shew, how to
lose without staking and how to pay without clearing himself of debt.'" I
had just finished Mamma's letter when Françoise returned to tell me that

she had in the house that very same slightly overbold young dairymaid of whom she had spoken to me. "She can quite well take Monsieur's note and bring back the answer, if it's not too far. Monsieur shall see her, she's just like a Little Red Ridinghood." Françoise withdrew to fetch the girl, and I could hear her leading the way and saying: "Come along now, you're frightened because there's a passage, stuff and nonsense, I never thought you would be such a goose. Have I got to lead you by the hand?" And Françoise, like a good and honest servant who means to see that her master is respected as she respects him herself, had draped herself in that majesty with ennobles the matchmaker in a picture by an old master where, in comparison with her, the lover and his mistress fade into insignificance. But Elstir when he gazed at them had no need to bother about what the violets were doing. The entry of the young dairymaid at once robbed me of my contemplative calm; I could think only of how to give plausibility to the fable of the letter that she was to deliver and I began to write quickly without venturing to cast more than a furtive glance at her, so that I might not seem to have brought her into my room to be scrutinised. She was invested for me with that charm of the unknown which I should not discover in a pretty girl whom I had found in one of those houses where they come to meet one. She was neither naked nor in disguise, but a genuine dairymaid, one of those whom we imagine to be so pretty, when we have not time to approach them; she possessed something of what constitutes the eternal desire, the eternal regret of life, the twofold current of which is at length diverted, directed towards us. Twofold, for if it is a question of the unknown, of a person who must, we guess, be divine, from her stature, her proportions, her indifferent glance, her haughty calm, on the other hand we wish this woman to be thoroughly specialised in her profession, allowing us to escape from ourselves into that world which a peculiar costume makes us romantically believe different. If for that matter we seek to comprise in a formula the law of our amorous curiosities, we should have to seek it in the maximum of difference between a woman of whom we have caught sight and one whom we have approached and caressed. If the women of what used at one time to be called the closed houses, if prostitutes themselves (provided that we know them to be prostitutes) attract us so little, it is not because they are less beautiful than other women, it is because they are ready and waiting; the very object that we are seeking to attain they offer us already; it is because they are not conquests. The difference there is at a minimum. A harlot smiles at us already in the street as she will smile when she is in our room. We are sculptors. We are anxious to obtain of a woman a statue entirely different from that which she has presented to us. We have seen a girl strolling, indifferent, insolent, along the seashore, we have seen a shop-assistant, serious and active, behind her counter, who will answer us stiffly, if only so as to escape the sarcasm of her comrades, a fruit seller who barely answers us at all. Well, we know no rest until we can discover by experiment whether the proud girl on the seashore, the shop-assistant on her high horse of 'What will people say?', the preoccupied fruit seller cannot be made, by skilful handling on our part, to relax their rectangular attitude, to throw about our neck their fruit-laden arms, to direct towards our lips, with a smile of consent, eyes hitherto frozen or absent—oh, the beauty of stern eyes—in working hours when the worker was so afraid of the gossip of her companions, eyes that avoided our beleaguering stare and, now that we have seen her alone and face to face, make their pupils yield beneath the sunlit burden of laughter when we speak of making love. Between the shopgirl, the laundress busy with her iron, the fruit seller, the dairymaid on the one hand, and the same girl when she is about to become our mistress, the maximum of difference is attained, stretched indeed to its extreme limits, and varied by those habitual gestures of her profession which make a pair of arms, during the hours of toil, something as different as possible (regarded as an arabesque pattern) from those supple bonds that already every evening are fastened about our throat while the mouth shapes itself for a kiss. And so we pass our whole life in uneasy advances, incessantly renewed, to respectable girls whom their calling seems to separate from us. Once they are in our arms, they are no longer anything more than they originally were, the gulf that we dreamed of crossing has been bridged. But we begin afresh with other women, we devote to these enterprises all our time, all our money, all our strength, our blood boils at the too cautious driver who is perhaps going to make us miss our first assignation, we work ourself into a fever. That first meeting, we know all the same that it will mean the vanishing of an illusion. It does not so much matter that the illusion still persists; we wish to see whether we can convert it into reality, and then we think of the laundress whose coldness we remarked. Amorous curiosity is like that which is aroused in us by the names of places; perpetually disappointed, it revives and remains for ever insatiable.

Alas! As soon as she stood before me, the fair dairymaid with the ribbed tresses, stripped of all that I had imagined and of the desire that had been aroused in me, was reduced to her own proportions. The throbbing cloud of my suppositions no longer enveloped her in a shimmering haze. She acquired an almost beggarly air from having (in place of the ten, the score that I recalled in turn without being able to fix any of them in my memory) but a single nose, rounder than I had thought, which made her appear rather a fool and had in any case lost the faculty of multiplying itself. This flyaway caught on the wing, inert, crushed, incapable of adding anything to its own paltry appearance, had no longer my imagination to collaborate with it. Fallen into the inertia of reality, I sought to rebound; her cheeks, which I had not seen in the shop, appeared to me so pretty that I became alarmed, and, to put myself in countenance, said to the young dairymaid: "Would you be so kind as to pass me the *Figaro* which is lying there, I must make sure of the address to which I am going to send you." Thereupon, as she picked up the newspaper, she disclosed as far as her elbow the red sleeve of her jersey and handed me the conservative sheet with a neat and courteous gesture which pleased me by its intimate rapidity, its pliable contour and its scarlet hue. While I was opening the *Figaro*, in order to say something and without raising my eyes, I asked the girl: "What do you call that red knitted thing you're wearing? It is very becoming." She replied: "It's my golf." For, by a slight downward tendency common to all fashions, the garments and styles which, a few years earlier, seemed to belong to the relatively smart world of Albertine's friends, were now the portion of working girls. "Are you quite sure it won't be giving you too much trouble," I said, while I pretended to be searching the columns of the *Figaro,* "if I send you rather a long way?" As soon as I myself appeared to find the service at all arduous that she would be performing by taking a message for me, she began to feel that it would be a trouble to her. "The only thing is, I have to be going out presently on my bike. Good lord, you know, Sunday's the only day we've got." "But won't you catch cold, going bare-headed like that?" "Oh, I shan't be bare-headed, I shall have my polo, and I could get on without it with all the hair I have." I raised my eyes tó the blaze of curling tresses and felt myself caught in their swirl and swept away, with a throbbing heart, amid the lightning and the blasts of a hurricane of beauty. I continued to study the newspaper, but albeit this was only to keep myself in countenance and to gain time, while I merely pretended to read, I took in nevertheless the meaning of the words that were before my eyes, and my attention was caught by the following: "To the programme already announced for this afternoon in the great hall of the Trocadéro must be added the name of Mlle. Léa who has consented to appear in *Les Fourberies de Nérine.* She will of course sustain the part of Nérine, in which she is astounding in her display of spirit and bewitching gaiety." It was as though a hand had brutally torn from my heart the bandage beneath which its wound had begun since my return from Balbec to heal. The flood of my anguish escaped in torrents, Léa, that was the actress friend of the two girls at Balbec whom Albertine, without appearing to see them, had, one afternoon at the Casino, watched in the mirror. It was true that at Balbec Albertine, at the name of Léa, had adopted a special tone of compunction in order to say to me, almost shocked that anyone could suspect such a pattern of virtue: "Oh no, she is not in the least that sort of woman, she is a very respectable person." Unfortunately for me, when Albertine made a statement of this sort, it was never anything but the first stage towards other, divergent statements. Shortly after the first, came this second: "I don't know her." In the third phase, after Albertine had spoken to me of somebody who was 'above suspicion' and whom (in the second place) she did not know, she first of all forgot that she had said that she did not know her and then, in a speech in which she contradicted herself unawares, informed me that she did know her. This first act of oblivion completed, and the fresh statement made, a second oblivion began, to wit that the person was above suspicion. "Isn't So-and-So," I would ask, "one of those women?" "Why, of course, everybody knows that!" Immediately the note of compunction was sounded afresh to utter a statement which was a vague echo, greatly reduced, of the first statement of all. "I'm bound to say that she has always behaved perfectly properly with me. Of course, she knows that I would send her about her business if she tried it on. Still, that makes no difference. I am obliged to give her credit for the genuine respect she has always shewn for me. It is easy to see she knew the sort of person she had to deal with." We remember the truth because it has a name, is rooted in the past, but a make-shift lie is quickly forgotten. Albertine forgot this latest lie, her fourth, and, one day when she was anxious to gain my confidence by confiding in me, went so far as to tell me, with regard to the same person who at the outset had been so respectable and whom she did not know: "She took quite a fancy to me at one time. She asked me, three or four times, to go home with her and to come upstairs to her room. I saw no harm in going home with her, where everybody could see us, in broad daylight, in the open air. But when we reached her front door I always made some excuse and I never went upstairs." Shortly after this, Albertine made an allusion to the beautiful things that this lady had in her room. By proceeding from one approximation to another, I should no doubt have arrived at making her tell me the truth which was perhaps less serious than I had been led to believe, for, although perhaps easy going with women, she preferred a male lover, and now that she had myself would not have given a thought to Léa. In any case, with regard to this person, I was still at the first stage of revelation and was not aware whether Albertine knew her. Already, in the case of many women at any rate, it would have been enough for me to collect and present to my mistress, in a synthesis, her contradictory statements, in order to convict her of her misdeeds (misdeeds which, like astronomical laws, it is a great deal easier to deduce by a process of rea-soning than to observe, to surprise in the act). But then she would have preferred to say that one of her statements had been a lie, the withdrawal of which would thus bring about the collapse of my whole system of evi-dence, rather than admit that everything which she had told me from the start was simply a tissue of falsehood. There are similar tissues in the *Thousand and One Nights,* which we find charming. They pain us, coming from a person whom we love, and thereby enable us to penetrate a little deeper in our knowledge of human nature instead of being content to play upon the surface. Grief penetrates into us and forces us out of painful curiosity to penetrate other people. Whence emerge truths which we feel that we have no right to keep hidden, so much so that a dying atheist who has discovered them, certain of his own extinction, indifferent to fame, will nevertheless devote his last hours on earth to an attempt to make them known.

Of course, I was still at the first stage of enlightenment with regard to Léa. I was not even aware whether Albertine knew her. No matter, it all came to the same thing. I must at all costs prevent her from—at the Troca-déro—renewing this acquaintance or making the acquaintance of this stranger. I have said that I did not know whether she knew Léa; I ought, however, to have learned it at Balbec, from Albertine herself. For defec-tive memory obliterated from my mind as well as from Albertine's a great many of the statements that she had made to me. Memory, instead of being a duplicate always present before our eyes of the various events of our life, is rather an abyss from which at odd moments a chance resem-blance enables us to draw up, restored to life, dead impressions; but even then there are innumerable little details which have not fallen into that potential reservoir of memory, and which will remain for ever beyond our control. To anything that we do not know to be related to the real life of the person whom we love we pay but scant attention, we forget immediately what she has said to us about some incident or people that we do not know, and her expression while she was saying it. And so when, in due course, our jealousy is aroused by these same people, and seeks to make sure that it is not mistaken, that it is they who are responsible for the haste which our mistress shews in leaving the house, her annoyance when we have prevented her from going out by returning earlier than usual; our jealousy ransacking the past in search of a clue can find nothing; always retrospective, it is like a historian who has to write the history of a period for which he has no documents; always belated, it dashes like a mad bull to the spot where it will not find the proud and brilliant creature who is infuriating it with his darts and whom the crowd admire for his splendour and his cunning. Jealousy fights the empty air, uncertain as we are in those dreams in which we are distressed because we cannot find in his empty house a person whom we have known well in life, but who here perhaps is really another person and has merely borrowed the features of our friend, uncertain as we are even more after we awake when we seek to identify this or that detail of our dream. What was our mistress's expression when she told us this; did she not look happy, was she not actually whistling, a thing that she never does unless there is some amorous thought in her mind? In the time of our love, if our presence teased her and irritated her a little, has she not told us something that is contradicted by what she now affirms, that she knows or does not know such and such a person? We do not know, we shall never find out; we strain after the unsubstantial fragments of a dream, and all the time our life with our mistress continues, our life indifferent to what we do not know to be important to us, attentive to what is perhaps of no importance, hagridden by people who have no real connexion with us, full of lapses of memory, gaps, vain anxieties, our life as fantastic as a dream.

I realised that the young dairymaid was still in the room. I told her that the place was certainly a long way off, that I did not need her. Whereupon she also decided that it would be too much trouble: "There's a fine match coming off, I don't want to miss it." I felt that she must already be devoted to sport and that in a few years' time she would be talking about 'living her own life.' I told her that I certainly did not need her any longer, and gave her five francs. Immediately, having little expected this largesse, and telling herself that if she earned five francs for doing nothing she would have a great deal more for taking my message, she began to find that her match was of no importance. "I could easily have taken your message. I can always find time." But I thrust her from the room, I needed to be alone, I must at all costs prevent Albertine from any risk of meeting Léa's girl friends at the Trocadéro. I must try, and I must succeed; to tell the truth I did not yet see how, and during these first moments I opened my hands, gazed at them, cracked my knuckles, whether because the mind which cannot find what it is seeking, in a fit of laziness allows itself to halt for an instant at a spot where the most unimportant things are distinctly visible to it, like the blades of grass on the embankment which we see from the carriage window trembling in the wind, when the train halts in the open country—an immobility that is not always more fertile than that of the captured animal which, paralysed by fear or fascinated, gazes without moving a muscle—or that I might hold my body in readiness—with my mind at work inside it and, in my mind, the means of action against this or that person—as though it were no more than a weapon from which would be fired the shot that was to separate Albertine from Léa and her two friends. It is true that earlier in the morning, when Françoise had come in to tell me that Albertine was going to the Trocadéro, I had said to myself: "Albertine is at liberty to do as she pleases" and had supposed that until evening came, in this radiant weather, her actions would remain without any perceptible importance to myself; but it was not only the morning sun, as I had thought, that had made me so careless; it was because, having obliged Albertine to abandon the plans that she might perhaps have initiated or even completed at the Verdurins', and having restricted her to attending a performance which I myself had chosen, so that she could not have made any preparations, I knew that whatever she did would of necessity be innocent. Just as, if Albertine had said a few moments later: "If I kill myself, it's all the same to me," it would have been because she was certain that she would not kill herself. Surrounding myself and Albertine there had been this morning (far more than the sunlight in the air) that atmosphere which we do not see, but by the translucent and changing medium of which we do see, I her actions, she the importance of her own life, that is to say those beliefs which we do not perceive but which are no more assimilable to a pure vacuum than is the air that surrounds us; composing round about us a variable atmosphere, sometimes excellent, often unbreathable, they deserve to be studied and recorded as carefully as the temperature, the barometric pressure, the weather, for our days have their own singularity, physical and moral. My belief, which I had failed to remark this morning, and yet in which I had been joyously enveloped until the moment when I had looked a second time at the *Figaro*, that Albertine would do nothing that was not harmless, this belief had vanished. I was living no longer in the fine sunny day, but in a day carved out of the other by my anxiety lest Albertine might renew her acquaintance with Léa and more easily still with the two girls, should they go, as seemed to me probable, to applaud the actress at the Trocadéro where it would not be difficult for them, in one of the intervals, to come upon Albertine. I no longer thought of Mlle. Vinteuil, the name of Léa had brought back to my mind, to make me jealous, the image of Albertine in the Casino watching the two girls. For I possessed in my memory only series of Albertines, separate from one another, incomplete, outlines, snapshots; and so my jealousy was restricted to an intermittent expression, at once fugitive and fixed, and to the people who had caused that expression to appear upon Albertine's face. I remembered her when, at Balbec, she received undue attention from the two girls or from women of that sort; I remembered the distress that I used to feel when I saw her face subjected to an active scrutiny, like that of a painter preparing to make a sketch, entirely covered by them, and, doubtless on account of my pres-

ence, submitting to this contact without appearing to notice it, with a
passivity that was perhaps clandestinely voluptuous. And before she recovered herself and spoke to me there was an instant during which Albertine
did not move, smiled into the empty air, with the same air of feigned spontaneity and concealed pleasure as if she were posing for somebody to take
her photograph; or even seeking to assume before the camera a more dashing pose—that which she had adopted at Doncières when we were walking
with Saint-Loup, and, laughing and passing her tongue over her lips, she
pretended to be teasing a dog. Certainly at such moments she was not at
all the same as when it was she that was interested in little girls who passed
us. Then, on the contrary, her narrow velvety gaze fastened itself upon,
glued itself to the passer-by, so adherent, so corrosive, that you felt that
when she removed it it must tear away the skin. But at that moment this
other expression, which did at least give her a serious air, almost as though
she were in pain, had seemed to me a pleasant relief after the toneless blissful expression she had worn in the presence of the two girls, and I should
have preferred the sombre expression of the desire that she did perhaps
feel at times to the laughing expression caused by the desire which she
aroused. However she might attempt to conceal her consciousness of it,
it bathed her, enveloped her, vaporous, voluptuous, made her whole face
appear rosy. But everything that Albertine held at such moments suspended in herself, that radiated round her and hurt me so acutely, how
could I tell whether, once my back was turned, she would continue to keep
it to herself, whether to the advances of the two girls, now that I was no
longer with her, she would not make some audacious response. Indeed,
these memories caused me intense grief, they were like a complete admission of Albertine's failings, a general confession of her infidelity against
which were powerless the various oaths that she swore to me and I wished
to believe, the negative results of my incomplete researches, the assurances,
made perhaps in connivance with her, of Andrée. Albertine might deny
specified betrayals; by words that she let fall, more emphatic than her
declarations to the contrary, by that searching gaze alone, she had made
confession of what she would fain have concealed, far more than any
specified incident, what she would have let herself be killed sooner than
admit: her natural tendency. For there is no one who will willingly deliver
up his soul. Notwithstanding the grief that these memories were causing
me, could I have denied that it was the programme of the matinée at the
Trocadéro that had revived my need of Albertine? She was one of those
women in whom their misdeeds may at a pinch take the place of absent
charms, and no less than their misdeeds the kindness that follows them and
restores to us that sense of comfort which in their company, like an invalid
who is never well for two days in succession, we are incessantly obliged to
recapture. And then, even more than their misdeeds while we are in love
with them, there are their misdeeds before we made their acquaintance,
and first and foremost: their nature. What makes this sort of love painful
is, in fact, that there preexists a sort of original sin of Woman, a sin which
makes us love them, so that, when we forget it, we feel less need of them,
and to begin to love afresh we must begin to suffer afresh. At this moment,

the thought that she must not meet the two girls again and the question whether or not she knew Léa were what was chiefly occupying my mind, in spite of the rule that we ought not to take an interest in particular facts except in relation to their general significance, and notwithstanding the childishness, as great as that of longing to travel or to make friends with women, of shattering our curiosity against such elements of the invisible torrent of painful realities which will always remain unknown to us as have happened to crystallise in our mind. But, even if we should succeed in destroying that crystallisation, it would at once be replaced by another. Yesterday I was afraid lest Albertine should go to see Mme. Verdurin. Now my only thought was of Léa. Jealousy, which wears a bandage over its eyes, is not merely powerless to discover anything in the darkness that enshrouds it, it is also one of those torments where the task must be incessantly repeated, like that of the Danaids, or of Ixion. Even if her friends were not there, what impression might she not form of Léa, beautified by her stage attire, haloed with success, what thoughts would she leave in Albertine's mind, what desires which, even if she repressed them, would in my house disgust her with a life in which she was unable to gratify them.

Besides, how could I tell that she was not acquainted with Léa, and would not pay her a visit in her dressing-room; and, even if Léa did not know her, who could assure me that, having certainly seen her at Balbec, she would not recognise her and make a signal to her from the stage that would entitle Albertine to seek admission behind the scenes? A danger seems easy to avoid after it has been conjured away. This one was not yet conjured, I was afraid that it might never be, and it seemed to me all the more terrible. And yet this love for Albertine which I felt almost vanish when I attempted to realise it, seemed in a measure to acquire a proof of its existence from the intensity of my grief at this moment. I no longer cared about anything else, I thought only of how I was to prevent her from remaining at the Trocadéro, I would have offered any sum in the world to Léa to persuade her not to go there. If then we prove our choice by the action that we perform rather than by the idea that we form, I must have been in love with Albertine. But this renewal of my suffering gave no further consistency to the image that I beheld of Albertine. She caused my calamities, like a deity that remains invisible. Making endless conjectures, I sought to shield myself from suffering without thereby realising my love. First of all, I must make certain that Léa was really going to perform at the Trocadéro. After dismissing the dairymaid, I telephoned to Bloch, whom I knew to be on friendly terms with Léa, in order to ask him. He knew nothing about it and seemed surprised that the matter could be of any importance to me. I decided that I must set to work immediately, remembered that Françoise was ready to go out and that I was not, and as I rose and dressed made her take a motor-car; she was to go to the Trocadéro, engage a seat, look high and low for Albertine and give her a note from myself. In this note I told her that I was greatly upset by a letter which I had just received from that same lady on whose account she would remember that I had been so wretched one night at Balbec.

I reminded her that, on the following day, she had reproached me for not having sent for her. And so I was taking the liberty, I informed her, of asking her to sacrifice her matinée and to join me at home so that we might take a little fresh air together, which might help me to recover from the shock. But as I should be a long time in getting ready, she would oblige me, seeing that she had Françoise as an escort, by calling at the Trois-Quartiers (this shop, being smaller, seemed to me less dangerous than the Bon Marché) to buy the scarf of white tulle that she required. My note was probably not superfluous. To tell the truth, I knew nothing that Albertine had done since I had come to know her, or even before. But in her conversation (she might, had I mentioned it to her, have replied that I had misunderstood her) there were certain contradictions, certain embellishments which seemed to me as decisive as catching her red-handed, but less serviceable against Albertine who, often caught out in wrongdoing like a child, had invariably, by dint of sudden, strategic changes of front, stultified my cruel onslaught and reestablished her own position. Cruel, most of all, to myself. She employed, not from any refinement of style, but in order to correct her imprudences, abrupt breaches of syntax not unlike that figure which the grammarians call anacoluthon or some such name. Having allowed herself, while discussing women, to say: "I remember, the other day, I . . . ," she would at once catch her breath, after which 'I' became 'she': it was something that she had witnessed as an innocent spectator, not a thing that she herself had done. It was not herself that was the heroine of the anecdote. I should have liked to recall how, exactly, the sentence began, so as to conclude for myself, since she had broken off in the middle, how it would have ended. But as I had heard the end, I found it hard to remember the beginning, from which perhaps my air of interest had made her deviate, and was left still anxious to know what she was really thinking, what she really remembered. The first stages of falsehood on the part of our mistress are like the first stages of our own love, or of a religious vocation. They take shape, accumulate, pass, without our paying them any attention. When we wish to remember in what manner we began to love a woman, we are already in love with her; when we dreamed about her before falling in love, we did not say to ourself: This is the prelude to a love affair, we must pay attention!—and our dreams took us by surprise, and we barely noticed them. So also, except in cases that are comparatively rare, it is only for the convenience of my narrative that I have frequently in these pages confronted one of Albertine's false statements with her previous assertion upon the same subject. This previous assertion, as often as not, since I could not read the future and did not at the time guess what contradictory affirmation was to form a pendant to it, had slipped past unperceived, heard it is true by my ears, but without my isolating it from the continuous flow of Albertine's speech. Later on, faced with the self-evident lie, or seized by an anxious doubt, I would fain have recalled it; but in vain; my memory had not been warned in time, and had thought it unnecessary to preserve a copy.

I urged Françoise, when she had got Albertine out of the hall, to let me know by telephone, and to bring her home, whether she was willing or not. "That would be the last straw, that she should not be willing to come and see Monsieur," replied Françoise. "But I don't know that she's as fond as all that of seeing me." "Then she must be an ungrateful wretch," went on Françoise, in whom Albertine was renewing after all these years the same torment of envy that Eulalie used at one time to cause her in my aunt's sickroom. Unaware that Albertine's position in my household was not of her own seeking but had been decided by myself (a fact which, from motives of self-esteem and to make Françoise angry, I preferred to conceal from her), she admired and execrated the girl's dexterity, called her when she spoke of her to the other servants a 'play-actress,' a wheedler who could twist me round her little finger. She dared not yet declare open war against her, shewed her a smiling countenance and sought to acquire merit in my sight by the services which she performed for her in her relations with myself, deciding that it was useless to say anything to me and that she would gain nothing by doing so; but if the opportunity ever arose, if ever she discovered a crack in Albertine's armour, she was fully determined to enlarge it, and to part us for good and all. "Ungrateful? No, Françoise, I think it is I that am ungrateful, you don't know how good she is to me." (It was so soothing to give the impression that I was loved.) "Be as quick as you can." "All right, I'll get a move on." Her daughter's influence was beginning to contaminate Françoise's vocabulary. So it is that all languages lose their purity by the admission of new words. For this decadence of Françoise's speech, which I had known in its golden period, I was myself indirectly responsible. Françoise's daughter would not have made her mother's classic language degenerate into the vilest slang, had she been content to converse with her in dialect. She had never given up the use of it, and when they were both in my room at once, if they had anything private to say, instead of shutting themselves up in the kitchen, they armed themselves, right in the middle of my room, with a screen more impenetrable than the most carefully shut door, by conversing in dialect. I supposed merely that the mother and daughter were not always on the best of terms, if I was to judge by the frequency with which they employed the only word that I could make out: *m'esasperate* (unless it was that the object of their exasperation was myself). Unfortunately the most unfamiliar tongue becomes intelligible in time when we are always hearing it spoken. I was sorry that this should be dialect, for I succeeded in picking it up, and should have been no less successful had Françoise been in the habit of expressing herself in Persian. In vain might Françoise, when she became aware of my progress, accelerate the speed of her utterance, and her daughter likewise, it was no good. The mother was greatly put out that I understood their dialect, then delighted to hear me speak it. I am bound to admit that her delight was a mocking delight, for albeit I came in time to pronounce the words more or less as she herself did, she found between our two ways of pronunciation an abyss of difference which gave her infinite joy, and she began to regret that she no longer saw people to whom she had not given a thought for years but who, it appeared, would have rocked with a laughter which it would have done her good to hear, if they could have heard me speaking their dialect so badly. In any case, no joy came to mitigate her sorrow that, however badly I might pronounce it, I understood well. Keys become useless when the person whom we seek to prevent from entering can avail himself of a skeleton key or a jemmy. Dialect having become useless as a means of defence, she took to conversing with her daughter in a French which rapidly became that of the most debased epochs.

I was now ready, but Françoise had not yet telephoned; I ought perhaps to go out without waiting for a message. But how could I tell that she would find Albertine, that the latter would not have gone behind the scenes, that even if Françoise did find her, she would allow herself to be taken away? Half an hour later the telephone bell began to tinkle and my heart throbbed tumultuously with hope and fear. There came, at the bidding of an operator, a flying squadron of sounds which with an instantaneous speed brought me the words of the telephonist, not those of Françoise whom an inherited timidity and melancholy, when she was brought face to face with any object unknown to her fathers, prevented from approaching a telephone receiver, although she would readily visit a person suffering from a contagious disease. She had found Albertine in the lobby by herself, and Albertine had simply gone to warn Andrée that she was not staying any longer and then had hurried back to Françoise. "She wasn't angry? Oh, I beg your pardon; will you please ask the person whether the young lady was angry?" "The lady asks me to say that she wasn't at all angry, quite the contrary, in fact; anyhow, if she wasn't pleased, she didn't shew it. They are starting now for the Trois-Quartiers, and will be home by two o'clock." I gathered that two o'clock meant three, for it was past two o'clock already. But Françoise suffered from one of those peculiar, permanent, incurable defects, which we call maladies; she was never able either to read or to announce the time correctly. I have never been able to understand what went on in her head. When Françoise, after consulting her watch, if it was two o'clock, said: "It is one" or "it is three o'clock," I have never been able to understand whether the phenomenon that occurred was situated in her vision or in her thought or in her speech; the one thing certain is that the phenomenon never failed to occur. Humanity is a very old institution. Heredity, cross-breeding have given an irresistible force to bad habits, to vicious reflexes. One person sneezes and gasps because he is passing a rosebush, another breaks out in an eruption at the smell of wet paint, has frequent attacks of colic if he has to start on a journey, and grandchildren of thieves who are themselves millionaires and generous cannot resist the temptation to rob you of fifty francs. As for knowing in what consisted Françoise's incapacity to tell the time correctly, she herself never threw any light upon the problem. For, notwithstanding the anger that I generally displayed at her inaccurate replies, Françoise never attempted either to apologise for her mistake or to explain it. She remained silent, pretending not to hear, and thereby making me lose my temper altogether. I should have liked to hear a few words of justification, were it only that I might smite her hip and thigh; but not a word, an indifferent silence. In any case, about the time-table for to-day there could be no doubt; Albertine was coming home with

Françoise at three o'clock, Albertine would not be meeting Léa or her friends. Whereupon the danger of her renewing relations with them, having been averted, at once began to lose its importance in my eyes and I was amazed, seeing with what ease it had been averted, that I should have supposed that I would not succeed in averting it. I felt a keen impulse of gratitude to Albertine, who, I could see, had not gone to the Trocadéro to meet Léa's friends, and shewed me, by leaving the performance and coming home at a word from myself, that she belonged to me more than I had imagined. My gratitude was even greater when a bicyclist brought me a line from her bidding me be patient, and full of the charming expressions that she was in the habit of using. "My darling, dear Marcel, I return less quickly than this cyclist, whose machine I would like to borrow in order to be with you sooner. How could you imagine that I might be angry or that I could enjoy anything better than to be with you? It will be nice to go out, just the two of us together; it would be nicer still if we never went out except together. The ideas you get into your head! What a Marcel! What a Marcel! Always and ever your Albertine."

The frocks that I bought for her, the yacht of which I had spoken to her, the wrappers from Fortuny's, all these things having in this obedience on Albertine's part not their recompense but their complement, appeared to me now as so many privileges that I was enjoying; for the duties and expenditure of a master are part of his dominion, and define it, prove it, fully as much as his rights. And these rights which she recognised in me were precisely what gave my expenditure its true character: I had a woman of my own, who, at the first word that I sent to her unexpectedly, made my messenger telephone humbly that she was coming, that she was allowing herself to be brought home immediately. I was more of a master than I had supposed. More of a master, in other words more of a slave. I no longer felt the slightest impatience to see Albertine. The certainty that she was at this moment engaged in shopping with Françoise, or that she would return with her at an approaching moment which I would willingly have postponed, illuminated like a calm and radiant star a period of time which I would now have been far better pleased to spend alone. My love for Albertine had made me rise and get ready to go out, but it would prevent me from enjoying my outing. I reflected that on a Sunday afternoon like this little shopgirls, midinettes, prostitutes must be strolling in the Bois. And with the words *midinettes, little shopgirls* (as had often happened to me with a proper name, the name of a girl read in the account of a ball), with the image of a white bodice, a short skirt, since beneath them I placed a stranger who might perhaps come to love me, I created out of nothing desirable women, and said to myself: "How charming they must be!" But of what use would it be to me that they were charming, seeing that I was not going out alone. Taking advantage of the fact that I still was alone, and drawing the curtains together so that the sun should not prevent me from reading the notes, I sat down at the piano, turned over the pages of Vinteuil's sonata which happened to be lying there, and began to play; seeing that Albertine's arrival was still a matter of some time but was on the other hand certain, I had at once time to spare and tranquillity of mind. Floating in the expectation, big with security, of her return escorted by Françoise and in my confidence in her docility as in the blessedness of an inward light as warming as the light of the sun, I might dispose of my thoughts, detach them for a moment from Albertine, apply them to the sonata. In the latter, indeed, I did not take pains to remark how the combinations of the voluptuous and anxious motives corresponded even more closely now to my love for Albertine, from which jealousy had been absent for so long that I had been able to confess to Swann my ignorance of that sentiment. No, taking the sonata from another point of view, regarding it in itself as the work of a great artist, I was carried back upon the tide of sound to the days at Combray—I do not mean at Montjouvain and along the Méséglise way, but to walks along the Guermantes way—when I had myself longed to become an artist. In definitely abandoning that ambition, had I forfeited something real? Could life console me for the loss of art, was there in art a more profound reality, in which our true personality finds an expression that is not afforded it by the activities of life? Every great artist seems indeed so different from all the rest, and gives us so strongly that sensation of individuality for which we seek in vain in our everyday existence. Just as I was thinking thus, I was struck by a passage in the sonata, a passage with which I was quite familiar, but sometimes our attention throws a different light upon things which we have long known, and we remark in them what we have never seen before. As I played the passage, and for all that in it Vinteuil had been trying to express a fancy which would have been wholly foreign to Wagner, I could not help murmuring 'Tristan,' with the smile of an old friend of the family discovering a trace of the grandfather in an intonation, a gesture of the grandson who never set eyes on him. And as the friend then examines a photograph which enables him to estimate the likeness, so, in front of Vinteuil's sonata, I set up on the music-rest the score of Tristan, a selection from which was being given that afternoon, as it happened, at the Lamoureux concert. I had not, in admiring the Bayreuth master, any of the scruples of those people whom, like Nietzsche, their sense of duty bids to shun in art as in life the beauty that tempts them, and who, tearing themselves from Tristan as they renounce Parsifal, and, in their spiritual asceticism, progressing from one mortification to another, arrive, by following the most bloody of viae Crucis, at exalting themselves to the pure cognition and perfect adoration of Le Postillon de Longjumeau. I began to perceive how much reality there is in the work of Wagner, when I saw in my mind's eye those insistent, fleeting themes which visit an act, withdraw only to return, and, sometimes distant, drowsy, almost detached, are at other moments, while remaining vague, so pressing and so near, so internal, so organic, so visceral, that one would call them the resumption not so much of a musical motive as of an attack of neuralgia.

Music, very different in this respect from Albertine's society, helped me to descend into myself, to make there a fresh discovery: that of the difference that I had sought in vain in life, in travel, a longing for which was given me, however, by this sonorous tide which sent its sunlit waves rolling to expire at my feet. A twofold difference. As the spectrum makes visible to us the composition of light, so the harmony of a Wagner, the colour of an Elstir enable us to know that essential quality of another person's sensations into which love for another person does not allow us to penetrate. Then there is diversity inside the work itself, by the sole means that it has of being effectively diverse, to wit combining diverse individualities. Where a minor composer would pretend that he was portraying a squire, or a knight, whereas he would make them both sing the same music, Wagner on the contrary allots to each denomination a different reality, and whenever a squire appears, it is an individual figure, at once complicated and simplified, that, with a joyous, feudal clash of warring sounds, inscribes itself in the vast, sonorous mass. Whence the completeness of a music that is indeed filled with so many different musics, each of which is a person. A person or the impression that is given us by a momentary aspect of nature. Even what is most independent of the sentiment that it makes us feel preserves its outward and entirely definite reality; the song of a bird, the ring of a hunter's horn, the air that a shepherd plays upon his pipe, cut out against the horizon their silhouette of sound. It is true that Wagner had still to bring these together, to make use of them, to introduce them into an orchestral whole, to make them subservient to the highest musical ideals, but always respecting their original nature, as a carpenter respects the grain, the peculiar essence of the wood that he is carving.

But notwithstanding the richness of these works in which the contemplation of nature has its place by the side of action, by the side of persons who are something more than proper names, I thought how markedly, all the same, these works participate in that quality of being—albeit marvellously—always incomplete, which is the peculiarity of all the great works of the nineteenth century, with which the greatest writers of that century have stamped their books, but, watching themselves at work as though they were at once author and critic, have derived from this self-contemplation a novel beauty, exterior and superior to the work itself, imposing upon it retrospectively a unity, a greatness which it does not possess. Without pausing to consider him who saw in his novels, after they had appeared, a *Human Comedy*, nor those who entitled heterogeneous poems or essays *The Legend of the Ages* or *The Bible of Humanity*, can we not say all the same of the last of these that he is so perfect an incarnation of the nineteenth century that the greatest beauties in Michelet are to be sought not so much in his work itself as in the attitudes that he adopts when he is considering his work, not in his *History of France* nor in his *History of the Revolution*, but in his prefaces to his books? *Prefaces*, that is to say pages written after the books themselves, in which he considers the books, and with which we must include here and there certain phrases beginning as a rule with a: "Shall I say?" which is not a scholar's precaution but a musician's cadence. The other musician, he who was delighting me at this moment, Wagner, retrieving some exquisite scrap from a drawer of his writing-table to make it appear as a theme, retrospectively necessary, in a work of which he had not been thinking at the moment when he composed it, then having composed a first mythological opera, and a second, and afterwards others still, and perceiving all of a sudden that he had written a tetralogy, must have felt something of the same exhilaration as Balzac, when, casting over his works the eye at once of a stranger and of a father, finding in one the purity of Raphael, in another the simplicity of the Gospel, he suddenly decided, as he shed a retrospective illumination upon them, that they would be better brought together in a cycle in which the same characters would reappear, and added to his work, in this act of joining it together, a stroke of the brush, the last and the most sublime. A unity that was ulterior, not artificial, otherwise it would have crumbled into dust like all the other systematisations of mediocre writers who with the elaborate assistance of titles and sub-titles give themselves the appearance of having pursued a single and transcendent design. Not fictitious, perhaps indeed all the more real for being ulterior, for being born of a moment of enthusiasm when it is discovered to exist among fragments which need only to be joined together. A unity that has been unaware of itself, therefore vital and not logical, that has not banned variety, chilled execution. It emerges (only applying itself this time to the work as a whole) like a fragment composed separately, born of an inspiration, not required by the artificial development of a theme, which comes in to form an integral part of the rest. Before the great orchestral movement that precedes the return of Yseult, it is the work itself that has attracted to it the half-forgotten air of a shepherd's pipe. And, no doubt, just as the swelling of the orchestra at the approach of the ship, when it takes hold of these notes on the pipe, transforms them, infects them with its own intoxication, breaks their rhythm, clarifies their tone, accelerates their movement, multiplies their instrumentation, so no doubt Wagner himself was filled with joy when he discovered in his memory a shepherd's air, incorporated it in his work, gave it its full wealth of meaning. This joy moreover never forsakes him. In him, however great the melancholy of the poet, it is consoled, surpassed—that is to say destroyed, alas, too soon— by the delight of the craftsman. But then, no less than by the similarity I had remarked just now between Vinteuil's phrase and Wagner's, I was troubled by the thought of this Vulcan-like craftsmanship. Could it be this that gave to great artists the illusory appearance of a fundamental originality, incommensurable with any other, the reflexion of a more than human reality, actually the result of industrious toil? If art be no more than that, it is not more real than life and I had less cause for regret. I went on playing *Tristan.* Separated from Wagner by the wall of sound, I could hear him exult, invite me to share his joy, I could hear ring out all the louder the immortally youthful laugh and the hammer-blows of Siegfried, in which, moreover, more marvellously struck were those phrases, the technical skill of the craftsman serving merely to make it easier for them to leave the earth, birds akin not to Lohengrin's swan but to that aeroplane which I had seen at Balbec convert its energy into vertical motion, float over the sea and lose itself in the sky. Perhaps, as the birds that soar highest and fly most swiftly have a stronger wing, one required one of these frankly material vehicles to explore the infinite, one of these 120 horse-

power machines, marked Mystery, in which nevertheless, however high
one flies, one is prevented to some extent from enjoying the silence of space
by the overpowering roar of the engine!

For some reason or other the course of my musings, which hitherto had
wandered among musical memories, turned now to those men who have
been the best performers of music in our day, among whom, slightly exaggerating his merit, I included Morel. At once my thoughts took a sharp
turn, and it was Morel's character, certain eccentricities of his nature that
I began to consider. As it happened—and this might be connected though
it should not be confused with the neurasthenia to which he was a prey—
Morel was in the habit of talking about his life, but always presented so
shadowy a picture of it that it was difficult to make anything out. For
instance, he placed himself entirely at M. de Charlus's disposal on the
understanding that he must keep his evenings free, as he wished to be able
after dinner to attend a course of lectures on algebra. M. de Charlus con-
ceded this, but insisted upon seeing him after the lectures. "Impossible,
it's an old Italian painting" (this witticism means nothing when written
down like this; but M. de Charlus having made Morel read *l'Éducation
sentimentale,* in the penultimate chapter of which Frédéric Moreau uses
this expression, it was Morel's idea of a joke never to say the word 'impossible' without following it up with "it's an old Italian painting") "the
lectures go on very late, and I've already given a lot of trouble to the lec-
turer, who naturally would be annoyed if I came away in the middle."
"But there's no need to attend lectures, algebra is not a thing like swim-
ming, or even English, you can learn it equally well from a book," replied
M. de Charlus, who had guessed from the first that these algebra lectures
were one of those images of which it was impossible to make out anything.
It was perhaps some affair with a woman, or, if Morel was seeking to earn
money in shady ways and had attached himself to the secret police, a nocturnal expedition with detectives, or possibly, what was even worse, an
engagement as one of the young men whose services may be required in a
brothel. "A great deal easier, from a book," Morel assured M. de Charlus,
"for it's impossible to make head or tail of the lectures." "Then why don't
you study it in my house, where you would be far more comfortable?"
M. de Charlus might have answered, but took care not to do so, knowing
that at once, preserving only the same essential element that the evening
hours must be set apart, the imaginary algebra course would change to a
compulsory lesson in dancing or in drawing. In which M. de Charlus might
have seen that he was mistaken, partially at least, for Morel did often
spend his time at the Baron's in solving equations. M. de Charlus did raise
the objection that algebra could be of little use to a violinist. Morel replied
that it was a distraction which helped him to pass the time and to conquer
his neurasthenia. No doubt M. de Charlus might have made inquiries, have
tried to find out what actually were these mysterious and ineluctable lectures on algebra that were delivered only at night. But M. de Charlus was
not qualified to unravel the tangled skein of Morel's occupations, being
himself too much caught in the toils of social life. The visits he received
or paid, the time he spent at his club, dinner-parties, evenings at the theatre

prevented him from thinking about the problem, or for that matter about the violent and vindictive animosity which Morel had (it was reported) indulged and at the same time sought to conceal in the various environments, the different towns in which his life had been spent, and where people still spoke of him with a shudder, with bated breath, never venturing to say anything definite about him.

It was unfortunately one of the outbursts of this neurotic irritability that I was privileged to hear that day when, rising from the piano, I went down to the courtyard to meet Albertine, who still did not appear. As I passed by Jupien's shop, in which Morel and the girl who, I supposed, was shortly to become his wife were by themselves, Morel was screaming at the top of his voice, thereby revealing an accent that I had never heard in his speech, a rustic tone, suppressed as a rule, and very strange indeed. His words were no less strange, faulty from the point of view of the French language, but his knowledge of everything was imperfect. "Will you get out of here, *grand pied de grue, grand pied de grue, grand pied de grue,*" he repeated to the poor girl who at first had certainly not understood what he meant, and now, trembling and indignant, stood motionless before him. "Didn't I tell you to get out of here, *grand pied de grue, grand pied de grue*; go and fetch your uncle till I tell him what you are, you whore." Just at that moment the voice of Jupien who was coming home talking to one of his friends was heard in the courtyard, and as I knew that Morel was an utter coward, I decided that it was unnecessary to join my forces with those of Jupien and his friend, who in another moment would have entered the shop, and I retired upstairs again to escape Morel, who, for all his having pretended to be so anxious that Jupien should be fetched (probably in order to frighten and subjugate the girl, an act of blackmail which rested probably upon no foundation), made haste to depart as soon as he heard his voice in the courtyard. The words I have set down here are nothing, they would not explain why my heart throbbed so as I went upstairs. These scenes of which we are witnesses in real life find an incalculable element of strength in what soldiers call, in speaking of a military offensive, the advantage of surprise, and however agreeably I might be soothed by the knowledge that Albertine, instead of remaining at the Trocadéro, was coming home to me, I still heard ringing in my ears the accent of those words ten times repeated: "*Grand pied de grue, grand pied de grue,*" which had so appalled me.

Gradually my agitation subsided. Albertine was on her way home. I should hear her ring the bell in a moment. I felt that my life was no longer what it might have become, and that to have a woman in the house like this with whom quite naturally, when she returned home, I should have to go out, to the adornment of whose person the strength and activity of my nature were to be ever more and more diverted, made me as it were a bough that has blossomed, but is weighed down by the abundant fruit into which all its reserves of strength have passed. In contrast to the anxiety that I had been feeling only an hour earlier, the calm that I now felt at the prospect of Albertine's return was more ample than that which I had felt in the morning before she left the house. Anticipating the future, of which my mistress's docility made me practically master, more resistant, as though it were filled and stabilised by the imminent, importunate, inevitable, gentle presence, it was the calm (dispensing us from the obligation to seek our happiness in ourselves) that is born of family feeling and domestic bliss. Family and domestic: such was again, no less than the sentiment that had brought me such great peace while I was waiting for Albertine, that which I felt later on when I drove out with her. She took off her glove for a moment, whether to touch my hand, or to dazzle me by letting me see on her little finger, next to the ring that Mme. Bontemps had given her, another upon which was displayed the large and liquid surface of a clear sheet of ruby. "What! Another ring, Albertine. Your aunt *is* generous!" "No, I didn't get this from my aunt," she said with a laugh. "It was I who bought it, now that, thanks to you, I can save up ever so much money. I don't even know whose it was before. A visitor who was short of money left it with the landlord of an hotel where I stayed at Le Mans. He didn't know what to do with it, and would have let it go for much less than it was worth. But it was still far too dear for me. Now that, thanks to you, I'm becoming a smart lady, I wrote to ask him if he still had it. And here it is." "That makes a great many rings, Albertine. Where will you put the one that I am going to give you? Anyhow, it is a beautiful ring, I can't quite make out what that is carved round the ruby, it looks like a man's head grinning. But my eyes aren't strong enough." "They might be as strong as you like, you would be no better off. I can't make it out either." In the past it had often happened, as I read somebody's memoirs, or a novel, in which a man always goes out driving with a woman, takes tea with her, that I longed to be able to do likewise. I had thought sometimes that I was successful, as for instance when I took Saint-Loup's mistress out with me, or went to dinner with her. But in vain might I summon to my assistance the idea that I was at that moment actually impersonating the character that I had envied in the novel, that idea assured me that I ought to find pleasure in Rachel's society, and afforded me none. For, whenever we attempt to imitate something that has really existed, we forget that this something was brought about not by the desire to imitate but by an unconscious force which itself also is real; but this particular impression which I had been unable to derive from all my desire to taste a delicate pleasure in going out with Rachel, behold I was now tasting it without having made the slightest effort to procure it, but for quite different reasons, sincere, profound; to take a single instance, for the reason that my jealousy prevented me from letting Albertine go out of my sight, and, the moment that I was able to leave the house, from letting her go anywhere without me. I tasted it only now, because our knowledge is not of the external objects which we try to observe, but of involuntary sensations, because in the past a woman might be sitting in the same carriage as myself, she was not *really* by my side, so long as she was not created afresh there at every moment by a need of her such as I felt of Albertine, so long as the constant caress of my gaze did not incessantly restore to her those tints that need to be perpetually refreshed, so long as my senses, appeased it might be but still endowed with memory, did not place beneath those colours savour and substance, so long as, combined with the senses and with the imagination that exalts them, jealousy was not maintaining the woman in equilibrium by my side by a compensated attraction as powerful as the law of gravity. Our motor-car passed swiftly along the boulevards, the avenues whose lines of houses, a rosy congelation of sunshine and cold, reminded me of calling upon Mme. Swann in the soft light of her chrysanthemums, before it was time to ring for the lamps.

I had barely time to make out, being divided from them by the glass of the motor-car as effectively as I should have been by that of my bedroom window, a young fruit seller, a dairymaid, standing in the doorway of her shop, illuminated by the sunshine like a heroine whom my desire was sufficient to launch upon exquisite adventures, on the threshold of a romance which I might never know. For I could not ask Albertine to let me stop, and already the young women were no longer visible whose features my eyes had barely distinguished, barely caressed their fresh complexions in the golden vapour in which they were bathed. The emotion that I felt grip me when I caught sight of a wine-merchant's girl at her desk or a laundress chatting in the street was the emotion that we feel on recognising a goddess. Now that Olympus no longer exists, its inhabitants dwell upon the earth. And when, in composing a mythological scene, painters have engaged to pose as Venus or Ceres young women of humble birth, who follow the most sordid callings, so far from committing sacrilege, they have merely added, restored to them the quality, the various attributes which they had forfeited. "What did you think of the Trocadéro, you little gadabout?" "I'm jolly glad I came away from it to go out with you. As architecture, it's pretty measly, isn't it? It's by Davioud, I fancy." "But how learned my little Albertine is becoming! Of course it was Davioud who built it, but I couldn't have told you offhand." "While you are asleep, I read your books, you old lazybones." "Listen, child, you are changing so fast and becoming so intelligent" (this was true, but even had it not been true I was not sorry that she should have the satisfaction, failing any other, of saying to herself that at least the time which she spent in my house was not being entirely wasted) "that I don't mind telling you things that would generally be regarded as false and which are all on the way to a truth that I am seeking. You know what is meant by impressionism?" "Of course!" "Very well then, this is what I mean: you remember the church at Marcouville l'Orgueilleuse which Elstir disliked because it was new. Isn't it rather a denial of his own impressionism when he subtracts such buildings from the general impression in which they are contained to bring them out of the light in which they are dissolved and scrutinise like an archaeologist their intrinsic merit? When he begins to paint, have not a hospital, a school, a poster upon a hoarding the same value as a priceless cathedral which stands by their side in a single indivisible image? Remember how the façade was baked by the sun, how that carved frieze of saints swam upon the sea of light. What does it matter that a building is new, if it appears to be old, or even if it does not. All the poetry that the old quarters contain has been squeezed out to the last drop, but if you look at some of the houses that have been built lately for rich tradesmen, in the new districts, where the stone is all freshly cut and still quite white, don't they seem to rend the torrid air of noon in July, at the hour when the shop-keepers go home to luncheon in the suburbs, with a cry as harsh as the odour of the cherries waiting for the meal to begin in the darkened dining-room, where the prismatic glass knife-rests project a multicoloured fire as beautiful as the windows of Chartres?" "How wonderful you are! If I ever do become clever, it will be entirely owing to you." "Why on a fine day tear your eyes away from the Trocadéro, whose giraffe-neck towers remind one of the Charterhouse of Pavia?" "It reminded me also, standing up like that on its hill, of a Mantegna that you have, I think it's of Saint Sebastian, where in the background there's a city like an amphitheatre, and you would swear you saw the Trocadéro." "There, you see! But how did you come across my Mantegna? You are amazing!" We had now reached a more plebeian quarter, and the installation of an ancillary Venus behind each counter made it as it were a suburban altar at the foot of which I would gladly have spent the rest of my life.

As one does on the eve of a premature death, I drew up a mental list of the pleasures of which I was deprived by Albertine's setting a full stop to my freedom. At Passy it was in the open street, so crowded were the foot-ways, that a group of girls, their arms encircling one another's waist, left me marvelling at their smile. I had not time to see it clearly, but it is hardly probable that I exaggerated it; in any crowd after all, in any crowd of young people, it is not unusual to come upon the effigy of a noble profile. So that these assembled masses on public holidays are to the voluptuary as precious as is to the archaeologist the congested state of a piece of ground in which digging will bring to light ancient medals. We arrived at the Bois. I reflected that, if Albertine had not come out with me, I might at this moment, in the enclosure of the Champs-Elysées, have been hearing the Wagnerian tempest set all the rigging of the orchestra ascream, draw to itself, like a light spindrift, the tune of the shepherd's pipe which I had just been playing to myself, set it flying, mould it, deform it, divide it, sweep it away in an ever-increasing whirlwind. I was determined, at any rate, that our drive should be short, and that we should return home early, for, without having mentioned it to Albertine, I had decided to go that evening to the Verdurins'. They had recently sent me an invitation which I had flung into the waste-paper basket with all the rest. But I changed my mind for this evening, for I meant to try to find out who the people were that Albertine might have been hoping to meet there in the afternoon. To tell the truth, I had reached that stage in my relations with Albertine when, if everything remains the same, if things go on normally, a woman ceases to serve us except as a starting point towards another woman. She still retains a corner in our heart, but a very small corner; we hasten out every evening in search of unknown women, especially unknown women who are known to her and can tell us about her life. Herself, after all, we have possessed, have exhausted everything that she has consented to yield to us of herself. Her life is still herself, but that part of herself which we do not know, the things as to which we have questioned her in vain and which we shall be able to gather from fresh lips.

If my life with Albertine was to prevent me from going to Venice, from travelling, at least I might in the meantime, had I been alone, have made the acquaintance of the young midinettes scattered about in the sunlight of this fine Sunday, in the sum total of whose beauty I gave a considerable place to the unknown life that animated them. The eyes that we see, are they not shot through by a gaze as to which we do not know what images, memories, expectations, disdains it carries, a gaze from which we cannot separate them? The life that the person who passes by is living, will it not impart, according to what it is, a different value to the knitting of those brows, to the dilatation of those nostrils? Albertine's presence debarred me from going to join them and perhaps also from ceasing to desire them. The man who would maintain in himself the desire to go on living, and his belief in something more delicious than the things of daily life, must go out driving; for the streets, the avenues are full of goddesses. But the goddesses do not allow us to approach them. Here and there, among the trees, at the entrance to some café, a waitress was watching like a nymph on the edge of a sacred grove, while beyond her three girls were seated by the sweeping arc of their bicycles that were stacked beside them, like three immortals leaning against the clouds or the fabulous coursers upon which they perform their mythological journeys. I remarked that, whenever Albertine looked for a moment at these girls, with a profound attention, she at once turned to gaze at myself. But I was not unduly troubled, either by the intensity of this contemplation, or by its brevity for which its intensity compensated; as for the latter, it often happened that Albertine, whether from exhaustion, or because it was an intense person's way of looking at other people, used to gaze thus in a sort of brown study at my father, it might be, or at Françoise; and as for the rapidity with which she turned to look at myself, it might be due to the fact that Albertine, knowing my suspicions, might prefer, even if they were not justified, to avoid giving them any foothold. This attention, moreover, which would have seemed to me criminal on Albertine's part (and quite as much so if it had been directed at young men), I fastened, without thinking myself reprehensible for an instant, almost deciding indeed that Albertine was reprehensible for preventing me, by her presence, from stopping the car and going to join them, upon all the midinettes. We consider it innocent to desire a thing and atrocious that the other person should desire it. And this contrast between what concerns ourselves on the one hand, and on the other the person with whom we are in love, is not confined only to desire, but extends also to falsehood. What is more usual than a lie, whether it is a question of masking the daily weakness of a constitution which we wish to be thought strong, of concealing a vice, or of going off, without offending the other person, to the thing that we prefer? It is the most necessary instrument of conversation, and the one that is most widely used. But it is this which we actually propose to banish from the life of her whom we love; we watch for it, scent it, detest it everywhere. It appalls us, it is sufficient to bring about a rupture, it seems to us to be concealing the most serious faults, except when it does so effectively conceal them that we do not suspect their existence. A strange state this in which we are so inordinately sensitive to a pathogenic agent which its universal swarming makes inoffensive to other people and so serious to the wretch who finds that he is no longer immune to it.

The life of these pretty girls (because of my long periods of seclusion, I so rarely met any) appeared to me as to everyone in whom facility of realisation has not destroyed the faculty of imagination, a thing as different from anything that I knew, as desirable as the most marvellous cities that travel holds in store for us.

The disappointment that I had felt with the women whom I had known, in the cities which I had visited, did not prevent me from letting myself be caught by the attraction of others or from believing in their reality; thus, just as seeing Venice—that Venice for which the spring weather too filled me with longing, and which marriage with Albertine would prevent me from knowing—seeing Venice in a panorama which Ski would perhaps have declared to be more beautiful in tone than the place itself, would to me have been no substitute for the journey to Venice the length of which, determined without any reference to myself, seemed to me an indispensable preliminary; similarly, however pretty she might be, the midinette whom a procuress had artificially provided for me could not possibly be a substitute for her who with her awkward figure was strolling at this moment under the trees, laughing with a friend. The girl that I might find in a house of assignation, were she even better-looking than this one, could not be the same thing, because we do not look at the eyes of a girl whom we do not know as we should look at a pair of little discs of opal or agate. We know that the little ray which colours them or the diamond dust that makes them sparkle is all that we can see of a mind, a will, a memory in which is contained the home life that we do not know, the intimate friends whom we envy. The enterprise of taking possession of all this, which is so difficult, so stubborn, is what gives its value to the gaze far more than its merely physical beauty (which may serve to explain why the same young man can awaken a whole romance in the imagination of a woman who has heard somebody say that he is the Prince of Wales, whereas she pays no more attention to him after learning that she is mistaken); to find the midinette in the house of assignation is to find her emptied of that unknown life which permeates her and which we aspire to possess with her, it is to approach a pair of eyes that have indeed become mere precious stones, a nose whose quivering is as devoid of meaning as that of a flower. No, that unknown midinette who was passing at that moment, it seemed to me as indispensable, if I wished to continue to believe in her reality, to test her resistance by adapting my behaviour to it, challenging a rebuff, returning to the charge, obtaining an assignation, waiting for her as she came away from her work, getting to know, episode by episode, all that composed the girl's life, traversing the space that, for her, enveloped the pleasure which I was seeking, and the distance which her different habits, her special mode of life, set between me and the attention, the favour which I wished to attain and capture, as making a long journey in the train if I wished to believe in the reality of Venice which I should see and which would not be merely a panoramic show in a World Exhibition. But this very parallel between desire and travel made me vow to myself that one day I would grasp a little more closely the nature of this force, invisible but as powerful as any faith, or as, in the world of physics, atmospheric pressure, which exalted to such a height cities and women so long as I did not know them, and slipped away from beneath them as soon as I had approached them, made them at once collapse and fall flat upon the dead level of the most commonplace reality.

Farther along another girl was kneeling beside her bicycle, which she was putting to rights. The repair finished, the young racer mounted her machine, but without straddling it as a man would have done. For a moment the bicycle swerved, and the young body seemed to have added to itself a sail, a huge wing; and presently we saw dart away at full speed the young creature half-human, half-winged, angel or peri, pursuing her course.

This was what a life with Albertine prevented me from enjoying. Prevented me, did I say? Should I not have thought rather: what it provided for my enjoyment. If Albertine had not been living with me, had been free, I should have imagined, and with reason, every woman to be a possible, a probable object of her desire, of her pleasure. They would have appeared to me like those dancers who, in a diabolical ballet, representing the Temptations to one person, plunge their darts in the heart of another. Midinettes, schoolgirls, actresses, how I should have hated them all! Objects of horror, I should have excepted them from the beauty of the universe. My bondage to Albertine, by permitting me not to suffer any longer on their account, restored them to the beauty of the world. Inoffensive, having lost the needle that stabs the heart with jealousy, I was able to admire them, to caress them with my eyes, another day more intimately perhaps. By secluding Albertine, I had at the same time restored to the universe all those rainbow wings which sweep past us in public gardens, ballrooms, theatres, and which became tempting once more to me because she could no longer succumb to their temptation. They composed the beauty of the world. They had at one time composed that of Albertine. It was because I had beheld her as a mysterious bird, then as a great actress of the beach, desired, perhaps won, that I had thought her wonderful. As soon as she was a captive in my house, the bird that I had seen one afternoon advancing with measured step along the front, surrounded by the congregation of the other girls like seagulls alighted from who knows whence, Albertine had lost all her colours, with all the chances that other people had of securing her for themselves. Gradually she had lost her beauty. It required excursions like this, in which I imagined her, but for my presence, accosted by some woman, or by some young man, to make me see her again amid the splendour of the beach, albeit my jealousy was on a different plane from the decline of the pleasures of my imagination. But notwithstanding these abrupt reversions in which, desired by other people, she once more became beautiful in my eyes, I might very well divide her visit to me in two periods, an earlier in which she was still, although less so every day, the glittering actress of the beach, and a later period in which, become the grey captive, reduced to her dreary self, I required those flashes in which I remembered the past to make me see her again in colour.

Sometimes, in the hours in which I felt most indifferent towards her, there came back to me the memory of a far-off moment when upon the beach, before I had made her acquaintance, a lady being near her with whom I was on bad terms and with whom I was almost certain now that she had had relations, she burst out laughing, staring me in the face in an insolent fashion. All round her hissed the blue and polished sea. In the sunshine of the beach, Albertine, in the midst of her friends, was the most beautiful of them all. She was a splendid girl, who in her familiar setting of boundless waters, had—precious in the eyes of the lady who admired her —inflicted upon me this unpardonable insult. It was unpardonable, for the lady would perhaps return to Balbec, would notice perhaps, on the luminous and echoing beach, that Albertine was absent. But she would not know that the girl was living with me, was wholly mine. The vast expanse of blue water, her forgetfulness of the fondness that she had felt for this particular girl and would divert to others, had closed over the outrage that Albertine had done me, enshrining it in a glittering and unbreakable casket. Then hatred of that woman gnawed my heart; of Albertine also, but a hatred mingled with admiration of the beautiful, courted girl, with her marvellous hair, whose laughter upon the beach had been an insult. Shame, jealousy, the memory of my earliest desires and of the brilliant setting had restored to Albertine the beauty, the intrinsic merit of other days. And thus there alternated with the somewhat oppressive boredom that I felt in her company a throbbing desire, full of splendid storms and of regrets; according to whether she was by my side in my bedroom or I set her at liberty in my memory upon the front, in her gay seaside frocks, to the sound of the musical instruments of the sea,—Albertine, now extracted from that environment, possessed and of no great value, now plunged back into it, escaping from me into a past which I should never be able to know, hurting me, in her friend's presence, as much as the splash of the wave or the heat of the sun,—Albertine restored to the beach or brought back again to my room, in a sort of amphibious love.

Farther on, a numerous band were playing ball. All these girls had come out to make the most of the sunshine, for these days in February, even when they are brilliant, do not last long and the splendour of their light does not postpone the hour of its decline. Before that hour drew near, we passed some time in twilight, because after we had driven as far as the Seine, where Albertine admired, and by her presence prevented me from admiring the reflexions of red sails upon the wintry blue of the water, a solitary house in the distance like a single red poppy against the clear horizon, of which Saint-Cloud seemed, farther off again, to be the fragmentary, crumbling, rugged petrification, we left our motor-car and walked a long way together; indeed for some moments I gave her my arm, and it seemed to me that the ring which her arm formed round it united our two persons in a single self and linked our separate destinies together.

At our feet, our parallel shadows, where they approached and joined, traced an exquisite pattern. No doubt it already seemed to me a marvellous thing at home that Albertine should be living with me, that it should be she that came and lay down on my bed. But it was so to speak the transporta-

tion of that marvel out of doors, into the heart of nature, that by the shore
of that lake in the Bois, of which I was so fond, beneath the trees, it should
be her and none but her shadow, the pure and simplified shadow of her
leg, of her bust, that the sun had to depict in monochrome by the side of
mine upon the gravel of the path. And I found a charm that was more
immaterial doubtless, but no less intimate, than in the drawing together,
the fusion of our bodies, in that of our shadows. Then we returned to our
car. And it chose, for our homeward journey, a succession of little winding
lanes along which the wintry trees, clothed, like ruins, in ivy and brambles,
seemed to be pointing the way to the dwelling of some magician. No sooner
had we emerged from their dusky cover than we found, upon leaving the
Bois, the daylight still so bright that I imagined that I should still have
time to do everything that I wanted to do before dinner, when, only a few
minutes later, at the moment when our car approached the Arc de Tri-
omphe, it was with a sudden start of surprise and dismay that I perceived,
over Paris, the moon prematurely full, like the face of a clock that has
stopped and makes us think that we are late for an engagement. We had
told the driver to take us home. To Albertine, this meant also coming to
my home. The company of those women, however dear to us, who are obliged to leave us and return home, does not bestow that peace which I
found in the company of Albertine seated in the car by my side, a company
that was conveying us not to the void in which lovers have to part but to
an even more stable and more sheltered union in my home, which was also
hers, the material symbol of my possession of her. To be sure, in order to
possess, one must first have desired. We do not possess a line, a surface, a
mass unless it is occupied by our love. But Albertine had not been for me
during our drive, as Rachel had been in the past, a futile dust of flesh and
clothing. The imagination of my eyes, my lips, my hands had at Balbec so
solidly built, so tenderly polished her body that now in this car, to touch
that body, to contain it, I had no need to press my own body against Albertine, nor even to see her; it was enough to hear her, and if she was silent
to know that she was by my side; my interwoven senses enveloped her altogether and when, as we arrived at the front door, she quite naturally
alighted, I stopped for a moment to tell the chauffeur to call for me later
on, but my gaze enveloped her still while she passed ahead of me under
the arch, and it was still the same inert, domestic calm that I felt as I saw
her thus, solid, flushed, opulent and captive, returning home quite naturally
with myself, as a woman who was my own property, and, protected by its
walls, disappearing into our house. Unfortunately, she seemed to feel herself a prisoner there, and to share the opinion of that Mme. de La Rochefoucauld who, when somebody asked her whether she was not glad to live
in so beautiful a home as Liancourt, replied: "There is no such thing as a
beautiful prison"; if I was to judge by her miserable, weary expression that
evening as we dined together in my room. I did not notice it at first; and
it was I that was made wretched by the thought that, if it had not been for
Albertine (for with her I should have suffered too acutely from jealousy in
an hotel where all day long she would have been exposed to contact with a
crowd of strangers), I might at that moment be dining in Venice in one of

those little restaurants, barrel-vaulted like the hold of a ship, from which one looks out on the Grand Canal through arched windows framed in Moorish mouldings.

I ought to add that Albertine greatly admired in my room a big bronze by Barbedienne which with ample justification Bloch considered extremely ugly. He had perhaps less reason to be surprised at my having kept it. I had never sought, like him, to furnish for artistic effect, to compose my surroundings, I was too lazy, too indifferent to the things that I was in the habit of seeing every day. Since my taste was not involved, I had a right not to harmonise my interior. I might perhaps, even without that, have discarded the bronze. But ugly and expensive things are of great use, for they enjoy, among people who do not understand us, who have not our taste and with whom we cannot fall in love, a prestige that would not be shared by some proud object that does not reveal its beauty. Now the people who do not understand us are precisely the people with regard to whom alone it may be useful to us to employ a prestige which our intellect is enough to assure us among superior people. Albertine might indeed be beginning to shew taste, she still felt a certain respect for the bronze, and this respect was reflected upon myself in a consideration which, coming from Albertine, mattered infinitely more to me than the question of keeping a bronze which was a trifle degrading, since I was in love with Albertine.

But the thought of my bondage ceased of a sudden to weigh upon me and I looked forward to prolonging it still further, because I seemed to perceive that Albertine was painfully conscious of her own. True that whenever I had asked her whether she was not bored in my house, she had always replied that she did not know where it would be possible to have a happier time. But often these words were contradicted by an air of nervous exhaustion, of longing to escape.

Certainly if she had the tastes with which I had credited her, this inhibition from ever satisfying them must have been as provoking to her as it was calming to myself, calming to such an extent that I should have decided that the hypothesis of my having accused her unjustly was the most probable, had it not been so difficult to fit into this hypothesis the extraordinary pains that Albertine was taking never to be alone, never to be disengaged, never to stop for a moment outside the front door when she came in, to insist upon being accompanied, whenever she went to the telephone, by some one who would be able to repeat to me what she had said, by Françoise or Andrée, always to leave me alone (without appearing to be doing so on purpose) with the latter, after they had been out together, so that I might obtain a detailed report of their outing. With this marvellous docility were contrasted certain quickly repressed starts of impatience, which made me ask myself whether Albertine was not planning to cast off her chain. Certain subordinate incidents seemed to corroborate my supposition. Thus, one day when I had gone out by myself, in the Passy direction, and had met Gisèle, we began to talk about one thing and another. Presently, not without pride at being able to do so, I informed her that I was constantly seeing Albertine. Gisèle asked me where she could find her, since there was something that she simply *must* tell her.

"Why, what is it?" "Something to do with some young friends of hers." "What friends? I may perhaps be able to tell you, though that need not prevent you from seeing her." "Oh, girls she knew years ago, I don't remember their names," Gisèle replied vaguely, and beat a retreat. She left me, supposing herself to have spoken with such prudence that the whole story must seem to me perfectly straightforward. But falsehood is so unexacting, needs so little help to make itself manifest! If it had been a question of friends of long ago, whose very names she no longer remembered, why *must* she speak about them to Albertine? This *'must,'* akin to an expression dear to Mme. Cottard: 'in the nick of time,' could be applicable only to something particular, opportune, perhaps urgent, relating to definite persons. Besides, something about her way of opening her mouth, as though she were going to yawn, with a vague expression, as she said to me (almost drawing back her body, as though she began to reverse her engine at this point in our conversation): "Oh, I don't know, I don't remember their names," made her face, and in harmony with it her voice, as clear a picture of falsehood as the wholly different air, tense, excited, of her previous *'must'* was of truth. I did not question Gisèle. Of what use would it have been to me? Certainly, she was not lying in the same fashion as Albertine. And certainly Albertine's lies pained me more. But they had obviously a point in common: the fact of the lie itself, which in certain cases is self-evident. Not evidence of the truth that the lie conceals. We know that each murderer in turn imagines that he has arranged everything so cleverly that he will not be caught, and so it is with liars, particularly the woman with whom we are in love. We do not know where she has been, what she has been doing. But at the very moment when she speaks, when she speaks of something else beneath which lies hidden the thing that she does not mention, the lie is immediately perceived, and our jealousy increased, since we are conscious of the lie, and cannot succeed in discovering the truth. With Albertine, the impression that she was lying was conveyed by many of the peculiarities which we have already observed in the course of this narrative, but especially by this, that, when she was lying, her story broke down either from inadequacy, omission, improbability, or on the contrary from a surfeit of petty details intended to make it seem probable. Probability, notwithstanding the idea that the liar has formed of it, is by no means the same as truth. Whenever, while listening to something that is true, we hear something that is only probable, which is perhaps more so than the truth, which is perhaps too probable, the ear that is at all sensitive feels that it is not correct, as with a line that does not scan or a word read aloud in mistake for another. Our ear feels this, and if we are in love our heart takes alarm. Why do we not reflect at the time, when we change the whole course of our life because we do not know whether a woman went along the Rue de Berri or the Rue Washington, why do we not reflect that these few hundred yards of difference, and the woman herself, will be reduced to the hundred millionth part of themselves (that is to say to dimensions far beneath our perception), if we only have the wisdom to remain for a few years without seeing the woman, and that she who has out-Gullivered Gulliver in our eyes will shrink to a Lilliputian whom no microscope—of the heart, at least, for that of the disinterested memory is more powerful and less fragile—can ever again perceive! However it may be, if there was a point in common—the lie itself—between Albertine's lies and Gisèle's, still Gisèle did not lie in the same fashion as Albertine, nor indeed in the same fashion as Andrée, but their respective lies dovetailed so neatly into one another, while presenting a great variety, that the little band had the impenetrable solidity of certain commercial houses, booksellers' for example or printing presses, where the wretched author will never succeed, notwithstanding the diversity of the persons employed in them, in discovering whether he is being swindled or not. The editor of the newspaper or review lies with an attitude of sincerity all the more solemn in that he is frequently obliged to conceal the fact that he himself does exactly the same things and indulges in the same commercial practices that he denounced in other editors or theatrical managers, in other publishers, when he chose as his battle-cry, when he raised against them the standard of Sincerity. The fact of a man's having proclaimed (as leader of a political party, or in any other capacity) that it is wicked to lie, obliges him as a rule to lie more than other people, without on that account abandoning the solemn mask, doffing the august tiara of sincerity. The 'sincere' gentleman's partner lies in a different and more ingenuous fashion. He deceives his author as he deceives his wife, with tricks from the vaudeville stage. The secretary of the firm, a blunt and honest man, lies quite simply, like an architect who promises that your house will be ready at a date when it will not have been begun. The head reader, an angelic soul, flutters from one to another of the three, and without knowing what the matter is, gives them, by a brotherly scruple and out of affectionate solidarity, the precious support of a word that is above suspicion. These four persons live in a state of perpetual dissension to which the arrival of the author puts a stop. Over and above their private quarrels, each of them remembers the paramount military duty of rallying to the support of the threatened 'corps.' Without realising it, I had long been playing the part of this author among the little band. If Gisèle had been thinking, when she used the word 'must,' of some one of Albertine's friends who was proposing to go abroad with her as soon as my mistress should have found some pretext or other for leaving me, and had meant to warn Albertine that the hour had now come or would shortly strike, she, Gisèle, would have let herself be torn to pieces rather than tell me so; it was quite useless therefore to ply her with questions. Meetings such as this with Gisèle were not alone in accentuating my doubts. For instance, I admired Albertine's sketches. Albertine's sketches, the touching distractions of the captive, moved me so that I congratulated her upon them. "No, they're dreadfully bad, but I've never had a drawing lesson in my life." "But one evening at Balbec you sent word to me that you had stayed at home to have a drawing lesson." I reminded her of the day and told her that I had realised at the time that people did not have drawing lessons at that hour in the evening. Albertine blushed. "It is true," she said, "I was not having drawing lessons, I told you a great many lies at first, that I admit. But I never lie to you now." I would so much have liked to know what were the many lies that she had told me at first, but I knew beforehand that her answers would be fresh lies. And so I contented myself with kissing her. I asked her to tell me one only of those lies. She replied: "Oh, well; for instance when I said that the sea air was bad for me." I ceased to insist in the face of this unwillingness to reveal.

To make her chain appear lighter, the best thing was no doubt to make her believe that I was myself about to break it. In any case, I could not at that moment confide this mendacious plan to her, she had been too kind in returning from the Trocadéro that afternoon; what I could do, far from distressing her with the threat of a rupture, was at the most to keep to myself those dreams of a perpetual life together which my grateful heart kept forming. As I looked at her, I found it hard to restrain myself from pouring them out to her, and she may perhaps have noticed this. Unfortunately the expression of such dreams is not contagious. The case of an affected old woman like M. de Charlus who, by dint of never seeing in his imagination anything but a stalwart young man, thinks that he has himself become a stalwart young man, all the more so the more affected and ridiculous he becomes, this case is more general, and it is the tragedy of an impassioned lover that he does not take into account the fact that while he sees in front of him a beautiful face, his mistress is seeing his face which is not made any more beautiful, far from it, when it is distorted by the pleasure that is aroused in it by the sight of beauty. Nor indeed does love exhaust the whole of this case; we do not see our own body, which other people see, and we 'follow' our own thought, the object invisible to other people which is before our eyes. This object the artist does sometimes enable us to see in his work. Whence it arises that the admirers of his work are disappointed in its author, upon whose face that internal beauty is imperfectly reflected.

Every person whom we love, indeed to a certain extent every person is to us like Janus, presenting to us the face that we like if that person leaves us, the repellent face if we know him or her to be perpetually at our disposal. In the case of Albertine, the prospect of her continued society was painful to me in another fashion which I cannot explain in this narrative. It is terrible to have the life of another person attached to our own like a bomb which we hold in our hands, unable to get rid of it without committing a crime. But let us take as a parallel the ups and downs, the dangers, the anxieties, the fear of seeing believed in time to come false and probable things which one will not be able then to explain, feelings that one experiences if one lives in the intimate society of a madman. For instance, I pitied M. de Charlus for living with Morel (immediately the memory of the scene that afternoon made me feel the left side of my breast heavier than the other); leaving out of account the relations that may or may not have existed between them, M. de Charlus must have been unaware at the outset that Morel was mad. Morel's beauty, his stupidity, his pride must have deterred the Baron from exploring so deeply, until the days of melancholy when Morel accused M. de Charlus of responsibility for his sorrows, without being able to furnish any explanation, abused him for his want of confidence, by the aid of false but extremely subtle reasoning, threatened him with desperate resolutions, while throughout all this there persisted the most cunning regard for his own most immediate interests. But all this is only a comparison. Albertine was not mad.

I learned that a death had occurred during the day which distressed me greatly, that of Bergotte. It was known that he had been ill for a long time past. Not, of course, with the illness from which he had suffered originally and which was natural. Nature hardly seems capable of giving us any but quite short illnesses. But medicine has annexed to itself the art of prolonging them. Remedies, the respite that they procure, the relapses that a temporary cessation of them provokes, compose a sham illness to which the patient grows so accustomed that he ends by making it permanent, just as children continue to give way to fits of coughing long after they have been cured of the whooping cough. Then remedies begin to have less effect, the doses are increased, they cease to do any good, but they have begun to do harm thanks to that lasting indisposition. Nature would not have offered them so long a tenure. It is a great miracle that medicine can almost equal nature in forcing a man to remain in bed, to continue on pain of death the use of some drug. From that moment the illness artificially grafted has taken root, has become a secondary but a genuine illness, with this difference only that natural illnesses are cured, but never those which medicine creates, for it knows not the secret of their cure.

For years past Bergotte had ceased to go out of doors. Anyhow, he had never cared for society, or had cared for it for a day only, to despise it as he despised everything else and in the same fashion, which was his own, namely to despise a thing not because it was beyond his reach but as soon as he had reached it. He lived so simply that nobody suspected how rich he was, and anyone who had known would still have been mistaken, for he would have thought him a miser, whereas no one was ever more generous. He was generous above all towards women,—girls, one ought rather to say—who were ashamed to receive so much in return for so little. He excused himself in his own eyes because he knew that he could never produce such good work as in an atmosphere of amorous feelings. Love is too strong a word, pleasure that is at all deeply rooted in the flesh is helpful to literary work because it cancels all other pleasures, for instance the pleasures of society, those which are the same for everyone. And even if this love leads to disillusionment, it does at least stir, even by so doing, the surface of the soul which otherwise would be in danger of becoming stagnant. Desire is therefore not without its value to the writer in detaching him first of all from his fellow men and from conforming to their standards, and afterwards in restoring some degree of movement to a spiritual machine which, after a certain age, tends to become paralysed. We do not succeed in being happy but we make observation of the reasons which prevent us from being happy and which would have remained invisible to us but for these loopholes opened by disappointment. Dreams are not to be converted into reality, that we know; we would not form any, perhaps, were it not for desire, and it is useful to us to form them in order to see them fail and to be instructed by their failure. And so Bergotte said to himself: "I am spending more than a multimillionaire would spend upon girls, but the pleasures or disappointments that they give me make me write a book which brings me money." Economically, this argument was absurd, but no doubt he found some charm in thus transmuting gold into caresses and caresses into gold. We saw, at the time of my grandmother's death, how a weary old age loves repose. Now in society, there is nothing but conversation. It may be stupid, but it has the faculty of suppressing women who are nothing more than questions and answers. Removed from society, women become once more what is so reposeful to a weary old man, an object of contemplation. In any case, it was no longer a question of anything of this sort. I have said that Bergotte never went out of doors, and when he got out of bed for an hour in his room, he would be smothered in shawls, plaids, all the things with which a person covers himself before exposing himself to intense cold or getting into a railway train. He would apologise to the few friends whom he allowed to penetrate to his sanctuary, and, pointing to his tartan plaids, his travelling-rugs, would say merrily: "After all, my dear fellow, life, as Anaxagoras has said, is a journey." Thus he went on growing steadily colder, a tiny planet that offered a prophetic image of the greater, when gradually heat will withdraw from the earth, then life itself. Then the resurrection will have come to an end, for if, among future generations, the works of men are to shine, there must first of all be men. If certain kinds of animals hold out longer against the invading chill, when there are no longer any men, and if we suppose Bergotte's fame to have lasted so long, suddenly it will be extinguished for all time. It will not be the last animals that will read him, for it is scarcely probable that, like the Apostles on the Day of Pentecost, they will be able to understand the speech of the various races of mankind without having learned it.

In the months that preceded his death, Bergotte suffered from insomnia, and what was worse, whenever he did fall asleep, from nightmares which, if he awoke, made him reluctant to go to sleep again. He had long been a lover of dreams, even of bad dreams, because thanks to them and to the contradiction they present to the reality which we have before us in our waking state, they give us, at the moment of waking if not before, the profound sensation of having slept. But Bergotte's nightmares were not like that. When he spoke of nightmares, he used in the past to mean unpleasant things that passed through his brain. Latterly, it was as though proceeding from somewhere outside himself that he would see a hand armed with a damp cloth which, passed over his face by an evil woman, kept scrubbing him awake, an intolerable itching in his thighs, the rage—because Bergotte had murmured in his sleep that he was driving badly—of a raving lunatic of a cabman who flung himself upon the writer, biting and gnawing his fingers. Finally, as soon as in his sleep it had grown sufficiently dark, nature arranged a sort of undress rehearsal of the apoplectic stroke that was to carry him off: Bergotte arrived in a carriage beneath the porch of Swann's new house, and tried to alight. A stunning giddiness glued him to his seat, the porter came forward to help him out of the carriage, he remained seated, unable to rise, to straighten his legs. He tried to pull himself up with the help of the stone pillar that was by his side, but did not find sufficient support in it to enable him to stand.

He consulted doctors who, flattered at being called in by him, saw in his virtue as an incessant worker (it was twenty years since he had written anything), in his overstrain, the cause of his ailments. They advised him not to read thrilling stories (he never read anything), to benefit more by the sunshine, which was 'indispensable to life' (he had owed a few years of comparative health only to his rigorous seclusion indoors), to take nourishment (which made him thinner, and nourished nothing but his nightmares). One of his doctors was blessed with the spirit of contradiction, and whenever Bergotte consulted him in the absence of the others, and, in order not to offend him, suggested to him as his own ideas what the others had advised, this doctor, thinking that Bergotte was seeking to have prescribed for him something that he himself liked, at once forbade it, and often for reasons invented so hurriedly to meet the case that in face of the material objections which Bergotte raised, this argumentative doctor was obliged in the same sentence to contradict himself, but, for fresh reasons, repeated the original prohibition. Bergotte returned to one of the first of these doctors, a man who prided himself on his cleverness, especially in the presence of one of the leading men of letters, and who, if Bergotte insinuated: "I seem to remember, though, that Dr. X—— told me—long ago, of course—that that might congest my kidneys and brain . . ." would smile sardonically, raise his finger and enounce: "I said use, I did not say abuse. Naturally every remedy, if one takes it in excess, becomes a two-edged sword." There is in the human body a certain instinct for what is beneficial to us, as there is in the heart for what is our moral duty, an instinct which no authorisation by a Doctor of Medicine or Divinity can replace. We know that cold baths are bad for us, we like them, we can always find a doctor to recommend them, not to prevent them from doing us harm. From each of these doctors Bergotte took something which, in his own wisdom, he had forbidden himself for years past. After a few weeks, his old troubles had reappeared, the new had become worse. Maddened by an unintermittent pain, to which was added insomnia broken only by brief spells of nightmare, Bergotte called in no more doctors and tried with success, but to excess, different narcotics, hopefully reading the prospectus that accompanied each of them, a prospectus which proclaimed the necessity of sleep but hinted that all the preparations which induce it (except that contained in the bottle round which the prospectus was wrapped, which never produced any toxic effect) were toxic, and therefore made the remedy worse than the disease. Bergotte tried them all. Some were of a different family from those to which we are accustomed, preparations for instance of amyl and ethyl. When we absorb a new drug, entirely different in composition, it is always with a delicious expectancy of the unknown. Our heart beats as at a first assignation. To what unknown forms of sleep, of dreams, is the newcomer going to lead us? He is inside us now, he has the control of our thoughts. In what fashion are we going to fall asleep? And, once we are asleep, by what strange paths, up to what peaks, into what unfathomed gulfs is he going to lead us? With what new grouping of sensations are we to become acquainted on this journey? Will it bring us in the end to illness? To blissful happiness? To death? Bergotte's death had come to him overnight, when he had thus entrusted himself to one of these friends (a friend? or an enemy, rather?) who proved too strong for him. The circumstances of his death were as follows. An attack of uraemia, by no means serious, had led to his being ordered to rest. But one of the critics having written somewhere that in Vermeer's *Street in Delft* (lent by the Gallery at The Hague for an exhibition of Dutch painting), a picture which he adored and imagined that he knew by heart, a little patch of yellow wall (which he could not remember) was so well painted that it was, if one looked at it by itself, like some priceless specimen of Chinese art, of a beauty that was sufficient in itself, Bergotte ate a few potatoes, left the house, and went to the exhibition. At the first few steps that he had to climb he was overcome by giddiness. He passed in front of several pictures and was struck by the stiffness and futility of so artificial a school, nothing of which equalled the fresh air and sunshine of a Venetian palazzo, or of an ordinary house by the sea. At last he came to the Vermeer which he remembered as more striking, more different from anything else that he knew, but in which, thanks to the critic's article, he remarked for the first time some small figures in blue, that the ground was pink, and finally the precious substance of the tiny patch of yellow wall. His giddiness increased; he fixed his eyes, like a child upon a yellow butterfly which it is trying to catch, upon the precious little patch of wall. "That is how I ought to have written," he said. "My last books are too dry, I ought to have gone over them with several coats of paint, made my language exquisite in itself, like this little patch of yellow wall." Meanwhile he was not unconscious of the gravity of his condition. In a celestial balance there appeared to him, upon one of its scales, his own life, while the other contained the little patch of wall so beautifully painted in yellow. He felt that he had rashly surrendered the former for the latter. "All the same," he said to himself, "I have no wish to provide the 'feature' of this exhibition for the evening papers."

He repeated to himself: "Little patch of yellow wall, with a sloping roof, little patch of yellow wall." While doing so he sank down upon a circular divan; and then at once he ceased to think that his life was in jeopardy and, reverting to his natural optimism, told himself: "It is just an ordinary indigestion from those potatoes; they weren't properly cooked; it is nothing." A fresh attack beat him down; he rolled from the divan to the floor, as visitors and attendants came hurrying to his assistance. He was dead. Permanently dead? Who shall say? Certainly our experiments in spiritualism prove no more than the dogmas of religion that the soul survives death. All that we can say is that everything is arranged in this life as though we entered it carrying the burden of obligations contracted in a former life; there is no reason inherent in the conditions of life on this earth that can make us consider ourselves obliged to do good, to be fastidious, to be polite even, nor make the talented artist consider himself obliged to begin over again a score of times a piece of work the admiration aroused by which will matter little to his body devoured by worms, like the patch of yellow wall painted with so much knowledge and skill by an artist who must for ever remain unknown and is barely identified under the name Vermeer. All these obligations which have not their sanction in our present life seem to belong to a different world, founded upon kindness, scrupulosity, self-sacrifice, a world entirely different from this, which we leave in order to be born into this world, before perhaps returning to the other to live once again beneath the sway of those unknown laws which we have obeyed because we bore their precepts in our hearts, knowing not whose hand had traced them there—those laws to which every profound work of the intellect brings us nearer and which are invisible only—and still!—to fools. So that the idea that Bergotte was not wholly and permanently dead is by no means improbable.

They buried him, but all through the night of mourning, in the lighted windows, his books arranged three by three kept watch like angels with outspread wings and seemed, for him who was no more, the symbol of his resurrection.

I learned, I have said, that day that Bergotte was dead. And I marvelled at the carelessness of the newspapers which—each of them reproducing the same paragraph—stated that he had died the day before. For, the day before, Albertine had met him, as she informed me that very evening, and indeed she had been a little late in coming home, for she had stopped for some time talking to him. She was doubtless the last person to whom he had spoken. She knew him through myself who had long ceased to see him, but, as she had been anxious to make his acquaintance, I had, a year earlier, written to ask the old master whether I might bring her to see him. He had granted my request, a trifle hurt, I fancy, that I should be visiting him only to give pleasure to another person, which was a proof of my indifference to himself. These cases are frequent: sometimes the man or woman whom we implore to receive us not for the pleasure of conversing with them again, but on behalf of a third person, refuses so obstinately that our protégée concludes that we have boasted of an influence which we do not possess; more often the man of genius or the famous beauty consents, but, humiliated in their glory, wounded in their affection, feel for us afterwards only a diminished, sorrowful, almost contemptuous attachment. I discovered long after this that I had falsely accused the newspapers of inaccuracy, since on the day in question Albertine had not met Bergotte, but at the time I had never suspected this for a single instant, so naturally had she told me of the incident, and it was not until much later that I discovered her charming skill in lying with simplicity. The things that she said, the things that she confessed were so stamped with the character of formal evidence—what we see, what we learn from an unquestionable source—that she sowed thus in the empty spaces of her life episodes of another life the falsity of which I did not then suspect and began to perceive only at a much later date. I have used the word 'confessed,' for the following reason. Sometimes a casual meeting gave me a jealous suspicion in which by her side there figured in the past, or alas in the future, another person. In order to appear certain of my facts, I mentioned the person's name, and Albertine said: "Yes, I met her, a week ago, just outside the house. I had to be polite and answer her when she spoke to me. I walked a little way with her. But there never has been anything between us. There never will be." Now Albertine had not even met this person, for the simple reason that the person had not been in Paris for the last ten months. But my mistress felt that a complete denial would sound hardly probable. Whence this imaginary brief encounter, related so simply that I could see the lady stop, bid her good day, walk a little way with her. The evidence of my senses, if I had been in the street at that moment, would perhaps have informed me that the lady had not been with Albertine. But if I had knowledge of the fact, it was by one of those chains of reasoning in which the words of people in whom we have confidence insert strong links, and not by the evidence of my senses. To invoke this evidence of the senses I should have had to be in the street at that particular moment, and I had not been. We may imagine, however, that such an hypothesis is not improbable: I might have gone out, and have been passing along the street at the time at which Albertine was to tell me in the evening (not having seen me there) that she had gone a little way with the lady, and I should then have known that Albertine was lying. But is that quite certain even then? A religious obscurity would have clouded my mind, I should have begun to doubt whether I had seen her by herself, I should barely have sought to understand by what optical illusion I had failed to perceive the lady, and should not have been greatly surprised to find myself mistaken, for the stellar universe is not so difficult of comprehension as the real actions of other people, especially of the people with whom we are in love, strengthened as they are against our doubts by fables devised for their protection. For how many years on end can they not allow our apathetic love to believe that they have in some foreign country a sister, a brother, a sister-in-law who have never existed!

The evidence of the senses is also an operation of the mind in which conviction creates the evidence. We have often seen her sense of hearing convey to Françoise not the word that was uttered but what she thought to be its correct form, which was enough to prevent her from hearing the correction implied in a superior pronunciation. Our butler was cast in a similar mould. M. de Charlus was in the habit of wearing at this time— for he was constantly changing—very light trousers which were recognisable a mile off. Now our butler, who thought that the word *pissotière* (the word denoting what M. de Rambuteau had been so annoyed to hear the Duc de Guermantes call a Rambuteau stall) was really *pistière*, never once in the whole of his life heard a single person say *pissotière*, albeit the word was frequently pronounced thus in his hearing. But error is more obstinate than faith and does not examine the grounds of its belief. Constantly the butler would say: "I'm sure M. le Baron de Charlus must have caught a disease to stand about as long as he does in a *pistière*. That's what comes of running after the girls at his age. You can tell what he is by his trousers. This morning, Madame sent me with a message to Neuilly. As I passed the *pistière* in the Rue de Bourgogne I saw M. le Baron de Charlus go in. When I came back from Neuilly, quite an hour later, I saw his yellow trousers in the same *pistière,* in the same place, in the middle stall where he always goes so that people shan't see him." I can think of no one more beautiful, more noble or more youthful than a certain niece of Mme. de Guermantes. But I have heard the porter of a restaurant where I used sometimes to dine say as she went by: "Just look at that old trollop, what a style! And she must be eighty, if she's a day." As far as age went, I find it difficult to believe that he meant what he said. But the pages clustered round him, who tittered whenever she went past the hotel on her way to visit, at their house in the neighbourhood, her charming great-aunts, Mmes. de Fezensac and de Bellery, saw upon the face of the young beauty the four-score years with which, seriously or in jest, the porter had endowed the 'old trollop.' You would have made them shriek with laughter had you told them that she was more distinguished than one of the two cashiers of the hotel, who, devoured by eczema, ridiculously stout, seemed to them a fine-looking woman. Perhaps sexual desire alone would have been capable of preventing their error from taking form, if it had been brought to bear upon the passage of the alleged old trollop, and if the pages had suddenly begun to covet the young goddess. But for reasons unknown, which were most probably of a social nature, this desire had not come into play. There is moreover ample room for discussion. The universe is true for us all and dissimilar to each of us. If we were not obliged, to preserve the continuity of our story, to confine ourselves to frivolous reasons, how many more serious reasons would permit us to demonstrate the falsehood and flimsiness of the opening pages of this volume in which, from my bed, I hear the world awake, now to one sort of weather, now to another. Yes, I have been forced to whittle down the facts, and to be a liar, but it is not one universe, there are millions, almost as many as the number of human eyes and brains in existence, that awake every morning.

To return to Albertine, I have never known any woman more amply endowed than herself with the happy aptitude for a lie that is animated, coloured with the selfsame tints of life, unless it be one of her friends— one of my blossoming girls also, rose-pink as Albertine, but one whose irregular profile, concave in one place, then convex again, was exactly like certain clusters of pink flowers the name of which I have forgotten, but which have long and sinuous concavities. This girl was, from the point of view of story-telling, superior to Albertine, for she never introduced any of those painful moments, those furious innuendoes, which were frequent with my mistress. I have said, however, that she was charming when she invented a story which left no room for doubt, for one saw then in front of her the thing—albeit imaginary—which she was saying, using it as an illustration of her speech. Probability alone inspired Albertine, never the desire to make me jealous. For Albertine, without perhaps any material interest, liked people to be polite to her. And if in the course of this work I have had and shall have many occasions to shew how jealousy intensifies love, it is the lover's point of view that I have adopted. But if that lover be only the least bit proud, and though he were to die of a separation, he will not respond to a supposed betrayal with a courteous speech, he will

turn away, or without going will order himself to assume a mask of coldness. And so it is entirely to her own disadvantage that his mistress makes
him suffer so acutely. If, on the contrary, she dispels with a tactful word,
with loving caresses, the suspicions that have been torturing him for all
his show of indifference, no doubt the lover does not feel that despairing
increase of love to which jealousy drives him, but ceasing in an instant to
suffer, happy, affectionate, relieved from strain as one is after a storm
when the rain has ceased and one barely hears still splash at long intervals
from the tall horse-chestnut trees the clinging drops which already the
reappearing sun has dyed with colour, he does not know how to express
his gratitude to her who has cured him. Albertine knew that I liked to
reward her for her kindnesses, and this perhaps explained why she used
to invent, to exculpate herself, confessions as natural as these stories the
truth of which I never doubted, one of them being that of her meeting
with Bergotte when he was already dead. Previously I had never known
any of Albertine's lies save those that, at Balbec for instance, Françoise
used to report to me, which I have omitted from these pages albeit they
hurt me so sorely: "As she didn't want to come, she said to me: 'Couldn't
you say to Monsieur that you didn't find me, that I had gone out?'" But
our 'inferiors,' who love us as Françoise loved me, take pleasure in wounding us in our self-esteem.

CHAPTER TWO

THE VERDURINS QUARREL WITH
M. DE CHARLUS

AFTER dinner, I told Albertine that, since I was out of bed, I might as well take the opportunity to go and see some of my friends, Mme. de Villeparisis, Mme. de Guermantes, the Cambremers, anyone in short whom I might find at home. I omitted to mention only the people whom I did intend to see, the Verdurins. I asked her if she would not come with me. She pleaded that she had no suitable clothes. "Besides, my hair is so awful. Do you really wish me to go on doing it like this?" And by way of farewell she held out her hand to me in that abrupt fashion, the arm outstretched, the shoulders thrust back, which she used to adopt on the beach at Balbec and had since then entirely abandoned. This forgotten gesture retransformed the body which it animated into that of the Albertine who as yet scarcely knew me. It restored to Albertine, ceremonious beneath an air of rudeness, her first novelty, her strangeness, even her setting. I saw the sea behind this girl whom I had never seen shake hands with me in this fashion since I was at the seaside. "My aunt thinks it makes me older," she added with a sullen air. "Oh that her aunt may be right!" thought I. "That Albertine by looking like a child should make Mme. Bontemps appear younger than she is, is all that her aunt would ask, and also that Albertine shall cost her nothing between now and the day when, by marrying me, she will repay what has been spent on her." But that Albertine should appear less young, less pretty, should turn fewer heads in the street, that is what I, on the contrary, hoped. For the age of a duenna is less reassuring to a jealous lover than the age of the woman's face whom he loves. I regretted only that the style in which I had asked her to do her hair should appear to Albertine an additional bolt on the door of her prison. And it was henceforward this new domestic sentiment that never ceased, even when I was parted from Albertine, to form a bond attaching me to her.

I said to Albertine, who was not dressed, or so she told me, to accompany me to the Guermantes' or the Cambremers', that I could not be certain where I should go, and set off for the Verdurins'. At the moment when the thought of the concert that I was going to hear brought back to my mind the scene that afternoon: *"Grand pied de grue, grand pied de grue,"* —a scene of disappointed love, of jealous love perhaps, but if so as bestial as the scene to which a woman might be subjected by, so to speak, an orang-outang that was, if one may use the expression, in love with her— at the moment when, having reached the street, I was just going to hail a cab, I heard the sound of sobs which a man who was sitting upon a curbstone was endeavouring to stifle. I came nearer; the man, who had buried his face in his hands, appeared to be quite young, and I was surprised to see, from the gleam of white in the opening of his cloak, that he was wearing evening clothes and a white tie. As he heard my step he uncovered a face bathed in tears, but at once, having recognised me, turned away. It was Morel. He guessed that I had recognised him and, checking his tears with an effort, told me that he had stopped to rest for a moment, he was in such pain. "I have grossly insulted, only to-day," he said, "a person for whom I had the very highest regard. It was a cowardly thing to do, for she loves me." "She will forget perhaps, as time goes on," I replied, without realising that by speaking thus I made it apparent that I had overheard the scene that afternoon. But he was so much absorbed in his own grief that it never even occurred to him that I might know something about the affair. "She may forget, perhaps," he said. "But I myself can never forget. I am too conscious of my degradation, I am disgusted with myself! However, what I have said I have said, and nothing can unsay it. When people make me lose my temper, I don't know what I am doing. And it is so bad for me, my nerves are all on edge," for, like all neurasthenics, he was keenly interested in his own health. If, during the afternoon, I had witnessed the amorous rage of an infuriated animal, this evening, within a few hours, centuries had elapsed and a fresh sentiment, a sentiment of shame, regret, grief, shewed that a great stage had been passed in the evolution of the beast destined to be transformed into a human being. Nevertheless, I still heard ringing in my ears his '*grand pied de grue*' and dreaded an imminent return to the savage state. I had only a very vague impression, however, of what had been happening, and this was but natural, for M. de Charlus himself was totally unaware that for some days past, and especially that day, even before the shameful episode which was not a direct consequence of the violinist's condition, Morel had been suffering from a recurrence of his neurasthenia. As a matter of fact, he had, in the previous month, proceeded as rapidly as he had been able, a great deal less rapidly than he would have liked, towards the seduction of Jupien's niece with whom he was at liberty, now that they were engaged, to go out whenever he chose. But whenever he had gone a trifle far in his attempts at violation, and especially when he suggested to his betrothed that she might make friends with other girls whom she would then procure for himself, he had met with a resistance that made him furious. All at once (whether she would have proved too chaste, or on the contrary would have surrendered herself) his desire had subsided. He had decided to break with her, but feeling that the Baron, vicious as he might be, was far more moral than himself, he was afraid lest, in the event of a rupture, M. de Charlus might turn him out of the house. And so he had decided, a fortnight ago, that he would not see the girl again, would leave M. de Charlus and Jupien to clean up the mess (he employed a more realistic term) by themselves, and, before announcing the rupture, to 'b—— off' to an unknown destination.

For all that his conduct towards Jupien's niece coincided exactly, in its minutest details, with the plan of conduct which he had outlined to the Baron as they were dining together at Saint-Mars le Vêtu, it is probable that his intention was entirely different, and that sentiments of a less atrocious nature, which he had not foreseen in his theory of conduct, had improved, had tinged it with sentiment in practice. The sole point in which, on the contrary, the practice was worse than the theory is this, that in theory it had not appeared to him possible that he could remain in Paris after such an act of betrayal. Now, on the contrary, actually to 'b——— off' for so small a matter seemed to him quite unnecessary. It meant leaving the Baron who would probably be furious, and forfeiting his own position. He would lose all the money that the Baron was now giving him. The thought that this was inevitable made his nerves give away altogether, he cried for hours on end, and in order not to think about it any more dosed himself cautiously with morphine. Then suddenly he hit upon an idea which no doubt had gradually been taking shape in his mind and gaining strength there for some time, and this was that a rupture with the girl would not inevitably mean a complete break with M. de Charlus. To lose all the Baron's money was a serious thing in itself. Morel in his uncertainty remained for some days a prey to dark thoughts, such as came to him at the sight of Bloch. Then he decided that Jupien and his niece had been trying to set a trap for him, that they might consider themselves lucky to be rid of him so cheaply. He found in short that the girl had been in the wrong in being so clumsy, in not having managed to keep him attached to her by a sensual attraction. Not only did the sacrifice of his position with M. de Charlus seem to him absurd, he even regretted the expensive dinners he had given the girl since they became engaged, the exact cost of which he knew by heart, being a true son of the valet who used to bring his 'book' every month for my uncle's inspection. For the word book, in the singular, which means a printed volume to humanity in general, loses that meaning among Royal Princes and servants. To the latter it means their house-keeping book, to the former the register in which we inscribe our names. (At Balbec one day when the Princesse de Luxembourg told me that she had not brought a book with her, I was about to offer her *Le Pêcheur d'Islande* and *Tartarin de Tarascon*, when I realised that she had meant not that she would pass the time less agreeably, but that I should find it more difficult to pay a call upon her.) Notwithstanding the change in Morel's point of view with regard to the consequences of his behaviour, albeit that behaviour would have seemed to him abominable two months earlier, when he was passionately in love with Jupien's niece, whereas during the last fortnight he had never ceased to assure himself that the same behaviour was natural, praiseworthy, it continued to intensify the state of nervous unrest in which, finally, he had announced the rupture that afternoon. And he was quite prepared to vent his anger, if not (save in a momentary outburst) upon the girl, for whom he still felt that lingering fear, the last trace of love, at any rate upon the Baron. He took care, however, not to say anything to him before dinner, for, valuing his own professional skill above everything, whenever he had any difficult music to play (as this evening at the Verdurins') he avoided (as far as possible, and the scene that afternoon was already more than ample) anything that might impair the flexibility of his wrists. Similarly a surgeon who is an enthusiastic motorist, does not drive when he has an operation to perform. This accounts to me for the fact that, while he was speaking to me, he kept bending his fingers gently one after another to see whether they had regained their suppleness. A slight frown seemed to indicate that there was still a trace of nervous stiffness. But, so as not to increase it, he relaxed his features, as we forbid ourself to grow irritated at not being able to sleep or to prevail upon a woman, for fear lest our rage itself may retard the moment of sleep or of satisfaction. And so, anxious to regain his serenity so that he might, as was his habit, absorb himself entirely in what he was going to play at the Verdurins', and anxious, so long as I was watching him, to let me see how unhappy he was, he decided that the simplest course was to beg me to leave him immediately. His request was superfluous, and it was a relief to me to get away from him. I had trembled lest, as we were due at the same house, within a few minutes, he might ask me to take him with me, my memory of the scene that afternoon being too vivid not to give me a certain distaste for the idea of having Morel by my side during the drive. It is quite possible that the love, and afterwards the indifference or hatred felt by Morel for Jupien's niece had been sincere. Unfortunately, it was not the first time that he had behaved thus, that he had suddenly 'dropped' a girl to whom he had sworn undying love, going so far as to produce a loaded revolver, telling her that he would blow out his brains if ever he was mean enough to desert her. He did nevertheless desert her in time, and felt instead of remorse, a sort of rancour against her. It was not the first time that he had behaved thus, it was not to be the last, with the result that the heads of many girls—girls less forgetful of him than he was of them—suffered—as Jupien's niece's head continued long afterwards to suffer, still in love with Morel although she despised him—suffered, ready to burst with the shooting of an internal pain because in each of them—like a fragment of a Greek carving—an aspect of Morel's face, hard as marble and beautiful as an antique sculpture, was embedded in her brain, with his blossoming hair, his fine eyes, his straight nose, forming a protuberance in a cranium not shaped to receive it, upon which no operation was possible. But in the fulness of time these stony fragments end by slipping into a place where they cause no undue discomfort, from which they never stir again; we are no longer conscious of their presence: I mean forgetfulness, or an indifferent memory.

Meanwhile I had gained two things in the course of the day. On the one hand, thanks to the calm that was produced in me by Albertine's docility, I found it possible, and therefore made up my mind, to break with her. There was on the other hand, the fruit of my reflexions during the interval that I had spent waiting for her, at the piano, the idea that Art, to which I would try to devote my reconquered liberty, was not a thing that justified one in making a sacrifice, a thing above and beyond life, that did not share in its fatuity and futility; the appearance of real individuality obtained in works of art being due merely to the illusion created by the artist's technical skill. If my afternoon had left behind it other deposits, possibly more profound, they were not to come to my knowledge until much later. As for the two which I was able thus to weigh, they were not to be permanent; for, from this very evening my ideas about art were to rise above the depression to which they had been subjected in the afternoon, while on the other hand my calm, and consequently the freedom that would enable me to devote myself to it, was once again to be withdrawn from me.

As my cab, following the line of the embankment, was coming near the Verdurins' house, I made the driver pull up. I had just seen Brichot alighting from the tram at the foot of the Rue Bonaparte, after which he dusted his shoes with an old newspaper and put on a pair of pearl grey gloves. I went up to him on foot. For some time past, his sight having grown steadily weaker, he had been endowed—as richly as an observatory—with new spectacles of a powerful and complicated kind, which, like astronomical instruments, seemed to be screwed into his eyes; he focussed their exaggerated blaze upon myself and recognised me. They—the spectacles—were in marvellous condition. But behind them I could see, minute, pallid, convulsive, expiring, a remote gaze placed under this powerful apparatus, as, in a laboratory equipped out of all proportion to the work that is done in it, you may watch the last throes of some insignificant animalcule through the latest and most perfect type of microscope. I offered him my arm to guide him on his way. "This time it is not by great Cherbourg that we meet," he said to me, "but by little Dunkerque," a remark which I found extremely tiresome, as I failed to understand what he meant; and yet I dared not ask Brichot, dreading not so much his scorn as his explanations. I replied that I was longing to see the room in which Swann used to meet Odette every evening. "What, so you know that old story, do you?" he said. "And yet from those days to the death of Swann is what the poet rightly calls: '*Grande spatium mortalis aevi.*'"

The death of Swann had been a crushing blow to me at the time. The death of Swann! Swann, in this phrase, is something more than a noun in the possessive case. I mean by it his own particular death, the death allotted by destiny to the service of Swann. For we talk of 'death' for convenience, but there are almost as many different deaths as there are people. We are not equipped with a sense that would enable us to see, moving at every speed in every direction, these deaths, the active deaths aimed by destiny at this person or that. Often there are deaths that will not be entirely relieved of their duties until two or even three years later. They come in haste to plant a tumour in the side of a Swann, then depart to attend to their other duties, returning only when, the surgeons having performed their operation, it is necessary to plant the tumour there afresh. Then comes the moment when we read in the *Gaulois* that Swann's health has been causing anxiety but that he is now making an excellent recovery. Then, a few minutes before the breath leaves our body, death, like a sister of charity who has come to nurse, rather than to destroy us, enters to preside over our last moments, crowns with a supreme halo the cold and stiffening creature whose heart has ceased to beat. And it is this diversity among deaths, the mystery of their circuits, the colour of their fatal badge, that makes so impressive a paragraph in the newspapers such as this:

"We regret to learn that M. Charles Swann passed away yesterday at his residence in Paris, after a long and painful illness. A Parisian whose intellectual gifts were widely appreciated, a discriminating but steadfastly loyal friend, he will be universally regretted, in those literary and artistic circles where the soundness and refinement of his taste made him a willing and a welcome guest, as well as at the Jockey Club of which he was one of the oldest and most respected members. He belonged also to the Union and Agricole. He had recently resigned his membership of the Rue Royale. His personal appearance and eminently distinguished bearing never failed to arouse public interest at all the great events of the musical and artistic seasons, especially at private views, at which he was a regular attendant until, during the last years of his life, he became almost entirely confined to the house. The funeral will take place, etc."

From this point of view, if one is not 'somebody,' the absence of a well known title makes the process of decomposition even more rapid. No doubt it is more or less anonymously, without any personal identity, that a man still remains Duc d'Uzès. But the ducal coronet does for some time hold the elements together, as their moulds keep together those artistically designed ices which Albertine admired, whereas the names of ultra-fashionable commoners, as soon as they are dead, dissolve and lose their shape. We have seen M. de Bréauté speak of Cartier as the most intimate friend of the Duc de La Trémoïlle, as a man greatly in demand in aristocratic circles. To a later generation, Cartier has become something so formless that it would almost be adding to his importance to make him out as related to the jeweller Cartier, with whom he would have smiled to think that anybody could be so ignorant as to confuse him! Swann on the contrary was a remarkable personality, in both the intellectual and the artistic worlds; and even although he had 'produced' nothing, still he had a chance of surviving a little longer. And yet, my dear Charles ——, whom I used to know when I was still so young and you were nearing your grave, it is because he whom you must have regarded as a little fool has made you the hero of one of his volumes that people are beginning to speak of you again and that your name will perhaps live. If in Tissot's picture representing the balcony of the Rue Royale club, where you figure with Galliffet, Edmond Polignac and Saint-Maurice, people are always drawing attention to yourself, it is because they know that there are some traces of you in the character of Swann.

To return to more general realities, it was of this foretold and yet unforeseen death of Swann that I had heard him speak himself to the Duchesse de Guermantes, on the evening of her cousin's party. It was the same death whose striking and specific strangeness had recurred to me one evening when, as I ran my eye over the newspaper, my attention was suddenly arrested by the announcement of it, as though traced in mysterious lines interpolated there out of place. They had sufficed to make of a living man some one who can never again respond to what you say to him, to reduce

him to a mere name, a written name, that has passed in a moment from
the real world to the realm of silence. It was they that even now made me
anxious to make myself familiar with the house in which the Verdurins
had lived, and where Swann, who at that time was not merely a row of
five letters printed in a newspaper, had dined so often with Odette. I must
add also (and this is what for a long time made Swann's death more painful than any other, albeit these reasons bore no relation to the individual
strangeness of his death) that I had never gone to see Gilberte, as I promised him at the Princesse de Guermantes's, that he had never told me what
the 'other reason' was, to which he alluded that evening, for his selecting
me as the recipient of his conversation with the Prince, that a thousand
questions occurred to me (as bubbles rise from the bottom of a pond)
which I longed to ask him about the most different subjects: Vermeer, M.
de Mouchy, Swann himself, a Boucher tapestry, Combray, questions that
doubtless were not very vital since I had put off asking them from day to
day, but which seemed to me of capital importance now that, his lips being
sealed, no answer would ever come.

"No," Brichot went on, "it was not here that Swann met his future wife,
or rather it was here only in the very latest period, after the disaster that
partially destroyed Mme. Verdurin's former home."

Unfortunately, in my fear of displaying before the eyes of Brichot an
extravagance which seemed to me out of place, since the professor had
no share in its enjoyment, I had alighted too hastily from the carriage and
the driver had not understood the words I had flung at him over my shoulder in order that I might be well clear of the carriage before Brichot caught
sight of me. The consequence was that the driver followed us and asked
me whether he was to call for me later; I answered hurriedly in the affirmative, and was regarded with a vastly increased respect by the professor who had come by omnibus.

"Ah! So you were in a carriage," he said in solemn tones. "Only by the
purest accident. I never take one as a rule. I always travel by omnibus or
on foot. However, it may perhaps entitle me to the great honour of taking
you home to-night if you will oblige me by consenting to enter that rattle-
trap; we shall be packed rather tight. But you are always so considerate
to me." Alas, in making him this offer, I am depriving myself of nothing
(I reflected) since in any case I shall be obliged to go home for Albertine's
sake. Her presence in my house, at an hour when nobody could possibly
call to see her, allowed me to dispose as freely of my time as I had that
afternoon, when, seated at the piano, I knew that she was on her way
back from the Trocadéro and that I was in no hurry to see her again. But
furthermore, as also in the afternoon, I felt that I had a woman in the
house and that on returning home I should not taste the fortifying thrill
of solitude. "I accept with great good will," replied Brichot. "At the period
to which you allude, our friends occupied in the Rue Montalivet a magnificent ground floor apartment with an upper landing, and a garden behind, less sumptuous of course, and yet to my mind preferable to the old
Venetian Embassy." Brichot informed me that this evening there was to
be at 'Quai Conti' (thus it was that the faithful spoke of the Verdurin

drawing-room since it had been transferred to that address) a great musical 'tow-row-row' got up by M. de Charlus. He went on to say that in the
old days to which I had referred, the little nucleus had been different, and
its tone not at all the same, not only because the faithful had then been
younger. He told me of elaborate jokes played by Elstir (what he called
'pure buffooneries'), as for instance one day when the painter, having
pretended to fail at the last moment, had come disguised as an extra
waiter and, as he handed round the dishes, whispered gallant speeches in
the ear of the extremely proper Baroness Putbus, crimson with anger and
alarm; then disappearing before the end of dinner he had had a hip-bath
carried into the drawing-room, out of which, when the party left the table,
he had emerged stark naked uttering fearful oaths; and also of supper
parties to which the guests came in paper costumes, designed, cut out and
coloured by Elstir, which were masterpieces in themselves, Brichot having
worn on one occasion that of a great nobleman of the court of Charles
VII, with long turned-up points to his shoes, and another time that of
Napoleon I, for which Elstir had fashioned a Grand Cordon of the Legion
of Honour out of sealing-wax. In short Brichot, seeing again with the eyes
of memory the drawing-room of those days with its high windows, its low
sofas devoured by the midday sun which had had to be replaced, declared
that he preferred it to the drawing-room of to-day. Of course, I quite understood that by 'drawing-room' Brichot meant—as the word church implies not merely the religious edifice but the congregation of worshippers
—not merely the apartment, but the people who visited it, the special
pleasures that they came to enjoy there, to which, in his memory, those
sofas had imparted their form upon which, when you called to see Mme.
Verdurin in the afternoon, you waited until she was ready, while the blossom on the horse chestnuts outside, and on the mantelpiece carnations in
vases seemed, with a charming and kindly thought for the visitor expressed
in the smiling welcome of their rosy hues, to be watching anxiously for
the tardy appearance of the lady of the house. But if the drawing-room
seemed to him superior to what it was now, it was perhaps because our
mind is the old Proteus who cannot remain the slave of any one shape
and, even in the social world, suddenly abandons a house which has slowly
and with difficulty risen to the pitch of perfection to prefer another which
is less brilliant, just as the 'touched-up' photographs which Odette had
had taken at Otto's, in which she queened it in a 'princess' gown, her hair
waved by Lenthéric, did not appeal to Swann so much as a little 'cabinet
picture' taken at Nice, in which, in a cloth cape, her loosely dressed hair
protruding beneath a straw hat trimmed with pansies and a bow of black
ribbon, instead of being twenty years younger (for women as a rule look
all the older in a photograph, the earlier it is), she looked like a little
servant girl twenty years older than she now was. Perhaps too he derived
some pleasure from praising to me what I myself had never known, from
shewing me that he had tasted delights that I could never enjoy. If so, he
was successful, for merely by mentioning the names of two or three people
who were no longer alive and to each of whom he imparted something mysterious by his way of referring to them, to that delicious intimacy, he made

me ask myself what it could have been like; I felt that everything that
had been told me about the Verdurins was far too coarse; and indeed, in
the case of Swann whom I had known, I reproached myself with not having
paid him sufficient attention, with not having paid attention to him in a
sufficiently disinterested spirit, with not having listened to him properly
when he used to entertain me while we waited for his wife to come home
for luncheon and he shewed me his treasures, now that I knew that he was
to be classed with the most brilliant talkers of the past. Just as we were
coming to Mme. Verdurin's doorstep, I caught sight of M. de Charlus,
steering towards us the bulk of his huge body, drawing unwillingly in his
wake one of those blackmailers or mendicants who nowadays, whenever
he appeared, sprang up without fail even in what were to all appearance
the most deserted corners, by whom this powerful monster was, evidently
against his will, invariably escorted, although at a certain distance, as is
the shark by its pilot, in short contrasting so markedly with the haughty
stranger of my first visit to Balbec, with his stern aspect, his affectation of
virility, that I seemed to be discovering, accompanied by its satellite, a
planet at a wholly different period of its revolution, when one begins to
see it full, or a sick man now devoured by the malady which a few years
ago was but a tiny spot which was easily concealed and the gravity of
which was never suspected. Although the operation that Brichot had undergone had restored a tiny portion of the sight which he had thought to be
lost for ever, I do not think he had observed the ruffian following in the
Baron's steps. Not that this mattered, for, ever since la Raspelière, and
notwithstanding the professor's friendly regard for M. de Charlus, the
sight of the latter always made him feel ill at ease. No doubt to every man
the life of every other extends along shadowy paths which he does not suspect. Falsehood, however, so often treacherous, upon which all conversation is based, conceals less perfectly a feeling of hostility, or of sordid
interest, or a visit which we wish to look as though we had not paid, or an
escapade with the mistress of a day which we are anxious to keep from
our wife, than a good reputation covers up—so as not to let their existence
be guessed—evil habits. They may remain unknown to us for a lifetime;
an accidental encounter upon a pier, at night, will disclose them; even then
this accidental discovery is frequently misunderstood and we require a
third person, who is in the secret, to supply the unimaginable clue of which
everyone is unaware. But, once we know about them, they alarm us because we feel that that way madness lies, far more than by their immorality.
Mme. de Surgis did not possess the slightest trace of any moral feeling,
and would have admitted anything of her sons that could be degraded and
explained by material interest, which is comprehensible to all mankind!
But she forbade them to go on visiting M. de Charlus when she learned
that, by a sort of internal clockwork, he was inevitably drawn upon each
of their visits, to pinch their chins and to make each of them pinch his
brother's. She felt that uneasy sense of a physical mystery which makes
us ask ourself whether the neighbour with whom we have been on friendly
terms is not tainted with cannibalism, and to the Baron's repeated in-
quiry: "When am I going to see your sons again?" she would reply, con-

scious of the thunderbolts that she was attracting to her defenceless head, that they were very busy working for examinations, preparing to go abroad, and so forth. Irresponsibility aggravates faults, and even crimes, whatever anyone may say. Landru (assuming that he really did kill his wives) if he did so from a financial motive, which it is possible to resist, may be pardoned, but not if his crime was due to an irresistible Sadism.

PART II

CHAPTER TWO (*continued*)

THE VERDURINS QUARREL WITH M. DE CHARLUS

BRICHOT'S coarse pleasantries, in the early days of his friendship with the Baron, had given place, as soon as it was a question, not of uttering commonplaces, but of understanding, to an awkward feeling which concealed a certain merriment. He reassured himself by recalling pages of Plato, lines of Virgil, because, being mentally as well as physically blind, he did not understand that in those days to fall in love with a young man was like, in our day (Socrates's jokes reveal this more clearly than Plato's theories), keeping a dancing girl before one marries and settles down. M. de Charlus himself would not have understood, he who confused his mania with friendship, which does not resemble it in the least, and the athletes of Praxiteles with obliging boxers. He refused to see that for the last nineteen hundred years ("a pious courtier under a pious prince would have been an atheist under an atheist prince," as Labruyère reminds us) all conventional homosexuality—that of Plato's young friends as well as that of Virgil's shepherds—has disappeared, that what survives and increases is only the involuntary, the neurotic kind, which we conceal from other people and disguise to ourselves. And M. de Charlus would have been wrong in not denying frankly the pagan genealogy. In exchange for a little plastic beauty, how vast the moral superiority! The shepherd in Theocritus who sighs for love of a boy, later on will have no reason to be less hard of heart, less dull of wit than the other shepherd whose flute sounds for Amaryllis. For the former is not suffering from a malady, he is conforming to the customs of his time. It is the homosexuality that survives in spite of obstacles, a thing of scorn and loathing, that is the only true form, the only form that can be found conjoined in a person with an enhancement of his moral qualities. We are appalled at the apparently close relation between these and our bodily attributes, when we think of the slight dislocation of a purely physical taste, the slight blemish in one of the senses, which explain why the world of poets and musicians, so firmly barred against the Duc de Guermantes, opens its portals to M. de Charlus. That the latter should shew taste in the furnishing of his home, which is that of an eclectic housewife, need not surprise us; but the narrow loophole that opens upon Beethoven and Veronese! This does not exempt the sane from a feeling of alarm when a madman who has composed a sublime poem, after explaining to them in the most logical fashion that he has been shut up by mistake, through his wife's machinations, imploring them to intercede for him with the governor of the asylum, complaining of the promiscuous company that is forced upon him, concludes as follows: "You see that man who is waiting to speak to me on the lawn, whom I am obliged to put up with; he thinks that he is Jesus Christ. That alone will shew you the sort of lunatics that I have to live among; he cannot be Christ, for I am Christ myself!" A moment earlier, you were on the point of going to assure the governor that a mistake had been made. At this final speech, even if you bear in mind the admirable poem at which this same man is working every day, you shrink from him, as Mme. de Surgis's sons shrank from M. de Charlus, not that he would have done them any harm, but because of his ceaseless invitations, the ultimate purpose of which was to pinch their chins. The poet is to be pitied, who must, with no Virgil to guide him, pass through the circles of an inferno of sulphur and brimstone, to cast himself into the fire that falls from heaven, in order to rescue a few of the inhabitants of Sodom! No charm in his work; the same severity in his life as in those of the unfrocked priests who follow the strictest rule of celibacy so that no one may be able to ascribe to anything but loss of faith their discarding of the cassock.

Making a pretence of not seeing the seedy individual who was following in his wake (whenever the Baron ventured into the Boulevards or crossed the waiting-room in Saint-Lazarre station, these followers might be counted by the dozen who, in the hope of 'touching him for a dollar,' never let him out of their sight), and afraid at the same time that the other might have the audacity to accost him, the Baron had devoutly lowered his darkened eyelids which, in contrast to his rice-powdered cheeks, gave him the appearance of a Grand Inquisitor painted by El Greco. But this priestly expression caused alarm, and he looked like an unfrocked priest, various compromises to which he had been driven by the need to apologise for his taste and to keep it secret having had the effect of bringing to the surface of his face precisely what the Baron sought to conceal, a debauched life indicated by moral decay. This last, indeed, whatever be its cause, is easily detected, for it is never slow in taking bodily form and proliferates upon a face, especially on the cheeks and round the eyes, as physically as the ochreous yellows accumulate there in a case of jaundice or repulsive reds in a case of skin disease. Nor was it merely in the cheeks, or rather the chaps of this painted face, in the mammiferous chest, the aggressive rump of this body allowed to deteriorate and invaded by obesity, upon which there now floated iridescent as a film of oil, the vice at one time so jealously confined by M. de Charlus in the most secret chamber of his heart. Now it overflowed in all his speech.

"So this is how you prowl the streets at night, Brichot, with a goodlooking young man," he said as he joined us, while the disappointed ruffian made off. "A fine example. We must tell your young pupils at the Sorbonne that this is how you behave. But, I must say, the society of youth seems to be good for you, Monsieur le Professeur, you are as fresh as a rosebud. I have interrupted you, you looked as though you were enjoying yourselves like a pair of giddy girls, and had no need of an old Granny Killjoy like myself. I shan't take it to the confessional, since you are

almost at your destination." The Baron's mood was all the more blithe
since he knew nothing whatever about the scene that afternoon, Jupien
having decided that it was better to protect his niece against a repetition
of the onslaught than to inform M. de Charlus. And so the Baron was still
looking forward to the marriage, and delighting in the thought of it. One
would suppose that it is a consolation to these great solitaries to give their
tragic celibacy the relief of a fictitious fatherhood. "But, upon my word,
Brichot," he went on, turning with a laugh to gaze at us, "I feel quite
awkward when I see you in such gallant company. You were like a pair of
lovers. Going along arm in arm, I say, Brichot, you do go the pace!"
Ought one to ascribe this speech to the senility of a particular state of
mind, less capable than in the past of controlling its reflexes, which in
moments of automatism lets out a secret that has been so carefully hidden
for forty years? Or rather to that contempt for plebeian opinion which
all the Guermantes felt in their hearts, and of which M. de Charlus's
brother, the Duke, was displaying a variant form when, regardless of the
fact that my mother could see him, he used to shave standing by his bedroom window in his unbuttoned nightshirt. Had M. de Charlus contracted,
during the roasting journeys between Doncières and Douville, the dangerous habit of making himself at ease, and, just as he would push back
his straw hat in order to cool his huge forehead, of unfastening—at first,
for a few moments only—the mask that for too long had been rigorously
imposed upon his true face? His conjugal attitude towards Morel might
well have astonished anyone who had observed it in its full extent. But
M. de Charlus had reached the stage when the monotony of the pleasures
that his vice has to offer became wearying. He had sought instinctively
for novel displays, and, growing tired of the strangers whom he picked
up, had passed to the opposite pole, to what he used to imagine that he
would always loathe, the imitation of family life, or of fatherhood. Sometimes even this did not suffice him, he required novelty, and would go
and spend the night with a woman, just as a normal man may, once in his
life, have wished to go to bed with a boy, from a curiosity similar though
inverse, and in either case equally unhealthy. The Baron's existence as
one of the 'faithful,' living, for Charlie's sake, entirely among the little
clan, had had, in stultifying the efforts that he had been making for years
to keep up lying appearances, the same influence that a voyage of exploration or residence in the colonies has upon certain Europeans who discard
the ruling principles by which they were guided at home. And yet, the
internal revolution of a mind, ignorant at first of the anomaly contained
in its body, then appalled at it after the discovery, and finally growing
so used to it as to fail to perceive that it is not safe to confess to other
people what the sinner has come in time to confess without shame to himself, had been even more effective in liberating M. de Charlus from the
last vestiges of social constraint than the time that he spent at the Verdurins'. No banishment, indeed, to the South Pole, or to the summit of
Mont Blanc, can separate us so entirely from our fellow creatures as a
prolonged residence in the seclusion of a secret vice, that is to say of a
state of mind that is different from theirs. A vice (so M. de Charlus used

at one time to style it) to which the Baron now gave the genial aspect of
a mere failing, extremely common, attractive on the whole and almost
amusing, like laziness, absent-mindedness or greed. Conscious of the
curiosity that his own striking personality aroused, M. de Charlus derived
a certain pleasure from satisfying, whetting, sustaining it. Just as a
Jewish journalist will come forward day after day as the champion of
Catholicism, not, probably, with any hope of being taken seriously, but
simply in order not to disappoint the good-natured amusement of his
readers, M. de Charlus would genially denounce evil habits among the
little clan, as he would have mimicked a person speaking English or
imitated Mounet-Sully, without waiting to be asked, so as to pay his scot
with a good grace, by displaying an amateur talent in society; so that
M. de Charlus now threatened Brichot that he would report to the Sorbonne that he was in the habit of walking about with young men, exactly
as the circumcised scribe keeps referring in and out of season to the 'Eldest
Daughter of the Church' and the 'Sacred Heart of Jesus,' that is to say
without the least trace of hypocrisy, but with a distinctly histrionic effect.
It was not only the change in the words themselves, so different from those
that he allowed himself to use in the past, that seemed to require some
explanation, there was also the change that had occurred in his intonations,
his gestures, all of which now singularly resembled the type M. de Charlus
used most fiercely to castigate; he would now utter unconsciously almost
the same little cries (unconscious in him, and all the more deep-rooted)
as are uttered consciously by the inverts who refer to one another as 'she';
as though this deliberate 'camping,' against which M. de Charlus had for
so long set his face, were after all merely a brilliant and faithful imitation
of the manner that men of the Charlus type, whatever they may say, are
compelled to adopt when they have reached a certain stage in their malady,
just as sufferers from general paralysis or locomotor ataxia inevitably end
by displaying certain symptoms. As a matter of fact—and this is what this
purely unconscious 'camping' revealed—the difference between the stern
Charlus, dressed all in black, with his stiffly brushed hair, whom I had
known, and the painted young men, loaded with rings, was no more than
the purely imaginary difference that exists between an excited person who
talks fast, keeps moving all the time, and a neurotic who talks slowly,
preserves a perpetual phlegm, but is tainted with the same neurasthenia
in the eyes of the physician who knows that each of the two is devoured
by the same anguish and marred by the same defects. At the same time
one could tell that M. de Charlus had aged from wholly different signs,
such as the extraordinary frequency in his conversation of certain expressions that had taken root in it and used now to crop up at every moment
(for instance: 'the chain of circumstances') upon which the Baron's
speech leaned in sentence after sentence as upon a necessary prop. "Is
Charlie here yet?" Brichot asked M. de Charlus as we came in sight of
the door. "Oh, I don't know," said the Baron, raising his arms and half-
shutting his eyes with the air of a person who does not wish anyone to
accuse him of being indiscreet, all the·more so as he had probably been
reproached by Morel for things which he had said and which the other,

as timorous as he was vain, and as ready to deny M. de Charlus as he was
to boast of his friendship, had considered serious albeit they were quite
unimportant. "You know, he never tells me what he's going to do." If the
conversations of two people bound by a tie of intimacy are full of falsehood, this occurs no less spontaneously in the conversations that a third
person holds with a lover on the subject of the person with whom the
latter is in love, whatever be the sex of that person.

"Have you seen him lately?" I asked M. de Charlus, with the object of
seeming at once not to be afraid of mentioning Morel to him and not to
believe that they were actually living together. "He came in, as it happened, for five minutes this morning while I was still half asleep, and sat
down on the side of my bed, as though he wanted to ravish me." I guessed
at once that M. de Charlus had seen Charlie within the last hour, for if
we ask a woman when she last saw the man whom we know to be—and
whom she may perhaps suppose that we suspect of being—her lover, if
she has just taken tea with him, she replies: "I saw him for an instant
before luncheon." Between these two incidents the only difference is that
one is false and the other true, but both are equally innocent, or, if you
prefer it, equally culpable. And so we should be unable to understand why
the mistress (in this case, M. de Charlus) always chooses the false version, did we not know that such replies are determined, unknown to the
person who utters them, by a number of factors which appear so out of
proportion to the triviality of the incident that we do not take the trouble
to consider them. But to a physicist the space occupied by the tiniest ball
of pith is explained by the harmony of action, the conflict or equilibrium,
of laws of attraction or repulsion which govern far greater worlds. Just
as many different laws acting in opposite directions dictate the more general
responses with regard to the innocence, the 'platonism,' or on the contrary the carnal reality of the relations that one has with the person whom
one says one saw in the morning when one has seen him or her in the evening. Here we need merely record, without pausing to consider them, the
desire to appear natural and fearless, the instinctive impulse to conceal a
secret assignation, a blend of modesty and ostentation, the need to confess
what one finds so delightful and to shew that one is loved, a divination of
what the other person knows or guesses—but does not say—a divination
which, exceeding or falling short of the other person's, makes one now
exaggerate, now under-estimate it, the spontaneous longing to play with
fire and the determination to rescue something from the blaze. At the same
time, speaking generally, let us say that M. de Charlus, notwithstanding
the aggravation of his malady which perpetually urged him to reveal, to
insinuate, sometimes boldly to invent compromising details, did intend,
during this period in his life, to make it known that Charlie was not a man
of the same sort as himself and that they were friends and nothing more.
This did not prevent him (even though it may quite possibly have been
true) from contradicting himself at times (as with regard to the hour at
which they had last met), whether he forgot himself at such moments and
told the truth, or invented a lie, boastingly or from a sentimental affectation or because he thought it amusing to baffle his questioner. "You know

that he is to me," the Baron went on, "the best of comrades, for whom I have the greatest affection, as I am certain" (was he uncertain of it, then, that he felt the need to say that he was certain?) "he has for me, but there is nothing at all between us, nothing of that sort, you understand, nothing of that sort," said the Baron, as naturally as though he had been speaking of a woman. "Yes, he came in this morning to pull me out of bed. Though he knows that I hate anybody to see me in bed. You don't mind? Oh, it's horrible, it's so disturbing, one looks so perfectly hideous, of course I'm no longer five-and-twenty, they won't choose me to be Queen of the May, still one does like to feel that one is looking one's best."

It is possible that the Baron was in earnest when he spoke of Morel as a good comrade, and that he was being even more truthful than he supposed when he said: "I never know what he's doing; he tells me nothing about his life."

Indeed we may mention (interrupting for a few moments our narrative, which shall be resumed immediately after the closure of this parenthesis which opens at the moment when M. de Charlus, Brichot and myself are arriving at Mme. Verdurin's front door), we may mention that shortly before this evening the Baron had been plunged in grief and stupefaction by a letter which he had opened by mistake and which was addressed to Morel. This letter, which by a repercussion was to cause intense misery to myself also, was written by the actress Léa, notorious for her exclusive interest in women. And yet her letter to Morel (whom M. de Charlus had never suspected of knowing her, even) was written in the most impassioned tone. Its indelicacy prevents us from reproducing it here, but we may mention that Léa addressed him throughout in the feminine gender, with such expressions as: "Go on, you bad woman!" or "Of course you are so, my pretty, you know you are." And in this letter reference was made to various other women who seemed to be no less Morel's friends than Léa's. On the other hand, Morel's sarcasm at the Baron's expense and Léa's at that of an officer who was keeping her, and of whom she said: "He keeps writing me letters begging me to be careful! What do you say to that, my little white puss," revealed to M. de Charlus a state of things no less unsuspected by him than were Morel's peculiar and intimate relations with Léa. What most disturbed the Baron was the word 'so.' Ignorant at first of its application, he had eventually, at a time already remote in the past, learned that he himself was 'so.' And now the notion that he had acquired of this word was again put to the challenge. When he had discovered that he was 'so,' he had supposed this to mean that his tastes, as Saint-Simon says, did not lie in the direction of women. And here was this word 'so' applied to Morel with an extension of meaning of which M. de Charlus was unaware, so much so that Morel gave proof, according to this letter, of his being 'so' by having the same taste as certain women for other women. From that moment the Baron's jealousy had no longer any reason to confine itself to the men of Morel's acquaintance, but began to extend to the women also. So that the people who were 'so' were not merely those that he had supposed to be 'so,' but a whole and vast section of the inhabitants of the planet, consisting of women as well as of men, loving not merely men but women also, and the Baron, in the face of this novel meaning of a word that was so familiar to him, felt himself tormented by an anxiety of the mind as well as of the heart, born of this twofold mystery which combined an extension of the field of his jealousy with the sudden inadequacy of a definition.

M. de Charlus had never in his life been anything but an amateur. That is to say, incidents of this sort could never be of any use to him. He worked off the painful impression that they might make upon him in violent scenes in which he was a past-master of eloquence, or in crafty intrigues. But to a person endowed with the qualities of a Bergotte, for instance, they might have been of inestimable value. This may indeed explain, to a certain extent (since we have to grope blindfold, but choose, like the lower animals, the herb that is good for us), why men like Bergotte have generally lived in the company of persons who were ordinary, false and malicious. Their beauty is sufficient for the writer's imagination, enhances his generosity, but does not in any way alter the nature of his companion, whose life, situated thousands of feet below the level of his own, her incredible stories, her lies carried farther, and, what is more, in another direction than what might have been expected, appear in occasional flashes. The lie, the perfect lie, about people whom we know, about the relations that we have had with them, about our motive for some action, a motive which we express in totally different terms, the lie as to what we are, whom we love, what we feel with regard to the person who loves us and believes that she has fashioned us in her own image because she keeps on kissing us morning, noon and night, that lie is one of the only things in the world that can open a window for us upon what is novel, unknown, that can awaken in us sleeping senses to the contemplation of universes that otherwise we should never have known. We are bound to say, in so far as M. de Charlus is concerned, that, if he was stupefied to learn with regard to Morel a certain number of things which the latter had carefully concealed from him, he was not justified in concluding from this that it was a mistake to associate too closely with the lower orders. We shall indeed see, in the concluding section of this work, M. de Charlus himself engaged in doing things which would have stupefied the members of his family and his friends far more than he could possibly have been stupefied by the revelations of Léa. (The revelation that he had found most painful had been that of a tour which Morel had made with Léa, whereas at the time he had assured M. de Charlus that he was studying music in Germany. He had found support for this falsehood in obliging friends in Germany to whom he had sent his letters, to be forwarded from there to M. de Charlus, who, as it happened, was so positive that Morel was there that he had not even looked at the postmark.) But it is time to rejoin the Baron as he advances with Brichot and myself towards the Verdurins' door.

"And what," he went on, turning to myself, "has become of your young Hebrew friend, whom we met at Douville? It occurred to me that, if you liked, one might perhaps invite him to the house one evening." For M. de Charlus, who did not shrink from employing a private detective to spy upon every word and action of Morel, for all the world like a husband or a lover, had not ceased to pay attention to other young men. The vigilance which he made one of his old servants maintain, through an agency, upon Morel, was so indiscreet that his footmen thought they were being watched, and one of the housemaids could not endure the suspense, never ventured into the street, always expecting to find a policeman at her heels. "She can do whatever she likes! It would be a waste of time and money to follow her! As if her goings on mattered to us!" the old servant ironically exclaimed, for he was so passionately devoted to his master that, albeit he in no way shared the Baron's tastes, he had come in time, with such ardour did he employ himself in their service, to speak of them as though they were his own. "He is the very best of good fellows," M. de Charlus would say of this old servant, for we never appreciate anyone so much as those who combine with other great virtues that of placing themselves unconditionally at the disposal of our vices. It was moreover of men alone that M. de Charlus was capable of feeling any jealousy so far as Morel was concerned. Women inspired in him no jealousy whatever. This is indeed an almost universal rule with the Charlus type. The love of the man with whom they are in love for women is something different, which occurs in another animal species (a lion does not interfere with tigers); does not distress them; if anything, reassures them. Sometimes, it is true, in the case of those who exalt their inversion to the level of a priesthood, this love creates disgust. These men resent their friends' having succumbed to it, not as a betrayal but as a lapse from virtue. A Charlus, of a different variety from the Baron, would have been as indignant at the discovery of Morel's relations with a woman as upon reading in a newspaper that he, the interpreter of Bach and Händel, was going to play Puccini. It is, by the way, for this reason that the young men who, with an eye to their own personal advantage, condescend to the love of men like Charlus, assure them that women inspire them only with disgust, just as they would tell a doctor that they never touch alcohol, and care only for spring water. But M. de Charlus, in this respect, departed to some extent from the general rule. Since he admired everything about Morel, the latter's successes with women caused him no annoyance, gave him the same joy as his successes on the platform, or at écarté. "But do you know, my dear fellow, he has women," he would say, with an air of disclosure, of scandal, possibly of envy, above all of admiration. "He is extraordinary," he would continue. "Everywhere, the most famous whores can look at nobody but him. They stare at him everywhere, whether it's on the underground or in the theatre. It's becoming a nuisance! I can't go out with him to a restaurant without the waiter bringing him notes from at least three women. And always pretty women too. Not that there's anything surprising in that. I was watching him yesterday, I can quite understand it, he has become so beautiful, he looks just like a Bronzino, he is really marvellous." But M. de Charlus liked to shew that he was in love with Morel, to persuade other people, possibly to persuade himself, that Morel was in love with him. He applied to the purpose of having Morel always with him (notwithstanding the harm that the young fellow might do to the Baron's social position) a sort of self-esteem. For (and this is frequent among men of good position, who are snobs, and, in their vanity, sever all their social ties in order to be seen everywhere with a mistress, a person of doubtful or a lady of tarnished reputation, whom nobody will invite, and with whom nevertheless it seems to them flattering to be associated) he had arrived at that stage at which self-esteem devotes all its energy to destroying the goals to which it has attained, whether because, under the influence of love, a man finds a prestige which he is alone in perceiving in ostentatious relations with the beloved object, or because, by the waning of social ambitions that have been gratified, and the rising of a tide of subsidiary curiosities all the more absorbing the more platonic they are, the latter have not only reached but have passed the level at which the former found it difficult to remain.

As for young men in general, M. de Charlus found that to his fondness for them Morel's existence was not an obstacle, and that indeed his brilliant reputation as a violinist or his growing fame as a composer and journalist might in certain instances prove an attraction. Did anyone introduce to the Baron a young composer of an agreeable type, it was in Morel's talents that he sought an opportunity of doing the stranger a favour. "You must," he would tell him, "bring me some of your work so that Morel can play it at a concert or on tour. There is hardly any decent music written, now, for the violin. It is a godsend to find anything new. And abroad they appreciate that sort of thing enormously. Even in the provinces there are little musical societies where they love music with a fervour and intelligence that are quite admirable." Without any greater sincerity (for all this could serve only as a bait and it was seldom that Morel condescended to fulfil these promises), Bloch having confessed that he was something of a poet (when he was 'in the mood,' he had added with the sarcastic laugh with which he would accompany a platitude, when he could think of nothing original), M. de Charlus said to me: "You must tell your young Israelite, since he writes verses, that he must really bring me some for Morel. For a composer, that is always the stumbling block, to find something decent to set to music. One might even consider a libretto. It would not be without interest, and would acquire a certain value from the distinction of the poet, from my patronage, from a whole chain of auxiliary circumstances, among which Morel's talent would take the chief place, for he is composing a lot just now, and writing too, and very pleasantly, I must talk to you about it. As for his talent as a performer (there, as you know, he is already a past-master), you shall see this evening how well the lad plays Vinteuil's music; he overwhelms me; at his age, to have such an understanding while he is still such a boy, such a kid! Oh, this evening is only to be a little rehearsal. The big affair is to come off in two or three days. But it will be much more distinguished this evening. And so we are delighted that you have come," he went on, employing the plural pronoun doubtless because a King says: "It is our wish." "The programme is so magnificent that I have advised Mme. Verdurin to give two parties. One in a few days' time, at which she will have all her own friends, the other to-night at which the hostess is, to use a legal expression, 'disseized.' It is I who have issued the invitations, and I have collected a few people from another sphere, who may be useful to Charlie, and whom it will be nice for the Verdurins to meet. Don't you agree, it is all very well to have the finest music played by the greatest artists, the effect of the performance remains muffled in cotton-wool, if the audience is composed of the milliner from across the way and the grocer from round the corner. You know what I think of the intellectual level of people in society, still they can play certain quite important parts, among others that which in public events devolves upon the press, and which is that of being an organ of publicity. You know what I mean; I have for instance invited my sister-in-law Oriane; it is not certain that she will come, but it is on the other hand certain that, if she does come, she will understand absolutely nothing. But one does not ask her to understand, which is beyond her capacity, but to talk, a task which is admirably suited to her, and which she never fails to perform. What is the result? To-morrow as ever is, instead of the silence of the milliner and the grocer, an animated conversation at the Mortemarts' with Oriane telling everyone that she has heard the most marvellous music, that a certain Morel, and so forth; unspeakable rage of the people not invited, who will say: 'Palamède thought, no doubt, that we were unworthy; anyhow, who are these people who were giving the party?' a counterblast quite as useful as Oriane's praises, because Morel's name keeps cropping up all the time and is finally engraved in the memory like a lesson that one has read over a dozen times. All this forms a chain of circumstances which may be of value to the artist, to the hostess, may serve as a sort of megaphone for a performance which will thus be made audible to a remote public. Really, it is worth the trouble; you shall see what progress Charlie has made. And what is more, we have discovered a new talent in him, my dear fellow, he writes like an angel. Like an angel, I tell you." M. de Charlus omitted to say that for some time past he had been employing Morel, like those great noblemen of the seventeenth century who scorned to sign and even to write their own slanderous attacks, to compose certain vilely calumnious little paragraphs at the expense of Comtesse Molé. Their insolence apparent even to those who merely glanced at them, how much more cruel were they to the young woman herself, who found in them, so skilfully introduced that nobody but herself saw the point, certain passages from her own correspondence, textually quoted, but interpreted in a sense which made them as deadly as the cruellest revenge. They killed the lady. But there is edited every day in Paris, Balzac would tell us, a sort of spoken newspaper, more terrible than its printed rivals. We shall see later on that this verbal press reduced to nothing the power of a Charlus who had fallen out of fashion, and exalted far above him a Morel who was not worth the millionth part of his former patron. Is this intellectual fashion really so simple, and does it sincerely believe in the nullity of a Charlus of genius, in the incontestable authority of a crass Morel? The Baron was not so innocent in his implacable vengeance. Whence, no doubt, that bitter venom on his tongue, the spreading of which seemed to dye his cheeks with jaundice when he was in a rage. "You who knew Bergotte," M. de Charlus went on, "I thought at one time that you might, perhaps, by refreshing his memory with regard to the youngster's writings, collaborate in short with myself, help me to assist a two-fold talent, that of a musician and a writer, which may one day acquire the prestige of that of Berlioz. As you know, the Illustrious have often other things to think about, they are smothered in flattery, they take little interest except in themselves. But Bergotte, who was genuinely unpretentious and obliging, promised me that he would get into the *Gaulois*, or some such paper, those little articles, a blend of the humourist and the musician, which he really does quite charmingly now, and I am really very glad that Charlie should combine with his violin this little stroke of Ingres's pen. I know that I am prone to exaggeration, when he is concerned, like all the old fairy godmothers of the Conservatoire. What, my dear fellow, didn't you know that? You have never observed my little weakness. I pace up and down for hours on end outside the examination hall. I'm as happy as a queen. As for Charlie's prose, Bergotte assured me that it was really very good indeed."

M. de Charlus, who had long been acquainted with Bergotte through Swann, had indeed gone to see him a few days before his death, to ask him to find an opening for Morel in some newspaper for a sort of commentary, half humorous, upon the music of the day. In doing so, M. de Charlus had felt some remorse, for, himself a great admirer of Bergotte, he was conscious that he never went to see him for his own sake, but in order, thanks to the respect, partly intellectual, partly social, that Bergotte felt for him, to be able to do a great service to Morel, or to some other of his friends. That he no longer made use of people in society for any other purpose did not shock M. de Charlus, but to treat Bergotte thus had appeared to him more offensive, for he felt that Bergotte had not the calculating nature of people in society, and deserved better treatment. Only, his was a busy life, and he could never find time for anything except when he was greatly interested in something, when, for instance, it. affected Morel. What was more, as he was himself extremely intelligent, the conversation of an intelligent man left him comparatively cold, especially that of Bergotte who was too much the man of letters for his liking and belonged to another clan, did not share his point of view. As for Bergotte, he had observed the calculated motive of M. de Charlus's visits, but had felt no resentment, for he had been incapable, throughout his life, of any consecutive generosity, but anxious to give pleasure, broadminded, insensitive to the pleasure of administering a rebuke. As for M. de Charlus's vice, he had never partaken of it to the smallest extent, but had found in it rather an element of colour in the person affected, *fas et nefas*, for an artist, consisting not in moral examples but in memories of Plato or of Sodom. "But you, fair youth, we never see you at Quai Conti. You don't abuse their hospitality!" I explained that I went out as a rule with my cousin. "Do you hear that! He goes out with his cousin! What a most particularly pure young man!" said M. de Charlus to Brichot. Then, turning again to myself: "But we are not asking you to give an account of your life, my boy. You are free to do anything that amuses you. We merely regret that we have no share in it. Besides, you shew very good taste, your cousin is charming, ask Brichot, she quite turned his head at Douville. We shall regret her absence this evening. But you did just as well, perhaps, not to bring her with you. Vinteuil's music is delightful. But I have heard that we are to meet the composer's daughter and her friend, who have a terrible reputation. That sort of thing is always awkward for a girl. They are sure to be there, unless the ladies have been detained in the country, for they were to have been present without fail all afternoon at a rehearsal which Mme. Verdurin was giving to-day, to which she had invited only the bores, her family, the people whom she could not very well have this evening. But a moment ago, before dinner, Charlie told us that the sisters Vinteuil. as we call them, for whom they were all waiting, never came." Notwithstanding the intense pain that I had felt at the sudden association with its effect, of which alone I had been aware, of the cause, at length discovered, of Albertine's anxiety to be there that afternoon, the presence publicly announced (but of which I had been ignorant) of Mlle. Vinteuil and her friend, my mind was still sufficiently detached to remark that M. de Charlus, who had told us, a few minutes earlier, that he had not seen Charlie since the morning, was now brazenly admitting that he had seen him before dinner. My pain became visible. "Why, what is the matter with you?" said the Baron. "You are quite green; come, let us go in, you will catch cold, you don't look at all well." It was not any doubt as to Albertine's virtue that M. de Charlus's words had awakened in me. Many other doubts had penetrated my mind already; at each fresh doubt we feel that the measure is heaped full, that we cannot cope with it, then we manage to find room for it all the same, and once it is introduced into our vital essence it enters into competition there with so many longings to believe, so many reasons to forget, that we speedily become accustomed to it, and end by ceasing to pay it any attention. There remains only, like a partly healed pain, the menace of possible suffering, which, the counterpart of desire, a feeling of the same order, and like it become the centre of our thoughts, radiates through them to an infinite circumference a wistful melancholy, as desire radiates pleasures whose origin we fail to perceive, wherever anything may suggest the idea of the person with whom we are in love. But pain revives as soon as a fresh doubt enters our mind complete; even if we assure ourself almost immediately: "I shall deal with this, there must be some method by which I need not suffer, it cannot be true," nevertheless there has been a first moment in which we suffered as though we believed it. If we had merely members, such as legs and arms, life would be endurable; unfortunately we carry inside us that little organ which we call the heart, which is subject to certain maladies in the course of which it is infinitely impressionable by everything that concerns the life of a certain person, so that a lie—that most harmless of things, in the midst of which we live so unconcernedly, if the lie be told by ourselves or by strangers—coming from that person, causes the little heart, which surgeons ought really to be able to excise from us, intolerable anguish. Let us not speak of the brain, for our mind may go on reasoning interminably in the course of this anguish, it does no more to mitigate it than by taking thought can we soothe an aching tooth. It is true that this person is to blame for having lied to us, for she had sworn to us that she would always tell us the truth.

But we know from our own shortcomings, towards other people, how little an oath is worth. And we have deliberately believed them when they came from her, the very person to whose interest it has always been to lie to us, and whom, moreover, we did not select for her virtues. It is true that, later on, she would almost cease to have any need to lie to us—at the moment when our heart will have grown indifferent to her falsehood—because then we shall not feel any interest in her life. We know this, and, notwithstanding, we deliberately sacrifice our own lives, either by killing ourselves for her sake, or by letting ourselves be sentenced to death for having murdered her, or simply by spending, in the course of a few evenings, our whole fortune upon her, which will oblige us presently to commit suicide because we have not a penny in the world. Besides, however calm we may imagine ourselves when we are in love, we always have love in our heart in a state of un-stable equilibrium. A trifle is sufficient to exalt it to the position of happi-ness, we radiate happiness, we smother in our affection not her whom we love, but those who have given us merit in her eyes, who have protected her from every evil temptation; we think that our mind is at ease, and a word is sufficient: 'Gilberte is not coming,' 'Mademoiselle Vinteuil is ex-pected,' to make all the preconceived happiness towards which we were rising collapse, to make the sun hide his face, to open the bag of the winds and let loose the internal tempest which one day we shall be incapable of resisting. That day, the day upon which the heart has become so frail, our friends who respect us are pained that such trifles, that certain persons, can so affect us, can bring us to death's door. But what are they to do? If a poet is dying of septic pneumonia, can one imagine his friends explain-ing to the pneumococcus that the poet is a man of talent and that it ought to let him recover? My doubt, in so far as it referred to Mlle. Vinteuil, was not entirely novel. But to a certain extent, my jealousy of the afternoon, inspired by Léa and her friends, had abolished it. Once that peril of the Trocadéro was removed, I had felt that I had recaptured for all time com-plete peace of mind. But what was entirely novel to me was a certain excur-sion as to which Andrée had told me: "We went to this place and that, we didn't meet anyone," and during which, on the contrary, Mlle. Vinteuil had evidently arranged to meet Albertine at Mme. Verdurin's. At this mo-ment I would gladly have allowed Albertine to go out by herself, to go wherever she might choose, provided that I might lock up Mlle. Vinteuil and her friend somewhere and be certain that Albertine would not meet them. The fact is that jealousy is, as a rule, partial, of intermittent appli-cation, whether because it is the painful extension of an anxiety which is provoked now by one person, now by another with whom our mistress may be in love, or because of the exiguity of our thought which is able to realise only what it can represent to itself and leaves everything else in an obscurity which can cause us only a proportionately modified anguish.

Just as we were about to ring the bell we were overtaken by Saniette who informed us that Princess Sherbatoff had died at six o'clock, and added that he had not at first recognised us. "I envisaged you, however, for some time," he told us in a breathless voice. "Is it aught but curious that I should have hesitated?" To say "Is it not curious" would have seemed to him wrong, and he had acquired a familiarity with obsolete forms of speech that was becoming exasperating. "Not but what you are people whom one may acknowledge as friends." His grey complexion seemed to be illuminated by the livid glow of a storm. His breathlessness, which had been noticeable, as recently as last summer, only when M. Verdurin 'jumped down his throat,' was now continuous. "I understand that an unknown work of Vinteuil is to be performed by excellent artists, and singularly by Morel." "Why singularly?" inquired the Baron who detected a criticism in the adverb. "Our friend Saniette," Brichot made haste to exclaim, acting as interpreter, "is prone to speak, like the excellent scholar that he is, the language of an age in which 'singularly' was equivalent to our 'especially.' "

As we entered the Verdurins' hall, M. de Charlus asked me whether I was engaged upon any work and as I told him that I was not, but that I was greatly interested at the moment in old dinner-services of plate and porcelain, he assured me that I could not see any finer than those that the Verdurins had; that moreover I might have seen them at la Raspelière, since, on the pretext that one's possessions are also one's friends, they were so silly as to cart everything down there with them; it would be less convenient to bring everything out for my benefit on the evening of a party; still, he would tell them to shew me anything that I wished to see. I begged him not to do anything of the sort. M. de Charlus unbuttoned his greatcoat, took off his hat, and I saw that the top of his head had now turned silver in patches. But like a precious shrub which is not only coloured with autumn tints but certain leaves of which are protected by bandages of wadding or incrustations of plaster, M. de Charlus received from these few white hairs at his crest only a further variegation added to those of his face. And yet, even beneath the layers of different expressions, paint and hypocrisy which formed such a bad 'make-up,' his face continued to hide from almost everyone the secret that it seemed to me to be crying aloud. I was almost put to shame by his eyes in which I was afraid of his surprising me in the act of reading it, as from an open book, by his voice which seemed to me to be repeating it in every tone, with an untiring indecency. But secrets are well kept by such people, for everyone who comes in contact with them is deaf and blind. The people who learned the truth from some one else, from the Verdurins for instance, believed it, but only for so long as they had not met M. de Charlus. His face, so far from spreading, dissipated every scandalous rumour. For we form so extravagant an idea of certain characters that we would be incapable of identifying one of them with the familiar features of a person of our acquaintance. And we find it difficult to believe in such a person's vices, just as we can never believe in the genius of a person with whom we went to the Opera last night.

M. de Charlus was engaged in handing over his greatcoat with the instructions of a familiar guest. But the footman to whom he was handing it was a newcomer, and quite young. Now M. de Charlus had by this time begun, as people say, to 'lose his bearings' and did not always remember what might and what might not be done. The praiseworthy desire that he had felt at Balbec to shew that certain topics did not alarm him, that he was not afraid to declare with regard to some one or other: "He is a nice-looking boy," to utter, in short, the same words as might have been uttered by somebody who was not like himself, this desire he had now begun to express by saying on the contrary things which nobody could ever have said who was not like him, things upon which his mind was so constantly fixed that he forgot that they do not form part of the habitual preoccupation of people in general. And so, as he gazed at the new footman, he raised his forefinger in the air in a menacing fashion and, thinking that he was making an excellent joke: "You are not to make eyes at me like that, do you hear?" said the Baron, and, turning to Brichot: "He has a quaint little face, that boy, his nose is rather fun," and, completing his joke, or yielding to a desire, he lowered his forefinger horizontally, hesitated for an instant, then, unable to control himself any longer, thrust it irresistibly forwards at the footman and touched the tip of his nose, saying "Pif!" "That's a rum card," the footman said to himself, and inquired of his companions whether it was a joke or what it was. "It is just a way he has," said the butler (who regarded the Baron as slightly 'touched,' 'a bit balmy'), "but he is one of Madame's friends for whom I have always had the greatest respect, he has a good heart."

"Are you coming back this year to Incarville?" Brichot asked me. "I believe that our hostess has taken la Raspelière again, for all that she has had a crow to pick with her landlords. But that is nothing, it is a cloud that passes," he added in the optimistic tone of the newspapers that say: "Mistakes have been made, it is true, but who does not make mistakes at times?" But I remembered the state of anguish in which I had left Balbec, and felt no desire to return there. I kept putting off to the morrow my plans for Albertine. "Why, of course he is coming back, we need him, he is indispensable to us," declared M. de Charlus with the authoritative and uncomprehending egoism of friendliness.

At this moment M. Verdurin appeared to welcome us. When we expressed our sympathy over Princess Sherbatoff, he said: "Yes, I believe she is rather ill." "No, no, she died at six o'clock," exclaimed Saniette. "Oh, you exaggerate everything," was M. Verdurin's brutal retort, for, since he had not cancelled his party, he preferred the hypothesis of illness, imitating unconsciously the Duc de Guermantes. Saniette, not without fear of catching cold, for the outer door was continually being opened, stood waiting resignedly for some one to take his hat and coat. "What are you hanging about there for, like a whipped dog?" M. Verdurin asked him. "I am waiting until one of the persons who are charged with the cloakroom can take my coat and give me a number." "What is that you say?" demanded M. Verdurin with a stern expression. " 'Charged with the cloakroom?' Are you going off your head? 'In charge of the cloakroom,' is what we say, if we've got to teach you to speak your own language, like a man who has had a stroke." "Charged with a thing is the correct form," murmured Saniette in a stifled tone; "the abbé Le Batteux. . . ." "You make me tired, you do," cried M. Verdurin in a voice of thunder. "How you do wheeze! Have you been running upstairs to an attic?" The effect of M.

Verdurin's rudeness was that the servants in the cloakroom allowed other guests to take precedence of Saniette and, when he tried to hand over his things, replied: "Wait for your turn, Sir, don't be in such a hurry." "There's system for you, competent fellows, that's right, my lads," said M. Verdurin with an approving smile, in order to encourage them in their tendency to keep Saniette waiting till the end. "Come along," he said to us, "the creature wants us all to catch our death hanging about in his beloved draught. Come and get warm in the drawing-room. 'Charged with the cloakroom,' indeed, what an idiot!" "He is inclined to be a little precious, but he's not a bad fellow," said Brichot. "I never said that he was a bad fellow, I said that he was an idiot," was M. Verdurin's harsh retort.

Meanwhile Mme. Verdurin was busily engaged with Cottard and Ski. Morel had just declined (because M. de Charlus could not be present) an invitation from some friends of hers to whom she had promised the services of the violinist. The reason for Morel's refusal to perform at the party which the Verdurins' friends were giving, a reason which we shall presently see reinforced by others of a far more serious kind, might have found its justification in a habit common to the leisured classes in general but specially distinctive of the little nucleus. To be sure, if Mme. Verdurin intercepted between a newcomer and one of the faithful a whispered speech which might let it be supposed that they were already acquainted, or wished to become more intimate ("On Friday, then, at So-and-So's," or "Come to the studio any day you like; I am always there until five o'clock, I shall look forward to seeing you"), agitated, supposing the newcomer to occupy a 'position' which would make him a brilliant recruit to the little clan, the Mistress, while pretending not to have heard anything, and preserving in her fine eyes, shadowed by the habit of listening to Debussy more than they would have been by that of sniffing cocaine, the extenuated expression that they derived from musical intoxication alone, revolved nevertheless behind her splendid brow, inflated by all those quartets and the headaches that were their consequence, thoughts which were not exclusively polyphonic, and unable to contain herself any longer, unable to postpone the injection for another instant, flung herself upon the speakers, drew them apart, and said to the newcomer, pointing to the 'faithful' one: "You wouldn't care to come and dine to meet *him*, next Saturday, shall we say, or any day you like, with some really nice people! Don't speak too loud, as I don't want to invite all this mob" (a word used to denote for five minutes the little nucleus, disdained for the moment in favour of the newcomer in whom so many hopes were placed).

But this infatuated impulse, this need to make friendly overtures, had its counterpart. Assiduous attendance at their Wednesdays aroused in the Verdurins an opposite tendency. This was the desire to quarrel, to hold aloof. It had been strengthened, had almost been wrought to a frenzy during the months spent at la Raspelière, where they were all together morning, noon and night. M. Verdurin went out of his way to prove one of his guests in the wrong, to spin webs in which he might hand over to his comrade spider some innocent fly. Failing a grievance, he would invent some absurdity. As soon as one of the faithful had been out of the house for half an hour, they would make fun of him in front of the others, would feign surprise that their guests had not noticed how his teeth were never clean, or how on the contrary he had a mania for brushing them twenty times a day. If any one took the liberty of opening a window, this want of breeding would cause a glance of disgust to pass between host and hostess. A moment later Mme. Verdurin would ask for a shawl, which gave M. Verdurin an excuse for saying in a tone of fury: "No, I shall close the window, I wonder who had the impertinence to open it," in the hearing of the guilty wretch who blushed to the roots of his hair. You were rebuked indirectly for the quantity of wine that you had drunk. "It won't do you any harm. Navvies thrive on it!" If two of the faithful went out together without first obtaining permission from the Mistress, their excursions led to endless comments, however innocent they might be. Those of M. de Charlus with Morel were not innocent. It was only the fact that M. de Charlus was not staying at la Raspelière (because Morel was obliged to live near his barracks) that retarded the hour of satiety, disgust, retching. That hour was, however, about to strike.

Mme. Verdurin was furious and determined to 'enlighten' Morel as to the ridiculous and detestable part that M. de Charlus was making him play. "I must add," she went on (Mme. Verdurin, when she felt that she owed anyone a debt of gratitude which would be a burden to him, and was unable to rid herself of it by killing him, would discover a serious defect in him which would honourably dispense her from shewing her gratitude), "I must add that he gives himself airs in my house which I do not at all like." The truth was that Mme. Verdurin had another more serious reason than Morel's refusal to play at her friends' party for picking a quarrel with M. de Charlus. The latter, overcome by the honour he was doing the Mistress in bringing to Quai Conti people who after all would never have come there for her sake, had, on hearing the first names that Mme. Verdurin had suggested as those of people who ought to be invited, pronounced the most categorical ban upon them in a peremptory tone which blended the rancorous pride of a crotchety nobleman with the dogmatism of the expert artist in questions of entertainment who would cancel his programme and withhold his collaboration sooner than agree to concessions which, in his opinion, would endanger the success of the whole. M. de Charlus had given his approval, hedging it round with reservations, to Saintine alone, with whom, in order not to be bothered with his wife, Mme. de Guermantes had passed, from a daily intimacy, to a complete severance of relations, but whom M. de Charlus, finding him intelligent, continued to see. True, it was among a middle-class set, with a cross-breeding of the minor nobility, where people are merely very rich and connected with an aristocracy whom the true aristocracy does not know, that Saintine, at one time the flower of the Guermantes set, had gone to seek his fortune and, he imagined, a social foothold. But Mme. Verdurin, knowing the blue-blooded pretensions of the wife's circle, and failing to take into account the husband's position (for it is what is immediately over our head that gives us the impression of altitude and not what is almost invisible to us, so far is it lost in the clouds), felt that she ought to justify an invitation of Saintine by pointing out that he knew a great many people, "having married Mlle. ———." The ignorance which this assertion, the direct opposite of the truth, revealed in Mme. Verdurin caused the Baron's painted lips to part in a smile of indulgent scorn and wide comprehension. He disdained a direct answer, but as he was always ready to express in social examples theories which shewed the fertility of his mind and the arrogance of his pride, with the inherited frivolity of his occupations: "Saintine ought to have come to me before marrying," he said, "there is such a thing as social as well as physiological eugenics, and I am perhaps the only specialist in existence. Saintine's case aroused no discussion, it was clear that, in making the marriage that he made, he was tying a stone to his neck, and hiding his light under a bushel. His social career was at an end. I should have explained this to him, and he would have understood me, for he is quite intelligent. On the other hand, there was a person who had everything that he required to make his position exalted, predominant, world-wide, only a terrible cable bound him to the earth. I helped him, partly by pressure, partly by force, to break his bonds and now he has won, with a triumphant joy, the freedom, the omnipotence that he owes to me; it required, perhaps, a little determination on his part, but what a reward! Thus a man can himself, when he has the sense to listen to me, become the midwife of his destiny." It was only too clear that M. de Charlus had not been able to influence his own; action is a different thing from speech, even eloquent speech, and from thought, even the thoughts of genius. "But, so far as I am concerned, I live the life of a philosopher who looks on with interest at the social reactions which I have foretold, but who does not assist them. And so I have continued to visit Saintine, who has always received me with the whole-hearted deference which is my due. I have even dined with him in his new abode, where one is heavily bored, in the midst of the most sumptuous splendour, as one used to be amused in the old days when, living from hand to mouth, he used to assemble the best society in a wretched attic. Him, then, you may invite, I give you leave, but I rule out with my veto all the other names that you have mentioned. And you will thank me for it, for, if I am an expert in arranging marriages, I am no less an expert in arranging parties. I know the rising people who give tone to a gathering, make it go; and I know also the names that will bring it down to the ground, make it fall flat." These exclusions were not always founded upon the Baron's personal resentments nor upon his artistic refinements, but upon his skill as an actor. When he had perfected, at the expense of somebody or something, an entirely successful epigram, he was anxious to let it be heard by the largest possible audience, but took care not to admit to the second performance the audience of the first who could have borne witness that the novelty was not novel. He would then rearrange his drawing-room, simply because he did not alter his programme, and, when he had scored a success in conversation, would, if need be, have organised a tour, and given exhibitions in the provinces. Whatever may have been the various motives for these exclusions, they did not merely annoy Mme. Verdurin, who felt her authority as a hostess impaired, they also did her great damage socially, and for two reasons. The first was that

M. de Charlus, even more susceptible than Jupien, used to quarrel, without anyone's ever knowing why, with the people who were most suited to be his friends. Naturally, one of the first punishments that he could inflict upon them was that of not allowing them to be invited to a party which he was giving at the Verdurins'. Now these pariahs were often people who are in the habit of ruling the roost, as the saying is, but who in M. de Charlus's eyes had ceased to rule it from the day on which he had quarrelled with them. For his imagination, in addition to finding people in the wrong in order to quarrel with them, was no less ingenious in stripping them of all importance as soon as they ceased to be his friends. If, for instance, the guilty person came of an extremely old family, whose dukedom, however, dates only from the nineteenth century, such a family as the Montesquiou, from that moment all that counted for M. de Charlus was the precedence of the dukedom, the family becoming nothing. "They are not even Dukes," he would exclaim. "It is the title of the abbé de Montesquiou which passed most irregularly to a collateral, less than eighty years ago. The present Duke, if Duke he can be called, is the third. You may talk to me if you like of people like the Uzès, the La Trémoïlle, the Luynes, who are tenth or fourteenth Dukes, or my brother who is twelfth Duc de Guermantes and seventeenth Prince of Cordova. The Montesquiou are descended from an old family, what would that prove, supposing that it were proved? They have descended so far that they have reached the fourteenth storey below stairs." Had he on the contrary quarrelled with a gentleman who possessed an ancient dukedom, who boasted the most magnificent connexions, was related to ruling princes, but to whose line this distinction had come quite suddenly without any length of pedigree, a Luynes for instance, the case was altered, pedigree alone counted. "I ask you;—M. Alberti, who does not emerge from the mire until Louis XIII. What can it matter to us that favouritism at court allowed them to pick up dukedoms to which they have no right?" What was more, with M. de Charlus, the fall came immediately after the exaltation because of that tendency peculiar to the Guermantes to expect from conversation, from friendship, something that these are incapable of giving, as well as the symptomatic fear of becoming the objects of slander. And the fall was all the greater, the higher the exaltation had been. Now nobody had ever found such favour with the Baron as he had markedly shewn for Comtesse Molé. By what sign of indifference did she reveal, one fine day, that she had been unworthy of it? The Comtesse always maintained that she had never been able to solve the problem. The fact remains that the mere sound of her name aroused in the Baron the most violent rage, provoked the most eloquent but the most terrible philippics. Mme. Verdurin, to whom Mme. Molé had been very kind, and who was founding, as we shall see, great hopes upon her and had rejoiced in anticipation at the thought that the Comtesse would meet in her house all the noblest names, as the Mistress said, "of France and Navarre," at once proposed to invite "Madame de Molé." "Oh, my God! Everyone has his own taste," M. de Charlus had replied, "and if you, Madame, feel a desire to converse with Mme. Pipelet, Mme. Gibout and Mme. Joseph Prudhomme, I ask nothing better, but let it be on an evening when I am not present. I could see as soon as you opened your mouth that we do not speak the same language, since I was mentioning the names of the nobility, and you retort with the most obscure names of professional and tradespeople, dirty scandalmongering little bounders, little women who imagine themselves patronesses of the arts because they repeat, an octave lower, the manners of my Guermantes sister-in-law, like a jay that thinks it is imitating a peacock. I must add that it would be positively indecent to admit to a party which I am pleased to give at Mme. Verdurin's a person whom I have with good reason excluded from my society, a sheep devoid of birth, loyalty, intelligence, who is so idiotic as to suppose that she is capable of playing the Duchesse de Guermantes and the Princesse de Guermantes, a combination which is in itself idiotic, since the Duchesse de Guermantes and the Princesse de Guermantes are poles apart. It is as though a person should pretend to be at once Reichenberg and Sarah Bernhardt. In any case, even if it were not impossible, it would be extremely ridiculous. Even though I may, myself, smile at times at the exaggeration of one and regret the limitations of the other, that is my right. But that upstart little frog trying to blow herself out to the magnitude of two great ladies who, at all events, always reveal the incomparable distinction of blood, it is enough, as the saying is, to make a cat laugh. The Molé! That is a name which must not be uttered in my hearing, or else I must simply withdraw," he concluded with a smile, in the tone of a doctor, who, thinking of his patient's interests in spite of that same patient's opposition, lets it be understood that he will not tolerate the collaboration of a homoeopath. On the other hand, certain persons whom M. de Charlus regarded as negligible might indeed be so for him but not for Mme. Verdurin. M. de Charlus, with his exalted birth, could afford to dispense with people in the height of fashion, the assemblage of whom would have made Mme. Verdurin's drawing-room one of the first in Paris. She, at the same time, was beginning to feel that she had already on more than one occasion missed the coach, not to mention the enormous retardation that the social error of the Dreyfus case had inflicted upon her, not without doing her a service all the same. I forget whether I have mentioned the disapproval with which the Duchesse de Guermantes had observed certain persons of her world who, subordinating everything else to the Case, excluded fashionable women from their drawing-rooms and admitted others who were not fashionable, because they were for or against the fresh trial, and had then been criticised in her turn by those same ladies, as lukewarm, unsound in her views, and guilty of placing social distinctions above the national interests; may I appeal to the reader, as to a friend with regard to whom one completely forgets, at the end of a conversation, whether one has remembered, or had an opportunity to tell him something important? Whether I have done so or not, the attitude of the Duchesse de Guermantes can easily be imagined, and indeed if we look at it in the light of subsequent history may appear, from the social point of view, perfectly correct. M. de Cambremer regarded the Dreyfus case as a foreign machination intended to destroy the Intelligence Service, to undermine discipline, to weaken the army, to divide the French people, to pave the way for invasion. Literature being, apart from a few of La Fontaine's fables, a sealed book to the Marquis, he left it to his wife to prove that the cruelly introspective writers of the day had, by creating a spirit of irreverence, arrived by a parallel course at a similar result. "M. Reinach and M. Hervieu are in the plot," she would say. Nobody will accuse the Dreyfus case of having premeditated such dark designs upon society. But there it certainly has broken down the hedges. The social leaders who refuse to allow politics into society are as foreseeing as the soldiers who refuse to allow politics to permeate the army. Society is like the sexual appetite; one does not know at what forms of perversion it may not arrive, once we have allowed our choice to be dictated by aesthetic considerations. The reason that they were Nationalists gave the Faubourg Saint-Germain the habit of entertaining ladies from another class of society; the reason vanished with Nationalism, the habit remained. Mme. Verdurin, by the bond of Dreyfusism, had attracted to her house certain writers of distinction who for the moment were of no advantage to her socially, because they were Dreyfusards. But political passions are like all the rest, they do not last. Fresh generations arise which are incapable of understanding them. Even the generation that felt them changes, feels political passions which, not being modelled exactly upon their predecessors, make it rehabilitate some of the excluded, the reason for exclusion having altered. Monarchists no longer cared, at the time of the Dreyfus case, whether a man had been a Republican, that is to say a Radical, that is to say Anticlerical, provided that he was an anti-Semite and a Nationalist. Should a war ever come, patriotism would assume another form and if a writer was chauvinistic nobody would stop to think whether he had or had not been a Dreyfusard. It was thus that, at each political crisis, at each artistic revival, Mme. Verdurin had collected one by one, like a bird building its nest, the several items, useless for the moment, of what would one day be her Salon. The Dreyfus case had passed, Anatole France remained. Mme. Verdurin's strength lay in her genuine love of art, the trouble that she used to take for her faithful, the marvellous dinners that she gave for them alone, without inviting anyone from the world of fashion. Each of the faithful was treated at her table as Bergotte had been treated at Mme. Swann's. When a boon companion of this sort had turned into an illustrious man whom everybody was longing to meet, his presence at Mme. Verdurin's had none of the artificial, composite effect of a dish at an official or farewell banquet, cooked by Potel or Chabot, but was merely a delicious 'ordinary' which you would have found there in the same perfection on a day when there was no party at all. At Mme. Verdurin's the cast was trained to perfection, the repertory most select, all that was lacking was an audience. And now that the public taste had begun to turn from the rational and French art of a Bergotte, and to go in, above all things, for exotic forms of music, Mme. Verdurin, a sort of official representative in Paris of all foreign artists, was not long in making her appearance, by the side of the exquisite Princess Yourbeletief, an aged Fairy Godmother, grim but all-powerful, to the Russian dancers. This charming invasion, against whose seductions only the stupidest of critics protested, infected Paris, as we know, with a fever of curiosity less burning, more purely aesthetic, but quite as intense perhaps as that aroused by the Dreyfus case. There again Mme. Verdurin, but with a very different result socially, was to take her place in the front row. Just as she had been seen by the side of Mme. Zola, immediately under the bench, during the trial in the Assize Court, so when the new generation of humanity, in their enthusiasm for the Russian ballet, thronged to the Opera, crowned with the latest novelty in aigrettes, they invariably saw in a stage box Mme. Verdurin by the side of Princess Your-beletief. And just as, after the emotions of the law courts, people used to go in the evening to Mme. Verdurin's, to meet Picquart or Labori in the flesh and what was more to hear the latest news of the Case, to learn what hopes might be placed in Zurlinden, Loubet, Colonel Jouaust, the Regulations, so now, little inclined for sleep after the enthusiasm aroused by the *Scheherazade* or *Prince Igor,* they repaired to Mme. Verdurin's, where under the auspices of Princess Yourbeletief and their hostess an exquisite supper brought together every night the dancers themselves, who had abstained from dinner so as to be more resilient, their director, their designers, the great composers Igor Stravinski and Richard Strauss, a permanent little nucleus, around which, as round the supper-table of M. and Mme. Helvétius, the greatest ladies in Paris and foreign royalties were not too proud to gather. Even those people in society who professed to be endowed with taste and drew unnecessary distinctions between the various Russian ballets, regarding the setting of the *Sylphides* as somehow 'purer' than that of *Scheherazade,* which they were almost prepared to attribute to Negro inspiration, were enchanted to meet face to face the great revivers of theatrical taste, who in an art that is perhaps a little more artificial than that of the easel had created a revolution as profound as Impressionism itself.

To revert to M. de Charlus, Mme. Verdurin would have not minded so much if he had placed on his Index only Comtesse Molé and Mme. Bontemps, whom she had picked out at Odette's on the strength of her love of the fine arts, and who during the Dreyfus case had come to dinner occasionally bringing her husband, whom Mme. Verdurin called 'lukewarm,' because he was not making any move for a fresh trial, but who, being extremely intelligent, and glad to form relations in every camp, was delighted to shew his independence by dining at the same table as Labori, to whom he listened without uttering a word that might compromise himself, but managed to slip in at the right moment a tribute to the loyalty, recognised by all parties, of Jaurès. But the Baron had similarly proscribed several ladies of the aristocracy whose acquaintance Mme. Verdurin, on the occasion of some musical festivity or a collection for charity, had recently formed and who, whatever M. de Charlus might think of them, would have been, far more than himself, essential to the formation of a fresh nucleus at Mme. Verdurin's, this time aristocratic. Mme. Verdurin had indeed been reckoning upon this party, to which M. de Charlus would be bringing her women of the same set, to mix her new friends with them, and had been relishing in anticipation the surprise that the latter would feel upon meeting at Quai Conti their own friends or relatives invited there by the Baron. She was disappointed and furious at his veto. It remained to be seen whether the evening, in these conditions, would result in profit or loss to herself. The loss would not be too serious if only M. de Charlus's guests came with so friendly a feeling for Mme. Verdurin that they would become her friends in the future. In this case the mischief would be only half done, these two sections of the fashionable world, which the Baron had insisted upon keeping apart, would be united later on, he himself being excluded, of course, when the time came. And so Mme. Verdurin was awaiting the Baron's guests with a certain emotion. She would not be slow in discovering the state of mind in which they came, and the degree of intimacy to which she might hope to attain. While she waited, Mme. Verdurin took counsel with the faithful, but, upon seeing M. de Charlus enter the room with Brichot and myself, stopped short. Greatly to our astonishment, when Brichot told her how sorry he was to learn that her dear friend was so seriously ill, Mme. Verdurin replied: "Listen, I am obliged to confess that I am not at all sorry. It is useless to pretend to feel what one does not feel." No doubt she spoke thus from want of energy, because she shrank from the idea of wearing a long face throughout her party, from pride, in order not to appear to be seeking excuses for not having cancelled her invitations, from self-respect also and social aptitude, because the absence of grief which she displayed was more honourable if it could be attributed to a peculiar antipathy, suddenly revealed, to the Princess, rather than to a universal insensibility, and because her hearers could not fail to be disarmed by a sincerity as to which there could be no doubt. If Mme. Verdurin had not been genuinely unaffected by the death of the Princess, would she have gone on to excuse herself for giving the party, by accusing herself of a far more serious fault? Besides, one was apt to forget that Mme. Verdurin would thus have admitted, while confessing her grief, that she had not had the strength of mind to forego a pleasure; whereas the indifference of the friend was something more shocking, more immoral, but less humiliating, and consequently easier to confess than the frivolity of the hostess. In matters of crime, where the culprit is in danger, it is his material interest that prompts the confession. Where the fault incurs no penalty, it is self-esteem. Whether it was that, doubtless feeling the pretext to be too hackneyed of the people who, so as not to allow a bereavement to interrupt their life of pleasure, go about saying that it seems to them useless to display the outward signs of a grief which they feel in their hearts, Mme. Verdurin preferred to imitate those intelligent culprits who are revolted by the commonplaces of innocence and whose defence—a partial admission, though they do not know it—consists in saying that they would see no harm in doing what they are accused of doing, although, as it happens, they have had no occasion to do it; or that, having adopted, to explain her conduct, the theory of indifference, she found, once she had started upon the downward slope of her unnatural feeling, that it was distinctly original to have felt it, that she displayed a rare perspicacity in having managed to diagnose her own symptoms, and a certain 'nerve' in proclaiming them; anyhow, Mme. Verdurin kept dwelling upon her want of grief, not without a certain proud satisfaction, as of a paradoxical psychologist and daring dramatist. "Yes, it is very funny," she said, "I hardly felt it. Of course, I don't mean to say that I wouldn't rather she were still alive, she was not a bad person." "Yes, she was," put in M. Verdurin. "Ah! He doesn't approve of her because he thought that I was doing myself harm by having her here, but he is quite pig-headed about that." "Do me the justice to admit," said M. Verdurin, "that I never approved of your having her. I always told you that she had a bad reputation." "But I have never heard a thing against her," protested Saniette. "What!" exclaimed Mme. Verdurin, "everybody knew; bad isn't the word, it was scandalous, appalling. No, it has nothing to do with that. I couldn't explain, myself, what I felt; I didn't dislike her, but I took so little interest in her that, when we heard that she was seriously ill, my husband himself was quite surprised, and said: 'Anyone would think that you didn't mind.' Why, this evening, he offered to put off the party, and I insisted upon having it, because I should have thought it a farce to shew a grief which I do not feel." She said this because she felt that it had a curious smack of the 'independent theatre,' and was at the same time singularly convenient; for an admitted insensibility or immorality simplifies life as much as does easy virtue; it converts reproachable actions, for which one no longer need seek any excuse, into a duty imposed by sincerity. And the faithful listened to Mme. Verdurin's speech with the blend of admiration and misgiving which certain cruelly realistic plays, that shewed a profound observation, used at one time to cause, and, while they marvelled to see their beloved Mistress display a novel aspect of her rectitude and independence, more than one of them, albeit he assured himself that after all it would not be the same thing, thought of his own death, and asked himself whether, on the day when death came to him, they would draw the blinds or give a party at Quai Conti. "I am very glad that the party has not been put off, for my guests' sake," said M. de Charlus, not realising that in expressing himself thus he was offending Mme. Verdurin. Meanwhile I was struck, as was everybody who approached Mme. Verdurin that evening, by a far from pleasant odour of rhinogomenol. The reason was as follows. We know that Mme. Verdurin never expressed her artistic feelings in a moral, but always in a physical fashion, so that they might appear more inevitable and more profound. So, if one spoke to her of Vinteuil's music, her favourite, she remained unmoved, as though she expected to derive no emotion from it. But after a few minutes of a fixed, almost abstracted gaze, in a sharp, matter of fact, scarcely civil tone (as though she had said to you: "I don't in the least mind your smoking, it's because of the carpet; it's a very fine one [not that that matters either], but it's highly inflammable, I'm dreadfully afraid of fire, and I shouldn't like to see you all roasted because some one had carelessly dropped a cigarette end on it"), she replied: "I have no fault to find with Vinteuil; to my mind, he is the greatest composer of the age, only I can never listen to that sort of stuff without weeping all the time" (she did not apply any pathos to the word 'weeping,' she would have used precisely the same tone for 'sleeping'; certain slandermongers used indeed to insist that the latter verb would have been more applicable, though no one could ever be certain, for she listened to the music with her face buried in her hands, and certain snoring sounds might after all have been sobs). "I don't mind weeping, not in the least; only I get the most appalling colds afterwards. It stuffs up my mucous membrane, and the day after I look like nothing on earth. I have to inhale for days on end before I can utter. However, one of Cottard's pupils, a charming person, has been treating me for it. He goes by quite an original rule: 'Prevention is better than cure.' And he greases my nose before the music begins. It is radical. I can weep like all the mothers who ever lost a child, not a trace of a cold. Sometimes a little conjunctivitis, that's all. It is absolutely efficacious. Otherwise I could never have gone on listening to Vinteuil. I was just going from one bronchitis to another." I could not refrain from alluding to Mlle. Vinteuil. "Isn't the composer's daughter to be here," I asked Mme. Verdurin, "with one of her friends?" "No, I have just had a telegram," Mme. Verdurin said evasively, "they have been obliged to remain in the country." I felt a momentary hope that there might never have been any question of their leaving it and that Mme. Verdurin had announced the presence of these representatives of the composer only in order to make a favourable impression upon the performers and their audience. "What, didn't they come, then, to the rehearsal this afternoon?" came with a feigned curiosity from the Baron who was anxious to let it appear that he had not seen Charlie. The latter came up to greet me. I whispered a question in his ear about Mlle. Vinteuil; he seemed to me to know little or nothing about her. I signalled to him not to let himself be heard and told him that we should discuss the question later on. He bowed, and assured me that he would be delighted to place himself entirely at my disposal. I observed that he was far more polite, more respectful, than he had been in the past. I spoke warmly of him—who might perhaps be able to help me to clear up my suspicions—to M. de Charlus who replied: "He only does what is natural, there would be no point in his living among respectable people if he didn't learn good manners." These, according to M. de Charlus, were the old manners of France, untainted by any British bluntness. Thus when Charlie, returning from a tour in the provinces or abroad, arrived in his travelling suit at the Baron's, the latter, if there were not too many people present, would kiss him without ceremony upon both cheeks, perhaps a little in order to banish by so ostentatious a display of his affection any idea of its being criminal, perhaps because he could not deny himself a pleasure, but still more, doubtless, from a literary sense, as upholding and illustrating the traditional manners of France, and, just as he would have countered the Munich or modern style of furniture by keeping in his rooms old armchairs that had come to him from a great-grandmother, countering the British phlegm with the affection of a warm-hearted father of the eighteenth century, unable to conceal his joy at beholding his son once more. Was there indeed a trace of incest in this paternal affection? It is more probable that the way in which M. de Charlus habitually appeased his vicious cravings, as to which we shall learn something in due course, was not sufficient for the need of affection, which had remained unsatisfied since the death of his wife; the fact remains that after having thought more than once of a second marriage, he was now devoured by a maniacal desire to adopt an heir. People said that he was going to adopt Morel, and there was nothing extraordinary in that. The invert who has been unable to feed his passion save on a literature written for women-loving men, who used to think of men when he read Musset's *Nuits*, feels the need to partake, nevertheless, in all the social activities of the man who is not an invert, to keep a lover, as the old frequenter of the Opera keeps ballet-girls, to settle down, to marry or form a permanent tie, to become a father.

M. de Charlus took Morel aside on the pretext of making him tell him what was going to be played, but above all finding a great consolation, while Charlie shewed him his music, in displaying thus publicly their secret intimacy. In the meantime I myself felt a certain charm. For albeit the little clan included few girls, on the other hand girls were abundantly invited on the big evenings. There were a number present, and very pretty girls too, whom I knew. They wafted smiles of greeting to me across the room. The air was thus decorated at every moment with the charming smile of some girl. That is the manifold, occasional ornament of evening parties, as it is of days. We remember an atmosphere because girls were smiling in it.

Many people might have been greatly surprised had they overheard the furtive remarks which M. de Charlus exchanged with a number of important gentlemen at this party. These were two Dukes, a distinguished General, a great writer, a great physician, a great barrister. And the remarks in question were: "By the way, did you notice the footman, I mean the little fellow they take on the carriage? At our cousin Guermantes', you don't know of anyone?" "At the moment, no." "I say, though, outside the door, where the carriages stop, there used to be a fair little person, in breeches, who seemed to me most attractive. She called my carriage most charmingly, I would gladly have prolonged the conversation." "Yes, but I believe she's altogether against it, besides, she puts on airs, you like to get to business at once, you would loathe her. Anyhow, I know there's nothing doing, a friend of mine tried." "That is a pity, I thought the profile very fine, and the hair superb." "Really, as much as that? I think, if you had seen a little more of her, you would have been disillusioned. No, in the supper-room, only two months ago you would have seen a real marvel, a great fellow six foot six, a perfect skin, and loves it, too. But he's gone off to Poland." "Ah, that is rather a long way." "You never know, he may come back, perhaps. One always meets again somewhere." There is no great social function that does not, if, in taking a section of it, we contrive to cut sufficiently deep, resemble those parties to which doctors invite their patients, who utter the most intelligent remarks, have perfect manners, and would never shew that they were mad did they not whisper in our ear, pointing to some old gentleman who goes past: "That's Joan of Arc."

"I feel that it is our duty to enlighten him," Mme. Verdurin said to Brichot. "Not that I have anything against Charlus, far from it. He is a pleasant fellow and as for his reputation, I don't mind saying that it is not of a sort that can do me any harm! As far as I'm concerned, in our little clan, in our table-talk, as I detest flirts, the men who talk nonsense to a woman in a corner instead of discussing interesting topics, I've never had any fear with Charlus of what happened to me with Swann, and Elstir, and lots of them. With him I was quite safe, he would come to my dinners, all the women in the world might be there, you could be certain that the general conversation would not be disturbed by flirtations and whisperings. Charlus is in a class of his own, one doesn't worry, he might be a priest. Only, he must not be allowed to take it upon himself to order about the young men who come to the house and make a nuisance of himself in our little nucleus, or he'll be worse than a man who runs after women." And Mme. Verdurin was sincere in thus proclaiming her indulgence towards Charlism. Like every ecclesiastical power she regarded human frailties as less dangerous than anything that might undermine the principle of authority, impair the orthodoxy, modify the ancient creed of her little Church. "If he does, then I shall bare my teeth. What do you say to a gentleman who tried to prevent Charlie from coming to a rehearsal because he himself was not invited? So he's going to be taught a lesson, I hope he'll profit by it, otherwise he can simply take his hat and go. He keeps the boy under lock and key, upon my word he does." And, using exactly the same expressions that almost anyone else might have used, for there are certain not in common currency which some particular subject, some given circumstance recalls almost inevitably to the mind of the speaker, who imagines that he is giving free expression to his thought when he is merely repeating mechanically the universal lesson, she went on: "It's impossible to see Morel nowadays without that great lout hanging round him, like an armed escort." M. Verdurin offered to take Charlie out of the room for a minute to explain things to him, on the pretext of asking him a question. Mme. Verdurin was afraid that this might upset him, and that he would play badly in consequence. It would be better to postpone this performance until after the other. Perhaps even until a later occasion. For however Mme. Verdurin might look forward to the delicious emotion that she would feel when she knew that her husband was engaged in enlightening Charlie in the next room, she was afraid, if the shot missed fire, that he would lose his temper and would fail to reappear on the sixteenth.

What ruined M. de Charlus that evening was the ill-breeding—so common in their class—of the people whom he had invited and who were now beginning to arrive. Having come there partly out of friendship for M. de Charlus and also out of curiosity to explore these novel surroundings, each Duchess made straight for the Baron as though it were he who was giving the party and said, within a yard of the Verdurins, who could hear every word: "Shew me which is mother Verdurin; do you think I really need speak to her? I do hope at least, that she won't put my name in the paper to-morrow, nobody would ever speak to me again. What! That woman with the white hair, but she looks quite presentable." Hearing some mention of Mlle. Vinteuil, who, however, was not in the room, more than one of them said: "Ah! The sonata-man's daughter? Shew me her" and, each finding a number of her friends, they formed a group by themselves,

watched, sparkling with ironical curiosity, the arrival of the faithful, able
at the most to point a finger at the odd way in which a person had done
her hair, who, a few years later, was to make this the fashion in the very
best society, and, in short, regretted that they did not find this house as
different from the houses that they knew, as they had hoped to find it,
feeling the disappointment of people in society who, having gone to the
Boîte à Bruant in the hope that the singer would make a butt of them,
find themselves greeted on their arrival with a polite bow instead of the
expected:

> *Ah! voyez c'te gueule, c'te binette.*
> *Ah! voyez c'te gueule qu'elle a.*

M. de Charlus had, at Balbec, given me a perspicacious criticism of
Mme. de Vaugoubert who, notwithstanding her keen intellect, had brought
about, after his unexpected prosperity, the irremediable disgrace of her
husband. The rulers to whose Court M. de Vaugoubert was accredited,
King Theodosius and Queen Eudoxia, having returned to Paris, but this
time for a prolonged visit, daily festivities had been held in their honour,
in the course of which the Queen, on the friendliest terms with Mme. de
Vaugoubert, whom she had seen for the last ten years in her own capital,
and knowing neither the wife of the President of the Republic nor those
of his Ministers, had neglected these ladies and kept entirely aloof with
the Ambassadress. This lady, believing her own position to be unassailable
—M. de Vaugoubert having been responsible for the alliance between King
Theodosius and France—had derived from the preference that the Queen
shewed for her society a proud satisfaction but no anxiety at the peril that
threatened her, which took shape a few months later in the fact, wrongly
considered impossible by the too confident couple, of the brutal dismissal
from the Service of M. de Vaugoubert. M. de Charlus, remarking in the
'crawler' upon the downfall of his lifelong friend, expressed his astonishment that an intelligent woman had not, in such circumstances, brought
all her influence with the King and Queen to bear, so as to secure that she
might not seem to possess any influence, and to make them transfer to the
wives of the President and his Ministers a civility by which those ladies
would have been all the more flattered, that is to say which would have
made them more inclined, in their satisfaction, to be grateful to the Vau-
gouberts, inasmuch as they would have supposed that civility to be spontaneous, and not dictated by them. But the man who can see the mistakes
of others need only be exhilarated by circumstances in order to succumb
to them himself. And M. de Charlus, while his guests fought their way
towards him, to come and congratulate him, thank him, as though he were
the master of the house, never thought of asking them to say a few words
to Mme. Verdurin. Only the Queen of Naples, in whom survived the same
noble blood that had flowed in the veins of her sisters the Empress Elisabeth
and the Duchesse d'Alençon, made a point of talking to Mme. Verdurin as
though she had come for the pleasure of meeting her rather than for the
music and for M. de Charlus, made endless pretty speeches to her hostess,
could not cease from telling her for how long she had been wishing to

make her acquaintance, expressed her admiration for the house and spoke to her of all manner of subjects as though she were paying a call. She would so much have liked to bring her niece Elisabeth, she said (the niece who shortly afterwards was to marry Prince Albert of Belgium), who would be so sorry. She stopped talking when she saw the musicians mount the platform, asking which of them was Morel. She can scarcely have been under any illusion as to the motives that led M. de Charlus to desire that the young virtuoso should be surrounded with so much glory. But the venerable wisdom of a sovereign in whose veins flowed the blood of one of the noblest races in history, one of the richest in experience, scepticism and pride, made her merely regard the inevitable defects of the people whom she loved best, such as her cousin Charlus (whose mother had been, like herself, a 'Duchess in Bavaria'), as misfortunes that rendered more precious to them the support that they might find in herself and consequently made it even more pleasant to her to provide that support. She knew that M. de Charlus would be doubly touched by her having taken the trouble to come, in the circumstances. Only, being as good as she had long ago shewn herself brave, this heroic woman who, a soldier-queen, had herself fired her musket from the ramparts of Gaeta, always ready to take her place chivalrously by the weaker side, seeing Mme. Verdurin alone and abandoned, and unaware (for that matter) that she ought not to leave the Queen, had sought to pretend that for her, the Queen of Naples, the centre of this party, the lodestone that had made her come was Mme. Verdurin. She expressed her regret that she would not be able to remain until the end, as she had, although she never went anywhere, to go on to another party, and begged that on no account, when she had to go, should any fuss be made for her, thus discharging Mme. Verdurin of the honours which the latter did not even know that she ought to render.

One must, however, do M. de Charlus the justice of saying that, if he entirely forgot Mme. Verdurin and allowed her to be ignored, to a scandalous extent, by the people 'of his own world' whom he had invited, he did, on the other hand, realise that he must not allow these people to display, during the 'symphonic recital' itself, the bad manners which they were exhibiting towards the Mistress. Morel had already mounted the platform, the musicians were assembling, and one could still hear conversations, not to say laughter, speeches such as "it appears, one has to be initiated to understand it." Immediately M. de Charlus, drawing himself erect, as though he had entered a different body from that which I had seen, not an hour ago, crawling towards Mme. Verdurin's door, assumed a prophetic expression and regarded the assembly with an earnestness which indicated that this was not the moment for laughter, whereupon one saw a rapid blush tinge the cheeks of more than one lady thus publicly rebuked, like a schoolgirl scolded by her teacher in front of the whole class. To my mind, M. de Charlus's attitude, noble as it was, was somehow slightly comic; for at one moment he pulverised his guests with a flaming glare, at another, in order to indicate to them as with a *vade mecum* the religious silence that ought to be observed, the detachment from every worldly consideration, he furnished in himself, as he raised to his fine brow his white-gloved hands, a model (to which they must conform) of gravity, already almost of ecstasy, without acknowledging the greetings of late-comers so indelicate as not to understand that it was now the time for High Art. They were all hypnotised; no one dared utter a sound, move a chair; respect for music— by virtue of Palamède's prestige—had been instantaneously inculcated in a crowd as ill-bred as it was exclusive.

When I saw appear on the little platform, not only Morel and a pianist, but performers upon other instruments as well, I supposed that the programme was to begin with works of composers other than Vinteuil. For I imagined that the only work of his in existence was his sonata for piano and violin.

Mme. Verdurin sat in a place apart, the twin hemispheres of her pale, slightly roseate brow magnificently curved, her hair drawn back, partly in imitation of an eighteenth century portrait, partly from the desire for coolness of a fever-stricken patient whom modesty forbids to reveal her condition, aloof, a deity presiding over musical rites, patron saint of Wagnerism and sick-headaches, a sort of almost tragic Norn, evoked by the spell of genius in the midst of all these bores, in whose presence she would more than ordinarily scorn to express her feelings upon hearing a piece of music which she knew better than they. The concert began, I did not know what they were playing, I found myself in a strange land. Where was I to locate it? Into what composer's country had I come? I should have been glad to know, and, seeing nobody near me whom I might question, I should have liked to be a character in those *Arabian Nights* which I never tired of reading and in which, in moments of uncertainty, there arose a genie or a maiden of ravishing beauty, invisible to everyone else but not to the embarrassed hero to whom she reveals exactly what he wishes to learn. Well, at this very moment I was favoured with precisely such a magical apparition. As, in a stretch of country which we suppose to be strange to us and which as a matter of fact we have approached from a new angle, when after turning out of one road we find ourself emerging suddenly upon another every inch of which is familiar only we have not been in the habit of entering it from that end, we say to ourself immediately: "Why, this is the lane that leads to the garden gate of my friends the X——; I shall be there in a minute," and there, indeed, is their daughter at the gate, come out to greet us as we pass; so, all of a sudden, I found myself, in the midst of this music that was novel to me, right in the heart of Vinteuil's sonata; and, more marvellous than any maiden, the little phrase, enveloped, harnessed in silver, glittering with brilliant effects of sound, as light and soft as silken scarves, came towards me, recognisable in this new guise. My joy at having found it again was enhanced by the accent, so friendlily familiar, which it adopted in addressing me, so persuasive, so simple, albeit without dimming the shimmering beauty with which it was resplendent. Its intention, however, was, this time, merely to shew me the way, which was not the way of the sonata, for this was an unpublished work of Vinteuil in which he had merely amused himself, by an allusion which was explained at this point by a sentence in the programme which one ought to have been reading simultaneously, in making the little phrase reappear for a moment. No sooner was it thus recalled than it vanished, and I found myself once more in an unknown world, but I knew now, and everything that followed only confirmed my knowledge, that this world was one of those which I had never even been capable of imagining that Vinteuil could have created, for when, weary of the sonata which was to me a universe thoroughly explored, I tried to imagine others equally beautiful but different, I was merely doing what those poets do who fill their artificial paradise with meadows, flowers and streams which duplicate those existing already upon Earth. What was now before me made me feel as keen a joy as the sonata would have given me if I had not already known it, and consequently, while no less beautiful, was different. Whereas the sonata opened upon a dawn of lilied meadows, parting its slender whiteness to suspend itself over the frail and yet consistent mingling of a rustic bower of honeysuckle with white geraniums, it was upon continuous, level surfaces like those of the sea that, in the midst of a stormy morning beneath an already lurid sky, there began, in an eery silence, in an infinite void, this new masterpiece, and it was into a roseate dawn that, in order to construct itself progressively before me, this unknown universe was drawn from silence and from night. This so novel redness, so absent from the tender, rustic, pale sonata, tinged all the sky, as dawn does, with a mysterious hope. And a song already thrilled the air, a song on seven notes, but the strangest, the most different from any that I had ever imagined, from any that I could ever have been able to imagine, at once ineffable and piercing, no longer the cooing of a dove as in the sonata, but rending the air, as vivid as the scarlet tinge in which the opening bars had been bathed, something like the mystical crow of a cock, an ineffable but over-shrill appeal of the eternal morning. The cold atmosphere, soaked in rain, electric—of a quality so different, feeling wholly other pressures, in a world so remote from that, virginal and endowed only with vegetable life, of the sonata—changed at every moment, obliterating the empurpled promise of the Dawn. At noon, however, beneath a scorching though transitory sun, it seemed to fulfil itself in a dull, almost rustic bliss in which the peal of clanging, racing bells (like those which kindled the blaze of the square outside the church of Combray, which Vinteuil, who must often have heard them, had perhaps discovered at that moment in his memory like a colour which the painter's hand has conveyed to his palette) seemed to materialise the coarsest joy. To be honest, from the aesthetic point of view, this joyous motive did not appeal to me, I found it almost ugly, its rhythm dragged so laboriously along the ground that one might have succeeded in imitating almost everything that was essential to it by merely making a noise, sounds, by the tapping of drumsticks upon a table. It seemed to me that Vinteuil had been lacking, here, in inspiration, and consequently I was a little lacking also in the power of attention.

I looked at the Mistress, whose sullen immobility seemed to be protesting against the noddings—in time with the music—of the empty heads of the ladies of the Faubourg. She did not say: "You understand that I know something about this music, and more than a little! If I had to express all that I feel, you would never hear the end of it!" She did not say this. But her upright, motionless body, her expressionless eyes, her straying locks said it for her. They spoke also of her courage, said that the musicians might go on, need not spare her nerves, that she would not flinch at the andante, would not cry out at the allegro. I looked at the musicians. The violoncellist dominated the instrument which he clutched between his knees, bowing his head to which its coarse features gave, in moments of mannerism, an involuntary expression of disgust; he leaned over it, fingered it with the same domestic patience with which he might have plucked a cabbage, while by his side the harpist (a mere girl) in a short skirt, bounded on either side by the lines of her golden quadrilateral like those which, in the magic chamber of a Sibyl, would arbitrarily denote the ether, according to the consecrated rules, seemed to be going in quest, here and there, at the point required, of an exquisite sound, just as though, a little allegorical deity, placed in front of the golden trellis of the heavenly vault, she were gathering, one by one, its stars. As for Morel, a lock, hitherto invisible and lost in the rest of his hair, had fallen loose and formed a curl upon his brow. I turned my head slightly towards the audience to discover what M. de Charlus might be feeling at the sight of this curl. But my eyes encountered only the face, or rather the hands of Mme. Verdurin, for the former was entirely buried in the latter.

But very soon, the triumphant motive of the bells having been banished, dispersed by others, I succumbed once again to the music; and I began to realise that if, in the body of this septet, different elements presented themselves in turn, to combine at the close, so also Vinteuil's sonata, and, as I was to find later on, his other works as well, had been no more than timid essays, exquisite but very slight, towards the triumphant and complete masterpiece which was revealed to me at this moment. And so too, I could not help recalling how I had thought of the other worlds which Vinteuil might have created as of so many universes as hermetically sealed as each of my own love-affairs, whereas in reality I was obliged to admit that in the volume of my latest love—that is to say, my love for Albertine—my first inklings of love for her (at Balbec at the very beginning, then after the game of ferret, then on the night when she slept at the hotel, then in Paris on the foggy afternoon, then on the night of the Guermantes' party, then at Balbec again, and finally in Paris where my life was now closely linked to her own) had been nothing more than experiments; indeed, if I were to consider, not my love for Albertine, but my life as a whole, my earlier love-affairs had themselves been but slight and timid essays, experiments, which paved the way to this vaster love: my love for Albertine. And I ceased to follow the music, in order to ask myself once again whether Albertine had or had not seen Mlle. Vinteuil during the last few days, as we interrogate afresh an internal pain, from which we have been distracted for a moment. For it was in myself that Albertine's possible actions were performed. Of each of the people whom we know we possess a double, but it is generally situated on the horizon of our imagination, of our memory; it remains more or less external to ourselves, and what it has done or may have done has no greater capacity to cause us pain than an object situated at a certain distance, which provides us with only the painless sensations of vision. The things that affect these people we perceive in a contemplative fashion, we are able to deplore them in appropriate language which gives other people a sense of our kindness of heart, we do not feel them; but since the wound inflicted on me at Balbec, it was in my heart, at a great depth, difficult to extract, that Albertine's double was lodged. What I saw of her hurt me, as a sick man would be hurt whose senses were so seriously deranged that the sight of a colour would be felt by him internally like a knife-thrust in his living flesh. It was fortunate that I had not already yielded to the temptation to break with Albertine; the boring thought that I should have to see her again presently, when I went home, was a trifling matter compared with the anxiety that I should have felt if the separation had been permanent at this moment when I felt a doubt about her before she had had time to become immaterial to me. At the moment when I pictured her thus to myself waiting for me at home, like a beloved wife who found the time of waiting long, and had perhaps fallen asleep for a moment in her room, I was caressed by the passage of a tender phrase, homely and domestic, of the septet. Perhaps—everything is so interwoven and superimposed in our inward life—it had been inspired in Vinteuil by his daughter's sleep—his daughter, the cause to-day of all my troubles—when it enveloped in its quiet, on peaceful evenings, the work of the composer, this phrase which calmed me so, by the same soft background of silence which pacifies certain of Schumann's reveries, during which, even when 'the Poet is speaking,' one can tell that 'the child is asleep.' Asleep, awake, I should find her again this evening, when I chose to return home, Albertine, my little child. And yet, I said to myself, something more mysterious than Albertine's love seemed to be promised at the outset of this work, in those first cries of dawn. I endeavoured to banish the thought of my mistress, so as to think only of the composer. Indeed, he seemed to be present. One would have said that, reincarnate, the composer lived for all time in his music; one could feel the joy with which he was choosing the colour of some sound, harmonising it with the rest. For with other and more profound gifts Vinteuil combined that which few composers, and indeed few painters have possessed, of using colours not merely so lasting but so personal that, just as time has been powerless to fade them, so the disciples who imitate him who discovered them, and even the masters who surpass him do not pale their originality. The revolution that their apparition has effected does not live to see its results merge unacknowledged in the work of subsequent generations; it is liberated, it breaks out again, and alone, whenever the innovator's works are performed in all time to come. Each note underlined itself in a colour which all the rules in the world could not have taught the most learned composers to imitate, with the result that Vinteuil, albeit he had appeared at his hour and was fixed in his place in the evolution of music, would always leave that place to stand in the forefront, whenever any of his compositions was performed, which would owe its appearance of having blossomed after the works of other more recent composers to this quality, apparently paradoxical and actually deceiving, of permanent novelty. A page of symphonic music by Vinteuil, familiar already on the piano, when one heard it ren-

dered by an orchestra, like a ray of summer sunlight which the prism of
the window disintegrates before it enters a dark dining-room, revealed like
an unsuspected, myriad-hued treasure all the jewels of the *Arabian Nights*.
But how can one compare to that motionless brilliance of light what was
life, perpetual and blissful motion? This Vinteuil, whom I had known so
timid and sad, had been capable—when he had to select a tone, to blend
another with it—of audacities, had enjoyed a good fortune, in the full
sense of the word, as to which the hearing of any of his works left one in no
doubt. The joy that such chords had aroused in him, the increase of strength
that it had given him wherewith to discover others led the listener on also
from one discovery to another, or rather it was the composer himself who
guided him, deriving from the colours that he had invented a wild joy
which gave him the strength to discover, to fling himself upon the others
which they seemed to evoke, enraptured, quivering, as though from the
shock of an electric spark, when the sublime came spontaneously to life
at the clang of the brass, panting, drunken, maddened, dizzy, while he
painted his great musical fresco, like Michelangelo strapped to his scaffold
and dashing, from his supine position, tumultuous brush-strokes upon the
ceiling of the Sistine Chapel. Vinteuil had been dead for many years; but
in the sound of these instruments which he had animated, it had been given
him to prolong, for an unlimited time, a part at least of his life. Of his
life as a man merely? If art was indeed but a prolongation of life, was it
worth while to sacrifice anything to it, was it not as unreal as life itself?
If I was to listen properly to this septet, I could not pause to consider the
question. No doubt the glowing septet differed singularly from the candid
sonata; the timid question to which the little phrase replied, from the
breathless supplication to find the fulfilment of the strange promise that
had resounded, so harsh, so supernatural, so brief, setting athrob the still
inert crimson of the morning sky, above the sea. And yet these so widely
different phrases were composed of the same elements, for just as there
was a certain universe, perceptible by us in those fragments scattered here
and there, in private houses, in public galleries, which were Elstir's universe, the universe which he saw, in which he lived, so to the music of
Vinteuil extended, note by note, key by key, the unknown colourings of
an inestimable, unsuspected universe, made fragmentary by the gaps
that occurred between the different occasions of hearing his work performed; those two so dissimilar questions which commanded the so different movements of the sonata and the septet, the former breaking
into short appeals a line continuous and pure, the latter welding together
into an indivisible structure a medley of scattered fragments, were nevertheless, one so calm and timid, almost detached and as though philo-
sophic, the other so anxious, pressing, imploring, were nevertheless the
same prayer, poured forth before different risings of the inward sun and
merely refracted through the different mediums of other thoughts, of
artistic researches carried on through the years in which he had tried to
create something new. A prayer, a hope which was at heart the same,
distinguishable beneath these disguises in the various works of Vinteuil,
and on the other hand not to be found elsewhere than in his works. For

these phrases historians of music might indeed find affinities, a pedigree in the works of other great composers, but merely for subordinate reasons, from external resemblances, from analogies which were ingeniously discovered by reasoning rather than felt by a direct impression. The impression that these phrases of Vinteuil imparted was different from any other, as though, notwithstanding the conclusions to which science seems to point, the individual did really exist. And it was precisely when he was seeking vigorously to be something new that one recognised beneath the apparent differences the profound similarities; and the deliberate resemblances that existed in the body of a work, when Vinteuil repeated once and again a single phrase, diversified it, amused himself by altering its rhythm, by making it reappear in its original form, these deliberate resemblances, the work of the intellect, inevitably superficial, never succeeded in being as striking as those resemblances, concealed, involuntary, which broke out in different colours, between the two separate masterpieces; for then Vinteuil, seeking to do something new, questioned himself, with all the force of his creative effort, reached his own essential nature at those depths, where, whatever be the question asked, it is in the same accent, that is to say its own, that it replies. Such an accent, the accent of Vinteuil, is separated from the accents of other composers by a difference far greater than that which we perceive between the voices of two people, even between the cries of two species of animal: by the difference that exists between the thoughts of those other composers and the eternal investigations of Vinteuil, the question that he put to himself in so many forms, his habitual speculation, but as free from analytical formulas of reasoning as if it were being carried out in the world of the angels, so that we can measure its depth, but without being any more able to translate it into human speech than are disincarnate spirits when, evoked by a medium, he questions them as to the mysteries of death. And even when I bore in mind the acquired originality which had struck me that afternoon, that kinship which musical critics might discover among them, it is indeed a unique accent to which rise, and return in spite of themselves those great singers that original composers are, which is a proof of the irreducibly individual existence of the soul. Though Vinteuil might try to make more solemn, more grand, or to make more sprightly and gay what he saw reflected in the mind of his audience, yet, in spite of himself, he submerged it all beneath an undercurrent which makes his song eternal and at once recognisable. This song, different from those of other singers, similar to all his own, where had Vinteuil learned, where had he heard it? Each artist seems thus to be the native of an unknown country, which he himself has forgotten, different from that from which will emerge, making for the earth, another great artist. When all is said, Vinteuil, in his latest works, seemed to have drawn nearer to that unknown country. The atmosphere was no longer the same as in the sonata, the questioning phrases became more pressing, more uneasy, the answers more mysterious; the clean-washed air of morning and evening seemed to influence even the instruments. Morel might be playing marvellously, the sounds that came from his violin seemed to me singularly piercing, almost blatant. This harshness was pleasing, and, as in certain voices, one felt in it a sort of moral virtue and intellectual superiority. But this might give offence. When his vision of the universe is modified, purified, becomes more adapted to his memory of the country of his heart, it is only natural that this should be expressed by a general alteration of sounds in the musician, as of colours in the painter. Anyhow, the more intelligent section of the public is not misled, since people declared later on that Vinteuil's last compositions were the most profound. Now no programme, no subject supplied any intellectual basis for judgment. One guessed therefore that it was a question of transposition, an increasing profundity of sound.

This lost country composers do not actually remember, but each of them remains all his life somehow attuned to it; he is wild with joy when he is singing the airs of his native land, betrays it at times in his thirst for fame, but then, in seeking fame, turns his back upon it, and it is only when he despises it that he finds it when he utters, whatever the subject with which he is dealing, that peculiar strain the monotony of which—for whatever its subject it remains identical in itself—proves the permanence of the elements that compose his soul. But is it not the fact then that from those elements, all the real residuum which we are obliged to keep to ourselves, which cannot be transmitted in talk, even by friend to friend, by master to disciple, by lover to mistress, that ineffable something which makes a difference in quality between what each of us has felt and what he is obliged to leave behind at the threshold of the phrases in which he can communicate with his fellows only by limiting himself to external points common to us all and of no interest, art, the art of a Vinteuil like that of an Elstir, makes the man himself apparent, rendering externally visible in the colours of the spectrum that intimate composition of those worlds which we call individual persons and which, without the aid of art, we should never know? A pair of wings, a different mode of breathing, which would enable us to traverse infinite space, would in no way help us, for, if we visited Mars or Venus keeping the same senses, they would clothe in the same aspect as the things of the earth everything that we should be capable of seeing. The only true voyage of discovery, the only fountain of Eternal Youth, would be not to visit strange lands but to possess other eyes, to behold the universe through the eyes of another, of a hundred others, to behold the hundred universes that each of them beholds, that each of them is; and this we can contrive with an Elstir, with a Vinteuil; with men like these we do really fly from star to star. The andante had just ended upon a phrase filled with a tenderness to which I had entirely abandoned myself; there followed, before the next movement, a short interval during which the performers laid down their instruments and the audience exchanged impressions. A Duke, in order to shew that he knew what he was talking about, declared: "It is a difficult thing to play well." Other more entertaining people conversed for a moment with myself. But what were their words, which like every human and external word, left me so indifferent, compared with the heavenly phrase of music with which I had just been engaged? I was indeed like an angel who, fallen from the inebriating bliss of paradise, subsides into the most humdrum reality. And, just as certain creatures are the last surviving testimony to a form of life which nature has discarded, I asked myself if music were not the unique example of what might have been—if there had not come the invention of language, the formation of words, the analysis of ideas—the means of communication between one spirit and another. It is like a possibility which has ended in nothing; humanity has developed along other lines, those of spoken and written language. But this return to the unanalysed was so inebriating, that on emerging from that paradise, contact with people who were more or less intelligent seemed to me of an extraordinary insignificance. People—I had been able during the music to remember them, to blend them with it; or rather I had blended with the music little more than the memory of one person only, which was Albertine. And the phrase that ended the andante seemed to me so sublime that I said to myself that it was a pity that Albertine did not know it, and, had she known it, would not have understood what an honour it was to be blended with anything so great as this phrase which brought us together, and the pathetic voice of which she seemed to have borrowed. But, once the music was interrupted, the people who were present seemed utterly lifeless. Refreshments were handed round. M. de Charlus accosted a footman now and then with: "How are you? Did you get my note? Can you come?" No doubt there was in these remarks the freedom of the great nobleman who thinks he is flattering his hearer and is himself more one of the people than a man of the middle classes; there was also the cunning of the criminal who imagines that anything which he volunteers is on that account regarded as innocent. And he added, in the Guermantes tone of Mme. de Villeparisis: "He's a good young fellow, such a good sort, I often employ him at home." But his adroitness turned against the Baron, for people thought his intimate conversation and correspondence with footmen extraordinary. The footmen themselves were not so much flattered as embarrassed, in the presence of their comrades. Meanwhile the septet had begun again and was moving towards its close; again and again one phrase or another from the sonata recurred, but always changed, its rhythm and harmony different, the same and yet something else, as things recur in life; and they were phrases of the sort which, without our being able to understand what affinity assigns to them as their sole and necessary home the past life of a certain composer, are to be found only in his work, and appear constantly in it, where they are the fairies, the dryads, the household gods; I had at the start distinguished in the septet two or three which reminded me of the sonata. Presently—bathed in the violet mist which rose particularly in Vinteuil's later work, so much so that, even when he introduced a dance measure, it remained captive in the heart of an opal—I caught the sound of another phrase from the sonata, still hovering so remote that I barely recognised it; hesitating, it approached, vanished as though in alarm, then returned, joined hands with others, come, as I learned later on, from other works, summoned yet others which became in their turn attractive and persuasive, as soon as they were tamed, and took their places in the ring, a ring divine but permanently invisible to the bulk of the audience, who, having before their eyes only a thick veil through which they saw nothing, punctuated arbitrarily with admiring exclamations a continuous boredom which was becoming deadly. Then they withdrew, save one which I saw reappear five times or six, without being able to distinguish its features, but so caressing, so different—as was no doubt the little phrase in Swann's sonata—from anything that any woman had ever made me desire, that this phrase which offered me in so sweet a voice a happiness which would really have been worth the struggle to obtain it, is perhaps— this invisible creature whose language I did not know and whom I under- stood so well—the only Stranger that it has ever been my good fortune to meet. Then this phrase broke up, was transformed, like the little phrase in the sonata, and became the mysterious appeal of the start. A phrase of a plaintive kind rose in opposition to it, but so profound, so vague, so internal, almost so organic and visceral that one could not tell at each of its repetitions whether they were those of a theme or of an attack of neuralgia. Presently these two motives were wrestling together in a close fight in which now one disappeared entirely, and now the listener could catch only a fragment of the other. A wrestling match of energies only, to tell the truth; for if these creatures attacked one another, it was rid of their physical bodies, of their appearance, of their names, and finding in me an inward spectator, himself indifferent also to their names and to all details, interested only in their immaterial and dynamic combat and following with passion its sonorous changes. In the end the joyous motive was left triumphant; it was no longer an almost anxious appeal addressed to an empty sky, it was an ineffable joy which seemed to come from paradise, a joy as different from that of the sonata as from a grave and gentle angel by Bellini, playing the theorbo, would be some archangel by Mantegna sounding a trump. I might be sure that this new tone of joy, this appeal to a super-terrestrial joy, was a thing that I would never forget. But should I be able, ever, to realise it? This question seemed to me all the more important, inasmuch as this phrase was what might have seemed most definitely to characterise—from its sharp contrast with all the rest of my life, with the visible world—those impressions which at remote intervals I recaptured in my life as starting-points, foundation- stones for the construction of a true life: the impression that I had felt at the sight of the steeples of Martinville, or of a line of trees near Balbec. In any case, to return to the particular accent of this phrase, how strange it was that the presentiment most different from what life assigns to us on earth, the boldest approximation to the bliss of the world beyond should have been materialised precisely in the melancholy, respectable little old man whom we used to meet in the Month of Mary at Combray; but, stranger still, how did it come about that this revelation, the strangest that I had yet received, of an unknown type of joy, should have come to me from him, since, it was understood, when he died he left nothing be- hind him but his sonata, all the rest being non-existent in indecipherable scribblings. Indecipherable they may have been, but they had neverthe- less been in the end deciphered, by dint of patience, intelligence and re- spect, by the only person who had lived sufficiently in Vinteuil's company

to understand his method of working, to interpret his orchestral indica-
tions: Mlle. Vinteuil's friend. Even in the lifetime of the great composer,
she had acquired from his daughter the reverence that the latter felt for
her father. It was because of this reverence that, in those moments in
which people run counter to their natural inclinations, the two girls had
been able to find an insane pleasure in the profanations which have already been narrated. (Her adoration of her father was the primary condition of his daughter's sacrilege. And no doubt they ought to have
foregone the delight of that sacrilege, but it did not express the whole of
their natures.) And, what is more, the profanations had become rarefied
until they disappeared altogether, in proportion as their morbid carnal
relations, that troubled, smouldering fire, had given place to the flame
of a pure and lofty friendship. Mlle. Vinteuil's friend was sometimes
worried by the importunate thought that she had perhaps hastened the
death of Vinteuil. At any rate, by spending years in poring over the cryptic
scroll left by him, in establishing the correct reading of those illegible
hieroglyphs, Mlle. Vinteuil's friend had the consolation of assuring the
composer whose grey hairs she had sent in sorrow to the grave an im-
mortal and compensating glory. Relations which are not consecrated by
the laws establish bonds of kinship as manifold, as complex, even more
solid than those which spring from marriage. Indeed, without pausing to
consider relations of so special a nature, do we not find every day that
adultery, when it is based upon genuine love, does not upset the family
sentiment, the duties of kinship, but rather revivifies them. Adultery brings
the spirit into what marriage would often have left a dead letter. A good-
natured girl who merely from convention will wear mourning for her
mother's second husband has not tears enough to shed for the man whom
her mother has chosen out of all the world as her lover. Anyhow, Mlle.
Vinteuil had acted only in a spirit of Sadism, which did not excuse her,
but it gave me a certain consolation to think so later on. She must indeed
have realised, I told myself, at the moment when she and her friend
profaned her father's photograph, that what they were doing was merely
morbidity, silliness, and not the true and joyous wickedness which she
would have liked to feel. This idea that it was merely a pretence of wickedness spoiled her pleasure. But if this idea recurred to her mind later
on, as it had spoiled her pleasure, so it must then have diminished her
grief. "It was not I," she must have told herself, "I was out of my mind.
I myself mean still to pray for my father's soul, not to despair of his
forgiveness." Only it is possible that this idea, which had certainly presented itself to her in her pleasure, may not have presented itself in her
grief. I would have liked to be able to put it into her mind. I am sure that
I should have done her good and that I should have been able to reestablish
between her and the memory of her father a pleasant channel of communication.

As in the illegible note-books in which a chemist of genius, who does
not know that death is at hand, jots down discoveries which will perhaps
remain forever unknown, Mlle. Vinteuil's friend had disentangled, from
papers more illegible than strips of papyrus, dotted with a cuneiform script,

the formula eternally true, forever fertile, of this unknown joy, the mystic hope of the crimson Angel of the dawn. And I to whom, albeit not so much perhaps as to Vinteuil, she had been also, she had been once more this very evening, by reviving afresh my jealousy of Albertine, she was above all in the future to be the cause of so many sufferings, it was thanks to her, in compensation, that there had been able to come to my ears the strange appeal which I should never for a moment cease to hear, as the promise and proof that there existed something other, realisable no doubt by art, than the nullity that I had found in all my pleasures and in love itself, and that if my life seemed to me so empty, at least there were still regions unexplored.

What she had enabled us, thanks to her labour, to know of Vinteuil was, to tell the truth, the whole of Vinteuil's work. Compared with this septet, certain phrases from the sonata which alone the public knew appeared so commonplace that one failed to understand how they could have aroused so much admiration. Similarly we are surprised that for years past, pieces as trivial as the *Evening Star* or *Elisabeth's Prayer* can have aroused in the concert-hall fanatical worshippers who wore themselves out in applause and in crying *encore* at the end of what after all is poor and trite to us who know *Tristan*, the *Rheingold* and the *Meistersinger*. We are left to suppose that those featureless melodies contained already nevertheless in infinitesimal, and for that reason, perhaps, more easily assimilable quantities, something of the originality of the masterpieces which, in retrospect, are alone of importance to us, but which their very perfection may perhaps have prevented from being understood; they have been able to prepare the way for them in our hearts. Anyhow it is true that, if they gave a confused presentiment of the beauties to come, they left these in a state of complete obscurity. It was the same with Vinteuil; if at his death he had left behind him—excepting certain parts of the sonata—only what he had been able to complete, what we should have known of him would have been, in relation to his true greatness, as little as, in the case of, say, Victor Hugo, if he had died after the *Pas d'Armes du Roi Jean*, the *Fiancée du Timbalier* and *Sarah la Baigneuse*, without having written a line of the *Légende des Siècles* or the *Contemplations*: what is to us his real work would have remained purely potential, as unknown as those universes to which our perception does not attain, of which we shall never form any idea.

Anyhow, the apparent contrast, that profound union between genius (talent too and even virtue) and the sheath of vices in which, as had happened in the case of Vinteuil, it is so frequently contained, preserved, was legible, as in a popular allegory, in the mere assembly of the guests among whom I found myself once again when the music had come to an end. This assembly, albeit limited this time to Mme. Verdurin's drawing-room, resembled many others, the ingredients of which are unknown to the general public, and which philosophical journalists, if they are at all well-informed, call Parisian, or Panamist, or Dreyfusard, never suspecting that they may equally well be found in Petersburg, Berlin, Madrid, and at every epoch; if as a matter of fact the Under Secretary of State for

Fine Arts, an artist to his fingertips, well-bred and smart, several Duchesses and three Ambassadors with their wives were present this evening at Mme. Verdurin's, the proximate, immediate cause of their presence lay in the relations that existed between M. de Charlus and Morel, relations which made the Baron anxious to give as wide a celebrity as possible to the artistic triumphs of his young idol, and to obtain for him the Cross of the Legion of Honour; the remoter cause which had made this assembly possible was that a girl living with Mlle. Vinteuil in the same way as the Baron was living with Charlie had brought to light a whole series of works of genius which had been such a revelation that before long a subscription was to be opened under the patronage of the Minister of Education, with the object of erecting a statue of Vinteuil. Moreover, these works had been assisted, no less than by Mlle. Vinteuil's relations with her friend, by the Baron's relations with Charlie, a sort of cross-road, a short cut, thanks to which the world was enabled to overtake these works without the preliminary circuit, if not of a want of comprehension which would long persist, at least of a complete ignorance which might have lasted for years. Whenever an event occurs which is within the range of the vulgar mind of the moralising journalist, a political event as a rule, the moralising journalists are convinced that there has been some great change in France, that we shall never see such evenings again, that no one will ever again admire Ibsen, Renan, Dostoievski, D'Annunzio, Tolstoi, Wagner, Strauss. For moralising journalists take their text from the equivocal undercurrents of these official manifestations, in order to find something decadent in the art which is there celebrated and which as often as not is more austere than any other. But there is no name among those most revered by these moralising journalists which has not quite naturally given rise to some such strange gathering, although its strangeness may have been less flagrant and better concealed. In the case of this gathering, the impure elements that associated themselves with it struck me from another aspect; to be sure, I was as well able as anyone to dissociate them, having learned to know them separately, but anyhow it came to pass that some of them, those which concerned Mlle. Vinteuil and her friend, speaking to me of Combray, spoke to me also of Albertine, that is to say of Balbec, since it was because I had long ago seen Mlle. Vinteuil at Montjouvain and had learned of her friend's intimacy with Albertine, that I was presently, when I returned home, to find, instead of solitude, Albertine awaiting me, and that the others, those which concerned Morel and M. de Charlus, speaking to me of Balbec, where I had seen, on the platform at Doncières, their intimacy begin, spoke to me of Combray and of its two 'ways,' for M. de Charlus was one of those Guermantes, Counts of Combray, inhabiting Combray without having any dwelling there, between earth and heaven, like Gilbert the Bad in his window: while, after all, Morel was the son of that old valet who had enabled me to know the lady in pink, and had permitted me, years after, to identify her with Mme. Swann.

M. de Charlus repeated, when, the music at an end, his guests came to say good-bye to him, the same error that he had made when they arrived. He did not ask them to shake hands with their hostess, to include her and her husband in the gratitude that was being showered on himself. There was a long queue waiting, but a queue that led to the Baron alone, a fact of which he must have been conscious, for as he said to me a little later: "The form of the artistic celebration ended in a 'few-words-in-the-vestry' touch that was quite amusing." The guests even prolonged their expressions of gratitude with indiscriminate remarks which enabled them to remain for a moment longer in the Baron's presence, while those who had not yet congratulated him on the success of his party hung wearily in the rear. A stray husband or two may have announced his intention of going; but his wife, a snob as well as a Duchess, protested: "No, no, even if we are kept waiting an hour, we cannot go away without thanking Palamède, who has taken so much trouble. There is nobody else left now who can give entertainments like this." Nobody would have thought of asking to be introduced to Mme. Verdurin any more than to the attendant in a theatre to which some great lady has for one evening brought the whole aristocracy. "Were you at Eliane de Montmorency's yesterday, cousin?" asked Mme. de Mortemart, seeking an excuse to prolong their conversation. "Good gracious, no; I like Eliane, but I never can understand her invitations. I must be very stupid, I'm afraid," he went on, parting his lips in a broad smile, while Mme. de Mortemart realised that she was to be made the first recipient of 'one of Palamède's' as she had often been of 'one of Oriane's.' "I did indeed receive a card a fortnight ago from the charming Eliane. Above the questionably authentic name of 'Montmorency' was the following kind invitation: 'My dear cousin, will you please remember me next Friday at half-past nine.' Beneath were written two less gratifying words: 'Czech Quartet.' These seemed to me incomprehensible, and in any case to have no more connexion with the sentence above than the words 'My dear ——,' which you find on the back of a letter, with nothing else after them, when the writer has already begun again on the other side, and has not taken a fresh sheet, either from carelessness or in order to save paper. I am fond of Eliane: and so I felt no annoyance, I merely ignored the strange and inappropriate allusion to a Czech Quartet, and, as I am a methodical man, I placed on my chimney-piece the invitation to remember Madame de Montmorency on Friday at half-past nine. Although renowned for my obedient, punctual and meek nature, as Buffon says of the camel"—at this, laughter seemed to radiate from M. de Charlus who knew that on the contrary he was regarded as the most impossible person to live with—"I was a few minutes late (it took me a few minutes to change my clothes), and without any undue remorse, thinking that half-past nine meant ten, at the stroke of ten in a comfortable dressing-gown, with warm slippers on my feet, I sat down in my chimney corner to remember Eliane as she had asked me and with a concentration which began to relax only at half-past ten. Tell her please that I complied strictly with her audacious request. I am sure she will be gratified." Mme. de Mortemart was helpless with laughter, in which M. de Charlus joined. "And to-morrow," she went on, forgetting that she had already long exceeded the time that might be allotted to her, "are

you going to our La Rochefoucauld cousins?" "Oh, that, now, is quite
impossible, they have invited me, and you too, I see, to a thing it is utterly
impossible to imagine, which is called, if I am to believe their card of
invitation, a 'dancing tea.' I used to be considered pretty nimble when
I was young, but I doubt whether I could ever decently have drunk a cup
of tea while I was dancing. No, I have never cared for eating or drinking
in unnatural positions. You will remind me that my dancing days are
done. But even sitting down comfortably to drink my tea—of the quality
of which I am suspicious since it is called 'dancing'—I should be afraid
lest other guests younger than myself, and less nimble possibly than I was
at their age, might spill their cups over my clothes which would interfere
with my pleasure in draining my own." Nor indeed was M. de Charlus
content with leaving Mme. Verdurin out of the conversation while he
spoke of all manner of subjects which he seemed to be taking pleasure in
developing and varying, that cruel pleasure which he had always enjoyed
of keeping indefinitely on their feet the friends who were waiting with
an excruciating patience for their turn to come; he even criticised all that
part of the entertainment for which Mme. Verdurin was responsible. "But,
talking about cups, what in the world are those strange little bowls which
remind me of the vessels in which, when I was a young man, people used
to get sorbets from Poiré-Blanche. Somebody said to me just now that they
were for 'iced coffee.' But if it comes to that, I have seen neither coffee
nor ice. What curious little objects—so very ambiguous." In saying this
M. de Charlus had placed his white-gloved hands vertically over his lips
and had modestly circumscribed his indicative stare as though he were
afraid of being heard, or even seen by his host and hostess. But this was a
mere feint, for in a few minutes he would be offering the same criticisms
to the Mistress herself, and a little later would be insolently enjoining:
"No more iced-coffee cups, remember! Give them to one of your friends
whose house you wish to disfigure. But warn her not to have them in
the drawing-room, or people might think that they had come into the
wrong room, the things are so exactly like chamberpots." "But, cousin,"
said the guest, lowering her own voice also, and casting a questioning
glance at M. de Charlus, for she was afraid of offending not Mme. Verdurin
but him, "perhaps she doesn't quite know yet. . . ." "She shall be taught."
"Oh!" laughed the guest, "she couldn't have a better teacher! She *is*
lucky! If you are in charge, one can be sure there won't be a false note."
"There wasn't one, if it comes to that, in the music." "Oh! It was sublime. One of those pleasures which can never be forgotten. Talking of that
marvellous violinist," she went on, imagining in her innocence that M.
de Charlus was interested in the violin 'pure and simple,' "do you happen
to know one whom I heard the other day playing too wonderfully a
sonata by Fauré, his name is Frank. . . ." "Oh, he's a horror," replied
M. de Charlus, overlooking the rudeness of a contradiction which implied
that his cousin was lacking in taste. "As far as violinists are concerned,
I advise you to confine yourself to mine." This paved the way to a fresh
exchange of glances, at once furtive and scrutinous, between M. de Charlus
and his cousin, for, blushing and seeking by her zeal to atone for her

blunder, Mme. de Mortemart went on to suggest to M. de Charlus that she might give a party, to hear Morel play. Now, so far as she was concerned, this party had not the object of bringing an unknown talent into prominence, an object which she would, however, pretend to have in mind, and which was indeed that of M. de Charlus. She regarded it only as an opportunity for giving a particularly smart party and was calculating already whom she would invite and whom she would reject. This business of selection, the chief preoccupation of people who give parties (even the people whom 'society' journalists are so impudent or so foolish as to call 'the élite'), alters at once the expression—and the handwriting—of a hostess more profoundly than any hypnotic suggestion. Before she had even thought of what Morel was to play (which she regarded, and rightly, as a secondary consideration, for even if everybody this evening, from fear of M. de Charlus, had observed a polite silence during the music, it would never have occurred to anyone to listen to it), Mme. de Mortemart, having decided that Mme. de Valcourt was not to be one of the elect, had automatically assumed that air of conspiracy, of a secret plotting which so degrades even those women in society who can most easily afford to ignore what 'people will say.' "Wouldn't it be possible for me to give a party, for people to hear your friend play?" murmured Mme. de Mortemart, who, while addressing herself exclusively to M. de Charlus, could not refrain, as though under a fascination, from casting a glance at Mme. de Valcourt (the rejected) in order to make certain that the other was too far away to hear her. "No she cannot possibly hear what I am saying," Mme. de Mortemart concluded inwardly, reassured by her own glance which as a matter of fact had had a totally different effect upon Mme. de Valcourt from that intended: "Why," Mme. de Valcourt had said to herself when she caught this glance, "Marie-Thérèse is planning something with Palamède which I am not to be told." "You mean my protégé," M. de Charlus corrected, as merciless to his cousin's choice of words as he was to her musical endowments. Then without paying the slightest attention to her silent prayers, as she made a smiling apology: "Why, yes . . ." he said in a loud tone, audible throughout the room, "although there is always a risk in that sort of exportation of a fascinating personality into surroundings that must inevitably diminish his transcendent gifts and would in any case have to be adapted to them." Madame de Mortemart told herself that the aside, the pianissimo of her question had been a waste of trouble, after the megaphone through which the answer had issued. She was mistaken. Mme. de Valcourt heard nothing, for the simple reason that she did not understand a single word. Her anxiety diminished and would rapidly have been extinguished had not Mme. de Mortemart, afraid that she might have been given away and afraid of having to invite Mme. de Valcourt, with whom she was on too intimate terms to be able to leave her out if the other knew about her party beforehand, raised her eyelids once again in Edith's direction, as though not to lose sight of a threatening peril, lowering them again briskly so as not to commit herself. She intended, on the morning after the party, to write her one of those letters, the complement of the revealing glance, letters which people suppose to be subtle and which are tantamount to a full and signed confession. For instance: "Dear Edith, I am so sorry about you, I did not really expect you last night" ("How could she have expected me," Edith would ask herself, "since she never invited me?") "as I know that you are not very fond of parties of that sort, which rather bore you. We should have been greatly honoured, all the same, by your company" (never did Mme. de Mortemart employ the word 'honoured,' except in the letters in which she attempted to cloak a lie in the semblance of truth). "You know that you are always at home in our house, however, you were quite right, as it was a complete failure, like everything that is got up at a moment's notice." But already the second furtive glance darted at her had enabled Edith to grasp everything that was concealed by the complicated language of M. de Charlus. This glance was indeed so violent that, after it had struck Mme. de Valcourt, the obvious secrecy and mischievous intention that it embodied rebounded upon a young Peruvian whom Mme. de Mortemart intended, on the contrary, to invite. But being of a suspicious nature, seeing all too plainly the mystery that was being made without realising that it was not intended to mystify him, he at once conceived a violent hatred of Mme. de Mortemart and determined to play all sorts of tricks upon her, such as ordering fifty iced coffees to be sent to her house on a day when she was not giving a party, or, when she was, inserting a paragraph in the newspapers announcing that the party was postponed, and publishing false reports of her other parties, in which would figure the notorious names of all the people whom, for various reasons, a hostess does not invite or even allow to be introduced to her. Mme. de Mortemart need not have bothered herself about Mme. de Valcourt. M. de Charlus was about to spoil, far more effectively than the other's presence could spoil it, the projected party. "But, my dear cousin," she said in response to the expression 'adapting the surroundings,' the meaning of which her momentary state of hyperaesthesia had enabled her to discern, "we shall save you all the trouble. I undertake to ask Gilbert to arrange everything." "Not on any account, all the more as he must not be invited to it. Nothing can be arranged except by myself. The first thing is to exclude all the people who have ears and hear not." M. de Charlus's cousin, who had been reckoning upon Morel as an attraction in order to give a party at which she could say that, unlike so many of her kinswomen, she had 'had Palamède,' carried her thoughts abruptly, from this prestige of M. de Charlus, to all sorts of people with whom he would get her into trouble if he began interfering with the list of her guests. The thought that the Prince de Guermantes (on whose account, partly, she was anxious to exclude Mme. de Valcourt, whom he declined to meet) was not to be invited, alarmed her. Her eyes assumed an uneasy expression. "Is the light, which is rather too strong, hurting you?" inquired M. de Charlus with an apparent seriousness the underlying irony of which she failed to perceive. "No, not at all, I was thinking of the difficulty, not for myself of course, but for my family, if Gilbert were to hear that I had given a party without inviting him, when he never has a cat on his housetop without. . . ." "Why of course, we must begin by eliminating the cat on the housetop, which could only miaow; I suppose that the din of talk has prevented you from realising that it was a question not of doing the civilities of a hostess but of proceeding to the rites customary at every true celebration." Then, deciding, not that the next person had been kept waiting too long, but that it did not do to exaggerate the favours shewn to one who had in mind not so much Morel as her own visiting-list, M. de Charlus, like a physician who cuts short a consultation when he considers that it has lasted long enough, gave his cousin a signal to withdraw, not by bidding her good night but by turning to the person immediately behind her. "Good evening, Madame de Montesquiou, marvellous, wasn't it? I have not seen Hélène, tell her that every general abstention, even the most noble, that is to say her own, must include exceptions, if they are brilliant, as has been the case to-night. To shew that one is rare is all very well, but to subordinate one's rarity, which is only negative, to what is precious is better still. In your sister's case, and I value more than anyone her systematic *absence* from places where what is in store for her is not worthy of her, here to-night, on the contrary, her presence at so memorable an exhibition as this would have been a *presidence*, and would have given your sister, already so distinguished, an additional distinction." Then he turned to a third person, M. d'Argencourt. I was greatly astonished to see in this room, as friendly and flattering towards M. de Charlus as he was severe with him elsewhere, insisting upon Morel's being introduced to him and telling him that he hoped he would come and see him, M. d'Argencourt, that terrible scourge of men such as M. de Charlus. At the moment he was living in the thick of them. It was certainly not because he had in any sense become one of them himself. But for some time past he had practically deserted his wife for a young woman in society whom he adored. Being intelligent herself, she made him share her taste for intelligent people, and was most anxious to have M. de Charlus in her house. But above all M. d'Argencourt, extremely jealous and not unduly potent, feeling that he was failing to satisfy his captive and anxious at once to introduce her to people and to keep her amused, could do so without risk to himself only by surrounding her with innocuous men, whom he thus cast for the part of guardians of his seraglio. These men found that he had become quite pleasant and declared that he was a great deal more intelligent than they had supposed, a discovery that delighted him and his mistress.

The remainder of M. de Charlus's guests drifted away fairly rapidly. Several of them said: "I don't want to call at the vestry" (the little room in which the Baron, with Charlie by his side, was receiving congratulations, and to which he himself had given the name), "but I must let Palamède see me so that he shall know that I stayed to the end." Nobody paid the slightest attention to Mme. Verdurin. Some pretended not to know which was she and said good night by mistake to Mme. Cottard, appealing to me for confirmation with a "That *is* Mme. Verdurin, ain't it?" Mme. d'Arpajon asked me, in the hearing of our hostess: "Tell me, has there ever been a Monsieur Verdurin?" The Duchesses, finding none of the oddities that they expected in this place which they had hoped to find more different from anything that they already knew, made the best of a bad job by going into fits of laughter in front of Elstir's paintings; for all the rest of the entertainment, which they found more in keeping than they had expected with the style with which they were familiar, they gave the credit to M. de Charlus, saying: "How clever Palamède is at arranging things; if he were to stage an opera in a stable or a bathroom, it would still be perfectly charming." The most noble ladies were those who shewed most fervour in congratulating M. de Charlus upon the success of a party, of the secret motive of which some of them were by no means unaware, without, however, being embarrassed by the knowledge, this class of society—remembering perhaps certain epochs in history when their own family had already arrived at an identical stage of brazenly conscious effrontery—carrying their contempt for scruples almost as far as their respect for etiquette. Several of them engaged Charlie on the spot for different evenings on which he was to come and play them Vinteuil's septet, but it never occurred to any of them to invite Mme. Verdurin. This last was already blind with fury when M. de Charlus who, his head in the clouds, was incapable of perceiving her condition, decided that it would be only decent to invite the Mistress to share his joy. And it was perhaps yielding to his literary preciosity rather than to an overflow of pride that this specialist in artistic entertainments said to Mme. Verdurin: "Well, are you satisfied? I think you have reason to be; you see that when I set to work to give a party there are no half-measures. I do not know whether your heraldic knowledge enables you to gauge the precise importance of the display, the weight that I have lifted, the volume of air that I have displaced for you. You have had the Queen of Naples, the brother of the King of Bavaria, the three premier peers. If Vinteuil is Mahomet, we may say that we have brought to him some of the least movable of mountains. Bear in mind that to attend your party the Queen of Naples has come up from Neuilly, which is a great deal more difficult for her than evacuating the Two Sicilies," he went on, with a deliberate sneer, notwithstanding his admiration for the Queen. "It is an historic event. Just think that it is perhaps the first time she has gone anywhere since the fall of Gaeta. It is probable that the dictionaries of dates will record as culminating points the day of the fall of Gaeta and that of the Verdurins' party. The fan that she laid down, the better to applaud Vinteuil, deserves to become more famous than the fan that Mme. de Metternich broke because the audience hissed Wagner." "Why, she has left it here," said Mme. Verdurin, momentarily appeased by the memory of the Queen's kindness to herself, and she shewed M. de Charlus the fan which was lying upon a chair. "Oh! What a touching spectacle!" exclaimed M. de Charlus, approaching the relic with veneration. "It is all the more touching, it is so hideous; poor little Violette is incredible!" And spasms of emotion and irony coursed through him alternately. "Oh dear, I don't know whether you feel this sort of thing as I do. Swann would positively have died of convulsions if he had seen it. I am sure, whatever price it fetches, I shall buy the fan at the Queen's sale. For she is bound to be sold up, she hasn't a penny," he went on, for he never ceased to intersperse the cruellest slanders with the most sincere veneration, albeit these sprang from two opposing natures, which, however, were combined in himself. They might even be brought to bear alternately upon the same incident. For M. de Charlus who in his comfortable state as a wealthy man ridiculed the poverty of the Queen was himself often to be heard extolling that poverty and, when anyone spoke of Princesse Murat, Queen of the Two Sicilies, would reply: "I do not know to whom you are alluding. There is only one Queen of Naples, who is a sublime person and does not keep a carriage. But from her omnibus she annihilates every vehicle on the street and one could kneel down in the dust on seeing her drive past." "I shall bequeath it to a museum. In the meantime, it must be sent back to her, so that she need not hire a cab to come and fetch it. The wisest thing, in view of the historical interest of such an object, would be to steal the fan. But that would be awkward for her—since it is probable that she does not possess another!" he added, with a shout of laughter. "Anyhow, you see that for my sake she came. And that is not the only miracle that I have performed. I do not believe that anyone at the present day has the power to move the people whom I have brought here. However, everyone must be given his due. Charlie and the rest of the musicians played divinely. And, my dear Mistress," he added condescendingly, "you yourself have played your part on this occasion. Your name will not be unrecorded. History has preserved that of the page who armed Joan of Arc when she set out for battle; indeed you have served as a connecting link, you have made possible the fusion between Vinteuil's music and its inspired interpreter, you have had the intelligence to appreciate the capital importance of the whole chain of circumstances which would enable the interpreter to benefit by the whole weight of a considerable—if I were not referring to myself, I would say providential—personage, whom you were clever enough to ask to ensure the success of the gathering, to bring before Morel's violin the ears directly attached to the tongues that have the widest hearing; no, no, it is not a small matter. There can be no small matter in so complete a realisation. Everything has its part. The Duras was marvellous. In fact, everything; that is why," he concluded, for he loved to administer a rebuke, "I set my face against your inviting those persons—divisors who, among the overwhelming people whom I brought you would have played the part of the decimal points in a sum, reducing the others to a merely fractional value. I have a very exact appreciation of that sort of thing. You understand, we must avoid blunders when we are giving a party which ought to be worthy of Vinteuil, of his inspired interpreter, of yourself, and, I venture to say, of me. You were prepared to invite the Molé, and everything would have been spoiled. It would have been the little contrary, neutralising drop which deprives a potion of its virtue. The electric lights would have fused, the pastry would not have come in time, the orangeade would have given everybody a stomachache. She was the one person not to invite. At the mere sound of her name, as in a fairy-tale, not a note would have issued from the brass; the flute and the hautboy would have been stricken with a sudden silence. Morel himself, even if he had succeeded in playing a few bars, would not have been in tune, and instead of Vinteuil's septet you would have had a parody of it by Beckmesser, ending amid catcalls. I, who believe strongly in personal influence, could feel quite plainly in the expansion of a certain largo, which opened itself right out like a flower, in the supreme satisfaction of the finale, which was not merely allegro but incomparably allegro, that the absence of the Molé was inspiring the musicians and was diffusing joy among the very instruments themselves. In any case, when one is at home to Queens one does not invite one's hall-portress." In calling her 'the Molé' (as for that matter he said quite affectionately 'the Duras') M. de Charlus was doing the lady justice. For all these women were the actresses of society and it is true also that, even regarding her from this point of view, Comtesse Molé did not justify the extraordinary reputation for intelligence that she had acquired, which made one think of those mediocre actors or novelists who, at certain periods, are hailed as men of genius, either because of the mediocrity of their competitors, among whom there is no artist capable of revealing what is meant by true talent, or because of the mediocrity of the public, which, did there exist an extraordinary individuality, would be incapable of understanding it. In Mme. Molé's case it is preferable, if not absolutely fair, to stop at the former explanation. The social world being the realm of nullity, there exist between the merits of women in society only insignificant degrees, which are at best capable of rousing to madness the rancours or the imagination of M. de Charlus. And certainly, if he spoke as he had just been speaking in this language which was a precious alloy of artistic and social elements, it was because his old-womanly anger and his culture as a man of the world furnished the genuine eloquence that he possessed with none but insignificant themes. Since the world of differences does not exist on the surface of the earth, among all the countries which our perception renders uniform, all the more reason why it should not exist in the social 'world.' Does it exist anywhere else? Vinteuil's septet had seemed to tell me that it did. But where? As M. de Charlus also enjoyed repeating what one person had said of another, seeking to stir up quarrels, to divide and reign, he added: "You have, by not inviting her, deprived Mme. Molé of the opportunity of saying: 'I can't think why this Mme. Verdurin should invite me. I can't imagine who these people are, I don't know them.' She was saying a year ago that you were boring her with your advances. She's a fool, never invite her again. After all, she's nothing so very wonderful. She can come to your house without making a fuss about it, seeing that I come here. In short," he concluded, "it seems to me that you have every reason to thank me, for, so far as it went, everything has been perfect. The Duchesse de Guermantes did not come, but one can't tell, it was better perhaps that she didn't. We shan't bear her any grudge, and we shall remember her all the same another time, not that one can help remembering her, her very eyes say to us 'Forget me not!', for they are a pair of myosotes" (here I thought to myself how strong the Guermantes spirit—the decision to go to one house and not to another—must be, to have outweighed in the Duchess's mind her fear of Palamède). "In the face of so complete a success, one is tempted like Bernardin de Saint-Pierre to see everywhere the hand of Providence. The Duchesse de Duras was enchanted. She even asked me to tell you so," added M. de Charlus, dwelling upon the words as though Mme. Verdurin must regard this as a sufficient honour. Sufficient and indeed barely credible, for he found it necessary, if he was to be believed, to add, completely carried away by the madness of those whom Jupiter has decided to ruin: "She has engaged Morel to come to her house, where the same programme will be repeated, and I even think of asking her for an invitation for M. Verdurin." This civility to the husband alone was, although no such idea even occurred to M. de Charlus, the most wounding outrage to the wife who, believing herself to possess, with regard to the violinist, by virtue of a sort of ukase which prevailed in the little clan, the right to forbid him to perform elsewhere without her express authorisation, was fully determined to forbid his appearance at Mme. de Duras's party.

The Baron's volubility was in itself an irritation to Mme. Verdurin who did not like people to form independent groups within their little clan. How often, even at la Raspelière, hearing M. de Charlus talking incessantly to Charlie instead of being content with taking his part in the so harmonious chorus of the clan, she had pointed to him and exclaimed: "What a rattle [1] he is! What a rattle! Oh, if it comes to rattles, he's a famous rattle!" But this time it was far worse. Inebriated with the sound of his own voice, M. de Charlus failed to realise that by cutting down the part assigned to Mme. Verdurin and confining it within narrow limits, he was calling forth that feeling of hatred which was in her only a special, social form of jealousy. Mme. Verdurin was genuinely fond of her regular visitors, the faithful of the little clan, but wished them to be entirely devoted to their Mistress. Willing to make some sacrifice, like those jealous lovers who will tolerate a betrayal, but only under their own roof and even before their eyes, that is to say when there is no betrayal, she would allow the men to have mistresses, lovers, on condition that the affair had no social consequence outside her own house, that the tie was formed and perpetuated in the shelter of her Wednesdays. In the old days, every furtive peal of laughter that came from Odette when she conversed with Swann had gnawed her heartstrings, and so of late had every aside exchanged by Morel and the Baron; she found one consolation alone for her griefs which was to destroy the happiness of other people. She had not been able to endure for long that of the Baron. And here was this rash person precipitating the catastrophe by appearing to be restricting the Mistress's place in her little clan. Already she could see Morel going into society, without her, under the Baron's aegis. There was but a single remedy, to make Morel choose between the Baron and herself, and, relying upon the ascendancy that she had acquired over Morel by the display that she made of an extraordinary perspicacity, thanks to reports

[1] Mme. Verdurin uses here the word *tapette*, being probably unaware of its popular meaning. C. K. S. M.

which she collected, to falsehoods which she invented, all of which served to corroborate what he himself was led to believe, and what would in time be made plain to him, thanks to the pitfalls which she was preparing, into which her unsuspecting victims would fall, relying upon this ascendancy, to make him choose herself in preference to the Baron. As for the society ladies who had been present and had not even asked to be introduced to her, as soon as she grasped their hesitations or indifference, she had said: "Ah! I see what they are, the sort of old good-for-nothings that are not our style, it's the last time they shall set foot in this house." For she would have died rather than admit that anyone had been less friendly to her than she had hoped. "Ah! My dear General," M. de Charlus suddenly exclaimed, abandoning Mme. Verdurin, as he caught sight of General Deltour, Secretary to the President of the Republic, who might be of great value in securing Charlie his Cross, and who, after asking some question of Cottard, was rapidly withdrawing: "Good evening, my dear, delightful friend. So this is how you slip away without saying good-bye to me," said the Baron with a genial, self-satisfied smile, for he knew quite well that people were always glad to stay behind for a moment to talk to himself. And as, in his present state of excitement, he would answer his own questions in a shrill tone: "Well, did you enjoy it? Wasn't it really fine? The andante, what? It's the most touching thing that was ever written. I defy anyone to listen to the end without tears in his eyes. Charming of you to have come. Listen, I had the most perfect telegram this morning from Froberville, who tells me that as far as the Grand Chancery goes the difficulties have been smoothed away, as the saying is." M. de Charlus's voice continued to soar at this piercing pitch, as different from his normal voice as is that of a barrister making an emphatic plea from his ordinary utterance, a phenomenon of vocal amplification by over-excitement and nervous tension analogous to that which, at her own dinner-parties, raised to so high a diapason the voice and gaze alike of Mme. de Guermantes. "I intended to send you a note to-morrow by a messenger to tell you of my enthusiasm, until I could find an opportunity of speaking to you, but you have been so surrounded! Froberville's support is not to be despised, but for my own part, I have the Minister's promise," said the General. "Ah! Excellent. Besides, you have seen for yourself that it is only what such talent deserves. Hoyos was delighted, I didn't manage to see the Ambassadress, was she pleased? Who would not have been, except those that have ears and hear not, which does not matter so long as they have tongues and can speak." Taking advantage of the Baron's having withdrawn to speak to the General, Mme. Verdurin made a signal to Brichot. He, not knowing what Mme. Verdurin was going to say, sought to amuse her, and never suspecting the anguish that he was causing me, said to the Mistress: "The Baron is delighted that Mlle. Vinteuil and her friend did not come. They shock him terribly. He declares that their morals are appalling. You can't imagine how prudish and severe the Baron is on moral questions." Contrary to Brichot's expectation, Mme. Verdurin was not amused: "He is obscene," was her answer. "Take him out of the room to smoke a cigarette with you, so that my husband can get hold of his Dulcinea without his noticing it and warn him of the abyss that is yawning at his feet." Brichot seemed to hesitate. "I don't mind telling you," Mme. Verdurin went on, to remove his final scruples, "that I do not feel at all safe with a man like that in the house. I know, there are all sorts of horrible stories about him, and the police have him under supervision." And, as she possessed a certain talent of improvisation when inspired by malice, Mme. Verdurin did not stop at this: "It seems, he has been in prison. Yes, yes, I have been told by people who knew all about it. I know, too, from a person who lives in his street, that you can't imagine the ruffians that go to his house." And as Brichot, who often went to the Baron's, began to protest, Mme. Verdurin, growing animated, exclaimed: "But I can assure you! It is I who am telling you," an expression with which she habitually sought to give weight to an assertion flung out more or less at random. "He will be found murdered in his bed one of these days, as those people always are. He may not go quite as far as that perhaps, because he is in the clutches of that Jupien whom he had the impudence to send to me, and who is an ex-convict, I know it, you yourself know it, yes, for certain. He has a hold on him because of some letters which are perfectly appalling, it seems. I know it from somebody who has seen them, and told me: 'You would be sick on the spot if you saw them.' That is how Jupien makes him toe the line and gets all the money he wants out of him. I would sooner die a thousand times over than live in a state of terror like Charlus. In any case, if Morel's family decides to bring an action against him, I have no desire to be dragged in as an accomplice. If he goes on, it will be at his own risk, but I shall have done my duty. What is one to do? It's no joke, I can tell you." And, agreeably warmed already by the thought of her husband's impending conversation with the violinist, Mme. Verdurin said to me: "Ask Brichot whether I am not a courageous friend, and whether I am not capable of sacrificing myself to save my comrades." (She was alluding to the circumstances in which she had, just in time, made him quarrel, first of all with his laundress, and then with Mme. de Cambremer, quarrels as a result of which Brichot had become almost completely blind, and [people said] had taken to morphia.) "An incomparable friend, farsighted and valiant," replied the Professor with an innocent emotion. "Mme. Verdurin prevented me from doing something extremely foolish," Brichot told me when she had left us. "She never hesitates to operate without anaesthetics. She is an interventionist, as our friend Cottard says. I admit, however, that the thought that the poor Baron is still unconscious of the blow that is going to fall upon him distresses me deeply. He is quite mad about that boy. If Mme. Verdurin should prove successful, there is a man who is going to be very miserable. However, it is not certain that she will not fail. I am afraid that she may only succeed in creating a misunderstanding between them, which, in the end, without parting them, will only make them quarrel with her." It was often thus with Mme. Verdurin and her faithful. But it was evident that in her the need to preserve their friendship was more and more dominated by the requirement that this friendship should never be challenged by that which they might feel for one another. Homosexuality did not disgust her so long as it did not tamper with orthodoxy, but like the Church she preferred any sacrifice rather than a concession of orthodoxy. I was beginning to be afraid lest her irritation with myself might be due to her having heard that I had prevented Albertine from going to her that afternoon, and that she might presently set to work, if she had not already begun, upon the same task of separating her from me which her husband, in the case of Charlus, was now going to attempt with the musician. "Come along, get hold of Charlus, find some excuse, there's no time to lose," said Mme. Verdurin, "and whatever you do, don't let him come back here until I send for you. Oh! What an evening," Mme. Verdurin went on, revealing thus the true cause of her anger. "Performing a masterpiece in front of those wooden images. I don't include the Queen of Naples, she is intelligent, she is a nice woman" (which meant: "She has been kind to me"). "But the others. Oh! It's enough to drive anyone mad. What can you expect, I'm no longer a girl. When I was young, people told me that one must put up with boredom, I made an effort, but now, oh no, it's too much for me, I am old enough to please myself, life is too short; bore myself, listen to idiots, smile, pretend to think them intelligent. No, I can't do it. Get along, Brichot, there's no time to lose." "I am going, Madame, I am going," said Brichot, as General Deltour moved away. But first of all the Professor took me aside for a moment: "Moral Duty," he said, "is less clearly imperative than our Ethics teach us. Whatever the Theosophical cafés and the Kantian beer-houses may say, we are deplorably ignorant of the nature of Good. I myself who, without wishing to boast, have lectured to my pupils, in all innocence, upon the philosophy of the said Immanuel Kant, I can see no precise ruling for the case of social casuistry with which I am now confronted in that Critique of Practical Reason in which the great renegade of Protestantism platonised in the German manner for a Germany prehistorically sentimental and aulic, ringing all the changes of a Pomeranian mysticism. It is still the Symposium, but held this time at Königsberg, in the local style, indigestible and reeking of sauerkraut, and without any good-looking boys. It is obvious on the one hand that I cannot refuse our excellent hostess the small service that she asks of me, in a fully orthodox conformity with traditional morals. One ought to avoid, above all things, for there are few that involve one in more foolish speeches, letting oneself be lured by words. But after all, let us not hesitate to admit that if the mothers of families were entitled to vote, the Baron would run the risk of being lamentably blackballed for the Chair of Virtue. It is unfortunately with the temperament of a rake that he pursues the vocation of a pedagogue; observe that I am not speaking evil of the Baron; that good man, who can carve a joint like nobody in the world, combines with a genius for anathema treasures of goodness. He can be most amusing as a superior sort of wag, whereas with a certain one of my colleagues, an Academician, if you please, I am bored, as Xenophon would say, at a hundred drachmae to the hour. But I am afraid that he is expending upon Morel rather more than a wholesome morality enjoins, and without knowing to what extent the young penitent shews himself docile or rebellious to the special exercises which his catechist imposes upon him by way of mortification, one need not be a learned clerk to be aware that we should be erring, as the other says, on the side of clemency with regard to this Rosicrucian who seems to have come down to us from Petronius, by way of Saint-Simon, if we granted him with our eyes shut, duly signed and sealed, permission to satanise. And yet, in keeping the man occupied while Mme. Verdurin, for the sinner's good and indeed rightly tempted by such a cure of souls, proceeds—by speaking to the young fool without any concealment—to remove from him all that he loves, to deal him perhaps a fatal blow, it seems to me that I am leading him into what one might call a man-trap, and I recoil as though from a base action." This said, he did not hesitate to commit it, but, taking him by the arm, began: "Come, Baron, let us go and smoke a cigarette, this young man has not yet seen all the marvels of the house." I made the excuse that I was obliged to go home. "Just wait a moment," said Brichot. "You remember, you are giving me a lift, and I have not forgotten your promise." "Wouldn't you like me, really, to make them bring out their plate, nothing could be simpler," said M. de Charlus. "You promised me, remember, not a word about Morel's decoration. I mean to give him the surprise of announcing it presently when people have begun to leave, although he says that it is of no importance to an artist, but that his uncle would like him to have it" (I blushed, for, I thought to myself, the Verdurins would know through my grandfather what Morel's uncle was). "Then you wouldn't like me to make them bring out the best pieces," said M. de Charlus. "Of course, you know them already, you have seen them a dozen times at la Raspelière." I dared not tell him that what might have interested me was not the mediocrity of even the most splendid plate in a middle-class household, but some specimen, were it only reproduced in a fine engraving, of Mme. Du Barry's. I was far too gravely preoccupied—even if I had not been by this revelation as to Mlle. Vinteuil's expected presence—always, in society, far too much distracted and agitated to fasten my attention upon objects that were more or less beautiful. It could have been arrested only by the appeal of some reality that addressed itself to my imagination, as might have been, this evening, a picture of that Venice of which I had thought so much during the afternoon, or some general element, common to several forms and more genuine than they, which, of its own accord, never failed to arouse in me an inward appreciation, normally lulled in slumber, the rising of which to the surface of my consciousness filled me with great joy. Well, as I emerged from the room known as the concert-room, and crossed the other drawing-rooms with Brichot and M. de Charlus, on discovering, transposed among others, certain pieces of furniture which I had seen at la Raspelière and to which I had paid no attention, I perceived, between the arrangement of the town house and that of the country house, a certain common air of family life, a permanent identity, and I understood what Brichot meant when he said to me with a smile: "There, look at this room, it may perhaps give you an idea of what things were like in Rue Montalivet, twenty-five years ago." From his smile, a tribute to the defunct drawing-room which he saw with his mind's eye, I understood that what Brichot, perhaps without realising it, preferred in the old room, more than the large windows, more than the gay youth of his hosts and their faithful, was that unreal part (which I myself could discern from some similarities between la Raspelière and Quai Conti) of which, in a drawing-room as in everything else, the external, actual part, liable to everyone's control, is but the prolongation, was that part become purely imaginary, of a colour which no longer existed save for my elderly guide, which he was incapable of making me see, that part which has detached itself from the outer world, to take refuge in our soul, to which it gives a surplus value, in which it is assimilated to its normal substance, transforming itself—houses that have been pulled down, people long dead, bowls of fruit at the suppers which we recall—into that translucent alabaster of our memories, the colour of which we are incapable of displaying, since we alone see it, which enables us to say truthfully to other people, speaking of things past, that they cannot form any idea of them, that they do not resemble anything that they have seen, while we are unable to think of them ourselves without a certain emotion, remembering that it is upon the existence of our thoughts that there depends, for a little time still, their survival, the brilliance of the lamps that have been extinguished and the fragrance of the arbours that will never bloom again. And possibly, for this reason, the drawing-room in Rue Montalivet disparaged, for Brichot, the Verdurins' present home. But on the other hand it added to this home, in the Professor's eyes, a beauty which it could not have in those of a stranger. Those pieces of the original furniture that had been transported here, and sometimes arranged in the same groups, and which I myself remembered from la Raspelière, introduced into the new drawing-room fragments of the old which, at certain moments, recalled it so vividly as to create a hallucination and then seemed themselves scarcely real from having evoked in the midst of the surrounding reality fragments of a vanished world which seemed to extend round about them. A sofa that had risen up from dreamland between a pair of new and thoroughly substantial armchairs, smaller chairs upholstered in pink silk, the cloth surface of a card-table raised to the dignity of a person since, like a person, it had a past, a memory, retaining in the chill and gloom of Quai Conti the tan of its roasting by the sun through the windows of Rue Montalivet (where it could tell the time of day as accurately as Mme. Verdurin herself) and through the glass doors at la Raspelière, where they had taken it and where it used to gaze out all day long over the flower-beds of the garden at the valley far below, until it was time for Cottard and the musician to sit down to their game; a posy of violets and pansies in pastel, the gift of a painter friend, now dead, the sole fragment that survived of a life that had vanished without leaving any trace, summarising a great talent and a long friendship, recalling his keen, gentle eyes, his shapely hand, plump and melancholy, while he was at work on it; the incoherent, charming disorder of the offerings of the faithful, which have followed the lady of the house on all her travels and have come in time to assume the fixity of a trait of character, of a line of destiny; a profusion of cut flowers, of

chocolate-boxes which here as in the country systematised their growth
in an identical mode of blossoming; the curious interpolation of those
singular and superfluous objects which still appear to have been just taken
from the box in which they were offered and remain for ever what they
were at first, New Year's Day presents; all those things, in short, which
one could not have isolated from the rest, but which for Brichot, an old
frequenter of the Verdurin parties, had that patina, that velvety bloom
of things to which, giving them a sort of profundity, an astral body has
been added; all these things scattered before him, sounded in his ear like
so many resonant keys which awakened cherished likenesses in his heart,
confused reminiscences which, here in this drawing-room of the present
day that was littered with them, cut out, defined, as on a fine day a shaft
of sunlight cuts a section in the atmosphere, the furniture and carpets, and
pursuing it from a cushion to a flower-stand, from a footstool to a lingering scent, from the lighting arrangements to the colour scheme, carved,
evoked, spiritualised, called to life a form which might be called the ideal
aspect, immanent in each of their successive homes, of the Verdurin
drawing-room. "We must try," Brichot whispered in my ear, "to get the
Baron upon his favourite topic. He is astounding." Now on the one hand
I was glad of an opportunity to try to obtain from M. de Charlus information as to the coming of Mlle. Vinteuil and her friend. On the other hand,
I did not wish to leave Albertine too long by herself, not that she could
(being uncertain of the moment of my return, not to mention that, at so
late an hour, she could not have received a visitor or left the house herself
without arousing comment) make any evil use of my absence, but simply
so that she might not find it too long. And so I told Brichot and M. de
Charlus that I must shortly leave them. "Come with us all the same," said
the Baron, whose social excitement was beginning to flag, but feeling that
need to prolong, to spin out a conversation, which I had already observed
in the Duchesse de Guermantes as well as in himself, and which, while
distinctive of their family, extends in a more general fashion to all those
people who, offering their minds no other realisation than talk, that is
to say an imperfect realisation, remain unassuaged even after hours spent
in one's company, and attach themselves more and more hungrily to their
exhausted companion, from whom they mistakenly expect a satiety which
social pleasures are incapable of giving. "Come, won't you," he repeated,
"this is the pleasant moment at a party, the moment when all the guests
have gone, the hour of Doña Sol; let us hope that it will end less tragi-
cally. Unfortunately you are in a hurry, in a hurry probably to go and
do things which you would much better leave undone. People are always
in a hurry and leave at the time when they ought to be arriving. We are
here like Couture's philosophers, this is the moment in which to go over
the events of the evening, to make what is called in military language a
criticism of the operations. We might ask Mme. Verdurin to send us in
a little supper to which we should take care not to invite her, and we might
request Charlie—still *Hernani*—to play for ourselves alone the sublime
adagio. Isn't it fine, that adagio? But where is the young violinist, I would
like to congratulate him, this is the moment for tender words and em-

braces. Admit, Brichot, that they played like gods, Morel especially. Did you notice the moment when that lock of hair came loose? Ah, then, my dear fellow, you saw nothing at all. There was an F sharp at which Enesco, Capet and Thibaut might have died of jealousy; I may have appeared calm enough, I can tell you that at such a sound my heart was so wrung that I could barely control my tears. The whole room sat breathless; Brichot, my dear fellow," cried the Baron, gripping the other's arm which he shook violently, "it was sublime. Only young Charlie preserved a stony immobility, you could not even see him breathe, he looked like one of those objects of the inanimate world of which Théodore Rousseau speaks, which make us think, but do not think themselves. And then, all of a sudden," cried M. de Charlus with enthusiasm, making a pantomime gesture, "then . . . the Lock! And all the time, the charming little country-dance of the allegro vivace. You know, that lock was the symbol of the revelation, even to the most obtuse. The Princess of Taormina, deaf until then, for there are none so deaf as those that have ears and hear not, the Princess of Taormina, confronted by the message of the miraculous lock, realised that it was music that they were playing and not poker. Oh, that was indeed a solemn moment." "Excuse me, Sir, for interrupting you," I said to M. de Charlus, hoping to bring him to the subject in which I was interested, "you told me that the composer's daughter was to be present. I should have been most interested to meet her. Are you certain that she was expected?" "Oh, that I can't say." M. de Charlus thus complied, perhaps unconsciously, with that universal rule by which people withhold information from a jealous lover, whether in order to shew an absurd 'comradeship,' as a point of honour, and even if they detest her, with the woman who has excited his jealousy, or out of malice towards her, because they guess that jealousy can only intensify love, or from that need to be disagreeable to other people which consists in revealing the truth to the rest of the world but concealing it from the jealous, ignorance increasing their torment, or so at least the tormentors suppose, who, in their desire to hurt other people are guided by what they themselves believe, wrongly perhaps, to be most painful. "You know," he went on, "in this house they are a trifle prone to exaggerate, they are charming people, still they do like to catch celebrities of one sort or another. But you are not looking well, and you will catch cold in this damp room," he said, pushing a chair towards me. "Since you have not been well, you must take care of yourself, let me go and find you your coat. No, don't go for it yourself, you will lose your way and catch cold. How careless people are; you might be an infant in arms, you want an old nurse like me to look after you." "Don't trouble, Baron, let me go," said Brichot, and left us immediately; not being precisely aware perhaps of the very warm affection that M. de Charlus felt for me and of the charming lapses into simplicity and devotion that alternated with his delirious crises of grandeur and persecution, he was afraid that M. de Charlus, whom Mme. Verdurin had entrusted like a prisoner to his vigilance, might simply be seeking, under the pretext of asking for my greatcoat, to return to Morel and might thus upset the Mistress's plan.

Meanwhile Ski had sat down, uninvited, at the piano, and assuming—with a playful knitting of his brows, a remote gaze and a slight twist of his lips—what he imagined to be an artistic air, was insisting that Morel should play something by Bizet. "What, you don't like it, that boyish music of Bizet. Why, my dear fellow," he said, with that rolling of the letter *r* which was one of his peculiarities, "it's rravishing." Morel, who did not like Bizet, said so in exaggerated terms and (as he had the reputation in the little clan of being, though it seems incredible, a wit) Ski, pretending to take the violinist's diatribes as paradoxes, burst out laughing. His laugh was not, like M. Verdurin's, the stifled gasp of a smoker. Ski first of all assumed a subtle air, then allowed to escape, as though against his will, a single note of laughter, like the first clang from a belfry, followed by a silence in which the subtle gaze seemed to be making a competent examination of the absurdity of what had been said, then a second peal of laughter shook the air, followed presently by a merry angelus.

I expressed to M. de Charlus my regret that M. Brichot should be taking so much trouble. "Not at all, he is delighted, he is very fond of you, everyone is fond of you. Somebody was saying only the other day: 'We never see him now, he is isolating himself!' Besides, he is such a good fellow, is Brichot," M. de Charlus went on, never suspecting probably, in view of the affectionate, frank manner in which the Professor of Moral Philosophy conversed with him, that he had no hesitation is slandering him behind his back. "He is a man of great merit, immensely learned, and not a bit spoiled, his learning hasn't turned him into a bookworm, like so many of them who smell of ink. He has retained a breadth of outlook, a tolerance, rare in his kind. Sometimes, when one sees how well he understands life, with what a natural grace he renders everyone his due, one asks oneself where a humble little Sorbonne professor, an ex-schoolmaster, can have picked up such breeding. I am astonished at it myself." I was even more astonished when I saw the conversation of this Brichot, which the least refined of Mme. de Guermantes's friends would have found so dull, so heavy, please the most critical of them all, M. de Charlus. But to achieve this result there had collaborated, among other influences, themselves distinct also, those by virtue of which Swann, on the one hand, had so long found favour with the little clan, when he was in love with Odette, and on the other hand, after he married, found an attraction in Mme. Bontemps who, pretending to adore the Swann couple, came incessantly to call upon the wife and revelled in all the stories about the husband. Just as a writer gives the palm for intelligence, not to the most intelligent man, but to the worldling who utters a bold and tolerant comment upon the passion of a man for a woman, a comment which makes the writer's blue-stocking mistress agree with him in deciding that of all the people who come to her house the least stupid is after all this old beau who shews experience in the things of love, so M. de Charlus found more intelligent than the rest of his friends Brichot, who was not merely kind to Morel, but would cull from the Greek philosophers, the Latin poets, the authors of Oriental tales, appropriate texts which decorated the Baron's propensity with a strange and charming anthology. M. de Charlus had reached the age at which a Victor Hugo chooses to surround himself, above all, with Vacqueries and Meurices. He preferred to all others those men who tolerated his outlook upon life. "I see a great deal of him," he went on, in a balanced, sing-song tone, allowing no movement of his lips to stir his grave, powdered mask over which were purposely lowered his prelatical eyelids. "I attend his lectures, that atmosphere of the Latin Quarter refreshes me, there is a studious, thoughtful adolescence of young bourgeois, more intelligent, better read than were, in a different sphere, my own contemporaries. It is a different world, which you know probably better than I, they are young *bourgeois*," he said, detaching the last word to which he prefixed a string of *b*s, and emphasising it from a sort of habit of elocution, corresponding itself to a taste for fine distinctions in past history, which was peculiar to him, but perhaps also from inability to resist the pleasure of giving me a flick of his insolence. This did not in any way diminish the great and affectionate pity that was inspired in me by M. de Charlus (after Mme. Verdurin had revealed her plan in my hearing), it merely amused me, and indeed on any other occasion, when I should not have felt so kindly disposed towards him, would not have offended me. I derived from my grandmother such an absence of any self-importance that I might easily be found wanting in dignity. Doubtless, I was scarcely aware of this, and by dint of having seen and heard, from my schooldays onwards, my most esteemed companions take offence if anyone failed to keep an appointment, refuse to overlook any disloyal behaviour, I had come in time to exhibit in my speech and actions a second nature which was stamped with pride. I was indeed considered extremely proud, because, as I had never been timid, I had been easily led into duels, the moral prestige of which, however, I diminished by making little of them, which easily persuaded other people that they were absurd; but the true nature which we trample underfoot continues nevertheless to abide within us. Thus it is that at times, if we read the latest masterpiece of a man of genius, we are delighted to find in it all those of our own reflexions which we have always despised, joys and sorrows which we have repressed, a whole world of feelings scorned by us, the value of which the book in which we discover them afresh at once teaches us. I had come in time to learn from my experience of life that it was a mistake to smile a friendly smile when somebody made a fool of me, instead of feeling annoyed. But this want of self-importance and resentment, if I had so far ceased to express it as to have become almost entirely unaware that it existed in me, was nevertheless the primitive, vital element in which I was steeped. Anger and spite came to me only in a wholly different manner, in furious crises. What was more, the sense of justice was so far lacking in me as to amount to an entire want of moral sense. I was in my heart of hearts entirely won over to the side of the weaker party, and of anyone who was in trouble. I had no opinion as to the proportion in which good and evil might be blended in the relations between Morel and M. de Charlus, but the thought of the sufferings that were being prepared for M. de Charlus was intolerable to me. I would have liked to warn him, but did not know how to do it. "The spectacle of all that laborious little world is very pleasant to an old stick like myself. I do not know them," he went on, raising his hand with an air of reserve—so as not to appear to be boasting of his own conquests, to testify to his own purity and not to allow any suspicion to rest upon that of the students—"but they are most civil, they often go so far as to keep a place for me, since I am a very old gentleman. Yes indeed, my dear boy, do not protest, I am past forty," said the Baron, who was past sixty. "It is a trifle stuffy in the hall in which Brichot lectures, but it is always interesting." Albeit the Baron preferred to mingle with the youth of the schools, in other words to be jostled by them, sometimes, to save him a long wait in the lecture-room, Brichot took him in by his own door. Brichot might well be at home in the Sorbonne, at the moment when the janitor, loaded with chains of office, stepped out before him, and the master admired by his young pupils followed, he could not repress a certain timidity, and much as he desired to profit by that moment in which he felt himself so important to shew consideration for Charlus, he was nevertheless slightly embarrassed; so that the janitor should allow him to pass, he said to him, in an artificial tone and with a preoccupied air: "Follow me, Baron, they'll find a place for you," then, without paying any more attention to him, to make his own entry, he advanced by himself briskly along the corridor. On either side, a double hedge of young lecturers greeted him; Brichot, anxious not to appear to be posing in the eyes of these young men to whom he knew that he was a great pontiff, bestowed on them a thousand glances, a thousand little nods of connivance, to which his desire to remain martial, thoroughly French, gave the effect of a sort of cordial encouragement by an old soldier saying: "Damn it all, we can face the foe." Then the applause of his pupils broke out. Brichot sometimes extracted from this attendance by M. de Charlus at his lectures an opportunity for giving pleasure, almost for returning hospitality. He would say to some parent, or to one of his middle-class friends: "If it would interest your wife or daughter, I may tell you that the Baron de Charlus, Prince de Carency, a scion of the House of Condé, attends my lectures. It is something to remember, having seen one of the last descendants of our aristocracy who preserves the type. If they care to come, they will know him because he will be sitting next to my chair. Besides he will be alone there, a stout man, with white hair and black moustaches, wearing the military medal." "Oh, thank you," said the father. And, albeit his wife had other engagements, so as not to disoblige Brichot, he made her attend the lecture, while the daughter, troubled by the heat and the crowd, nevertheless devoured eagerly with her eyes the descendant of Condé, marvelling all the same that he was not crowned with strawberry-leaves and looked just like anybody else of the present day. He meanwhile had no eyes for her, but more than one student, who did not know who he was, was amazed at his friendly glances, became self-conscious and stiff, and the Baron left the room full of dreams and melancholy. "Forgive me if I return to the subject," I said quickly to M. de Charlus, for I could hear Brichot returning, "but could you let me know by wire if you should hear that Mlle. Vinteuil or her friend is expected in Paris, letting me know exactly how long they will be staying and without telling anybody that I asked you." I had almost ceased to believe that she had been expected, but I wished to guard myself thus for the future. "Yes, I will do that for you, first of all because I owe you a great debt of gratitude. By not accepting what, long ago, I had offered you, you rendered me, to your own loss, an immense service, you left me my liberty. It is true that I have abdicated it in another fashion," he added in a melancholy tone beneath which was visible a desire to take me into his confidence; "that is what I continue to regard as the important fact, a whole combination of circumstances which you failed to turn to your own account, possibly because fate warned you at that precise minute not to cross my path. For always man proposes and God disposes. Who knows whether if, on the day when we came away together from Mme. de Villeparisis's, you had accepted, perhaps many things that have since happened would never have occurred?" In some embarrassment, I turned the conversation, seizing hold of the name of Mme. de Villeparisis, and sought to find out from him, so admirably qualified in every respect, for what reasons Mme. de Villeparisis seemed to be held aloof by the aristocratic world. Not only did he not give me the solution of this little social problem, he did not even appear to me to be aware of its existence. I then realised that the position of Mme. de Villeparisis, if it was in later years to appear great to posterity, and even in the Marquise's lifetime to the ignorant rich, had appeared no less great at the opposite extremity of society, that which touched Mme. de Villeparisis, that of the Guermantes. She was their aunt; they saw first and foremost birth, connexions by marriage, the opportunity of impressing some sister-in-law with the importance of their own family. They regarded this less from the social than from the family point of view. Now this was more brilliant in the case of Mme. de Villeparisis than I had supposed. I had been impressed when I heard that the title Villeparisis was falsely assumed. But there are other examples of great ladies who have made degrading marriages and preserved a predominant position. M. de Charlus began by informing me that Mme. de Villeparisis was a niece of the famous Duchesse de ——, the most celebrated member of the great aristocracy during the July Monarchy, albeit she had refused to associate with the Citizen King and his family. I had so longed to hear stories about this Duchess! And Mme. de Villeparisis, the kind Mme. de Villeparisis, with those cheeks that to me had been the cheeks of an ordinary woman, Mme. de Villeparisis who sent me so many presents and whom I could so easily have seen every day, Mme. de Villeparisis was her niece brought up by her, in her home, at the Hôtel de ——. "She asked the Duc de Doudeauville," M. de Charlus told me, "speaking of the three sisters, 'Which of the sisters do you prefer?' And when Doudeauville said: 'Madame de Villeparisis,' the Duchesse de —— replied 'Pig!' For the Duchess was extremely *witty*," said M. de Charlus, giving the word the importance and the special pronunciation in use among the Guermantes. That he should have thought the expression so 'witty' did not, however, surprise me, for I had on many other occasions remarked the centrifugal, objective tendency which leads men to abdicate, when they are relishing the wit of others, the severity with which they would criticise their own, and to observe, to record faithfully, what they would have scorned to create. "But what on earth is he doing, that is my greatcoat he is bringing," he said, on seeing that Brichot had made so long a search to no better result. "I would have done better to go for it myself. However, you can put it on now. Are you aware that it is highly compromising, my dear boy, it is like drinking out of the same glass, I shall be able to read your thoughts. No, not like that, come, let me do it," and as he put me into his greatcoat, he pressed it down on my shoulders, fastened it round my throat, and brushed my chin with his hand, making the apology: "At his age, he doesn't know how to put on a coat, one has to titivate him, I have missed my vocation, Brichot, I was born to be a nursery-maid." I wanted to go home, but as M. de Charlus had expressed his intention of going in search of Morel, Brichot detained us both. Moreover, the certainty that when I went home I should find Albertine there, a certainty as absolute as that which I had felt in the afternoon that Albertine would return home from the Trocadéro, made me at this moment as little impatient to see her as I had been then when I was si:ting at the piano, after Françoise had sent me her telephone message. And it was this calm that enabled me, whenever, in the course of this conversation, I attempted to rise, to obey Brichot's injunctions who was afraid that my departure might prevent Charlus from remaining with him until the moment when Mme. Verdurin was to come and fetch us. "Come," he said to the Baron, "stay a little here with us, you shall give him the accolade presently," Brichot added, fastening upon myself his almost sightless eyes to which the many operations that he had undergone had restored some degree of life, but which had not all the same the mobility necessary to the sidelong expression of malice. "The accolade, how absurd!" cried the Baron, in a shrill and rapturous tone. "My boy, I tell you, he imagines he is at a prize-giving, he is dreaming of his young pupils. I ask myself whether he don't sleep with them." "You wish to meet Mlle. Vinteuil," said Brichot, who had overheard the last words of our conversation. "I promise to let you know if she comes, I shall hear of it from Mme. Verdurin," for he doubtless foresaw that the Baron was in peril of an immediate exclusion from the little clan. "I see, so you think that I have less claim than yourself upon Mme. Verdurin," said M. de Charlus, "to be informed of the coming of these terribly disreputable persons. You know that they are quite notorious. Mme. Verdurin is wrong to allow them to come here, they are all very well for the fast set. They are friends with a terrible band of women. They meet in the most appalling places." At each of these words, my suffering was increased by the addition of a fresh suffering, changing in form. "Certainly not, I don't suppose that I have any better claim than yourself upon Mme. Verdurin," Brichot protested, punctuating his words, for he was afraid that he might have aroused the Baron's suspicions. And as he saw that I was determined to go, seeking to detain me with the bait of the promised entertainment: "There is one thing which the Baron seems to me not to have taken into account when he speaks of the reputation of these two ladies, namely that a person's reputation may be at the same time appalling and undeserved. Thus for instance, in the more notorious group which I shall call parallel, it is certain that the errors of justice are many and that history has registered convictions for sodomy against illustrious men who were wholly innocent of the charge. The recent discovery of Michelangelo's passionate love for a woman is a fresh fact which should entitle the friend of Leo X to the benefit of a posthumous retrial. The Michelangelo case seems to me clearly indicated to excite the snobs and mobilise the Villette, when another case in which anarchism reared its head and became the fashionable sin of our worthy dilettantes, but which must not even be mentioned now for fear of stirring up quarrels, shall have run its course." From the moment when Brichot began to speak of masculine reputations, M. de Charlus betrayed on every one of his features that special sort of impatience which one sees on the face of a medical or military expert when society people who know nothing about the subject begin to talk nonsense about points of therapeutics or strategy. "You know absolutely nothing about the matter," he said at length to Brichot. "Quote me a single reputation that is undeserved. Mention names. Oh yes, I know the whole story," was his brutal retort to a timid interruption by Brichot, "the people who tried it once long ago out of curiosity, or out of affection for a dead friend, and the man who, afraid he has gone too far, if you speak to him of the beauty of a man, replies that that is Chinese to him, that he can no more distinguish between a beautiful man and an ugly one than between the engines of two motorcars, mechanics not being in his line. That's all stuff and nonsense. Mind you, I don't mean to say that a bad (or what is conventionally so called) and yet undeserved reputation is absolutely impossible. It is so exceptional, so rare, that for practical purposes it does not exist. At the same time I, who have a certain curiosity in ferreting things out, have known cases which were not mythical. Yes, in the course of my life, I have established (scientifically speaking, of course, you mustn't take me too literally) two unjustified reputations. They generally arise from a similarity of names, or from certain outward signs, a profusion of rings, for instance, which persons who are not qualified to judge imagine to be characteristic of what you were mentioning, just as they think that a peasant never utters a sentence without adding: 'Jarnignié,' or an Englishman: 'Goddam.' Dialogue for the boulevard theatres. What will surprise you is that the unjustified are those most firmly established in the eyes of the public. You yourself, Brichot, who would thrust your hand in the flames to answer for the virtue of some man or other who comes to this house and whom the enlightened know to be a wolf in sheep's clothing, you feel obliged to believe like every Tom, Dick and Harry in what is said about some man in the public eye who is the incarnation of those propensities to the common herd, when as a matter of fact, he doesn't care twopence for that sort of thing. I say twopence, because if we were to offer five-and-twenty louis, we should see the number of plaster saints dwindle down to nothing. As things are, the average rate of sanctity, if you see any sanctity in that sort of thing, is somewhere between thirty and forty per cent." If Brichot had transferred to the male sex the question of evil reputations, with me it was, inversely, to the female sex that, thinking of Albertine, I applied the Baron's words. I was appalled at his statistics, even when I bore in mind that he was probably enlarging his figures to reach the total that he would like to believe true, and had based them moreover upon the reports of persons who were scandalmongers and possibly liars, and had in any case been led astray by their own desire, which, coming in addition to that of M. de Charlus, doubtless falsified the Baron's calculations. "Thirty per cent!" exclaimed Brichot. "Why, even if the proportions were reversed I should still have to multiply the guilty a hundredfold. If it is as you say, Baron, and you are not mistaken, then we must confess that you are one of those rare visionaries who discern a truth which nobody round them has ever suspected. Just as Barrès made discoveries as to parliamentary corruption, the truth of which was afterwards established, like the existence of Leverrier's planet. Mme. Verdurin would prefer not to name who detected in the Intelligence Bureau, in the General Staff, activities inspired, I am sure, by patriotic zeal, which I had never imagined. Upon free-masonry, German espionage, morphinomania, Léon Daudet builds up, day by day, a fantastic fairy-tale which turns out to be the barest truth. Thirty per cent!" Brichot repeated in stupefaction. It is only fair to say that M. de Charlus taxed the great majority of his contemporaries with inversion, always excepting those men with whom he himself had had relations, their case, provided that they had introduced the least trace of romance into those relations, appearing to him more complex. So it is that we see men of the world, who refuse to believe in women's honour, allow some remnants of honour only to the woman who has been their mistress, as to whom they protest sincerely and with an air of mystery: "No, you are mistaken, she is not that sort of girl." This unlooked-for tribute is dictated partly by their own self-respect which is flattered by the supposition that such favours have been reserved for them alone, partly by their simplicity which has easily swallowed everything that their mistress has given them to believe, partly from that sense of the complexity of life which brings it about that, as soon as we approach other people, other lives, ready-made labels and classifications appear unduly crude. "Thirty per cent! But have a care; less fortunate than the historians whose conclusions the future will justify, Baron, if you were to present to posterity the statistics that you offer us, it might find them erroneous. Posterity judges only from documentary evidence, and will insist on being assured of your facts. But as no document would be forthcoming to authenticate this sort of collective phenomena which the few persons who are enlightened are only too ready to leave in obscurity, the best minds would be moved to indignation, and you would be regarded as nothing more than a slanderer or a lunatic. After having, in the social examination, obtained top marks and the primacy upon this earth, you would taste the sorrows of a blackball beyond the grave. That is not worth powder and shot, to quote—may God forgive me—our friend Bossuet." "I am not interested in history," replied M. de Charlus, "this life is sufficient for me, it is quite interesting enough, as poor Swann used to say." "What, you knew Swann, Baron, I was not aware of that. Tell me, was he that way inclined?" Brichot inquired with an air of misgiving! "What a mind the man has! So you suppose that I only know men like that. No,

I don't think so," said Charlus, looking to the ground and trying to weigh
the pros and cons. And deciding that, since he was dealing with Swann
whose hostility to that sort of thing had always been notorious, a half-
admission could only be harmless to him who was its object and flattering
to him who allowed it to escape in an insinuation: "I don't deny that long
ago in our schooldays, once by accident," said the Baron, as though unwillingly and as though he were thinking aloud, then recovering himself:
"But that was centuries ago, how do you expect me to remember, you are
making a fool of me," he concluded with a laugh. "In any case, he was
never what you'd call a beauty!" said Brichot who, himself hideous,
thought himself good-looking and was always ready to believe that other
men were ugly. "Hold your tongue," said the Baron, "you don't know
what you're talking about, in those days he had a peach-like complexion,
and," he added, finding a fresh note for each syllable, "he was as beautiful
as Cupid himself. Besides he was always charming. The women were madly
in love with him." "But did you ever know his wife?" "Why, it was through
me that he came to know her. I thought her charming in her disguise one
evening when she played Miss Sacripant; I was with some fellows from
the club, each of us took a woman home with him, and, although all that
I wanted was to go to sleep, slanderous tongues alleged, for it is terrible
how malicious people are, that I went to bed with Odette. Only she took
advantage of the slanders to come and worry me, and I thought I might
get rid of her by introducing her to Swann. From that moment she never
let me go, she couldn't spell the simplest word, it was I who wrote all her
letters for her. And it was I who, afterwards, had to take her out. That,
my boy, is what comes of having a good reputation, you see. Though I
only half deserved it. She forced me to help her to betray him, with five,
with six other men." And the lovers whom Odette had had in succession
(she had been with this man, then with that, those men not one of whose
names had ever been guessed by poor Swann, blinded in turn by jealousy
and by love, reckoning the chances and believing in oaths more affirmative
than a contradiction which escapes from the culprit, a contradiction far
more unseizable, and at the same time far more significant, of which the
jealous lover might take advantage more logically than of the information
which he falsely pretends to have received, in the hope of confusing his
mistress), these lovers M. de Charlus began to enumerate with as absolute
a certainty as if he had been repeating the list of the Kings of France.
And indeed the jealous lover is, like the contemporaries of an historical
event, too close, he knows nothing, and it is in the eyes of strangers that
the comic aspect of adultery assumes the precision of history, and prolongs
itself in lists of names which are, for that matter, unimportant and become
painful only to another jealous lover, such as myself, who cannot help
comparing his own case with that which he hears mentioned and asks
himself whether the woman of whom he is suspicious cannot boast an
equally illustrious list. But he can never know anything more, it is a sort
of universal conspiracy, a 'blindman's buff' in which everyone cruelly
participates, and which consists, while his mistress flits from one to another,
in holding over his eyes a bandage which he is perpetually attempting to

tear off without success, for everyone keeps him blindfold, poor wretch,
the kind out of kindness, the wicked out of malice, the coarse-minded out
of their love of coarse jokes, the well-bred out of politeness and good-
breeding, and all alike respecting one of those conventions which are called
principles. "But did Swann never know that you had enjoyed her favours?"
"What an idea! If you had suggested such a thing to Charles! It's enough
to make one's hair stand up on end. Why, my dear fellow, he would have
killed me on the spot, he was as jealous as a tiger. Any more than I ever
confessed to Odette, not that she would have minded in the least, that
. . . but you must not make my tongue run away with me. And the joke
of it is that it was she who fired a revolver at him, and nearly hit me. Oh!
I used to have a fine time with that couple; and naturally it was I who
was obliged to act as his second against d'Osmond, who never forgave me.
D'Osmond had carried off Odette and Swann, to console himself, had
taken as his mistress, or make-believe mistress, Odette's sister. But really
you must not begin to make me tell you Swann's story, we should be here
for ten years, don't you know, nobody knows more about him than I do.
It was I who used to take Odette out when she did not wish to see Charles.
It was all the more awkward for me as I have a quite near relative who
bears the name Crécy, without of course having any manner of right to
it, but still he was none too well pleased. For she went by the name of
Odette de Crécy, as she very well might, being merely separated from a
Crécy whose wife she still was, and quite an authentic person, a highly
respectable gentleman out of whom she had drained his last farthing. But
why should I have to tell you about this Crécy, I have seen you with him
on the crawler, you used to have him to dinner at Balbec. He must have
needed those dinners, poor fellow, he lived upon a tiny allowance that
Swann made him; I am greatly afraid that, since my friend's death, that
income must have stopped altogether. What I do not understand," M. de
Charlus said to me, "is that, since you used often to go to Charles's, you
did not ask me this evening to present you to the Queen of Naples. In
fact I can see that you are less interested in *people* than in curiosities,
and that continues to surprise me in a person who knew Swann, in whom
that sort of interest was so far developed that it is impossible to say whether
it was I who initiated him in these matters or he myself. It surprises me
as much as if I met a person who had known Whistler and remained ignorant of what is meant by taste. By Jove, it is Morel that ought really
to have been presented to her, he was passionately keen on it too, for he is
the most intelligent fellow you could imagine. It is a nuisance that she
has left. However, I shall effect the conjunction one of these days. It is
indispensable that he should know her. The only possible obstacle would
be if she were to die in the night. Well, we may hope that it will not happen." All of a sudden Brichot, who was still suffering from the shock of
the proportion 'thirty per cent' which M. de Charlus had revealed to him,
Brichot who had continued all this time in the pursuit of his idea, with
an abruptness which suggested that of an examining magistrate seeking
to make a prisoner confess, but which was in reality the result of the Professor's desire to appear perspicacious and of the misgivings that he felt

about launching so grave an accusation, spoke. "Isn't Ski like that?" he inquired of M. de Charlus with a sombre air. To make us admire his alleged power of intuition, he had chosen Ski, telling himself that since there were only three innocent men in every ten, he ran little risk of being mistaken if he named Ski who seemed to him a trifle odd, suffered from insomnia, scented himself, in short was not entirely normal. *"Nothing of the sort!"* exclaimed the Baron with a bitter, dogmatic, exasperated irony. "What you say is utterly false, absurd, fantastic. Ski is like that precisely to the people who know nothing about it; if he was, he would not look so like it, be it said without any intention to criticise, for he has a certain charm, indeed I find something very attractive about him." "But give us a few names, then," Brichot pursued with insistence. M. de Charlus drew himself up with a forbidding air. "Ah! my dear Sir, I, as you know, live in a world of abstraction, all that sort of thing interests me only from a transcendental point of view," he replied with the touchy susceptibility peculiar to men of his kind, and the affectation of grandiloquence that characterised his conversation. "To me, you understand, it is only general principles that are of any interest, I speak to you of this as I might of the law of gravitation." But these moments of irritable reaction in which the Baron sought to conceal his true life lasted but a short time compared with the hours of continual progression in which he allowed it to be guessed, displayed it with an irritating complacency, the need to confide being stronger in him than the fear of divulging his secret. "What I was trying to say," he went on, "is that for one evil reputation that is unjustified there are hundreds of good ones which are no less so. Obviously, the number of those who do not merit their reputations varies according to whether you rely upon what is said by men of their sort or by the others. And it is true that if the malevolence of the latter is limited by the extreme difficulty which they would find in believing that a vice as horrible to them as robbery or murder is being practised by men whom they know to be sensitive and sincere, the malevolence of the former is stimulated to excess by the desire to regard as—what shall I say?—accessible, men who appeal to them, upon the strength of information given them by people who have been led astray by a similar desire, in fact by the very aloofness with which they are generally regarded. I have heard a man, viewed with considerable disfavour on account of these tastes, say that he supposed that a certain man in society shared them. And his sole reason for believing it was that this other man had been polite to him! So many reasons for *optimism*," said the Baron artlessly, "in the computation of the number. But the true reason of the enormous difference that exists between the number calculated by the profane, and that calculated by the initiated, arises from the mystery with which the latter surround their actions, in order to conceal them from the rest, who, lacking any source of information, would be literally stupefied if they were to learn merely a quarter of the truth." "Then in our days, things are as they were among the Greeks," said Brichot. "What do you mean, among the Greeks? Do you suppose that it has not been going on ever since? Take the reign of Louis XIV, you have young Vermandois, Molière, Prince Louis of Baden, Brunswick, Charolais, Boufflers, the

Great Condé, the Duc de Brissac." "Stop a moment, I knew about Monsieur, I knew about Brissac from Saint-Simon, Vendôme of course, and many. others as well. But that old pest Saint-Simon often refers to the Great Condé and Prince Louis of Baden and never mentions it." "It seems a pity, I must say, that it should fall to me to teach a Professor of the Sorbonne his history. But, my dear Master, you are as ignorant as a carp." "You are harsh, Baron, but just. And, wait a moment, now this will please you, I remember now a song of the period composed in macaronic verse about a certain storm which surprised the Great Condé as he was going down the Rhône in the company of his friend, the Marquis de La Moussaye. Condé says:

> Carus Amicus Mussaeus,
> Ah! Quod tempus, bonus Deus,
>   Landerirette
> Imbre sumus perituri.

And La Moussaye reassures him with:

> Securae sunt nostrae vitae
> Sumus enim Sodomitae
> Igne tantum perituri
> Landeriri."

"I take back what I said," said Charlus in a shrill and mannered tone, "you are a well of learning, you will write it down for me, won't you, I must preserve it in my family archives, since my great-great-great-grandmother was a sister of M. le Prince." "Yes, but, Baron, with regard to Prince Louis of Baden I can think of nothing. However, at that period, I suppose that generally speaking the art of war. . . ." "What nonsense, Vendôme, Villars, Prince Eugène, the Prince de Conti, and if I were to tell you of all the heroes of Tonkin, Morocco, and I am thinking of men who are truly sublime, and pious, and 'new generation,' I should astonish you greatly. Ah! I should have something to teach the people who are making inquiries about the new generation which has rejected the futile complications of its elders, M. Bourget tells us! I have a young friend out there, who is highly spoken of, who has done great things, however, I am not going to tell tales out of school, let us return to the seventeenth century, you know that Saint-Simon says of the Maréchal d'Huxelles—one among many: 'Voluptuous in Grecian debaucheries which he made no attempt to conceal, he used to get hold of young officers whom he trained to his purpose, not to mention stalwart young valets, and this openly, in the army and at Strasbourg.' You have probably read Madame's Letters, all his men called him 'Putain.' She is quite outspoken about it." "And she was in a good position to know, with her husband." "Such an interesting character, Madame," said M. de Charlus. "One might base upon her the lyrical synthesis of 'Wives of Aunties.' First of all, the masculine type; generally the wife of an Auntie is a man, that is what makes it so easy for her to bear him children. Then Madame does not mention Monsieur's vices, but she does mention incessantly the same vice in other men, writing as a well-informed woman, from that tendency which makes us enjoy finding in other people's families the same defects as afflict us in our own, in order to prove to ourselves that there is nothing exceptional or degrading in them. I was saying that things have been much the same in every age. Nevertheless, our own is quite remarkable in that respect. And notwithstanding the instances that I have borrowed from the seventeenth century, if my great ancestor François C. de La Rochefoucauld were alive in these days, he might say of them with even more justification than of his own—come, Brichot, help me out: 'Vices are common to every age; but if certain persons whom everyone knows had appeared in the first centuries of our era, would anyone speak to-day of the prostitutions of Heliogabalus?' *'Whom everyone knows'* appeals to me immensely. I see that my sagacious kinsman understood the tricks of his most illustrious contemporaries as I understand those of my own. But men of that sort are not only far more frequent to-day. They have also special characteristics." I could see that M. de Charlus was about to tell us in what fashion these habits had evolved. The insistence with which M. de Charlus kept on reverting to this topic—into which, moreover, his intellect, constantly trained in the same direction, had acquired a certain penetration—was, in a complicated way, distinctly trying. He was as boring as a specialist who can see nothing outside his own subject, as irritating as a well-informed man whose vanity is flattered by the secrets which he possesses and is burning to divulge, as repellent as those people who, whenever their own defects are mentioned, spread themselves without noticing that they are giving offence, as obsessed as a maniac and as uncontrollably imprudent as a criminal. These characteristics which, at certain moments, became as obvious as those that stamp a madman or a criminal, brought me, as it happened, a certain consolation. For, making them undergo the necessary transposition in order to be able to draw from them deductions with regard to Albertine, and remembering her attitude towards Saint-Loup, and towards myself, I said to myself, painful as one of these memories and melancholy as the other was to me, I said to myself that they seemed to exclude the kind of deformity so plainly denounced, the kind of specialisation inevitably exclusive, it appeared, which was so vehemently apparent in the conversation as in the person of M. de Charlus. But he, as ill luck would have it, made haste to destroy these grounds for hope in the same way as he had furnished me with them, that is to say unconsciously. "Yes," he said, "I am no longer in my teens, and I have already seen many things change round about me, I no longer recognise either society, in which the barriers are broken down, in which a mob, devoid of elegance and decency, dance the tango even in my own family, or fashions, or politics, or the arts, or religion, or anything. But I must admit that the thing which has changed most of all is what the Germans call homosexuality. Good God, in my day, apart from the men who loathed women, and those who, caring only for women, did the other thing merely with an eye to profit, the homosexuals were sound family men and never kept mistresses except to screen themselves. If I had had a daughter to give away, it is among them that I should have looked for my son-in-law if I had wished to be certain that she would not be unhappy. Alas! Things have changed entirely. Nowadays they are recruited also from the men who are the most insatiable with women. I thought I possessed a certain instinct, and that when I said to myself: 'Certainly not,' I could not have been mistaken. Well, I give it up. One of my friends, who is well-known for that sort of thing, had a coachman whom my sister-in-law Oriane found for him, a lad from Combray who was something of a jack of all trades, but particularly in trading with women, and who, I would have sworn, was as hostile as possible to anything of that sort. He broke his mistress's heart by betraying her with two women whom he adored, not to mention the others, an actress and a girl from a bar. My cousin the Prince de Guermantes, who has that irritating intelligence of people who are too ready to believe anything, said to me one day: 'But why in the world does not X—— have his coachman? It might be a pleasure to Théodore' (which is the coachman's name) 'and he may be annoyed at finding that his master does not make advances to him.' I could not help telling Gilbert to hold his tongue; I was overwrought both by that boasted perspicacity which, when it is exercised indiscriminately, is a want of perspicacity, and also by the silver-lined malice of my cousin who would have liked X—— to risk taking the first steps so that, if the going was good, he might follow." "Then the Prince de Guermantes is like that, too?" asked Brichot with a blend of astonishment and dismay. "Good God," replied M. de Charlus, highly delighted, "it is so notorious that I don't think I am guilty of an indiscretion if I tell you that he is. Very well, the year after this, I went to Balbec, where I heard from a sailor who used to take me out fishing occasionally, that my Théodore, whose sister, I may mention, is the maid of a friend of Mme. Verdurin, Baroness Putbus, used to come down to the harbour to pick up now one sailor, now another, with the most infernal cheek, to go for a trip on the sea 'with extras.'" It was now my turn to inquire whether his employer, whom I had identified as the gentleman who at Balbec used to play cards all day long with his mistress, and who was the leader of the little group of four boon companions, was like the Prince of Guermantes. "Why, of course, everyone knows about him, he makes no attempt to conceal it." "But he had his mistress there with him." "Well, and what difference does that make? How innocent these children are," he said to me in a fatherly tone, little suspecting the grief that I extracted from his words when I thought of Albertine. "She is charming, his mistress." "But then his three friends are like himself." "Not at all," he cried, stopping his ears as though, in playing some instrument, I had struck a wrong note. "Now he has gone to the other extreme. So a man has no longer the right to have friends? Ah! Youth, youth; it gets everything wrong. We shall have to begin your education over again, my boy. Well," he went on, "I admit that this case, and I know of many others, however open a mind I may try to keep for every form of audacity, does embarrass me. I may be very old-fashioned, but I fail to understand," he said in the tone of an old Gallican speaking of some development of Ultramontanism, of a Liberal Royalist speaking of the *Action Française* or of a disciple of Claude Monet speaking of the Cubists. "I do not reproach these innovators, I envy them if anything, I try to understand them, but I do not succeed. If they are so passionately fond of woman, why, and especially in this workaday world where that sort of thing is so frowned upon, where they conceal themselves from a sense of shame, have they any need of what they call 'a bit of brown'? It is because it represents to them something else. What?" "What else can a woman represent to Albertine," I thought, and there indeed lay the cause of my anguish. "Decidedly, Baron," said Brichot, "should the Board of Studies ever think of founding a Chair of Homosexuality, I shall see that your name is the first to be submitted. Or rather, no; an Institute of Psycho-physiology would suit you better. And I can see you, best of all, provided with a Chair in the Collège de France, which would enable you to devote yourself to personal researches the results of which you would deliver, like the Professor of Tamil or Sanskrit, to the handful of people who are interested in them. You would have an audience of two, with your assistant, not that I mean to cast the slightest suspicion upon our corps of janitors, whom I believe to be above suspicion." "You know nothing about them," the Baron retorted in a harsh and cutting tone. "Besides yóu are wrong in thinking that so few people are interested in the subject. It is just the opposite." And without stopping to consider the incompatibility between the invariable trend of his own conversation and the reproach which he was about to heap upon other people: "It is, on the contrary, most alarming," said the Baron, with a scandalised and contrite air, "people are talking about nothing else. It is a scandal, but I am not exaggerating, my dear fellow! It appears that, the day before yesterday, at the Duchesse d'Agen's, they talked about nothing else for two hours on end; you can imagine, if women have taken to discussing that sort of thing, it is a positive scandal! What is vilest of all is that they get their information," he went on with an extraordinary fire and emphasis, "from pests, regular harlots like young Châtellerault, who has the worst reputation in the world, who tell them stories about other men. I have been told that he said more than enough to hang me, but I don't care, I am convinced that the mud and filth flung by an individual who barely escaped being turned out of the Jockey for cheating at cards can only fall back upon himself. I am sure that if I were Jane d'Agen, I should have sufficient respect for my drawing-room not to allow such subjects to be discussed in it, nor to allow my own flesh and blood to be dragged through the mire in my house. But there is no longer any society, any rules, any conventions, in conversation any more than in dress. Ah, my dear fellow, it is the end of the world. Everyone has become so malicious. The prize goes to the man who can speak most evil of his fellows. It is appalling."

As cowardly still as I had been long ago in my boyhood at Combray when I used to run away in order not to see my grandfather tempted with brandy and the vain efforts of my grandmother imploring him not to drink it, I had but one thought in my mind, which was to leave the Verdurins' house before the execution of M. de Charlus occurred. "I simply must go," I said to Brichot. "I am coming with you," he replied, "but we cannot slip away, English fashion. Come and say good-bye to Mme. Verdurin," the Professor concluded, as he made his way to the drawing-room with the air of a man who, in a guessing game, goes to find out whether he may 'come back.'

While we conversed, M. Verdurin, at a signal from his wife, had taken Morel aside. Indeed, had Mme. Verdurin decided, after considering the matter in all its aspects, that it was wiser to postpone Morel's enlightenment, she was powerless now to prevent it. There are certain desires, some of them confined to the mouth, which, as soon as we have allowed them to grow, insist upon being gratified, whatever the consequences may be; we are unable to resist the temptation to kiss a bare shoulder at which we have been gazing for too long and at which our lips strike like a serpent at a bird, to bury our sweet tooth in a cake that has fascinated and famished it, nor can we forego the delight of the amazement, anxiety, grief or mirth to which we can move another person by some unexpected communication. So, in a frenzy of melodrama, Mme. Verdurin had ordered her husband to take Morel out of the room and, at all costs, to explain matters to him. The violinist had begun by deploring the departure of the Queen of Naples before he had had a chance of being presented to her. M. de Charlus had told him so often that she was the sister of the Empress Elisabeth and of the Duchesse d'Alençon that Her Majesty had assumed an extraordinary importance in his eyes. But the Master explained to him that it was not to talk about the Queen of Naples that they had withdrawn from the rest, and then went straight to the root of the matter. "Listen," he had concluded after a long explanation; "listen; if you like, we can go and ask my wife what she thinks. I give you my word of honour, I've said nothing to her about it. We shall see how she looks at it. My advice is perhaps not the best, but you know how sound her judgment is; besides, she is extremely attached to yourself, let us go and submit the case to her." And while Mme. Verdurin, awaiting with impatience the emotions that she would presently be relishing as she talked to the musician, and again, after he had gone, when she made her husband give her a full report of their conversation, continued to repeat: "But what in the world can they be doing? I do hope that my husband, in keeping him all this time, has managed to give him his cue," M. Verdurin reappeared with Morel who seemed greatly moved. "He would like to ask your advice," M. Verdurin said to his wife, in the tone of a man who does not know whether his prayer will be heard. Instead of replying to M. Verdurin, it was to Morel that, in the heat of her passion, Mme. Verdurin addressed herself. "I agree entirely with my husband, I consider that you cannot tolerate this sort of thing for another instant," she exclaimed with violence, discarding as a useless fiction her agreement with her husband that she was supposed to know nothing of what he had been saying to the violinist. "How do you mean? Tolerate what?" stammered M. Verdurin, endeavouring to feign astonishment and seeking, with an awkwardness that was explained by his dismay, to defend his falsehood. "I guessed what you were saying to him," replied Mme. Verdurin, undisturbed by the improbability of this explanation, and caring little what, when he recalled this scene, the violinist might think of the Mistress's veracity. "No," Mme. Verdurin continued, "I feel that you ought not to endure any longer this degrading

promiscuity with a tainted person whom nobody will have in her house,"
she went on, regardless of the fact that this was untrue and forgetting
that she herself entertained him almost daily. "You are the talk of the
Conservatoire," she added, feeling that this was the argument that carried
most weight; "another month of this life and your artistic future is shattered, whereas, without Charlus, you ought to be making at least a hundred thousand francs a year." "But I have never heard anyone utter a
word, I am astounded, I am very grateful to you," Morel murmured, the
tears starting to his eyes. But, being obliged at once to feign astonishment
and to conceal his shame, he had turned redder and was perspiring more
abundantly than if he had played all Beethoven's sonatas in succession,
and tears welled from his eyes which the Bonn Master would certainly not
have drawn from him. "If you have never heard anything, you are unique
in that respect. He is a gentleman with a vile reputation and the most
shocking stories are told about him. I know that the police are watching
him and that is perhaps the best thing for him if he is not to end like all
those men, murdered by hooligans," she went on, for as she thought of
Charlus the memory of Mme. de Duras recurred to her, and in her frenzy
of rage she sought to aggravate still further the wounds that she was in-
flicting on the unfortunate Charlie, and to avenge herself for those that
she had received in the course of the evening. "Anyhow, even financially,
he can be of no use to you, he is completely ruined since he has become
the prey of people who are blackmailing him, and who can't even make
him fork out the price of the tune they call, still less can he pay you for
your playing, for it is all heavily mortgaged, town house, country house,
everything." Morel was all the more ready to believe this lie since M. de
Charlus liked to confide in him his relations with hooligans, a race for
which the son of a valet, however debauched he may be, professes a feeling
of horror as strong as his attachment to Bonapartist principles.

Already, in the cunning mind of Morel, a plan was beginning to take
shape similar to what was called in the eighteenth century the reversal
of alliances. Determined never to speak to M. de Charlus again, he would
return on the following evening to Jupien's niece, and see that everything
was made straight with her. Unfortunately for him this plan was doomed
to failure, M. de Charlus having made an appointment for that very evening with Jupien, which the ex-tailor dared not fail to keep, in spite of
recent events. Other events, as we shall see, having followed upon Morel's
action, when Jupien in tears told his tale of woe to the Baron, the latter,
no less wretched, assured him that he would adopt the forsaken girl, that
she should assume one of the titles that were at his disposal, probably that
of Mlle. d'Oloron, that he would see that she received a thorough education,
and furnish her with a rich husband. Promises which filled Jupien with
joy and left his niece unmoved, for she was still in love with Morel, who,
from stupidity or cynicism, used to come into the shop and tease her in
Jupien's absence. "What is the matter with you," he would say with a
laugh, "with those black marks under your eyes? A broken heart? Gad,
the years pass and people change. After all, a man is free to try on a shoe,
all the more a woman, and if she doesn't fit him. . . ." He lost his temper

once only, because she cried, which he considered cowardly, unworthy of her. People are not always very tolerant of the tears which they themselves have provoked.

But we have looked too far ahead, for all this did not happen until after the Verdurins' party which we have interrupted, and we must go back to the point at which we left off. "I should never have suspected it," Morel groaned, in answer to Mme. Verdurin. "Naturally people do not say it to your face, that does not prevent your being the talk of the Conservatoire," Mme. Verdurin went on wickedly, seeking to make it plain to Morel that it was not only M. de Charlus that was being criticised, but himself also. "I can well believe that you know nothing about it; all the same, people are quite outspoken. Ask Ski what they were saying the other day at Chevillard's within a foot of us when you came into my box. I mean to say, people point you out. As far as I'm concerned, I don't pay the slightest attention, but what I do feel is that it makes a man supremely ridiculous and that he becomes a public laughing-stock for the rest of his life." "I don't know how to thank you," said Charlie in the tone we use to a dentist who has just caused us terrible pain while we tried not to let him see it, or to a too bloodthirsty second who has forced us into a duel on account of some casual remark of which he has said: "You can't swallow that." "I believe that you have plenty of character, that you are a man," replied Mme. Verdurin, "and that you will be capable of speaking out boldly, although he tells everybody that you would never dare, that he holds you fast." Charlie, seeking a borrowed dignity in which to cloak the tatters of his own, found in his memory something that he had read or, more probably, heard quoted, and at once proclaimed: "I was not brought up to eat that sort of bread. This very evening I will break with M. de Charlus. The Queen of Naples has gone, hasn't she? Otherwise, before breaking with him, I should like to ask him. . . ." "It is not necessary to break with him altogether," said Mme. Verdurin, anxious to avoid a disruption of the little nucleus. "There is no harm in your seeing him here, among our little group, where you are appreciated, where no one speaks any evil of you. But insist upon your freedom, and do not let him drag you about among all those sheep who are friendly to your face; I wish you could have heard what they were saying behind your back. Anyhow, you need feel no regret, not only are you wiping off a stain which would have marked you for the rest of your life, from the artistic point of view, even if there had not been this scandalous presentation by Charlus, I don't mind telling you that wasting yourself like this in this sham society will make people suppose that you aren't serious, give you an amateur reputation, as a little drawing-room performer, which is a terrible thing at your age. I can understand that to all those fine ladies it is highly convenient to be able to return their friends' hospitality by making you come and play for nothing, but it is your future as an artist that would foot the bill. I don't say that you shouldn't go to one or two of them. You were speaking of the Queen of Naples—who has left, for she had to go on to another party—now she is a splendid woman, and I don't mind saying that I think she has a poor opinion of Charlus and came here chiefly to please me. Yes, yes, I know she was longing to meet us, M. Verdurin and myself. That is a house in which you might play. And then I may tell you that if I take you—because the artists all know me, you understand, they have always been most obliging to me, and regard me almost as one of themselves, as their Mistress—that is a very different matter. But whatever you do, you must never go near Mme. de Duras! Don't go and make a stupid blunder like that! I know several artists who have come here and told me all about her. They know they can trust me," she said, in the sweet and simple tone which she knew how to adopt in an instant, imparting an appropriate air of modesty to her features, an appropriate charm to her eyes, "they come here, just like that, to tell me all their little troubles; the ones who are said to be most silent, go on chatting to me sometimes for hours on end and I can't tell you how interesting they are. Poor Chabrier used always to say: 'There's nobody like Mme. Verdurin for getting them to talk.' Very well, don't you know, all of them, without one exception, I have seen them in tears because they had gone to play for Mme. de Duras. It is not only the way she enjoys making her servants humiliate them, they could never get an engagement anywhere else again. The agents would say: 'Oh yes, the fellow who plays at Mme. de Duras's.' That settled it. There is nothing like that for ruining a man's future. You know what society people are like, it's not taken seriously, you may have all the talent in the world, it's a dreadful thing to have to say, but one Mme. de Duras is enough to give you the reputation of an amateur. And among artists, don't you know, well I, you can ask yourself whether I know them, when I have been moving among them for forty years, launching them, taking an interest in them; very well, when they say that somebody is an amateur, that finishes it. And people were beginning to say it of you. Indeed, at times I have been obliged to take up the cudgels, to assure them that you would not play in some absurd drawing-room! Do you know what the answer was: 'But he will be forced to go, Charlus won't even consult him, he never asks him for his opinion.' Somebody thought he would pay him a compliment and said: 'We greatly admire your friend Morel.' Can you guess what answer he made, with that insolent air which you know? 'But what do you mean by calling him my friend, we are not of the same class, say rather that he is my creature, my protégé.' " At this moment there stirred beneath the convex brows of the musical deity the one thing that certain people cannot keep to themselves, a saying which it is not merely abject but imprudent to repeat. But the need to repeat it is stronger than honour, than prudence. It was to this need that, after a few convulsive movements of her spherical and sorrowful brows, the Mistress succumbed: "Some one actually told my husband that he had said 'my servant,' but for that I cannot vouch," she added. It was a similar need that had compelled M. de Charlus, shortly after he had sworn to Morel that nobody should ever know the story of his birth, to say to Mme. Verdurin: "His father was a flunkey." A similar need again, now that the story had been started, would make it circulate from one person to another, each of whom would confide it under the seal of a secrecy which would be promised and not kept by the hearer, as by the informant himself. These stories would end, as in the game called hunt-the-thimble, by being traced back to Mme. Verdurin, bringing down upon her the wrath of the person concerned, who would at last have learned the truth. She knew this, but could not repress the words that were burning her tongue. Anyhow, the word 'servant' was bound to annoy Morel. She said 'servant' nevertheless, and if she added that she could not vouch for the word, this was so as at once to appear certain of the rest, thanks to this hint of uncertainty, and to shew her impartiality. This impartiality that she shewed, she herself found so touching that she began to speak affectionately to Charlie: "For, don't you see," she went on, "I am not blaming him, he is dragging you down into his abyss, it is true, but it is not his fault, since he wallows in it himself, since he wallows in it," she repeated in a louder tone, having been struck by the aptness of the image which had taken shape so quickly that her attention only now overtook it and was trying to give it prominence. "No, the fault that I do find with him," she said in a melting tone—like a woman drunken with her own success—"is a want of delicacy towards yourself. There are certain things which one does not say in public. Well, this evening, he was betting that he would make you blush with joy, by telling you (stuff and nonsense, of course, for his recommendation would be enough to prevent your getting it) that you were to have the Cross of the Legion of Honour. Even that I could overlook, although I have never quite liked," she went on with a delicate, dignified air, "hearing a person make a fool of his friends, but, don't you know, there are certain little things that one does resent. Such as when he told us, with screams of laughter, that if you want the Cross it's to please your uncle and that your uncle was a footman." "He told you that!" cried Charlie, believing, on the strength of this adroitly interpolated quotation, in the truth of everything that Mme. Verdurin had said! Mme. Verdurin was overwhelmed with the joy of an old mistress who, just as her young lover was on the point of deserting her, has succeeded in breaking off his marriage, and it is possible that she had not calculated her lie, that she was not even consciously lying. A sort of sentimental logic, something perhaps more elementary still, a sort of nervous reflex urging her, in order to brighten her life and preserve her happiness, to stir up trouble in the little clan, may have brought impulsively to her lips, without giving her time to check their veracity, these assertions diabolically effective if not rigorously exact. "If he had only repeated it to us, it wouldn't matter," the Mistress went on, "we know better than to listen to what he says, besides, what does a man's origin matter, you have your own value, you are what you make yourself, but that he should use it to make Mme. de Portefin laugh" (Mme. Verdurin named this lady on purpose because she knew that Charlie admired her) "that is what vexes me: my husband said to me when he heard him: 'I would sooner he had struck me in the face.' For he is as fond of you as I am, don't you know, is Gustave" (from this we learn that M. Verdurin's name was Gustave). "He is really very sensitive." "But I never told you I was fond of him," muttered M. Verdurin, acting the kind-hearted curmudgeon. "It is Charlus that is fond of him." "Oh, no! Now I realise the difference, I was betrayed by a scoundrel and you, you are good," Charlie exclaimed in all sincerity. "No, no," murmured Mme. Verdurin, seeking to retain her victory, for she felt that her Wednesdays were safe, but not to abuse it: "scoundrel is too strong; he does harm, a great deal of harm, unconsciously; you know that tale about the Legion of Honour was the affair of a moment. And it would be painful to me to repeat all that he said about your family," said Mme. Verdurin, who would have been greatly embarrassed had she been asked to do so. "Oh, even if it only took a moment, it proves that he is a traitor," cried Morel. It was at this moment that we returned to the drawing-room. "Ah!" exclaimed M. de Charlus when he saw that Morel was in the room, advancing upon him with the alacrity of the man who has skillfully organised a whole evening's entertainment with a view to an assignation with a woman, and in his excitement never imagines that he has with his own hands set the snare in which he will presently be caught and publicly thrashed by bravoes stationed in readiness by her husband. "Well, after all it is none too soon; are you satisfied, young glory, and presently young knight of the Legion of Honour? For very soon you will be able to sport your Cross," M. de Charlus said to Morel with a tender and triumphant air, but by the very mention of the decoration endorsed Mme. Verdurin's lies, which appeared to Morel to be indisputable truth. "Leave me alone, I forbid you to come near me," Morel shouted at the Baron. "You know what I mean, all right, I'm not the first young man you've tried to corrupt!" My sole consolation lay in the thought that I was about to see Morel and the Verdurins pulverised by M. de Charlus. For a thousand times less an offence I had been visited with his furious rage, no one was safe from it, a king would not have intimidated him. Instead of which, an extraordinary thing happened. One saw M. de Charlus dumb, stupefied, measuring the depths of his misery without understanding its cause, finding not a word to utter, raising his eyes to stare at each of the company in turn, with a questioning, outraged, suppliant air, which seemed to be asking them not so much what had happened as what answer he ought to make. And yet M. de Charlus possessed all the resources, not merely of eloquence but of audacity, when, seized by a rage which had long been simmering against some one, he reduced him to desperation, with the most outrageous speeches, in front of a scandalised society which had never imagined that anyone could go so far. M. de Charlus, on these occasions, burned, convulsed with a sort of epilepsy, which left everyone trembling. But in these instances he had the initiative, he launched the attack, he said whatever came into his mind (just as Bloch was able to make fun of Jews and blushed if the word Jew was uttered in his hearing). Perhaps what struck him speechless was—when he saw that M. and Mme. Verdurin turned their eyes from him and that no one was coming to his rescue—his anguish at the moment and, still more, his dread of greater anguish to come; or else that, not having lost his temper in advance, in imagination, and forged his thunderbolt, not having his rage ready as a weapon in his hand, he had been seized and dealt a mortal blow at the moment when he was unarmed (for, sensitive, neurotic, hysterical, his impulses were genuine, but his courage was a sham; indeed, as I had always thought, and this was what made me like him, his malice was a sham also: the people whom he hated, he hated because he thought that they looked down upon him; had they been civil to him, instead of flying into a furious rage with them, he would have taken them to his bosom, and he did not shew the normal reactions of a man of honour who has been insulted); or else that, in a sphere which was not his own, he felt himself less at his ease and less courageous than he would have been in the Faubourg. The fact remains that, in this drawing-room which he despised, this great nobleman (in whom his sense of superiority to the middle classes was no less essentially inherent than it had been in any of his ancestors who had stood in the dock before the Revolutionary Tribunal) could do nothing, in a paralysis of all his members, including his tongue, but cast in every direction glances of terror, outraged by the violence that had been done to him, no less suppliant than questioning. In a situation so cruelly unforeseen, this great talker could do no more than stammer: "What does it all mean, what has happened?" His question was not even heard. And the eternal pantomime of panic terror has so little altered, that this elderly gentleman, to whom a disagreeable incident had just occurred in a Parisian drawing-room, unconsciously repeated the various formal attitudes in which the Greek sculptors of the earliest times symbolised the terror of nymphs pursued by the Great Pan.

The ambassador who has been recalled, the undersecretary placed suddenly on the retired list, the man about town whom people began to cut, the lover who has been shewn the door examine sometimes for months on end the event that has shattered their hopes; they turn it over and over like a projectile fired at them they know not whence or by whom, almost as though it were a meteorite. They would fain know the elements that compose this strange engine which has burst upon them, learn what hostilities may be detected in them. Chemists have at least the power of analysis; sick men suffering from a malady the origin of which they do not know can send for the doctor; criminal mysteries are more or less solved by the examining magistrate. But when it comes to the disconcerting actions of our fellow-men, we rarely discover their motives. Thus M. de Charlus, to anticipate the days that followed this party to which we shall presently return, could see in Charlie's attitude one thing alone that was self-evident. Charlie, who had often threatened the Baron that he would tell people of the passion that he inspired in him, must have seized the opportunity to do so when he considered that he had now sufficiently 'arrived' to be able to fly unaided. And he must, out of sheer ingratitude, have told Mme. Verdurin everything. But how had she allowed herself to be taken in (for the Baron, having made up his mind to deny the story, had already persuaded himself that the sentiments for which he was blamed were imaginary)? Some friends of Mme. Verdurin, who themselves perhaps felt a passion for Charlie, must have prepared the ground. Accordingly, M. de Charlus during the next few days wrote terrible letters to a number of the faithful, who were entirely innocent and concluded that he must be mad; then he went to Mme. Verdurin with a long and moving tale, which had not at all the effect that he desired. For in the first place Mme. Verdurin repeated to the Baron: "All you need do is not to bother about him, treat him with scorn, he is a mere boy." Now the Baron longed only for a reconciliation. In the second place, to bring this about, by depriving Charlie of everything of which he had felt himself assured, he asked Mme. Verdurin not to invite him again; a request which she met with a refusal that brought upon her angry and sarcastic letters from M. de Charlus. Flitting from one supposition to another, the Baron never arrived at the truth, which was that the blow had not come from Morel. It is true that he might have learned this by asking him for a few minutes' conversation. But he felt that this would injure his dignity and would be against the interests of his love. He had been insulted, he awaited an explanation. There is, for that matter, almost invariably, attached to the idea of a conversation which might clear up a misunderstanding, another idea which, whatever the reason, prevents us from agreeing to that conversation. The man who is abased and has shewn his weakness on a score of occasions, will furnish proofs of pride on the twenty-first, the only occasion on which it would serve him not to adopt a headstrong and arrogant attitude but to dispel an error which will take root in his adversary failing a contradiction. As for the social side of the incident, the rumour spread abroad that M. de Charlus had been turned out of the Verdurins' house at the moment when he was attempting to rape a young musician. The effect of this rumour was that nobody was surprised when M. de Charlus did not appear again at the Verdurins', and whenever he happened by chance to meet, anywhere else, one of the faithful whom he had suspected and insulted, as this person had a grudge against the Baron who himself abstained from greeting him, people were not surprised, realising that no member of the little clan would ever wish to speak to the Baron again.

While M. de Charlus, rendered speechless by Morel's words and by the attitude of the Mistress, stood there in the pose of the nymph a prey to Panic terror, M. and Mme. Verdurin had retired to the outer drawing-room, as a sign of diplomatic rupture, leaving M. de Charlus by himself, while on the platform Morel was putting his violin in its case. "Now you must tell us exactly what happened," Mme. Verdurin appealed avidly to her husband. "I don't know what you can have said to him, he looked quite upset," said Ski, "there are tears in his eyes." Pretending not to have understood: "I'm sure, nothing that I said could make any difference to him," said Mme. Verdurin, employing one of those stratagems which do not deceive everybody, so as to force the sculptor to repeat that Charlie was in tears, tears which filled the Mistress with too much pride for her to be willing to run the risk that one or other of the faithful, who might not have heard what was said, remained in ignorance of them. "No, it has made a difference, for I saw big tears glistening in his eyes," said the sculptor in a low tone with a smile of malicious connivance, and a sidelong glance to make sure that Morel was still on the platform and could not overhear the conversation. But there was somebody who did overhear, and whose presence, as soon as it was observed, was to restore to Morel one of the hopes that he had forfeited. This was the Queen of Naples, who, having left her fan behind, had thought it more polite, on coming away from another party to which she had gone on, to call for it in person. She had entered the room quite quietly, as though she were ashamed of herself, prepared to make apologies for her presence, and to pay a little call upon her hostess now that all the other guests had gone. But no one had heard her come in, in the heat of the incident the meaning of which she had at once gathered, and which set her ablaze with indignation. "Ski says that he had tears in his eyes, did you notice that? I did not see any tears. Ah, yes, I remember now," she corrected herself, in the fear that her denial might not be believed. "As for Charlus, he's not far off them, he ought to take a chair, he's tottering on his feet, he'll be on the floor in another minute," she said with a pitiless laugh. At that moment Morel hastened towards her: "Isn't that lady the Queen of Naples?" he asked (albeit he knew quite well that she was), pointing to Her Majesty who was making her way towards Charlus. "After what has just happened, I can no longer, I'm afraid, ask the Baron to present me." "Wait, I shall take you to her myself," said Mme. Verdurin, and, followed by a few of the faithful, but not by myself and Brichot who made haste to go and call for our hats and coats, she advanced upon the Queen who was talking to M. de Charlus. He had imagined that the realisation of his great desire that Morel should be presented to the Queen of Naples could be prevented only by the improbable demise of that lady. But we picture the future as a reflexion of the present projected into empty space, whereas it is the result, often almost immediate, of causes which for the most part escape our notice. Not an hour had passed, and now M. de Charlus would have given everything he possessed in order that Morel should not be presented to the Queen. Mme. Verdurin made the Queen a curtsey. Seeing that the other appeared not to recognise her: "I am Mme. Verdurin. Your Majesty does not remember me." "Quite well," said the Queen as she continued so naturally to converse with M. de Charlus and with an air of such complete indifference that Mme. Verdurin doubted whether it was to herself that this 'Quite well' had been addressed, uttered with a marvellously detached intonation, which wrung from M. de Charlus, despite his broken heart, a smile of expert and delighted appreciation of the art of impertinence. Morel, who had watched from the distance the preparations for his presentation, now approached. The Queen offered her arm to M. de Charlus. With him, too, she was vexed, but only because he did not make a more energetic stand against vile detractors. She was crimson with shame for him whom the Verdurins dared to treat in this fashion. The entirely simple civility which she had shewn them a few hours earlier, and the arrogant pride with which she now stood up to face them, had their source in the same region of her heart. The Queen, as a woman full of good nature, regarded good nature first and foremost in the form of an unshakable attachment to the people whom she liked, to her own family, to all the Princes of her race, among whom was M. de Charlus, and, after them, to all the people of the middle classes or of the humblest populace who knew how to respect those whom she liked and felt well-disposed towards them. It was as to a woman endowed with these sound instincts that she had shewn kindness to Mme. Verdurin. And, no doubt, this is a narrow conception, somewhat Tory, and increasingly obsolete, of good nature. But this does not mean that her good nature was any less genuine or ardent. The ancients were no less strongly attached to the group of humanity to which they devoted themselves because it did not exceed the limits of their city, nor are the men of to-day to their country than will be those who in the future love the United States of the World. In my own immediate surroundings, I have had an example of this in my mother whom Mme. de Cambremer and Mme. de Guermantes could never persuade to take part in any philanthropic undertaking, to join any patriotic workroom, to sell or to be a patroness at any bazaar. I do not go so far as to say that she was right in doing good only when her heart had first spoken, and in reserving for her own family, for her servants, for the unfortunate whom chance brought in her way, her treasures of love and generosity, but I do know that these, like those of my grandmother, were unbounded and exceeded by far anything that Mme. de Guermantes or Mme. de Cambremer ever could have done or did. The case of the Queen of Naples was altogether different, but even here it must be admitted that her conception of deserving people was not at all that set forth in those novels of Dostoievski which Albertine had taken from my shelves and devoured, that is to say in the guise of wheedling parasites, thieves, drunkards, at one moment stupid, at another insolent, debauchees, at a pinch murderers. Extremes, however, meet, since the noble man, the brother, the outraged kinsman whom the Queen sought to defend, was M. de Charlus, that is to say, notwithstanding his birth and all the family ties that bound him to the Queen, a man whose virtue was hedged round by many vices. "You do not look at all well, my dear cousin," she said to M. de Charlus. "Lean upon my arm. Be sure that it will still support you. It is firm enough for that." Then, raising her eyes proudly to face her adversaries (at that moment, Ski told me, there were in front of her Mme. Verdurin and Morel), "You know that, in the past, at Gaeta, it held the mob in defiance. It will be able to serve you as a rampart." And it was thus, taking the Baron on her arm and without having allowed Morel to be presented to her, that the splendid sister of the Empress Elisabeth left the house. It might be supposed, in view of M. de Charlus's terrible nature, the persecutions with which he terrorised even his own family, that he would, after the events of this evening, let loose his fury and practise reprisals upon the Verdurins. We have seen why nothing of this sort occurred at first. Then the Baron, having caught cold shortly afterwards, and contracted the septic pneumonia which was very rife that winter, was for long regarded by his doctors, and regarded himself, as being at the point of death, and lay for many months suspended between it and life. Was there simply a physical change, and the substitution of a different malady for the neurosis that had previously made him lose all control of himself in his outbursts of rage? For it is too obvious to suppose that, having never taken the Verdurins seriously, from the social point of view, but having come at last to understand the part that they had played, he was unable to feel the resentment that he would have felt for any of his equals; too obvious also to remember that neurotics, irritated on the slightest provocation by imaginary and inoffensive enemies, become on the contrary inoffensive as soon as anyone takes the offensive against them, and that we can calm them more easily by flinging cold water in their faces than by attempting to prove to them the inanity of their grievances. It is probably not in a physical change that we ought to seek the explanation of this absence of rancour, but far more in the malady itself. It exhausted the Baron so completely that he had little leisure left in which to think about the Verdurins. He was almost dead. We mentioned offensives; even those which have only a posthumous effect require, if we are to 'stage' them properly, the sacrifice of a part of our strength. M. de Charlus had too little strength left for the activity of a preparation. We hear often of mortal enemies who open their eyes to gaze upon one another in the hour of death and close them again, made happy. This must be a rare occurrence, except when death surprises us in the midst of life. It is, on the contrary, at the moment when we have nothing left to lose, that we are not bothered by the risks which, when full of life, we would lightly have undertaken. The spirit of vengeance forms part of life, it abandons us as a rule—notwith-standing certain exceptions which, occurring in the heart of the same person, are, as we shall see, human contradictions,—on the threshold of death. After having thought for a moment about the Verdurins, M. de Charlus felt that he was too weak, turned his face to the wall, and ceased to think about anything. If he often lay silent like this, it was not that he had lost his eloquence. It still flowed from its source, but it had changed. Detached from the violence which it had so often adorned, it was no more now than an almost mystic eloquence decorated with words of meekness, words from the Gospel, an apparent resignation to death. He talked especially on the days when he thought that he would live. A relapse made him silent. This Christian meekness into which his splendid violence was transposed (as is in *Esther* the so different genius of *Andromaque*) pro-voked the admiration of those who came to his bedside. It would have provoked that of the Verdurins themselves, who could not have helped adoring a man whom his weakness had made them hate. It is true that thoughts which were Christian only in appearance rose to the surface. He implored the Archangel Gabriel to appear and announce to him, as to the Prophet, at what time the Messiah would come to him. And, breaking off with a sweet and sorrowful smile, he would add: "But the Archangel must not ask me, as he asked Daniel, to have patience for 'seven weeks, and threescore and two weeks,' for I should be dead before then." The person whom he awaited thus was Morel. And so he asked the Archangel Raphael to bring him to him, as he had brought the young Tobias. And, introducing more human methods (like sick Popes who, while ordering masses to be said, do not neglect to send for their doctors), he insinuated to his visitors that if Brichot were to bring him without delay his young Tobias, perhaps the Archangel Raphael would consent to restore Brichot's sight, as he had done to the father of Tobias, or as had happened in the sheep-pool of Bethesda. But, notwithstanding these human lapses, the moral purity of M. de Charlus's conversation had none the less become alarming. Vanity, slander, the insanity of malice and pride, had alike disappeared. Morally M. de Charlus had been raised far above the level at which he had lived in the past. But this moral perfection, as to the reality of which his oratorical art was for that matter capable of deceiving more than one of his com-passionate audience, this perfection vanished with the malady which had laboured on its behalf. M. de Charlus returned along the downward slope with a rapidity which, as we shall see, continued steadily to increase. But the Verdurins' attitude towards him was by that time no more than a somewhat distant memory which more immediate outbursts prevented from reviving.

To turn back to the Verdurins' party, when the host and hostess were by themselves, M. Verdurin said to his wife: "You know where Cottard has gone? He is with Saniette: he has been speculating to put himself straight and has gone smash. When he got home just now after leaving us, and learned that he hadn't a penny in the world and nearly a million francs of debts, Saniette had a stroke." "But then, why did he gamble, it's idiotic, he was the last person in the world to succeed at that game. Cleverer men than he get plucked at it, and he was born to let himself be swindled by every Tom, Dick and Harry." "Why, of course, we have always known that he was an idiot," said M. Verdurin. "Anyhow, this is the result. Here you have a man who will be turned out of house and home to-morrow by his landlord, who is going to find himself utterly penniless; his family don't like him, Forcheville is the last man in the world to do anything for him. And so it occurred to me, I don't wish to do anything that doesn't meet with your approval, but we might perhaps be able to scrape up a small income for him so that he shan't be too conscious of his ruin, so that he can keep a roof over his head." "I entirely agree with you, it is very good of you to have thought of it. But you say 'a roof'; the imbecile has kept on an apartment beyond his means, he can't remain in it, we shall have to find him a couple of rooms somewhere. I understand that at the present moment he is still paying six or seven thousand francs for his apartment." "Six thousand, five hundred. But he is greatly attached to his home. In short, he has had his first stroke, he can scarcely live more than two or three years. Suppose we were to allow him ten thousand francs for three years. It seems to me that we should be able to afford that. We might for instance this year, instead of taking la Raspelière again, get hold of something on a simpler scale. With our income, it seems to me that to sacrifice ten thousand francs a year for three years is not out of the question." "Very well, there's only the nuisance that people will get to know about it, we shall be expected to do it again for others." "Believe me, I have thought about that. I shall do it only upon the express condition that nobody knows anything about it. Thank you, I have no desire that we should become the benefactors of the human race. No philanthropy! What we might do is to tell him that the money has been left to him by Princess Sherbatoff." "But will he believe it? She consulted Cottard about her will." "If the worse comes to the worst, we might take Cottard into our confidence, he is used to professional secrecy, he makes an enormous amount of money, he won't be like one of those busybodies one is obliged to hush up. He may even be willing to say, perhaps, that it was himself that the Princess appointed as her agent. In that way we shouldn't even appear. That would avoid all the nuisance of scenes, and gratitude, and speeches." M. Verdurin added an expression which made quite plain the kind of touching scenes and speeches which they were anxious to avoid. But it cannot have been reported to me correctly, for it was not a French expression, but one of those terms that are to be found in certain families to denote certain things, annoying things especially, probably because people wish to indicate them in the hearing of the persons concerned without being understood! An expression of this sort is generally a survival from an earlier condition of the family. In a Jewish family, for instance, it will be a ritual term diverted from its true meaning, and perhaps the only Hebrew word with which the family, now thoroughly French, is still acquainted. In a family that is strongly provincial, it will be a term in the local dialect, albeit the family no longer speaks or even understands that dialect. In a family that has come from South America and no longer speaks anything but French, it will be a Spanish word. And, in the next generation, the word will no longer exist save as a childish memory. They may remember quite well that their parents at table used to allude to the servants who were waiting, without being understood by them, by employing some such word, but the children cannot tell exactly what the word meant, whether it was Spanish, Hebrew, German, dialect, if indeed it ever belonged to any language and was not a proper name or a word entirely forged. The uncertainty can be cleared up only if they have a great-uncle, a cousin still surviving who must have used the same expression. As I never knew any relative of the Verdurins, I have never been able to reconstruct the word. All I know is that it certainly drew a smile from Mme. Verdurin, for the use of this language less general, more personal, more secret, than their everyday speech inspires in those who use it among themselves a sense of self-importance which is always accompanied by a certain satisfaction. After this moment of mirth: "But if Cottard talks," Mme. Verdurin objected. "He will not talk." He did mention it, to myself at least, for it was from him that I learned of this incident a few years later, actually at the funeral of Saniette. I was sorry that I had not known of it earlier. For one thing the knowledge would have brought me more rapidly to the idea that we ought never to feel resentment towards other people, ought never to judge them by some memory of an unkind action, for we do not know all the good that, at other moments, their hearts may have sincerely desired and realised; no doubt the evil form which we have established once and for all will recur, but the heart is far more rich than that, has many other forms that will recur, also, to these people, whose kindness we refuse to admit because of the occasion on which they behaved badly. Furthermore, this revelation by Cottard must inevitably have had an effect upon me, because by altering my opinion of the Verdurins, this revelation, had it been made to me earlier, would have dispelled the suspicions that I had formed as to the part that the Verdurins might be playing between Albertine and myself, would have dispelled them, wrongly perhaps as it happened, for if M. Verdurin— whom I supposed, with increasing certainty, to be the most malicious man alive—had certain virtues, he was nevertheless tormenting to the point of the most savage persecution, and so jealous of his domination over the little clan as not to shrink from the basest falsehoods, from the fomentation of the most unjustified hatreds, in order to sever any ties between the faithful which had not as their sole object the strengthening of the little group. He was a man capable of disinterested action, of unostentatious generosity, that does not necessarily mean a man of feeling, nor a pleasant man, nor a scrupulous, nor a truthful, nor always a good man. A partial goodness, in which there persisted, perhaps, a trace of the family whom my great-aunt had known, existed probably in him in view of this action before I discovered it, as America or the North Pole existed before Columbus or Peary. Nevertheless, at the moment of my discovery, M. Verdurin's nature offered me a new and unimagined aspect; and so I am brought up against the difficulty of presenting a permanent image as well of a character as of societies and passions. For it changes no less than they, and if we seek to portray what is relatively unchanging in it, we see it present in succession different aspects (implying that it cannot remain still but keeps moving) to the disconcerted artist.

CHAPTER THREE

FLIGHT OF ALBERTINE

SEEING how late it was, and fearing that Albertine might be growing impatient, I asked Brichot, as we left the Verdurins' party, to be so kind as to drop me at my door. My carriage would then take him home. He congratulated me upon going straight home like this (unaware that a girl was waiting for me in the house), and upon ending so early, and so wisely, an evening of which, on the contrary, all that I had done was to postpone the actual beginning. Then he spoke to me about M. de Charlus. The latter would doubtless have been stupefied had he heard the Professor, who was so kind to him, the Professor who always assured him: "I never repeat anything," speaking of him and of his life without the slightest reserve. And Brichot's indignant amazement would perhaps have been no less sincere if M. de Charlus had said to him: "I am told that you have been speaking evil of me." Brichot did indeed feel an affection for M. de Charlus and, if he had had to call to mind some conversation that had turned upon him, would have been far more likely to remember the friendly feeling that he had shewn for the Baron, while he said the same things about him that everyone was saying, than to remember the things that he had said. He would not have thought that he was lying if he had said: "I who speak of you in so friendly a spirit," since he did feel a friendly spirit while he was speaking of M. de Charlus. The Baron had above all for Brichot the charm which the Professor demanded before everything else in his social existence, and which was that of furnishing real examples of what he had long supposed to be an invention of the poets. Brichot, who had often expounded the second Eclogue of Virgil without really knowing whether its fiction had any basis in reality, found later on in conversing with Charlus some of the pleasure which he knew that his masters, M. Mérimée and M. Renan, his colleague M. Maspéro had felt, when travelling in Spain, Palestine, and Egypt, upon recognising in the scenery and the contemporary peoples of Spain, Palestine and Egypt, the setting and the invariable actors of the ancient scenes which they themselves had expounded in their books. "Be it said without offence to that knight of noble lineage," Brichot declared to me in the carriage that was taking us home, "he is simply prodigious when he illustrates his satanic catechism with a distinctly Bedlamite vigour and the persistence, I was going to say the candour, of Spanish whitewash and of a returned *émigré*. I can assure you, if I dare express myself like Mgr. d'Hulst, I am by no means bored upon the days when I receive a visit from that feudal lord who, seeking to defend Adonis against our age of miscreants, has followed the instincts of his race, and, in all sodomist innocence, has gone crusading." I listened to

Brichot, and I was not alone with him. As, for that matter, I had never ceased to feel since I left home that evening, I felt myself, in however obscure a fashion, tied fast to the girl who was at that moment in her room. Even when I was talking to some one or other at the Verdurins', I had felt, confusedly, that she was by my side, I had that vague impression of her that we have of our own limbs, and if I happened to think of her it was as we think, with disgust at being bound to it in complete subjection, of our own body. "And what a fund of scandal," Brichot went on, "sufficient to supply all the appendices of the *Causeries du Lundi*, is the conversation of that apostle. Imagine that I have learned from him that the ethical treatise which I had always admired as the most splendid moral composition of our age was inspired in our venerable colleague X by a young telegraph messenger. Let us not hesitate to admit that my eminent friend omitted to give us the name of this ephebe in the course of his demonstrations. He has shewn in so doing more human respect, or, if you prefer, less gratitude than Phidias who inscribed the name of the athlete whom he loved upon the ring of his Olympian Zeus. The Baron had not heard that story. Needless to say, it appealed to his orthodox mind. You can readily imagine that whenever I have to discuss with my colleague a candidate's thesis, I shall find in his dialectic, which for that matter is extremely subtle, the additional savour which spicy revelations added, for Sainte-Beuve, to the insufficiently confidential writings of Chateaubriand. From our colleague, who is a goldmine of wisdom but whose gold is not legal tender, the telegraph-boy passed into the hands of the Baron, 'all perfectly proper, of course,' (you ought to hear his voice when he says it). And as this Satan is the most obliging of men, he has found his protégé a post in the Colonies, from which the young man, who has a sense of gratitude, sends him from time to time the most excellent fruit. The Baron offers these to his distinguished friends; some of the young man's pineapples appeared quite recently on the table at Quai Conti, drawing from Mme. Verdurin, who at that moment put no malice into her words: 'You must have an uncle or a nephew in America, M. de Charlus, to get pineapples like these!' I admit that if I had known the truth then I should have eaten them with a certain gaiety, repeating to myself *in petto* the opening lines of an Ode of Horace which Diderot loved to recall. In fact, like my colleague Boissier, strolling from the Palatine to Tibur, I derive from the Baron's conversation a singularly more vivid and more savoury idea of the writers of the Augustan age. Let us not even speak of those of the Decadence, nor let us hark back to the Greeks, although I have said to that excellent Baron that in his company I felt like Plato in the house of Aspasia. To tell the truth, I had considerably enlarged the scale of the two characters and, as La Fontaine says, my example was taken 'from lesser animals.' However it be, you do not, I imagine, suppose that the Baron took offence. Never have I seen him so ingenuously delighted. A childish excitement made him depart from his aristocratic phlegm. 'What flatterers all these Sorbonnards are!' he exclaimed with rapture. 'To think that I should have had to wait until my age before being compared to Aspasia! An old image like me! Oh, my youth!' I should like you to have seen him as he said that, outrageously powdered as he always is, and, at his age, scented like a young coxcomb. All the same, beneath his genealogical obsessions, the best fellow in the world. For all these reasons, I should be distressed were this evening's rupture to prove final. What did surprise me was the way in which the young man turned upon him. His manner towards the Baron has been, for some time past, that of a violent partisan, of a feudal vassal, which scarcely betokened such an insurrection. I hope that, in any event, even if (*Dii omen avertant*) the Baron were never to return to Quai Conti, this schism is not going to involve myself. Each of us derives too much advantage from the exchange that we make of my feeble stock of learning with his experience." (We shall see that if M. de Charlus, after having hoped in vain that Brichot would bring Morel back to him, shewed no violent rancour against him, at any rate his affection for the Professor vanished so completely as to allow him to judge him without any indulgence.) "And I swear to you that the exchange is so much in my favour that when the Baron yields up to me what his life has taught him, I am unable to endorse the opinion of Sylvestre Bonnard that a library is still the best place in which to ponder the dream of life."

We had now reached my door. I got out of the carriage to give the driver Brichot's address. From the pavement, I could see the window of Albertine's room, that window, formerly quite black, at night, when she was not staying in the house, which the electric light inside, dissected by the slats of the shutters, striped from top to bottom with parallel bars of gold. This magic scroll, clear as it was to myself, tracing before my tranquil mind precise images, near at hand, of which I should presently be taking possession, was completely invisible to Brichot who had remained in the carriage, almost blind, and would moreover have been completely incomprehensible to him could he have seen it, since, like the friends who called upon me before dinner, when Albertine had returned from her drive, the Professor was unaware that a girl who was all my own was waiting for me in a bedroom adjoining mine. The carriage drove on. I remained for a moment alone upon the pavement. To be sure, these luminous rays which I could see from below and which to anyone else would have seemed merely superficial, I endowed with the utmost consistency, plenitude, solidity, in view of all the significance that I placed behind them, in a treasure unsuspected by the rest of the world which I had concealed there and from which those horizontal rays emanated, a treasure if you like, but a treasure in exchange for which I had forfeited my freedom, my solitude, my thought. If Albertine had not been there, and indeed if I had merely been in search of pleasure, I would have gone to demand it of unknown women, into whose life I should have attempted to penetrate, at Venice perhaps, or at least in some corner of nocturnal Paris. But now all that I had to do when the time came for me to receive caresses, was not to set forth upon a journey, was not even to leave my own house, but to return there. And to return there not to find myself alone, and, after taking leave of the friends who furnished me from outside with food for thought, to find myself at any rate compelled to seek it in myself, but to be on the contrary less alone than when I was at the Verdurins', welcomed as I should be by the person to whom I abdicated, to whom I handed over most completely my own person, without having for an instant the leisure to think of myself nor even requiring the effort, since she would be by my side, to think of her. So that as I raised my eyes to look for the last time from outside at the window of the room in which I should presently find myself, I seemed to behold the luminous gates which were about to close behind me and of which I myself had forged, for an eternal slavery, the unyielding bars of gold.

Our engagement had assumed the form of a criminal trial and gave Albertine the timidity of a guilty party. Now she changed the conversation whenever it turned upon people, men or women, who were not of mature years. It was when she had not yet suspected that I was jealous of her that I could have asked her to tell me what I wanted to know. We ought always to take advantage of that period. It is then that our mistress tells us of her pleasures and even of the means by which she conceals them from other people. She would no longer have admitted to me now as she had admitted at Balbec (partly because it was true, partly in order to excuse herself for not making her affection for myself more evident, for I had already begun to weary her even then, and she had gathered from my kindness to her that she need not shew it to me as much as to other men in order to obtain more from me than from them); she would no longer have admitted to me now as she had admitted then: "I think it stupid to let people see that one is in love; I'm just the opposite, as soon as a person appeals to me, I pretend not to take any notice of him. In that way, nobody knows anything about it."

What, it was the same Albertine of to-day, with her pretensions to frankness and indifference to all the world who had told me this! She would never have informed me of such a rule of conduct now! She contented herself when she was talking to me with applying it, by saying of somebody or other who might cause me anxiety: "Oh, I don't know, I never noticed them, they don't count." And from time to time, to anticipate discoveries which I might make, she would proffer those confessions which their accent, before one knows the reality which they are intended to alter, to render innocent, denounces already as being falsehoods.

Albertine had never told me that she suspected me of being jealous of her, preoccupied with everything that she did. The only words—and that, I must add, was long ago—which we had exchanged with regard to jealousy seemed to prove the opposite. I remembered that, on a fine moonlight evening, towards the beginning of our intimacy, on one of the first occasions when I had accompanied her home, and when I would have been just as glad not to do so and to leave her in order to run after other girls, I had said to her: "You know, if I am offering to take you home, it is not from jealousy; if you have anything else to do, I shall slip discreetly away." And she had replied: "Oh, I know quite well that you aren't jealous and that it's all the same to you, but I've nothing else to do except to stay with you." Another occasion was at la Raspelière, when M. de Charlus, not without casting a covert glance at Morel, had made a display of friendly gallantry toward Albertine; I had said to her: "Well, he gave you a good hug, I hope." And as I had added half ironically: "I suffered all the torments of jealousy," Albertine, employing the language proper either to the vulgar class from which she sprang or to that other, more vulgar still, which she frequented, replied: "What a fusspot you are! I know quite well you're not jealous. For one thing, you told me so, and besides, it's perfectly obvious, get along with you!" She had never told me since then that she had changed her mind; but there must all the same have developed in her, upon that subject, a number of fresh ideas, which she concealed from me but which an accident might, in spite of her, betray, for this evening when, having gone indoors, after going to fetch her from her own room and taking her to mine, I had said to her (with a certain awkwardness which I did not myself understand, for I had indeed told Albertine that I was going to pay a call, and had said that I did not know where, perhaps upon Mme. de Villeparisis, perhaps upon Mme. de Guermantes, perhaps upon Mme. de Cambremer; it is true that I had not actually mentioned the Verdurins): "Guess where I have been, at the Verdurins'," I had barely had time to utter the words before Albertine, a look of utter consternation upon her face, had answered me in words which seemed to explode of their own accord with a force which she was unable to contain: "I thought as much." "I didn't know that you would be annoyed by my going to see the Verdurins." It is true that she did not tell me that she was annoyed, but that was obvious; it is true also that I had not said to myself that she would be annoyed. And yet in the face of the explosion of her wrath, as in the face of those events which a sort of retrospective second sight makes us imagine that we have already known in the past, it seemed to me that I could never have expected anything else. "Annoyed? What do you suppose I care, where you've been. It's all the same to me. Wasn't Mlle. Vinteuil there?" Losing all control of myself at these words: "You never told me that you had met her the other day," I said to her, to shew her that I was better informed than she knew. Believing that the person whom I reproached her for having met without telling me was Mme. Verdurin, and not, as I meant to imply, Mlle. Vinteuil: "Did I meet her?" she inquired with a pensive air, addressing at once herself as though she were seeking to collect her fugitive memories and myself as though it were I that ought to have told her of the meeting; and no doubt in order that I might say what I knew, perhaps also in order to gain time before making a difficult response. But I was preoccupied with the thought of Mlle. Vinteuil, and still more with a dread which had already entered my mind but which now gripped me in a violent clutch, the dread that Albertine might be longing for freedom. When I came home I had supposed that Mme. Verdurin had purely and simply invented, to enhance her own renown, the story of her having expected Mlle. Vinteuil and her friend, so that I was quite calm. Albertine, merely by saying: "Wasn't Mlle. Vinteuil there?" had shewn me that I had not been mistaken in my original suspicion; but anyhow my mind was set at rest in that quarter for the future, since by giving up her plan of visiting the Verdurins' and going instead to the Trocadéro, Albertine had sacrificed

Mlle. Vinteuil. But, at the Trocadéro, from which, for that matter, she had come away in order to go for a drive with myself, there had been as a reason to make her leave it the presence of Léa. As I thought of this I mentioned Léa by name, and Albertine, distrustful, supposing that I had perhaps heard something more, took the initiative and exclaimed volubly, not without partly concealing her face: "I know her quite well; we went last year, some of my friends and I, to see her act: after the performance we went behind to her dressing-room, she changed in front of us. It was most interesting." Then my mind was compelled to relinquish Mlle. Vinteuil and, in a desperate effort, racing through the abysses of possible reconstructions, attached itself to the actress, to that evening when Albertine had gone behind to her dressing-room. On the other hand, after all the oaths that she had sworn to me, and in so truthful a tone, after the so complete sacrifice of her freedom, how was I to suppose that there was any evil in all this affair? And yet, were not my suspicions feelers pointing in the direction of the truth, since if she had made me a sacrifice of the Verdurins in order to go to the Trocadéro, nevertheless at the Verdurins' Mlle. Vinteuil was expected, and, at the Trocadéro, there had been Léa, who seemed to me to be disturbing me without cause and whom all the same, in that speech which I had not demanded of her, she admitted that she had known upon a larger scale than that of my fears, in circumstances that were indeed shady? For what could have induced her to go behind like that to that dressing-room? If I ceased to suffer because of Mlle. Vinteuil when I suffered because of Léa, those two tormentors of my day, it was either on account of the inability of my mind to picture too many scenes at one time, or on account of the interference of my nervous emotions of which my jealousy was but the echo. I could induce from them only that she had belonged no more to Léa than to Mlle. Vinteuil and that I was thinking of Léa only because the thought of her still caused me pain. But the fact that my twin jealousies were dying down—to revive now and then, alternately—does not, in any way, mean that they did not on the contrary correspond each to some truth of which I had had a foreboding, that of these women I must not say to myself none, but all. I say a foreboding, for I could not project myself to all the points of time and space which I should have had to visit, and besides, what instinct would have given me the coordinate of one with another necessary to enable me to surprise Albertine, here, at one moment, with Lea, or with the Balbec girls, or with that friend of Mme. Bontemps whom she had jostled, or with the girl on the tennis-court who had nudged her with her elbow, or with Mlle. Vinteuil?

I must add that what had appeared to me most serious, and had struck me as most symptomatic, was that she had forestalled my accusation, that she had said to me: "Wasn't Mlle. Vinteuil there?" to which I had replied in the most brutal fashion imaginable: "You never told me that you had met her." Thus as soon as I found Albertine no longer obliging, instead of telling her that I was sorry, I became malicious. There was then a moment in which I felt a sort of hatred of her which only intensified my need to keep her in captivity.

"Besides," I said to her angrily, "there are plenty of other things which you hide from me, even the most trivial things, such as for instance when you went for three days to Balbec, I mention it in passing." I had added the words "I mention it in passing" as a complement to "even the most trivial things" so that if Albertine said to me "What was there wrong about my trip to Balbec?" I might be able to answer: "Why, I've quite forgotten. I get so confused about the things people tell me, I attach so little importance to them." And indeed if I referred to those three days which she had spent in an excursion with the chauffeur to Balbec, from where her postcards had reached me after so long an interval, I referred to them purely at random and regretted that I had chosen so bad an example, for in fact, as they had barely had time to go there and return, it was certainly the one excursion in which there had not even been time for the interpolation of a meeting at all protracted with anybody. But Albertine supposed, from what I had just said, that I was fully aware of the real facts, and had merely concealed my knowledge from her; so she had been convinced, for some time past, that, in one way or another, I was having her followed, or in short was somehow or other, as she had said the week before to Andrée, better informed than herself about her own life. And so she interrupted me with a wholly futile admission, for certainly I suspected nothing of what she now told me, and I was on the other hand appalled, so vast can the disparity be between the truth which a liar has disguised and the idea which, from her lies, the man who is in love with the said liar has formed of the truth. Scarcely had I uttered the words: "When you went for three days to Balbec, I mention it in passing," before Albertine, cutting me short, declared as a thing that was perfectly natural: "You mean to say that I never went to Balbec at all? Of course I didn't! And I have always wondered why you pretended to believe that I had. All the same, there was no harm in it. The driver had some business of his own for three days. He didn't like to mention it to you. And so, out of kindness to him (it was my doing! Besides it is always I that have to bear the brunt), I invented a trip to Balbec. He simply put me down at Auteuil, with my friend in the Rue de l'Assomption, where I spent the three days bored to tears. You see it is not a serious matter, there's nothing broken. I did indeed begin to suppose that you perhaps knew all about it, when I saw how you laughed when the postcards began to arrive, a week late. I quite see that it was absurd, and that it would have been better not to send any cards. But that wasn't my fault. I had bought the cards beforehand and given them to the driver before he dropped me at Auteuil, and then the fathead put them in his pocket and forgot about them instead of sending them on in an envelope to a friend of his near Balbec who was to forward them to you. I kept on supposing that they would turn up. He forgot all about them for five days, and instead of telling me the idiot sent them on at once to Balbec. When he did tell me, I fairly broke it over him, I can tell you! And you go and make a stupid fuss, when it's all the fault of that great fool, as a reward for my shutting myself up for three whole days, so that he might go and look after his family affairs. I didn't even venture to go out into Auteuil for fear of being seen. The only time that I did go out, I was dressed as a man, and that was a funny business. And it was just my luck, which follows me wherever I go, that the first person I came across was your Yid friend Bloch. But I don't believe it was from him that you learned that my trip to Balbec never existed except in my imagination, for he seemed not to recognise me."

I did not know what to say, not wishing to appear astonished, while I was appalled by all these lies. With a sense of horror, which gave me no desire to turn Albertine out of the house, far from it, was combined a strong inclination to burst into tears. This last was caused not by the lie itself and by the annihilation of everything that I had so stoutly believed to be true that I felt as though I were in a town that had been razed to the ground, where not a house remained standing, where the bare soil was merely heaped with rubble—but by the melancholy thought that, during those three days when she had been bored to tears in her friend's house at Auteuil, Albertine had never once felt any desire, the idea had perhaps never occurred to her to come and pay me a visit one day on the quiet, or to send a message asking me to go and see her at Auteuil. But I had not time to give myself up to these reflexions. Whatever happened, I did not wish to appear surprised. I smiled with the air of a man who knows far more than he is going to say: "But that is only one thing out of a thousand. For instance, you knew that Mlle. Vinteuil was expected at Mme. Verdurin's, this afternoon when you went to the Trocadéro." She blushed: "Yes, I knew that." "Can you swear to me that it was not in order to renew your relations with her that you wanted to go to the Verdurins'." "Why, of course I can swear. Why do you say renew, I never had any relations with her, I swear it." I was appalled to hear Albertine lie to me like this, deny the facts which her blush had made all too evident. Her mendacity appalled me. And yet, as it contained a protestation of innocence which, almost unconsciously, I was prepared to accept, it hurt me less than her sincerity when, after I had asked her: "Can you at least swear to me that the pleasure of seeing Mlle. Vinteuil again had nothing to do with your anxiety to go this afternoon to the Verdurins' party?" she replied: "No, that I cannot swear. It would have been a great pleasure to see Mlle. Vinteuil again." A moment earlier, I had been angry with her because she concealed her relations with Mlle. Vinteuil, and now her admission of the pleasure that she would have felt in seeing her again turned my bones to water. For that matter, the mystery in which she had cloaked her intention of going to see the Verdurins ought to have been a sufficient proof. But I had not given the matter enough thought. Although she was now telling me the truth, why did she admit only half, it was even more stupid than it was wicked and wretched. I was so crushed that I had not the courage to insist upon this question, as to which I was not in a strong position, having no damning evidence to produce, and to recover my ascendancy, I hurriedly turned to a subject which would enable me to put Albertine to rout: "Listen, only this evening, at the Verdurins', I learned that what you had told me about Mlle. Vinteuil. . . ." Albertine gazed at me fixedly with a tormented air, seeking to read in my eyes how much I knew. Now, what I knew and what I was about to tell her as to Mlle. Vinteuil's true nature, it was true that it was not at the Verdurins' that I had learned it, but at Montjouvain long ago. Only, as I had always refrained, deliberately, from mentioning it to Albertine, I could now appear to have learned it only this evening. And I could almost feel a joy—after having felt, on the little tram, so keen an anguish—at possessing this memory of Montjouvain, which I postdated, but which would nevertheless be the unanswerable proof, a crushing blow to Albertine. This time at least, I had no need to "seem to know" and to "make Albertine speak"; I did know, I had seen through the lighted window at Montjouvain. It had been all very well for Albertine to tell me that her relations with Mlle. Vinteuil and her friend had been perfectly pure, how could she when I swore to her (and swore without lying) that I knew the habits of these two women, how could she maintain any longer that, having lived in a daily intimacy with them, calling them "my big sisters," she had not been approached by them with suggestions which would have made her break with them, if on the contrary she had not complied? But I had no time to tell her what I knew. Albertine, imagining, as in the case of the pretended excursion to Balbec, that I had learned the truth, either from Mlle. Vinteuil, if she had been at the Verdurins', or simply from Mme. Verdurin herself who might have mentioned her to Mlle. Vinteuil, did not allow me to speak but made a confession, the exact opposite of what I had supposed, which nevertheless, by shewing me that she had never ceased to lie to me, caused me perhaps just as much grief (especially since I was no longer, as I said a moment ago, jealous of Mlle. Vinteuil); in short, taking the words out of my mouth, Albertine proceeded to say: "You mean to tell me that you found out this evening that I lied to you when I pretended that I had been more or less brought up by Mlle. Vinteuil's friend. It is true that I did lie to you a little. But I felt that you despised me so, I saw too that you were so keen upon that man Vinteuil's music that as one of my school friends—this is true, I swear to you—had been a friend of Mlle. Vinteuil's friend, I stupidly thought that I might make myself seem interesting to you by inventing the story that I had known the girls quite well. I felt that I was boring you, that you thought me a goose, I thought that if I told you that those people used to see a lot of me, that I could easily tell you all sorts of things about Vinteuil's work, I should acquire a little importance in your eyes, that it would draw us together. When I lie to you, it is always out of affection for you. And it needed this fatal Verdurin party to open your eyes to the truth, which has been a bit exaggerated besides. I bet, Mlle. Vinteuil's friend told you that she did not know me. She met me at least twice at my friend's house. But of course, I am not smart enough for people like that who have become celebrities. They prefer to say that they have never met me." Poor Albertine, when she imagined that to tell me that she had been so intimate with Mlle. Vinteuil's friend would postpone her own dismissal, would draw her nearer to me, she had, as so often happens, attained the truth by a different road from that which she had intended to take. Her shewing herself better informed about music than I had supposed would never have prevented me from breaking with her that evening, on the little tram; and yet it was indeed that speech, which she had made with that object, which had immediately brought about far more than the impossibility of a rupture. Only she made an error in her interpretation, not of the effect which that speech was to have, but of the cause by virtue of which it was to produce that effect, a cause which was my discovery not of her musical culture, but of her evil associations. What had abruptly drawn me to her, what was more, merged me in her was not the expectation of a pleasure—and pleasure is too strong a word, a slight interest—it was a wringing grief.

Once again I had to be careful not to keep too long a silence which might have led her to suppose that I was surprised. And so, touched by the discovery that she was so modest and had thought herself despised in the Verdurin circle, I said to her tenderly: "But, my darling, I would gladly give you several hundred francs to let you go and play the fashionable lady wherever you please and invite M. and Mme. Verdurin to a grand dinner." Alas! Albertine was several persons in one. The most mysterious, most simple, most atrocious revealed herself in the answer which she made me with an air of disgust and the exact words to tell the truth I could not quite make out (even the opening words, for she did not finish her sentence). I succeeded in establishing them only a little later when I had guessed what was in her mind. We hear things retrospectively when we have understood them. "Thank you for nothing! Fancy spending a cent upon those old frumps, I'd a great deal rather you left me alone for once in a way so that I can go and get some one decent to break my. . . ." As she uttered the words, her face flushed crimson, a look of terror came to her eyes, she put her hand over her mouth as though she could have thrust back the words which she had just uttered and which I had completely failed to understand. "What did you say, Albertine?" "No, nothing, I was half asleep and talking to myself." "Not a bit of it, you were wide awake." "I was thinking about asking the Verdurins to dinner, it is very good of you." "No, I mean what you said just now." She gave me endless versions, none of which agreed in the least, I do not say with her words which, being interrupted, remained vague, but with the interruption itself and the sudden flush that had accompanied it. "Come, my darling, that is not what you were going to say, otherwise why did you stop short." "Because I felt that my request was indiscreet." "What request?" "To be allowed to give a dinner-party." "No, it is not that, there is no need of discretion between you and me." "Indeed there is, we ought never to take advantage of the people we love. In any case, I swear to you that that was all." On the one hand it was still impossible for me to doubt her sworn word, on the other hand her explanations did not satisfy my critical spirit. I continued to press her. "Anyhow, you might at least have the courage to finish what you were saying, you stopped short at *break*." "No, leave me alone!" "But why?" "Because it is dreadfully vulgar, I should be ashamed to say such a thing in front of you. I don't know what I was thinking of, the words—I don't even know what they mean, I heard them used in the street one day by some very low people—just came to my lips without rhyme or reason. It had nothing to do with me or anybody else, I was simply dreaming aloud." I felt that I should extract nothing more from

Albertine. She had lied to me when she had sworn, a moment ago, that what had cut her short had been a social fear of being indiscreet, since it had now become the shame of letting me hear her use a vulgar expression. Now this was certainly another lie. For when we were alone together there was no speech too perverse, no word too coarse for us to utter among our embraces. Anyhow, it was useless to insist at that moment. But my memory remained obsessed by the word "break." Albertine frequently spoke of 'breaking sticks' or 'breaking sugar' over some one, or would simply say: "Ah! I fairly broke it over him!" meaning "I fairly gave it to him!" But she would say this quite freely in my presence, and if it was this that she had meant to say, why had she suddenly stopped short, why had she blushed so deeply, placed her hands over her mouth, given a fresh turn to her speech, and, when she saw that I had heard the word 'break,' offered a false explanation. But as soon as I had abandoned the pursuit of an interrogation from which I received no response, the only thing to do was to appear to have lost interest in the matter, and, retracing my thoughts to Albertine's reproaches of me for having gone to the Mistress's, I said to her, very awkwardly, making indeed a sort of stupid excuse for my conduct: "Why, I had been meaning to ask you to come to the Verdurins' party this evening," a speech that was doubly maladroit, for if I meant it, since I had been with her all the day, why should I not have made the suggestion? Furious at my lie and emboldened by my timidity: "You might have gone on asking me for a thousand years," she said, "I would never have consented. They are people who have always been against me, they have done everything they could to upset me. There was nothing I didn't do for Mme. Verdurin at Balbec, and I've been finely rewarded. If she summoned me to her deathbed, I wouldn't go. There are some things which it is impossible to forgive. As for you, it's the first time you've treated me badly. When Françoise told me that you had gone out (she enjoyed telling me that, I don't think), you might have knocked me down with a feather. I tried not to shew any sign, but never in my life have I been so insulted." While she was speaking, there continued in myself, in the thoroughly alive and creative sleep of the unconscious (a sleep in which the things that barely touch us succeed in carving an impression, in which our hands take hold of the key that turns the lock, the key for which we have sought in vain), the quest of what it was that she had meant by that interrupted speech the end of which I was so anxious to know. And all of a sudden an appalling word, of which I had never dreamed, burst upon me: 'pot.' I cannot say that it came to me in a single flash, as when, in a long passive submission to an incomplete memory, while we try gently, cautiously, to draw it out, we remain fastened, glued to it. No, in contrast to the ordinary process of my memory, there were, I think, two parallel quests; the first took into account not merely Albertine's words, but her look of extreme annoyance when I had offered her a sum of money with which to give a grand dinner, a look which seemed to say: "Thank you, the idea of spending money upon things that bore me, when without money I could do things that I enjoy doing!" And it was perhaps the memory of this look that she had given me which made me alter my method in dis-

covering the end of her unfinished sentence. Until then I had been hypnotised by her last word: 'break,' she had meant to say break what? Break
wood? No. Sugar? No. Break, break, break. And all at once the look that
she had given me at the moment of my suggestion that she should give a
dinner-party, turned me back to the words that had preceded. And immediately I saw that she had not said 'break' but 'get some one to break.'
Horror! It was this that she would have preferred. Twofold horror! For
even the vilest of prostitutes, who consents to that sort of thing, or desires
it, does not employ to the man who yields to her desires that appalling expression. She would feel the degradation too great. To a woman alone, if
she loves women, she says this, as an excuse for giving herself presently to
a man. Albertine had not been lying when she told me that she was speaking in a dream. Distracted, impulsive, not realising that she was with me,
she had, with a shrug of her shoulders, begun to speak as she would have
spoken to one of those women, to one, perhaps, of my young budding girls.
And abruptly recalled to reality, crimson with shame, thrusting back between her lips what she was going to say, plunged in despair, she had
refused to utter another word. I had not a moment to lose if I was not to
let her see how desperate I was. But already, after my sudden burst of
rage, the tears came to my eyes. As at Balbec, on the night that followed
her revelation of her friendship with the Vinteuil pair, I must immediately
invent a plausible excuse for my grief, and one that was at the same time
capable of creating so profound an effect upon Albertine as to give me a
few days' respite before I came to a decision. And so, at the moment when
she told me that she had never received such an insult as that which I had
inflicted upon her by going out, that she would rather have died than hear
Françoise tell her of my departure, when, as though irritated by her absurd
susceptibility, I was on the point of telling her that what I had done was
nothing, that there was nothing that could offend her in my going out—as,
during these moments, moving on a parallel course, my unconscious quest
for what she had meant to say after the word 'break' had proved successful, and the despair into which my discovery flung me could not be completely hidden, instead of defending, I accused myself. "My little Albertine," I said to her in a gentle voice which was drowned in my first
tears, "I might tell you that you are mistaken, that what I did this evening
is nothing, but I should be lying; it is you that are right, you have realised
the truth, my poor child, which is that six months ago, three months ago,
when I was still so fond of you, never would I have done such a thing. It
is a mere nothing, and it is enormous, because of the immense change in
my heart of which it is the sign. And since you have detected this change
which I hoped to conceal from you, that leads me on to tell you this: My
little Albertine" (and here I addressed her with a profound gentleness and
melancholy), "don't you see, the life that you are leading here is boring to
you, it is better that we should part, and as the best partings are those that
are ended at once, I ask you, to cut short the great sorrow that I am bound
to feel, to bid me good-bye to-night and to leave in the morning without
my seeing you again, while I am asleep." She appeared stupefied, still
incredulous and already disconsolate: "To-morrow? You really mean it?"

And notwithstanding the anguish that I felt in speaking of our parting as though it were already in the past—partly perhaps because of that very anguish—I began to give Albertine the most precise instructions as to certain things which she would have to do after she left the house. And passing from one request to another, I soon found myself entering into the minutest details. "Be so kind," I said, with infinite melancholy, "as to send me back that book of Bergotte's which is at your aunt's. There is no hurry about it, in three days, in a week, whenever you like, but remember that I don't want to have to write and ask you for it, that would be too painful. We have been happy together, we feel now that we should be unhappy." "Don't say that we feel that we should be unhappy," Albertine interrupted me, "don't say 'we,' it is only you who feel that." "Yes, very well, you or I, as you like, for one reason or another. But it is absurdly late, you must go to bed—we have decided to part to-night." "Pardon me, *you* have decided, and I obey you because I do not wish to cause you any trouble." "Very well, it is I who have decided, but that makes it none the less painful for me. I do not say that it will be painful for long, you know that I have not the faculty of remembering things for long, but for the first few days I shall be so miserable without you. And so I feel that it will be useless to revive the memory with letters, we must end everything at once." "Yes, you are right," she said to me with a crushed air, which was enhanced by the strain of fatigue upon her features due to the lateness of the hour; "rather than have one finger chopped off, then another, I prefer to lay my head on the block at once." "Heavens, I am appalled when I think how late I am keeping you out of bed, it is madness. However, it's the last night! You will have plenty of time to sleep for the rest of your life." And as I suggested to her thus that it was time to say good night I sought to postpone the moment when she would have said it. "Would you like me, as a distraction during the first few days, to tell Bloch to send his cousin Esther to the place where you will be staying, he will do that for me." "I don't know why you say that" (I had said it in an endeavour to wrest a confession from Albertine); "there is only one person for whom I care, which is yourself," Albertine said to me, and her words filled me with comfort. But, the next moment, what a blow she dealt me! "I remember, of course, that I did give Esther my photograph because she kept on asking me for it and I saw that she would like to have it, but as for feeling any liking for her or wishing ever to see her again. . . ." And yet Albertine was of so frivolous a nature that she went on: "If she wants to see me, it is all the same to me, she is very nice, but I don't care in the least either way." And so when I had spoken to her of the photograph of Esther which Bloch had sent me (and which I had not even received when I mentioned it to Albertine) my mistress had gathered that Bloch had shewn me a photograph of herself, given by her to Esther. In my worst suppositions, I had never imagined that any such intimacy could have existed between Albertine and Esther. Albertine had found no words in which to answer me when I spoke of the photograph. And now, supposing me, wrongly, to be in the know, she thought it better to confess. I was appalled. "And, Albertine, let me ask you to do me one more favour, never attempt to see me again. If at any time, as may happen in a year, in two years, in three years, we should find ourselves in the same town, keep away from me." Then, seeing that she did not reply in the affirmative to my prayer: "My Albertine, never see me again in this world. It would hurt me too much. For I was really fond of you, you know. Of course, when I told you the other day that I wanted to see the friend again whom I mentioned to you at Balbec, you thought that it was all settled. Not at all, I assure you, it was quite immaterial to me. You were convinced that I had long made up my mind to leave you, that my affection was all make-believe." "No indeed, you are mad, I never thought so," she said sadly. "You are right, you must never think so, I did genuinely feel for you, not love perhaps, but a great, a very great affection, more than you can imagine." "I can, indeed. And do you suppose that I don't love you!" "It hurts me terribly to have to give you up." "It hurts me a thousand times more," replied Albertine. A moment earlier I had felt that I could no longer restrain the tears that came welling up in my eyes. And these tears did not spring from at all the same sort of misery which I had felt long ago when I said to Gilberte: "It is better that we should not see one another again, life is dividing us." No doubt when I wrote this to Gilberte, I said to myself that when I should be in love not with her but with another, the excess of my love would diminish that which I might perhaps have been able to inspire, as though two people must inevitably have only a certain quantity of love at their disposal; of which the surplus taken by one is subtracted from the other, and that from her too, as from Gilberte, I should be doomed to part. But the situation was entirely different for several reasons, the first of which (and it had, in its turn, given rise to the others) was that the lack of will-power which my grandmother and mother had observed in me with alarm, at Combray, and before which each of them, so great is the energy with which a sick man imposes his weakness upon others, had capitulated in turn, this lack of will-power had gone on increasing at an ever accelerated pace. When I felt that my company was boring Gilberte, I had still enough strength left to give her up; I had no longer the same strength when I had made a similar discovery with regard to Albertine, and could think only of keeping her at any cost to myself. With the result that, whereas I wrote to Gilberte that I would not see her again, meaning quite sincerely not to see her, I said this to Albertine as a pure falsehood, and in the hope of bringing about a reconciliation. Thus we presented each to the other an appearance which was widely different from the reality. And no doubt it is always so when two people stand face to face, since each of them is ignorant of a part of what exists in the other (even what he knows, he can understand only in part) and since both of them display what is the least personal thing about them, whether because they have not explored themselves and regard as negligible what is most important, or because insignificant advantages which have no place in themselves seem to them more important and more flattering. But in love this misunderstanding is carried to its supreme pitch because, except perhaps when we are children, we endeavour to make the appearance that we assume, rather than reflect exactly what is in our mind, be what our mind considers best adapted to enable us to obtain what we desire, which in my case, since my return to the house, was to be able to keep Albertine as docile as she had been in the past, was that she should not in her irritation ask me for a greater freedom, which I intended to give her one day, but which at this moment, when I was afraid of her cravings for independence, would have made me too jealous. After a certain age, from self-esteem and from sagacity, it is to the things which we most desire that we pretend to attach no importance. But in love, our mere sagacity—which for that matter is probably not the true wisdom—forces us speedily enough to this genius for duplicity. All that I had dreamed, as a boy, to be the sweetest thing in love, what had seemed to me to be the very essence of love, was to pour out freely, before the feet of her whom I loved, my affection, my gratitude for her kindness, my longing for a perpetual life together. But I had become only too well aware, from my own experience and from that of my friends, that the expression of such sentiments is far from being contagious. Once we have observed this, we no longer 'let ourself go'; I had taken good care in the afternoon not to tell Albertine how grateful I was to her that she had not remained at the Trocadéro. And to-night, having been afraid that she might leave me, I had feigned a desire to part from her, a feint which for that matter was not suggested to me merely by the enlightenment which I supposed myself to have received from my former loves and was seeking to bring to the service of this.

The fear that Albertine was perhaps going to say to me: "I wish to be allowed to go out by myself at certain hours, I wish to be able to stay away for a night," in fact any request of that sort, which I did not attempt to define, but which alarmed me, this fear had entered my mind for a moment before and during the Verdurins' party. But it had been dispelled, contradicted moreover by the memory of how Albertine assured me incessantly how happy she was with me. The intention to leave me, if it existed in Albertine, was made manifest only in an obscure fashion, in certain sorrowful glances, certain gestures of impatience, speeches which meant nothing of the sort, but which, if one analysed them (and there was not even any need of analysis, for we can immediately detect the language of passion, the lower orders themselves understand these speeches which can be explained only by vanity, rancour, jealousy, unexpressed as it happens, but revealing itself at once to the listener by an intuitive faculty which, like the 'good sense' of which Descartes speaks, is the most widespread thing in the world), revealed the presence in her of a sentiment which she concealed and which might lead her to form plans for another life apart from myself. Just as this intention was not expressed in her speech in a logical fashion, so the presentiment of this intention, which I had felt to-night, remained just as vague in myself. I continued to live by the hypothesis which admitted as true everything that Albertine told me. But it may be that in myself, during this time, a wholly contrary hypothesis, of which I refused to think, never left me; this is all the more probable since, otherwise, I should have felt no hesitation in telling Albertine that I had been to the Verdurins', and, indeed, my want of astonishment at her anger would not have been comprehensible. So that what probably existed in me was the idea of an Albertine entirely opposite to that which my reason formed of her, to that also which her own speech portrayed, an Albertine that all the same was not wholly invented, since she was like a prophetic mirror of certain impulses that occurred in her, such as her ill humour at my having gone to the Verdurins'. Besides, for a long time past, my frequent anguish, my fear of telling Albertine that I loved her, all this corresponded to another hypothesis which explained many things besides, and had also this to be said for it, that, if one adopted the first hypothesis, the second became more probable, for by allowing myself to give way to effusive tenderness for Albertine, I obtained from her nothing but irritation (to which moreover she assigned a different cause).

If I analyse my feelings by this hypothesis, by the invariable system of retorts expressing the exact opposite of what I was feeling, I can be quite certain that if, to-night, I told her that I was going to send her away, it was—at first, quite unconsciously—because I was afraid that she might desire her freedom (I should have been put to it to say what this freedom was that made me tremble, but anyhow some state of freedom in which she would have been able to deceive me, or, at least, I should no longer have been able to be certain that she was not) and wished to shew her, from pride, from cunning, that I was very far from fearing anything of the sort, as I had done already, at Balbec, when I was anxious that she should have a good opinion of me, and later on, when I was anxious that she should not have time to feel bored with me. In short, the objection that might be offered to this second hypothesis—which I did not formulate,—that everything that Albertine said to me indicated on the contrary that the life which she preferred was the life in my house, resting, reading, solitude, a loathing of Sapphic loves, and so forth, need not be considered seriously. For if on her part Albertine had chosen to interpret my feelings from what I said to her, she would have learned the exact opposite of the truth, since I never expressed a desire to part from her except when I was unable to do without her, and at Balbec I had confessed to her that I was in love with another woman, first Andrée, then a mysterious stranger, on the two occasions on which jealousy had revived my love for Albertine. My words, therefore, did not in the least reflect my sentiments. If the reader has no more than a faint impression of these, that is because, as narrator, I reveal my sentiments to him at the same time as I repeat my words. But if I concealed the former and he were acquainted only with the latter, my actions, so little in keeping with my speech, would so often give him the impression of strange revulsions of feeling that he would think me almost mad. A procedure which would not, for that matter, be much more false than that which I have adopted, for the images which prompted me to action, so opposite to those which were portrayed in my speech, were at that moment extremely obscure; I was but imperfectly aware of the nature which guided my actions; at present, I have a clear conception of its subjective truth. As for its objective truth, that is to say whether the inclinations of that nature grasped more exactly than my reason Albertine's true intentions, whether I was right to trust to that nature or on the contrary it did not corrupt Albertine's intentions instead of making them plain, that

I find difficult to say. That vague fear which I had felt at the Verdurins' that Albertine might leave me had been at once dispelled. When I returned home, it had been with the feeling that I myself was a captive, not with that of finding a captive in the house. But the dispelled fear had gripped me all the more violently when, at the moment of my informing Albertine that I had been to the Verdurins', I saw her face veiled with a look of enigmatic irritation which moreover was not making itself visible for the first time. I knew quite well that it was only the crystallisation in the flesh of reasoned complaints, of ideas clear to the person who forms and does not express them, a synthesis rendered visible but not therefore rational, which the man who gathers its precious residue from the face of his beloved, endeavours in his turn, so that he may understand what is occurring in her, to reduce by analysis to its intellectual elements. The approximate equation of that unknown quantity which Albertine's thoughts were to me, had given me, more or less: "I knew his suspicions, I was sure that he would attempt to verify them, and so that I might not hinder him, he has worked out his little plan in secret." But if this was the state of mind (and she had never expressed it to me) in which Albertine was living, must she not regard with horror, find the strength fail her to carry on, might she not at any moment decide to terminate an existence in which, if she was, in desire at any rate, guilty, she must feel herself exposed, tracked down, prevented from ever yielding to her instincts, without thereby disarming my jealousy, and if innocent in intention and fact, she had had every right, for some time past, to feel discouraged, seeing that never once, from Balbec, where she had shewn so much perseverance in avoiding the risk of her ever being left alone with Andrée, until this very day when she had agreed not to go to the Verdurins' and not to stay at the Trocadéro, had she succeeded in regaining my confidence. All the more so as I could not say that her behaviour was not exemplary. If at Balbec, when anyone mentioned girls who had a bad style, she used often to copy their laughter, their wrigglings, their general manner, which was a torture to me because of what I supposed that it must mean to her girl friends, now that she knew my opinion on the subject, as soon as anyone made an allusion to things of that sort, she ceased to take part in the conversation, not only in speech but with the expression on her face. Whether it was in order not to contribute her share to the slanders that were being uttered about some woman or other, or for a quite different reason, the only thing that was noticeable then, upon those so mobile features, was that from the moment in which the topic was broached they had made their inattention evident, while preserving exactly the same expression that they had worn a moment earlier. And this immobility of even a light expression was as heavy as a silence; it would have been impossible to say that she blamed, that she approved, that she knew or did not know about these things. None of her features bore any relation to anything save another feature. Her nose, her mouth, her eyes formed a perfect harmony, isolated from everything else; she looked like a pastel, and seemed to have no more heard what had just been said than if it had been uttered in front of a portrait by Latour.

My serfdom, of which I had already been conscious when, as I gave the driver Brichot's address, I caught sight of the light in her window, had ceased to weigh upon me shortly afterwards, when I saw that Albertine appeared so cruelly conscious of her own. And in order that it might seem to her less burdensome, that she might not decide to break her bonds of her own accord, I had felt that the most effective plan was to give her the impression that it would not be permanent and that I myself was looking forward to its termination. Seeing that my feint had proved successful, I might well have thought myself fortunate, in the first place because what I had so greatly dreaded, Albertine's determination (as I supposed) to leave me, was shewn to be non-existent, and secondly, because, quite apart from the object that I had had in mind, the very success of my feint, by proving that I was something more to Albertine than a scorned lover, whose jealousy is flouted, all of his ruses detected in advance, endowed our love afresh with a sort of virginity, revived for it the days in which she could still, at Balbec, so readily believe that I was in love with another woman. For she would probably not have believed that any longer, but she was taking seriously my feigned determination to part from her now and for ever. She appeared to suspect that the cause of our parting might be something that had happened at the Verdurins'. Feeling a need to soothe the anxiety into which I was worked by my pretence of a rupture, I said to her: "Albertine, can you swear that you have never lied to me?" She gazed fixedly into the air before replying: "Yes, that is to say no. I ought not to have told you that Andrée was greatly taken with Bloch, we never met him." "Then why did you say so?" "Because I was afraid that you had believed other stories about her, that's all." I told her that I had met a dramatist who was a great friend of Léa, and to whom Léa had told some strange things (I hoped by telling her this to make her suppose that I knew a great deal more than I cared to say about Bloch's cousin's friend. She stared once again into vacancy and then said: "I ought not, when I spoke to you just now about Léa, to have kept from you a three weeks' trip that I took with her once. But I knew you so slightly in those days!" "It was before Balbec?" "Before the second time, yes." And that very morning, she had told me that she did not know Léa, and, only a moment ago, that she had met her once only in her dressing-room! I watched a tongue of flame seize and devour in an instant a romance which I had spent millions of minutes in writing. To what end? To what end? Of course I understood that Albertine had revealed these facts to me because she thought that I had learned them indirectly from Léa; and that there was no reason why a hundred similar facts should not exist. I realised thus that Albertine's utterances, when one interrogated her, did not ever contain an atom of truth, that the truth she allowed to escape only in spite of herself, as though by a sudden combination in her mind of the facts which she had previously been determined to conceal with the belief that I had been informed of them. "But two things are nothing," I said to Albertine, "let us have as many as four, so that you may leave me some memories of you. What other revelations have you got for me?" Once again she stared into vacancy. To what belief in a future life was she adapting her falsehood, with what Gods less unstable than she had supposed was she seeking to ally herself? This cannot have been an easy matter, for her silence and the fixity of her gaze continued for some time. "No, nothing else," she said at length. And, notwithstanding my persistence, she adhered, easily now, to "nothing else." And what a lie! For, from the moment when she had acquired those tastes until the day when she had been shut up in my house, how many times, in how many places, on how many excursions must she have gratified them! The daughters of Gomorrah are at once so rare and so frequent that, in any crowd of people, one does not pass unperceived by the other. From that moment a meeting becomes easy.

I remembered with horror an evening which at the time had struck me as merely absurd. One of my friends had invited me to dine at a restaurant with his mistress and another of his friends who had also brought his own. The two women were not long in coming to an understanding, but were so impatient to enjoy one another that, with the soup, their feet were searching for one another, often finding mine. Presently their legs were interlaced. My two friends noticed nothing; I was on tenterhooks. One of the women, who could contain herself no longer, stooped under the table, saying that she had dropped something. Then one of them complained of a headache and asked to go upstairs to the lavatory. The other discovered that it was time for her to go and meet a woman friend at the theatre. Finally I was left alone with my two friends who suspected nothing. The lady with the headache reappeared, but begged to be allowed to go home by herself to wait for her lover at his house, so that she might take a dose of antipyrin. They became great friends, used to go about together, one of them, dressed as a man, picking up little girls and taking them to the other, initiating them. One of them had a little boy who, she pretended, was troublesome, and handed him over for punishment to her friend, who set to work with a strong arm. One may say that there was no place, however public, in which they did not do what is most secret.

"But Léa behaved perfectly properly with me all the time," Albertine told me. "She was indeed a great deal more reserved than plenty of society women." "Are there any society women who have shewn a want of reserve with you, Albertine?" "Never." "Then what do you mean?" "O, well, she was less free in her speech." "For instance?" "She would never, like many of the women you meet, have used the expression 'rotten,' or say: 'I don't care a damn for anybody.'" It seemed to me that a part of the romance which the flames had so far spared was crumbling at length in ashes.

My discouragement might have persisted. Albertine's words, when I thought of them, made it give place to a furious rage. This succumbed to a sort of tender emotion. I also, when I came home and declared that I wished to break with her, had been lying. And this desire for a parting, which I had feigned with perseverance, gradually affected me with some of the misery which I should have felt if I had really wished to part from Albertine.

Besides, even when I thought in fits and starts, in twinges, as we say of other bodily pains, of that orgiastic life which Albertine had led before she met me, I admired all the more the docility of my captive and ceased to feel any resentment.

No doubt, never, during our life together, had I failed to let Albertine know that such a life would in all probability be merely temporary, so that Albertine might continue to find some charm in it. But to-night I had gone further, having feared that vague threats of separation were no longer sufficient, contradicted as they would doubtless be, in Albertine's mind, by her idea of a strong and jealous love of her, which must have made me, she seemed to imply, go in quest of information to the Verdurins'.

To-night I thought that, among the other reasons which might have made me decide of a sudden, without even realising except as I went on what I was doing, to enact this scene of rupture, there was above all the fact that, when, in one of those impulses to which my father was liable, I threatened another person in his security, as I had not, like him, the courage to carry a threat into practice, in order not to let it be supposed that it had been but empty words, I would go to a considerable length in pretending to carry out my threat and would recoil only when my adversary, having had a genuine illusion of my sincerity, had begun seriously to tremble. Besides, in these lies, we feel that there is indeed a grain of truth, that, if life does not bring any alteration of our loves, it is ourselves who will seek to bring or to feign one, so strongly do we feel that all love, and everything else evolves rapidly towards a farewell. We would like to shed the tears that it will bring long before it comes. No doubt there had been, on this occasion, in the scene that I had enacted, a practical value. I had suddenly determined to keep Albertine because I felt that she was distributed among other people whom I could not prevent her from joining. But had she renounced them all finally for myself, I should have been all the more firmly determined never to let her go, for a parting is, by jealousy, rendered cruel, but, by gratitude, impossible. I felt that in any case I was fighting the decisive battle in which I must conquer or fall. I would have offered Albertine in an hour all that I possessed, because I said to myself: "Everything depends upon this battle, but such battles are less like those of old days which lasted for a few hours than a battle of to-day which does not end on the morrow, nor on the day after, nor in the following week. We give all our strength, because we steadfastly believe that we shall never need any strength again. And more than a year passes without bringing a 'decisive' victory. Perhaps an unconscious reminiscence of lying scenes enacted by M. de Charlus, in whose company I was when the fear of Albertine's leaving me had seized hold of me, was added to the rest. But, later on, I heard my mother say something of which I was then unaware and which leads me to believe that I found all the elements of this scene in myself, in those obscure reserves of heredity which certain emotions, acting in this respect as, upon the residue of our stored-up strength, drugs such as alcohol and coffee act, place at our disposal. When my aunt Léonie learned from Eulalie that Françoise, convinced that her mistress would never again leave the house, had secretly planned some outing of which my aunt was to know nothing, she, the day before, would pretend to have made up her mind that she would attempt an excursion on the morrow.

The incredulous Françoise was ordered not only to prepare my aunt's clothes beforehand, to give an airing to those that had been put away for too long, but to order a carriage, to arrange, to within a quarter of an hour, all the details of the day. It was only when Françoise, convinced or at any rate shaken, had been forced to confess to my aunt the plan that she herself had formed, that my aunt would publicly abandon her own, so as not, she said, to interfere with Françoise's arrangements. Similarly, so that Albertine might not believe that I was exaggerating and to make her proceed as far as possible in the idea that we were to part, drawing myself the obvious deductions from the proposal that I had advanced, I had begun to anticipate the time which was to begin on the morrow and was to last for ever, the time in which we should be parted, addressing to Albertine the same requests as if we were not to be reconciled almost immediately. Like a general who considers that if a feint is to succeed in deceiving the enemy it must be pushed to extremes, I had employed in this feint almost as much of my store of sensibility as if it had been genuine. This fictitious parting scene ended by causing me almost as much grief as if it had been real, possibly because one of the actors, Albertine, by believing it to be real, had enhanced the other's illusion. While we were living, from day to day, in a day which, even if painful, was still endurable, held down to earth by the ballast of habit and by that certainty that the morrow, should it prove a day of torment, would contain the presence of the person who is all in all, here was I stupidly destroying all that oppressive life. I was destroying it, it is true, only in a fictitious fashion, but this was enough to make me wretched; perhaps because the sad words which we utter, even when we are lying, carry in themselves their sorrow and inject it deeply into us; perhaps because we do not realise that, by feigning farewells, we evoke by anticipation an hour which must inevitably come later on; then we cannot be certain that we have not released the mechanism which will make it strike. In every bluff there is an element, however small, of uncertainty as to what the person whom we are deceiving is going to do. If this make-believe of parting should lead to a parting! We cannot consider the possibility, however unlikely it may seem, without a clutching of the heart. We are doubly anxious, because the parting would then occur at the moment when it would be intolerable, when we had been made to suffer by the woman who would be leaving us before she had healed, or at least appeased us. In short, we have no longer the solid ground of habit upon which we rest, even in our sorrow. We have deliberately deprived ourselves of it, we have given the present day an exceptional importance, have detached it from the days before and after it; it floats without roots like a day of departure; our imagination ceasing to be paralysed by habit has awakened, we have suddenly added to our everyday love sentimental dreams which enormously enhance it, make indispensable to us a presence upon which, as a matter of fact, we are no longer certain that we can rely. No doubt it is precisely in order to assure ourselves of that presence for the future that we have indulged in the make-believe of being able to dispense with it. But this make-believe, we have ourselves been taken in by it, we have begun to suffer afresh because we have created something new, unfamiliar which thus resembles those cures that are destined in time to heal the malady from which we are suffering, but the first effects of which are to aggravate it.

I had tears in my eyes, like the people who, alone in their bedrooms, imagining, in the wayward course of their meditations, the death of some one whom they love, form so detailed a picture of the grief that they would feel that they end by feeling it. And so as I multiplied my advice to Albertine as to the way in which she would have to behave in relation to myself after we had parted, I seemed to be feeling almost as keen a distress as though we had not been on the verge of a reconciliation. Besides, was I so certain that I could bring about this reconciliation, bring Albertine back to the idea of a life shared with myself, and, if I succeeded for the time being, that in her, the state of mind which this scene had dispelled would not revive? I felt myself, but did not believe myself to be master of the future, because I realised that this sensation was due merely to the fact that the future did not yet exist, and that thus I was not crushed by its inevitability. In short, while I lied, I was perhaps putting into my words more truth than I supposed. I had just had an example of this, when I told Albertine that I should quickly forget her; this was what had indeed happened to me in the case of Gilberte, whom I now refrained from going to see in order to escape not a grief but an irksome duty. And certainly I had been grieved when I wrote to Gilberte that I would not come any more, and I had gone to see her only occasionally. Whereas the whole of Albertine's time belonged to me, and in love it is easier to relinquish a sentiment than to lose a habit. But all these painful words about our parting, if the strength to utter them had been given me because I knew them to be untrue, were on the other hand sincere upon Albertine's lips when I heard her exclaim: "Ah! I promise, I will never see you again. Anything sooner than see you cry like that, my darling. I do not wish to cause you any grief. Since it must be, we will never meet again." They were sincere, as they could not have been coming from me, because, for one thing, as Albertine felt nothing stronger for me than friendship, the renunciation that they promised cost her less; because, moreover, in a scene of parting, it is the person who is not genuinely in love that makes the tender speeches, since love does not express itself directly; because, lastly, my tears, which would have been so small a matter in a great love, seemed to her almost extraordinary and overwhelmed her, transposed into the region of that state of friendship in which she dwelt, a friendship greater than mine for her, to judge by what she had just said, which was perhaps not altogether inexact, for the thousand kindnesses of love may end by arousing, in the person who inspires without feeling it, an affection, a gratitude less selfish than the sentiment that provoked them, which, perhaps, after years of separation, when nothing of that sentiment remains in the former lover, will still persist in the beloved.

"My little Albertine," I replied, "it is very good of you to make me this promise. Anyhow, for the first few years at least, I shall avoid the places where I might meet you. You don't know whether you will be going to Balbec this year? Because in that case I should arrange not to go there myself." But now, if I continued to progress thus, anticipating time to come in my lying inventions, it was with a view no less to inspiring fear in Albertine than to making myself wretched. As a man who at first had no serious reason for losing his temper, becomes completely intoxicated by the sound of his own voice, and lets himself be carried away by a fury engendered not by his grievance but by his anger which itself is steadily growing, so I was falling ever faster and faster down the slope of my wretchedness, towards an ever more profound despair, and with the inertia of a man who feels the cold grip him, makes no effort to resist it and even finds a sort of pleasure in shivering. And if I had now at length, as I fully supposed, the strength to control myself, to react and to reverse my engines, far more than from the grief which Albertine had caused me by so unfriendly a greeting on my return, it was from that which I had felt in imagining, so as to pretend to be outlining them, the formalities of an imaginary separation, in foreseeing its consequences, that Albertine's kiss, when the time came for her to bid me good night, would have to console me now. In any case, it must not be she that said this good night of her own accord, for that would have made more difficult the revulsion by which I would propose to her to abandon the idea of our parting. And so I continued to remind her that the time to say good night had long since come and gone, a method which, by leaving the initiative to me, enabled me to put it off for a moment longer. And thus I scattered with allusions to the lateness of the hour, to our exhaustion, the questions with which I was plying Albertine. "I don't know where I shall be going," she replied to the last of these, in a worried tone. "Perhaps I shall go to Touraine, to my aunt's." And this first plan that she suggested froze me as though it were beginning to make definitely effective our final separation. She looked round the room, at the pianola, the blue satin armchairs. "I still cannot make myself realise that I shall not see all this again, to-morrow, or the next day, or ever. Poor little room. It seems to me quite impossible; I cannot get it into my head." "It had to be; you were unhappy here." "No, indeed, I was not unhappy, it is now that I shall be unhappy." "No, I assure you, it is better for you." "For you, perhaps!" I began to stare fixedly into vacancy, as though, worried by an extreme hesitation, I was debating an idea which had occurred to my mind. Then, all of a sudden: "Listen, Albertine, you say that you are happier here, that you are going to be unhappy." "Why, of course." "That appalls me; would you like us to try to carry on for a few weeks? Who knows, week by week, we may perhaps go on for a long time; you know that there are temporary arrangements which end by becoming permanent." "Oh, how kind you are!" "Only in that case it is ridiculous of us to have made ourselves wretched like this over nothing for hours on end, it is like making all the preparations for a long journey and then staying at home. I am shattered with grief." I made her sit on my knee, I took Bergotte's manuscript which she so longed to have and wrote on the cover: "To my little Albertine, in memory of a new lease of life." "Now," I said to her, "go and sleep until to-morrow, my darling, for you must be worn out." "I am very glad, all the same." "Do you love me a little bit?" "A hundred times more than ever."

I should have been wrong in being delighted with this little piece of play-acting, had it not been that I had carried it to the pitch of a real scene on the stage. Had we done no more than quite simply discuss a separation, even that would have been a serious matter. In conversations of this sort, we suppose that we are speaking not merely without sincerity, which is true, but freely. Whereas they are generally, though we know it not, murmured in spite of us; the first murmur of a storm which we do not suspect. In reality, what we express at such times is the opposite of our desire (which is to live for ever with her whom we love), but there is also that impossibility of living together which is the cause of our daily suffering, a suffering preferred by us to that of a parting, which will, however, end, in spite of ourselves, in parting us. Generally speaking, not, however, at once. As a rule, it happens—this was not, as we shall see, my case with Albertine—that, some time after the words in which we did not believe, we put into action a vague attempt at a deliberate separation, not painful, temporary. We ask the woman, so that afterwards she may be happier in our company, so that we on the other hand may momentarily escape from continual worries and fatigues, to go without us, or to let us go without her, for a few days elsewhere, the first days that we have—for a long time past—spent, as would have seemed to us impossible, away from her. Very soon she returns to take her place by our fireside. Only this separation, short, but made real, is not so arbitrarily decided upon, not so certainly the only one that we have in mind. The same sorrows begin afresh, the same difficulty in living together becomes accentuated, only a parting is no longer so difficult as before; we have begun mentioning it, and have then put it into practice in a friendly fashion. But these are only preliminary ventures whose nature we have not recognised. Presently, to the momentary and smiling separation will succeed the terrible and final separation for which we have, without knowing it, paved the way.

"Come to my room in five minutes and let me see something of you, my dearest boy. You are full of kindness. But afterwards I shall fall asleep at once, for I am almost dead." It was indeed a dead woman that I beheld when, presently, I entered her room. She had gone to sleep immediately she lay down, the sheets wrapped like a shroud about her body had assumed, with their stately folds, a stony rigidity. One would have said that, as in certain Last Judgments of the Middle Ages, her head alone was emerging from the tomb, awaiting in its sleep the Archangel's trumpet. This head had been surprised by sleep almost flung back, its hair bristling. And as I saw the expressionless body extended there, I asked myself what logarithmic table it constituted so that all the actions in which it might have been involved, from the nudge of an elbow to the brushing of a skirt, were able to cause me, stretched out to the infinity of all the points that it had occupied in space and time, and from time to time sharply reawakened in my memory, so intense an anguish, albeit I knew those actions to have been determined in her by impulses, desires, which in another person, in herself five years earlier, or five years later, would have left me quite indifferent. All this was a lie, but a lie for which I had not the courage to seek any solution other than my own death. And so I remained, in the fur coat which I had not taken off since my return from the Verdurins', before that bent body, that figure allegorical of what? Of my death? Of my love? Presently I began to hear her regular breathing. I went and sat down on the edge of her bed to take that soothing cure of fresh air and contemplation. Then I withdrew very gently so as not to awaken her.

It was so late that, in the morning, I warned Françoise to tread very softly when she had to pass by the door of Albertine's room. And so Françoise, convinced that we had spent the night in what she used to call orgies, ironically warned the other servants not to 'wake the Princess.' And this was one of the things that I dreaded, that Françoise might one day be unable to contain herself any longer, might treat Albertine with insolence, and that this might introduce complications into our life. Françoise was now no longer, as at the time when it distressed her to see Eulalie treated generously by my aunt, of an age to endure her jealousy with courage. It distorted, paralysed our old servant's face to such an extent that at times I asked myself whether she had not, after some outburst of rage, had a slight stroke. Having thus asked that Albertine's sleep should be respected, I was unable to sleep myself. I endeavoured to understand the true state of Albertine's mind. By that wretched farce which I had played, was it a real peril that I had averted, and, notwithstanding her assurance that she was so happy living with me, had she really felt at certain moments a longing for freedom, or on the contrary was I to believe what she said?

Which of these two hypotheses was the truth? If it often befell me, if it was in a special case to befall me that I must extend an incident in my past life to the dimensions of history, when I made an attempt to understand some political event; inversely, this morning, I did not cease to identify, in spite of all the differences and in an attempt to understand its bearing, our scene overnight with a diplomatic incident that had just occurred. I had perhaps the right to reason thus. For it was highly probable that, without my knowledge, the example of M. de Charlus had guided me in that lying scene which I had so often seen him enact with such authority; on the other hand, was it in him anything else than an unconscious importation into the domain of his private life of the innate tendency of his Germanic stock, provocative from guile and, from pride, belligerent at need. Certain persons, among them the Prince of Monaco, having suggested the idea to the French Government that, if it did not dispense with M. Delcassé, a menacing Germany would indeed declare war, the Minister for Foreign Affairs had been asked to resign. So that the French Government had admitted the hypothesis of an intention to make war upon us if we did not yield. But others thought that it was all a mere 'bluff' and that if France had stood firm Germany would not have drawn the sword. No doubt the scenario was not merely different but almost opposite, since the threat of a rupture had not been put forward by Albertine; but a series of impressions had led me to believe that she was thinking of it, as France had been led to believe about Germany. On the other hand, if Germany desired peace, to have provoked in the French Government the idea that she was anxious for war was a disputable and dangerous trick. Certainly, my conduct had been skilful enough, if it was the thought that I would

never make up my mind to break with her that provoked in Albertine
sudden longings for independence. And was it not difficult to believe that
she did not feel them, to shut one's eyes to a whole secret existence, directed
towards the satisfaction of her vice, simply on remarking the anger with
which she had learned that I had gone to see the Verdurins', when she
exclaimed: "I thought as much," and went on to reveal everything by saying: "Wasn't Mlle. Vinteuil there?" All this was corroborated by Albertine's meeting with Mme. Verdurin of which Andrée had informed me.
But perhaps all the same these sudden longings for independence (I told
myself, when I tried to go against my own instinct) were caused—supposing them to exist—or would eventually be caused by the opposite theory,
to wit that I had never had any intention of marrying her, that it was when
I made, as though involuntarily, an allusion to our approaching separation
that I was telling the truth, that I would whatever happened part from
her one day or another, a belief which the scene that I had made overnight
could then only have confirmed and which might end by engendering in
her the resolution: "If this is bound to happen one day or another, better
to end everything at once." The preparations for war which the most misleading of proverbs lays down as the best way to secure the triumph of
peace, create first of all the belief in each of the adversaries that the other
desires a rupture, a belief which brings the rupture about, and, when it
has occurred, this further belief in each of them that it is the other that
has sought it. Even if the threat was not sincere, its success encourages a
repetition. But the exact point to which a bluff may succeed is difficult to
determine; if one party goes too far, the other which has previously yielded,
advances in its turn; the first party, no longer able to change its method,
accustomed to the idea that to seem not to fear a rupture is the best way
of avoiding one (which is what I had done overnight with Albertine), and
moreover driven to prefer, in its pride, to fall rather than yield, perseveres
in its threat until the moment when neither can draw back any longer.
The bluff may also be blended with sincerity, may alternate with it, and
it is possible that what was a game yesterday may become a reality to-
morrow. Finally it may also happen that one of the adversaries is really
determined upon war, it might be that Albertine, for instance, had the
intention of, sooner or later, not continuing this life any longer, or on the
contrary that the idea had never even entered her mind and that my imagination had invented the whole thing from start to finish. Such were the
different hypotheses which I considered while she lay asleep that morning.
And yet as to the last I can say that I never, in the period that followed,
threatened Albertine with a rupture unless in response to an idea of an evil
freedom on her part, an idea which she did not express to me, but which
seemed to me to be implied by certain mysterious dissatisfactions, certain
words, certain gestures, of which that idea was the only possible explanation and of which she refused to give me any other. Even then, quite often,
I remarked them without making any allusion to a possible separation,
hoping that they were due to a fit of ill temper which would end that same
day. But it continued at times without intermission for weeks on end,
during which Albertine seemed anxious to provoke a conflict, as though

there had been at the time, in some region more or less remote, pleasures of which she knew, of which her seclusion in my house was depriving her, and which would continue to influence her until they came to an end, like those atmospheric changes which, even by our own fireside, affect our nerves, even when they are occurring as far away as the Balearic islands.

This morning, while Albertine lay asleep and I was trying to guess what was concealed in her, I received a letter from my mother in which she expressed her anxiety at having heard nothing of what we had decided in this phrase of Mme. de Sévigné: "In my own mind I am convinced that he will not marry; but then, why trouble this girl whom he will never marry? Why risk making her refuse suitors at whom she will never look again save with scorn? Why disturb the mind of a person whom it would be so easy to avoid?" This letter from my mother brought me back to earth. "What am I doing, seeking a mysterious soul, interpreting a face and feeling myself overawed by presentiments which I dare not explore?" I asked myself. "I have been dreaming, the matter is quite simple. I am an undecided young man, and it is a question of one of those marriages as to which it takes time to find out whether they will happen or not. There is nothing in this peculiar to Albertine." This thought gave me an immense but a short relief. Very soon I said to myself: "One can after all reduce everything, if one regards it in its social aspect, to the most commonplace item of newspaper gossip. From outside, it is perhaps thus that I should look at it. But I know well that what is true, what at least is also true, is everything that I have thought, is what I have read in Albertine's eyes, is the fears that torment me, is the problem that I incessantly set myself with regard to Albertine. The story of the hesitating bridegroom and the broken engagement may correspond to this, as the report of a theatrical performance made by an intelligent reporter may give us the subject of one of Ibsen's plays. But there is something beyond those facts which are reported. It is true that this other thing exists perhaps, were we able to discern it, in all hesitating bridegrooms and in all the engagements that drag on, because there is perhaps an element of mystery in our everyday life." It was possible for me to neglect it in the lives of other people, but Albertine's life and my own I was living from within.

Albertine no more said to me after this midnight scene than she had said before it: "I know that you do not trust me, I am going to try to dispel your suspicions." But this idea, which she never expressed in words, might have served as an explanation of even her most trivial actions. Not only did she take care never to be alone for a moment, so that I might not lack information as to what she had been doing, if I did not believe her own statements, but even when she had to telephone to Andrée, or to the garage, or to the livery stable or elsewhere, she pretended that it was such a bore to stand about by herself waiting to telephone, what with the time the girls took to give you your number, and took care that I should be with her at such times, or, failing myself, Françoise, as though she were afraid that I might imagine reprehensible conversations by telephone in which she would make mysterious assignations. Alas, all this did not set my mind at rest. I had a day of discouragement. Aimé had sent me back Esther's photograph, with a message that she was not the person. And so Albertine had other intimate friends as well as this girl to whom, through her misunderstanding of what I said, I had, when I meant to refer to something quite different, discovered that she had given her photograph. I sent this photograph back to Bloch. What I should have liked to see was the photograph that Albertine had given to Esther. How was she dressed in it? Perhaps with a bare bosom, for all I knew. But I dared not mention it to Albertine (for it would then have appeared that I had not seen the photograph), or to Bloch, since I did not wish him to think that I was interested in Albertine. And this life, which anyone who knew of my suspicions and her bondage would have seen to be agonising to myself and to Albertine, was regarded from without, by Françoise, as a life of unmerited pleasures of which full advantage was cunningly taken by that 'trickstress' and (as Françoise said, using the feminine form far more often than the masculine, for she was more envious of women) 'charlatante.' Indeed, as Françoise, by contact with myself, had enriched her vocabulary with fresh terms, but had adapted them to her own style, she said of Albertine that she had never known a person of such 'perfidity,' who was so skilful at 'drawing my money' by play-acting (which Françoise, who was as prone to mistake the particular for the general as the general for the particular and who had but a very vague idea of the various kinds of dramatic art, called 'acting a pantomime'). Perhaps for this error as to the true nature of the life led by Albertine and myself, I was myself to some extent responsible owing to the vague confirmations of it which, when I was talking to Françoise, I skilfully let fall, from a desire either to tease her or to appear, if not loved, at any rate happy. And yet my jealousy, the watch that I kept over Albertine, which I would have given anything for Françoise not to suspect, she was not long in discovering, guided, like the thought-reader who, groping blindfold, finds the hidden object, by that intuition which she possessed for anything that might be painful to me, which would not allow itself to be turned aside by the lies that I might tell in the hope of distracting her, and also by that clairvoyant hatred which urged her—even more than it urged her to believe her enemies more prosperous, more skilful hypocrites than they really were—to discover the secret that might prove their undoing and to precipitate their downfall. Françoise certainly never made any scenes with Albertine. But I was acquainted with Françoise's art of insinuation, the advantage that she knew how to derive from a significant setting, and I cannot believe that she resisted the temptation to let Albertine know, day by day, what a degraded part she was playing in the household, to madden her by a description, cunningly exaggerated, of the confinement to which my mistress was subjected. On one occasion I found Françoise, armed with a huge pair of spectacles, rummaging through my papers and replacing among them a sheet on which I had jotted down a story about Swann and his utter inability to do without Odette. Had she maliciously left it lying in Albertine's room? Besides, above all Françoise's innuendoes which had merely been, in the bass, the muttering and perfidious orchestration, it is probable that there must have risen, higher, clearer, more pressing, the accusing and calumnious voice of the Verdurins, annoyed to see that Albertine was involuntarily keeping me and that I was voluntarily keeping her away from the little clan. As for the money that I was spending upon Albertine, it was almost impossible for me to conceal it from Françoise, since I was unable to conceal any of my expenditure from her. Françoise had few faults, but those faults had created in her, for their service, positive talents which she often lacked apart from the exercise of those faults. Her chief fault was her curiosity as to all money spent by us upon people other than herself. If I had a bill to pay, a gratuity to give, it was useless my going into a corner, she would find a plate to be put in the right place, a napkin to be picked up, which would give her an excuse for approaching. And however short a time I allowed her, before dismissing her with fury, this woman who had almost lost her sight, who could barely add up a column of figures, guided by the same expert sense which makes a tailor, on catching sight of you, instinctively calculate the price of the stuff of which your coat is made, while he cannot resist finger-ing it, or makes a painter responsive to a colour effect, Françoise saw by stealth, calculated instantaneously the amount that I was giving. And when, so that she might not tell Albertine that I was corrupting her chauf-feur, I took the initiative and, apologising for the tip, said: "I wanted to be generous to the chauffeur, I gave him ten francs"; Françoise, pitiless, to whom a glance, that of an old and almost blind eagle, had been sufficient, replied: "No indeed, Monsieur gave him a tip of 43 francs. He told Mon-sieur that the charge was 45 francs, Monsieur gave him 100 francs, and he handed back only 12 francs." She had had time to see and to reckon the amount of the gratuity which I myself did not know. I asked myself whether Albertine, feeling herself watched, would not herself put into effect that separation with which I had threatened her, for life in its chang-ing course makes realities of our fables. Whenever I heard a door open, I felt myself shudder as my grandmother used to shudder in her last mo-ments whenever I rang my bell. I did not believe that she would leave the house without telling me, but it was my unconscious self that thought so, as it was my grandmother's unconscious self that throbbed at the sound of the bell, when she was no longer conscious. One morning indeed, I felt a sudden misgiving that she not only had left the house but had gone for good: I had just heard the sound of a door which seemed to me to be that of her room. On tiptoe I crept towards the room, opened the door, stood upon the threshold. In the dim light the bedclothes bulged in a semi-circle, that must be Albertine who, with her body bent, was sleeping with her feet and face to the wall. Only, overflowing the bed, the hair upon that head, abundant and dark, made me realise that it was she, that she had not opened her door, had not stirred, and I felt that this motionless and living semi-circle, in which a whole human life was contained and which was the only thing to which I attached any value, I felt that it was there, in my despotic possession.

If Albertine's object was to restore my peace of mind, she was partly successful; my reason moreover asked nothing better than to prove to me that I had been mistaken as to her crafty plans, as I had perhaps been mis-taken as to her vicious instincts. No doubt I added to the value of the arguments with which my reason furnished me my own desire to find them sound. But, if I was to be fair and to have a chance of perceiving the truth, unless we admit that it is never known save by presentiment, by a telepathic emanation, must I not say to myself that if my reason, in seeking to bring about my recovery, let itself be guided by my desire, on the other hand, so far as concerned Mlle. Vinteuil, Albertine's vices, her intention to lead a different life, her plan of separation, which were the corollaries of her vices, my instinct had been capable, in the attempt to make me ill, of being led astray by my jealousy. Besides, her seclusion, which Albertine herself contrived so ingeniously to render absolute, by removing my suffering, removed by degrees my suspicion and I could begin again, when the night brought back my uneasiness, to find in Albertine's presence the consolation of earlier days. Seated beside my bed, she spoke to me of one of those dresses or one of those presents which I never ceased to give her in the effort to enhance the comfort of her life and the beauty of her prison. Albertine had at first thought only of dresses and furniture. Now silver had begun to interest her. And so I had questioned M. de Charlus about old French silver, and had done so because, when we had been planning to have a yacht—a plan which Albertine decided was impracticable, as I did also whenever I had begun to believe in her virtue, with the result that my jealousy, as it declined, no longer held in check other desires in which she had no place and which also needed money for their satisfaction—we had, to be on the safe side, not that she supposed that we should ever have a yacht, asked Elstir for his advice. Now, just as in matters of women's dress, the painter was a refined and sensitive critic of the furnishing of yachts. He would allow only English furniture and old silver. This had led Albertine, since our return from Balbec, to read books upon the silversmith's art, upon the handiwork of the old chasers. But as our old silver was melted twice over, at the time of the Treaty of Utrecht when the King himself, setting the example to his great nobles, sacrificed his plate, and again in 1789, it is now extremely rare. On the other hand, it is true that modern silversmiths have managed to copy all this old plate from the drawings of Le Pont-aux-Choux, Elstir considered this modern antique unworthy to enter the home of a woman of taste, even a floating home. I knew that Albertine had read the description of the marvels that Roelliers had made for Mme. du Barry. If any of these pieces remained, she was dying to see them, and I to give them to her. She had even begun to form a neat collection which she installed with charming taste in a glass case and at which I could not look without emotion and alarm, for the art with which she arranged them was that born of patience, ingenuity, home-sickness, the need to forget, in which prisoners excel. In the matter of dress, what appealed to her most at this time was everything that was made by Fortuny. These Fortuny gowns, one of which I had seen Mme. de Guermantes wearing, were those of which Elstir, when he told us about the magnificent garments of the women of Carpaccio's and Titian's day, had prophesied the speedy return, rising from their ashes, sumptuous, for everything must return in time, as it is written beneath the vaults of Saint Mark's, and proclaimed, where they drink from the urns of marble and jasper of the byzantine capitals, by the birds which symbolise at once death and resurrection. As soon as women had begun to wear them, Albertine had remembered Elstir's prophecy, she had desired to have one and we were to go and choose it. Now these gowns, even if they were not those genuine antiques in which women to-day seem a little too much 'in fancy dress' and which it is preferable to keep as pieces in a collection (I was in search of these also, as it happens, for Albertine), could not be said to have the chilling effect of the artificial, the sham antique. Like the theatrical designs of Sert, Bakst and Benoist who at that moment were recreating in the Russian ballet the most cherished periods of art—with the aid of works of art impregnated with their spirit and yet original—these Fortuny gowns, faithfully antique but markedly original, brought before the eye like a stage setting, with an even greater suggestiveness than a setting, since the setting was left to the imagination, that Venice loaded with the gorgeous East from which they had been taken, of which they were, even more than a relic in the shrine of Saint Mark suggesting the sun and a group of turbaned heads, the fragmentary, mysterious and complementary colour. Everything of those days had perished, but everything was born again, evoked to fill the space between them with the splendour of the scene and the hum of life, by the reappearance, detailed and surviving, of the fabrics worn by the Doges' ladies. I had tried once or twice to obtain advice upon this subject from Mme. de Guermantes. But the Duchess cared little for garments which form a 'costume.' She herself, though she possessed several, never looked so well as in black velvet with diamonds. And with regard to gowns like Fortuny's, her advice was not of any great value. Besides, I felt a scruple, if I asked for it, lest she might think that I called upon her only when I happened to need her help, whereas for a long time past I had been declining several invitations from her weekly. It was not only from her, moreover, that I received them in such profusion. Certainly, she and many other women had always been extremely kind to me. But my seclusion had undoubtedly multiplied their hospitality tenfold. It seems that in our social life, a minor echo of what occurs in love, the best way for a man to make himself sought-after is to withhold himself. A man calculates everything that he can possibly cite to his credit, in order to find favour with a woman, changes his clothes all day long, pays attention to his appearance, she does not pay him a single one of the attentions which he receives from the other woman to whom, while he betrays her, and in spite of his appearing before her ill-dressed and without any artifice to attract, he has endeared himself for ever. Similarly, if a man were to regret that he was not sufficiently courted in society, I should not advise him to pay more calls, to keep an even finer carriage, I should tell him not to accept any invitation, to live shut up in his room, to admit nobody, and that then there would be a queue outside his door. Or rather I should not tell him so. For it is a certain road to success which succeeds only like the road to love, that is to say if one has not adopted it with that object in view, if, for instance, you confine yourself to your room because you are seriously ill, or are supposed to be, or are keeping a mistress shut up with you whom you prefer to society (or for all these reasons at once), this will justify another person, who is not aware of the woman's existence, and simply because you decline to see him, in preferring you to all the people who offer themselves, and attaching himself to you.

"We shall have to begin to think soon about your Fortuny gowns," I said to Albertine one evening. Surely, to her who had long desired them, who chose them deliberately with me, who had a place reserved for them beforehand not only in her wardrobe but in her imagination, the possession of these gowns, every detail of which, before deciding among so many, she carefully examined, was something more than it would have been to an overwealthy woman who has more dresses than she knows what to do with and never even looks at them. And yet, notwithstanding the smile with which Albertine thanked me, saying: "You are too kind," I noticed how weary, and even wretched, she was looking.

While we waited for these gowns to be ready, I used to borrow others of the kind, sometimes indeed merely the stuffs, and would dress Albertine in them, drape them over her; she walked about my room with the majesty of a Doge's wife and the grace of a mannequin. Only my captivity in Paris was made more burdensome by the sight of these garments which suggested Venice. True, Albertine was far more of a prisoner than I. And it was curious to remark how, through the walls of her prison, destiny, which transforms people, had contrived to pass, to change her in her very essence, and turn the girl I had known at Balbec into a tedious and docile captive. Yes, the walls of her prison had not prevented that influence from reaching her; perhaps indeed it was they that had produced it. It was no longer the same Albertine, because she was not, as at Balbec, incessantly in flight upon her bicycle, never to be found owing to the number of little watering-places where she would go to spend the night with her girl friends and where moreover her untruths made it more difficult to lay hands upon her; because confined to my house, docile and alone, she was no longer even what at Balbec, when I had succeeded in finding her, she used to be upon the beach, that fugitive, cautious, cunning creature, whose presence was enlarged by the thought of all those assignations which she was skilled in concealing, which made one love her because they made one suffer, in whom, beneath her coldness to other people and her casual answers, one could feel yesterday's assignation and to-morrow's, and for myself a contemptuous, deceitful thought; because the sea breeze no longer buffeted her skirts, because, above all, I had clipped her wings, she had ceased to be a Victory, was a burdensome slave of whom I would fain have been rid.

Then, to change the course of my thoughts, rather than begin a game of cards or draughts with Albertine, I asked her to give me a little music. I remained in bed, and she went and sat down at the end of the room before the pianola, between the two bookcases. She chose pieces which were quite new or which she had played to me only once or twice, for, as she began to know me better, she had learned that I liked to fix my thoughts only upon what was still obscure to me, glad to be able, in the course of these successive renderings, to join together, thanks to the increasing but, alas, distorting and alien light of my intellect, the fragmentary and interrupted lines of the structure which at first had been almost hidden in the mist. She knew and, I think, understood, the joy that my mind derived, at these first hearings, from this task of modelling a still shapeless nebula. She guessed that at the third or fourth repetition my intellect, having reached, having consequently placed at the same distance, all the parts, and having no longer any activity to spare for them, had reciprocally extended and arrested them upon a uniform plane. She did not, however, proceed at once to a fresh piece, for, without perhaps having any clear idea of the process that was going on in my mind, she knew that at the moment when the effort of my intellect had succeeded in dispelling the mystery of a work, it was very rarely that, in compensation, it did not, in the course of its task of destruction, pick up some profitable reflexion. And when in time Albertine said: "We might give this roll to Françoise and get her to change it for something else," often there was for me a piece of music less in the world, perhaps, but a truth the more. While she was playing, of all Albertine's multiple tresses I could see but a single loop of black hair in the shape of a heart trained at the side of her ear like the riband of a Velasquez Infanta. Just as the substance of that Angel musician was constituted by the multiple journeys between the different points in past time which the memory of her occupied in myself, and its different abodes, from my vision to the most inward sensations of my being, which helped me to descend into the intimacy of hers, so the music that she played had also a volume, produced by the inconstant visibility of the different phrases, accordingly as I had more or less succeeded in throwing a light upon them and in joining together the lines of a structure which at first had seemed to me to be almost completely hidden in the fog.

I was so far convinced that it was absurd to be jealous of Mlle. Vinteuil and her friend, inasmuch as Albertine since her confession had made no attempt to see them and among all the plans for a holiday in the country which we had formed had herself rejected Combray, so near to Montjouvain, that, often, what I would ask Albertine to play to me, without its causing me any pain, would be some music by Vinteuil. Once only this music had been an indirect cause of my jealousy. This was when Albertine, who knew that I had heard it performed at Mme. Verdurin's by Morel, spoke to me one evening about him, expressing a keen desire to go and hear him play and to make his acquaintance. This, as it happened, was shortly after I had learned of the letter, unintentionally intercepted by M. de Charlus, from Léa to Morel. I asked myself whether Léa might not have mentioned him to Albertine. The words: 'You bad woman, you naughty old girl' came to my horrified mind. But precisely because Vinteuil's music was in this way painfully associated with Léa—and no longer with Mlle. Vinteuil and her friend—when the grief that Léa caused me was soothed, I could then listen to this music without pain; one malady had made me immune to any possibility of the others. In this music of Vinteuil, phrases that I had not noticed at Mme. Verdurin's, obscure phantoms that were then indistinct, turned into dazzling architectural structures; and some of them became friends, whom I had barely made out at first, who at best had appeared to me to be ugly, so that I could never have supposed that they were like those people, unattractive at first sight, whom we discover to be what they really are only after we have come to know them well. From one state to the other was a positive transmutation. On the other hand, phrases that I had distinguished at once in the music that I had heard at Mme. Verdurin's, but had not then recognised, I identified now with phrases from other works, such as that phrase from the Sacred Variation for the Organ which, at Mme. Verdurin's, had passed unperceived by me in the septet, where nevertheless, a saint that had stepped down from the sanctuary, it found itself consorting with the composer's familiar fays. Finally, the phrase that had seemed to me too little melodious, too mechanical in its rhythm, of the swinging joy of bells at noon, had now become my favourite, whether because I had grown accustomed to its ugliness or because I had discovered its beauty. This reaction from the disappointment which great works of art cause at first may in fact be attributed to a weakening of the initial impression or to the effort necessary to lay bare the truth. Two hypotheses which suggest themselves in all important questions, questions of the truth of Art, of the truth of the Immortality of the Soul; we must choose between them; and, in the case of Vinteuil's music, this choice presented itself at every moment under a variety of forms. For instance, this music seemed to me to be something truer than all the books that I knew. Sometimes I thought that this was due to the fact that what we feel in life, not being felt in the form of ideas, its literary (that is to say an intellectual) translation in giving an account of it, explains it, analyses it, but does not recompose it as does music, in which the sounds seem to assume the inflexion of the thing itself, to reproduce that interior and extreme point of our sensation which is the part that gives us that peculiar exhilaration which we recapture from time to time and which when we say: "What a fine day! What glorious sunshine!" we do not in the least communicate to our neighbour, in whom the same sun and the same weather arouse wholly different vibrations. In Vinteuil's music, there were thus some of those visions which it is impossible to express and almost forbidden to record, since, when at the moment of falling asleep we receive the caress of their unreal enchantment, at that very moment in which reason has already deserted us, our eyes are already sealed, and before we have had time to know not merely the ineffable but the invisible, we are asleep. It seemed to me indeed when I abandoned myself to this hypothesis that art might be real, that it was something even more than the simply nervous joy of a fine day or an opiate night that music can give; a more real, more fruitful exhilaration, to judge at least by what I felt. It is not possible that a piece of sculpture, a piece of music which gives us an emotion which we feel to be more exalted, more pure, more true, does not correspond to some definite spiritual reality. It is surely symbolical of one, since it gives that impression of profundity and truth. Thus nothing resembled more closely than some such phrase of Vinteuil the peculiar pleasure which I had felt at certain moments in my life, when gazing, for instance, at the steeples of Martinville, or at certain trees along a road near Balbec, or, more simply, in the first part of this book, when I tasted a certain cup of tea.

Without pressing this comparison farther, I felt that the clear sounds, the blazing colours which Vinteuil sent to us from the world in which he

composed, paraded before my imagination with insistence but too rapidly
for me to be able to apprehend it, something which I might compare to the
perfumed silkiness of a geranium. Only, whereas, in memory, this vagueness
may be, if not explored, at any rate fixed precisely, thanks to a guiding line
of circumstances which explain why a certain savour has been able to recall
to us luminous sensations, the vague sensations given by Vinteuil coming
not from a memory but from an impression (like that of the steeples of
Martinville), one would have had to find, for the geranium scent of his
music, not a material explanation, but the profound equivalent, the unknown and highly coloured festival (of which his works seemed to be the
scattered fragments, the scarlet-flashing rifts), the mode in which he
'heard' the universe and projected it far beyond himself. This unknown
quality of a unique world which no other composer had ever made us see,
perhaps it is in this, I said to Albertine, that the most authentic proof of
genius consists, even more than in the content of the work itself. "Even
in literature?" Albertine inquired. "Even in literature." And thinking again
of the monotony of Vinteuil's works, I explained to Albertine that the great
men of letters have never created more than a single work, or rather have
never done more than refract through various mediums an identical beauty
which they bring into the world. "If it were not so late, my child," I said
to her, "I would shew you this quality in all the writers whose works you
read while I am asleep, I would shew you the same identity as in Vinteuil.
These typical phrases, which you are beginning to recognise as I do, my
little Albertine, the same in the sonata, in the septet, in the other works,
would be for instance, if you like, in Barbey d'Aurevilly, a hidden reality
revealed by a material trace, the physiological blush of *l'Ensorcelée,* of
Aimée de Spens, of *la Clotte,* the hand of the *Rideau Cramoisi,* the old
manners and customs, the old words, the ancient and peculiar trades behind
which there is the Past, the oral history compiled by the rustics of the
manor, the noble Norman cities redolent of England and charming as a
Scots village, the cause of curses against which one can do nothing, the
Vellini, the Shepherd, a similar sensation of anxiety in a passage, whether
it be the wife seeking her husband in *Une Vieille Maîtresse,* or the husband
in *l'Ensorcelée* scouring the plain and the 'Ensorcelée' herself coming out
from Mass. There are other typical phrases in Vinteuil like that stone-
mason's geometry in the novels of Thomas Hardy."

Vinteuil's phrases made me think of the 'little phrase' and I told Albertine
that it had been so to speak the national anthem of the love of Swann and
Odette, "the parents of Gilberte whom you know. You told me that she was
not a bad girl. But didn't she attempt to have relations with you? She
has mentioned you to me." "Yes, you see, her parents used to send a carriage to fetch her from our lessons when the weather was bad, I believe
she took me home once and kissed me," she said, after a momentary pause,
with a laugh, and as though it were an amusing confession. "She asked me
all of a sudden whether I was fond of women." (But if she only believed
that she remembered that Gilberte had taken her home, how could she say
with such precision that Gilberte had asked her this odd question?) "In
fact, I don't know what absurd idea came into my head to make a fool of

her, I told her that I was." (One would have said that Albertine was afraid that Gilberte had told me this and did not wish me to come to the conclusion that she was lying.) "But we did nothing at all." (It was strange, if they had exchanged confidences, that they should have done nothing, especially as, before this, they had kissed, according to Albertine.) "She took me home like that four or five times, perhaps more, and that is all." It cost me a great effort not to ply her with further questions, but, mastering myself so as to appear not to be attaching any importance to all this, I returned to Thomas Hardy. "Do you remember the stonemasons in *Jude the Obscure*, in *The Well-Beloved*, the blocks of stone which the father hews out of the island coming in boats to be piled up in the son's studio where they are turned into statues; in *A Pair of Blue Eyes* the parallelism of the tombs, and also the parallel line of the vessel, and the railway coaches containing the lovers and the dead woman; the parallelism between *The Well-Beloved*, where the man is in love with three women, and *A Pair of Blue Eyes* where the woman is in love with three men, and in short all those novels which can be laid one upon another like the vertically piled houses upon the rocky soil of the island. I cannot summarise the greatest writers like this in a moment's talk, but you would see in Stendhal a certain sense of altitude combining with the life of the spirit: the lofty place in which Julien Sorel is imprisoned, the tower on the summit of which Fabrice is confined, the belfry in which the Abbé Blanès pores over his astrology and from which Fabrice has such a magnificent bird's-eye view. You told me that you had seen some of Vermeer's pictures, you must have realised that they are fragments of an identical world, that it is always, however great the genius with which they have been recreated, the same table, the same carpet, the same woman, the same novel and unique beauty, an enigma, at that epoch in which nothing resembles or explains it, if we seek to find similarities in subjects but to isolate the peculiar impression that is produced by the colour. Well, then, this novel beauty remains identical in all Dostoievski's works, the Dostoievski woman (as distinctive as a Rembrandt woman) with her mysterious face, whose engaging beauty changes abruptly, as though her apparent good nature had been but make-believe, to a terrible insolence (although at heart it seems that she is more good than bad), is she not always the same, whether it be Nastasia Philipovna writing love letters to Aglaé and telling her that she hates her, or in a visit which is wholly identical with this—as also with that in which Nastasia Philipovna insults Vania's family—Grouchenka, as charming in Katherina Ivanovna's house as the other had supposed her to be terrible, then suddenly revealing her malevolence by insulting Katherina Ivanovna (although Grouchenka is good at heart); Grouchenka, Nastasia, figures as original, as mysterious not merely as Carpaccio's courtesans but as Rembrandt's Bathsheba. As, in Vermeer, there is the creation of a certain soul, of a certain colour of fabrics and places, so there is in Dostoievski creation not only of people but of their homes, and the house of the Murder in *Crime and Punishment* with its dvornik, is it not almost as marvellous as the masterpiece of the House of Murder in Dostoievski, that sombre house, so long, and so high, and so huge, of Rogojin in which he kills

Nastasia Philipovna. That novel and terrible beauty of a house, that novel beauty blended with a woman's face, that is the unique thing which Dostoievski has given to the world, and the comparisons that literary critics may make, between him and Gogol, or between him and Paul de Kock, are of no interest, being external to this secret beauty. Besides, if I have said to you that it is, from one novel to another, the same scene, it is in the compass of a single novel that the same scenes, the same characters reappear if the novel is at all long. I could illustrate this to you easily in *War and Peace*, and a certain scene in a carriage. . . ." "I didn't want to interrupt you, but now that I see that you are leaving Dostoievski, I am afraid of forgetting. My dear boy, what was it you meant the other day when you said: 'It is, so to speak, the Dostoievski side of Mme. de Sévigné.' I must confess that I did not understand. It seems to me so different." "Come, little girl, let me give you a kiss to thank you for remembering so well what I say, you shall go back to the pianola afterwards. And I must admit that what I said was rather stupid. But I said it for two reasons. The first is a special reason. What I meant was that Mme. de Sévigné, like Elstir, like Dostoievski, instead of presenting things in their logical sequence, that is to say beginning with the cause, shews us first of all the effect, the illusion that strikes us. That is how Dostoievski presents his characters. Their actions seem to us as misleading as those effects in Elstir's pictures where the sea appears to be in the sky. We are quite surprised to find that some sullen person is really the best of men, or vice versa." "Yes, but give me an example in Mme. de Sévigné." "I admit," I answered her with a laugh, "that I am splitting hairs very fine, but still I could find examples." "But did he ever murder anyone, Dostoievski? The novels of his that I know might all be called *The Story of a Crime*. It is an obsession with him, it is not natural that he should always be talking about it." "I don't think so, dear Albertine, I know little about his life. It is certain that, like everyone else, he was acquainted with sin, in one form or another, and probably in a form which the laws condemn. In that sense he must have been more or less criminal, like his heroes (not that they are altogether heroes, for that matter), who are found guilty with attenuating circumstances. And it is not perhaps necessary that he himself should have been a criminal. I am not a novelist; it is possible that creative writers are tempted by certain forms of life of which they have no personal experience. If I come with you to Versailles as we arranged, I shall shew you the portrait of the ultra-respectable man, the best of husbands, Choderlos de Laclos, who wrote the most appallingly corrupt book, and facing it that of Mme. de Genlis who wrote moral tales and was not content with betraying the Duchesse d'Orléans but tormented her by turning her children against her. I admit all the same that in Dostoievski this preoccupation with murder is something extraordinary which makes him very alien to me. I am stupefied enough when I hear Baudelaire say:

> *Si le viol, le poison, le poignard, l'incendie*
> *N'ont pas encor brodé de leurs plaisants dessins*
> *Le canevas banal de nos piteux destins,*
> *C'est que notre âme, hélas! n'est pas assez hardie.*

But I can at least assume that Baudelaire is not sincere. Whereas Dostoievski. . . . All that sort of thing seems to me as remote from myself as possible, unless there are parts of myself of which I know nothing, for we realise our own nature only in course of time. In Dostoievski I find the deepest penetration but only into certain isolated regions of the human soul. But he is a great creator. For one thing, the world which he describes does really appear to have been created by him. All those buffoons who keep on reappearing, like Lebedeff, Karamazoff, Ivolghin, Segreff, that incredible procession, are a humanity more fantastic than that which peoples Rembrandt's *Night Watch*. And perhaps it is fantastic only in the same way, by the effect of lighting and costume, and is quite normal really. In any case it is at the same time full of profound and unique truths, which belong only to Dostoievski. They almost suggest, those buffoons, some trade or calling that no longer exists, like certain characters in the old drama, and yet how they reveal true aspects of the human soul! What astonishes me is the solemn manner in which people talk and write about Dostoievski. Have you ever noticed the part that self-respect and pride play in his characters? One would say that, to him, love and the most passionate hatred, goodness and treachery, timidity and insolence are merely two states of a single nature, their self-respect, their pride preventing Aglaé, Nastasia, the Captain whose beard Mitia pulls, Krassotkin, Aliosha's enemy-friend, from shewing themselves in their true colours. But there are many other great passages as well. I know very few of his books. But is it not a sculpturesque and simple theme, worthy of the most classical art, a frieze interrupted and resumed on which the tale of vengeance and expiation is unfolded, the crime of old Karamazoff getting the poor idiot with child, the mysterious, animal, unexplained impulse by which the mother, herself unconsciously the instrument of an avenging destiny, obeying also obscurely her maternal instinct, feeling perhaps a combination of physical resentment and gratitude towards her seducer, comes to bear her child on old Karamazoff's ground. This is the first episode, mysterious, grand, august as a Creation of Woman among the sculptures at Orvieto. And as counterpart, the second episode more than twenty years later, the murder of old Karamazoff, the disgrace brought upon the Karamazoff family by this son of the idiot, Smerdiakoff, followed shortly afterwards by another action, as mysteriously sculpturesque and unexplained, of a beauty as obscure and natural as that of the childbirth in old Karamazoff's garden, Smerdiakoff hanging himself, his crime accomplished. As for Dostoievski, I was not straying so far from him as you thought when I mentioned Tolstoi who has imitated him closely. In Dostoievski there is, concentrated and fretful, a great deal of what was to blossom later on in Tolstoi. There is, in Dostoievski, that proleptic gloom of the primitives which their disciples will brighten and dispel." "My dear boy, what a terrible thing it is that you are so lazy. Just look at your view of literature, so far more interesting than the way we were made to study it; the essays that they used to make us write upon *Esther*: 'Monsieur,'—you remember," she said with a laugh, less from a desire to make fun of her masters and herself than from the pleasure of finding in her memory, in our common memory, a relic that was already almost venerable. But while she was speaking, and I continued to think of Vinteuil, it was the other, the materialist hypothesis, that of there being nothing, that in turn presented itself to my mind. I began to doubt, I said to myself that after all it might be the case that, if Vinteuil's phrases seemed to be the expression of certain states of the soul analogous to that which I had experienced when I tasted the madeleine that had been dipped in a cup of tea, there was nothing to assure me that the vagueness of such states was a sign of their profundity rather than of our not having learned yet to analyse them, so that there need be nothing more real in them than in other states. And yet that happiness, that sense of certainty in happiness while I was drinking the cup of tea, or when I smelt in the Champs-Elysées a smell of mouldering wood, was not an illusion. In any case, whispered the spirit of doubt, even if these states are more profound than others that occur in life, and defy analysis for the very reason that they bring into play too many forces which we have not yet taken into consideration, the charm of certain phrases of Vinteuil's music makes us think of them because it too defies analysis, but this does not prove that it has the same depth; the beauty of a phrase of pure music can easily appear to be the image of or at least akin to an intellectual impression which we have received, but simply because it is unintellectual. And why then do we suppose to be specially profound those mysterious phrases which haunt certain works, including this septet by Vinteuil?

It was not, however, his music alone that Albertine played me; the pianola was to us at times like a scientific magic lantern (historical and geographical) and on the walls of this room in Paris, supplied with inventions more modern than that of Combray days, I would see, accordingly as Albertine played me Rameau or Borodin, extend before me now an eighteenth century tapestry sprinkled with cupids and roses, now the Eastern steppe in which sounds are muffled by boundless distances and the soft carpet of snow. And these fleeting decorations were as it happened the only ones in my room, for if, at the time of inheriting my aunt Léonie's fortune, I had vowed that I would become a collector like Swann, would buy pictures, statues, all my money went upon securing horses, a motorcar, dresses for Albertine. But did not my room contain a work of art more precious than all these—Albertine herself? I looked at her. It was strange to me to think that it was she, she whom I had for so long thought it impossible even to know, who now, a wild beast tamed, a rosebush to which I had acted as trainer, as the framework, the trellis of its life, was seated thus, day by day, at home, by my side, before the pianola, with her back to my bookcase. Her shoulders, which I had seen bowed and resentful when she was carrying her golf-clubs, were leaning against my books. Her shapely legs, which at first I had quite reasonably imagined as having trodden throughout her girlhood the pedals of a bicycle, now rose and fell alternately upon those of the pianola, upon which Albertine who had acquired a distinction which made me feel her more my own, because it was from myself that it came, pressed her shoes of cloth of gold. Her fingers, at one time trained to the handle-bars, now rested upon the keys like those of a Saint Cecilia. Her throat the curve of which, seen from my bed, was strong and full, at that distance and in the lamplight appeared more rosy, less rosy, however, than her face presented in profile, to which my gaze, issuing from the innermost depths of myself, charged with memories and burning with desire, added such a brilliancy, such an intensity of life that its relief seemed to stand out and turn with almost the same magic power as on the day, in the hotel at Balbec, when my vision was clouded by my overpowering desire to kiss her; I prolonged each of its surfaces beyond what I was able to see and beneath what concealed it from me and made me feel all the more strongly—eyelids which half hid her eyes, hair that covered the upper part of her cheeks—the relief of those superimposed planes. Her eyes shone like, in a matrix in which the opal is still embedded, the two facets which alone have as yet been polished, which, become more brilliant than metal, reveal, in the midst of the blind matter that encumbers them, as it were the mauve, silken wings of a butterfly placed under glass. Her dark, curling hair, presenting a different appearance whenever she turned to ask me what she was to play next, now a splendid wing, sharp at the tip, broad at the base, feathered and triangular, now weaving the relief of its curls in a strong and varied chain, a mass of crests, of watersheds, of precipices, with its incisions so rich and so multiple, seemed to exceed the variety that nature normally realises and to correspond rather to the desire of a sculptor who accumulates difficulties in order to bring into greater prominence the suppleness, the fire, the moulding, the life of his execution, and brought out more strongly, by interrupting in order to resume them, the animated curve, and, as it were, the rotation of the smooth and rosy face, of the polished dulness of a piece of painted wood. And, in contrast with all this relief, by the harmony also which united them with her, which had adapted her attitude to their form and purpose, the pianola which half concealed her like the keyboard of an organ, the bookcase, the whole of that corner of the room seemed to be reduced to nothing more than the lighted sanctuary, the shrine of this angel musician, a work of art which, presently, by a charming magic, was to detach itself from its niche and offer to my kisses its precious, rosy substance. But no, Albertine was in no way to me a work of art. I knew what it meant to admire a woman in an artistic fashion, I had known Swann. For my own part, moreover, I was, no matter who the woman might be, incapable of doing so, having no sort of power of detached observation, never knowing what it was that I beheld, and I had been amazed when Swann added retrospectively for me an artistic dignity—by comparing her, as he liked to do with gallantry to her face, to some portrait by Luini, by finding in her attire the gown or the jewels of a picture by Giorgione—to a woman who had seemed to me to be devoid of interest. Nothing of that sort with me. The pleasure and the pain that I derived from Albertine never took, in order to reach me, the line of taste and intellect; indeed, to tell the truth, when I began to regard Albertine as an angel musician glazed with a marvellous patina whom I congratulated myself upon possessing, it was not long before I found her uninteresting; I soon became bored in her company, but these moments were of brief duration; we love only that in which we pursue something inaccessible, we love only what we do not possess, and very soon I returned to the conclusion that I did not possess Albertine. In her eyes I saw pass now the hope, now the memory, perhaps the regret of joys which I could not guess, which in that case she preferred to renounce rather than tell me of them, and which, gathering no more of them than certain flashes in her pupils, I no more perceived than does the spectator who has been refused admission to the theatre, and who, his face glued to the glass panes of the door, can take in nothing of what is happening upon the stage. I do not know whether this was the case with her, but it is a strange thing, and so to speak a testimony by the most incredulous to their belief in good, this perseverance in falsehood shewn by all those who deceive us. It is no good our telling them that their lie hurts us more than a confession, it is no good their realising this for themselves, they will start lying again a moment later, to remain consistent with their original statement of how much we meant to them. Similarly an atheist who values his life will let himself be burned alive rather than allow any contradiction of the popular idea of his courage. During these hours, I used sometimes to see hover over her face, in her gaze, in her pout, in her smile, the reflexion of those inward visions the contemplation of which made her on these evenings unlike her usual self, remote from me to whom they were denied. "What are you thinking about, my darling?" "Why, nothing." Sometimes, in answer to this reproach that she told me nothing, she would at one moment tell me things which she was not unaware that I knew as well as anyone (like those statesmen who will never give you the least bit of news, but speak to you instead of what you could read for yourself in the papers the day before), at another would describe without the least precision, in a sort of false confidence, bicycle rides that she had taken at Balbec, the year before our first meeting. And as though I had guessed aright long ago, when I inferred from it that she must be a girl who was allowed a great deal of freedom, who went upon long jaunts, the mention of those rides insinuated between Albertine's lips the same mysterious smile that had captivated me in those first days on the front at Balbec. She spoke to me also of the excursions that she had made with some girl-friends through the Dutch countryside, of returning to Amsterdam in the evening, at a late hour, when a dense and happy crowd of people almost all of whom she knew, thronged the streets, the canal towpaths, of which I felt that I could see reflected in Albertine's brilliant eyes as in the glancing windows of a fast-moving carriage, the innumerable, flickering fires. Since what is called aesthetic curiosity would deserve rather the name of indifference in comparison with the painful, unwearying curiosity that I felt as to the places in which Albertine had stayed, as to what she might have been doing on a particular evening, her smiles, the expressions in her eyes, the words that she had uttered, the kisses that she had received. No, never would the jealousy that I had felt one day of Saint-Loup, if it had persisted, have caused me this immense uneasiness. This love of woman for woman was something too unfamiliar; nothing enabled me to form a certain, an accurate idea of its pleasures, its quality. How many people, how many places (even places which did not concern her directly, vague pleasure resorts where she might have enjoyed some pleasure), how many scenes (wherever there was a crowd, where people could brush against her) Albertine—like a person who, shepherding all her escort, a whole company, past the barrier in front of her, secures their admission to the theatre—from the threshold of my imagination or of my memory, where I paid no attention to them, had introduced into my heart! Now the knowledge that I had of them was internal, immediate, spasmodic, painful. Love, what is it but space and time rendered perceptible by the heart.

And yet perhaps, had I myself been entirely faithful, I should have suffered because of infidelities which I would have been incapable of conceiving, whereas what it tortured me to imagine in Albertine was my own perpetual desire to find favour with fresh ladies, to plan fresh romances, was to suppose her guilty of the glance which I had been unable to resist casting, the other day, even when I was by her side, at the young bicyclists seated at tables in the Bois de Boulogne. As we have no personal knowledge, one might almost say that we can feel no jealousy save of ourselves. Observation counts for little. It is only from the pleasure that we ourselves have felt that we can derive knowledge and grief.

At moments, in Albertine's eyes, in the sudden inflammation of her cheeks, I felt as it were a gust of warmth pass furtively into regions more inaccessible to me than the sky, in which Albertine's memories, unknown to me, lived and moved. Then this beauty which, when I thought of the various years in which I had known Albertine whether upon the beach at Balbec or in Paris, I found that I had but recently discovered in her, and which consisted in the fact that my mistress was developing upon so many planes and embodied so many past days, this beauty became almost heart-rending. Then beneath that blushing face I felt that there yawned like a gulf the inexhaustible expanse of the evenings when I had not known Albertine. I might, if I chose, take Albertine upon my knee, take her head in my hands; I might caress her, pass my hands slowly over her, but, just as if I had been handling a stone which encloses the salt of immemorial oceans or the light of a star, I felt that I was touching no more than the sealed envelope of a person who inwardly reached to infinity. How I suffered from that position to which we are reduced by the carelessness of nature which, when instituting the division of bodies, never thought of making possible the interpenetration of souls (for if her body was in the power of mine, her mind escaped from the grasp of mine). And I became aware that Albertine was not even for me the marvellous captive with whom I had thought to enrich my home, while I concealed her presence there as completely, even from the friends who came to see me and never suspected that she was at the end of the corridor, in the room next to my own, as did that man of whom nobody knew that he kept sealed in a bottle the Princess of China; urging me with a cruel and fruitless pressure to the remembrance of the past, she resembled, if anything, a mighty goddess of Time. And if it was necessary that I should lose for her sake years, my fortune—and provided that I can say to myself, which is by no means certain, alas, that she herself lost nothing—I have nothing to regret. No doubt solitude would have been better, more fruitful, less painful. But if I had led the life of a collector which Swann counselled (the joys of which M. de Charlus reproached me with not knowing, when, with a blend of wit, insolence and good taste, he said to me: "How ugly your rooms are!") what statues, what pictures long pursued, at length possessed, or even, to put it in the best light, contemplated with detachment, would, like the little wound which healed quickly enough, but which the unconscious clumsiness of Albertine, of people generally, or of my own thoughts was never long in reopening, have given me access beyond my own boundaries, upon that avenue which, private though it be, debouches upon the high road along which passes what we learn to know only from the day on which it has made us suffer, the life of other people?

Sometimes the moon was so bright that, an hour after Albertine had gone to bed, I would go to her bedside to tell her to look at it through the window. I am certain that it was for this reason that I went to her room and not to assure myself that she was really there. What likelihood was there of her being able, had she wished, to escape? That would have required an improbable collusion with Françoise. In the dim room, I could see nothing save on the whiteness of the pillow a slender diadem of dark hair. But I could hear Albertine's breath. Her slumber was so profound that I hesitated at first to go as far as the bed. Then I sat down on the edge of it. Her sleep continued to flow with the same murmur. What I find it impossible to express is how gay her awakenings were. I embraced her, shook her. At once she ceased to sleep, but, without even a moment's interval, broke out in a laugh, saying as she twined her arms about my neck: "I was just beginning to wonder whether you were coming," and she laughed a tender, beautiful laugh. You would have said that her charming head, when she slept, was filled with nothing but gaiety, affection and laughter. And in waking her I had merely, as when we cut a fruit, released the gushing juice which quenches our thirst.

Meanwhile winter was at an end; the fine weather returned, and often when Albertine had just bidden me good night, my room, my curtains, the wall above the curtains being still quite dark, in the nuns' garden next door I could hear, rich and precious in the silence like a harmonium in church, the modulation of an unknown bird which, in the Lydian mode, was already chanting matins, and into the midst of my darkness flung the rich dazzling note of the sun that it could see. Once indeed, we heard all of a sudden the regular cadence of a plaintive appeal. It was the pigeons beginning to coo. "That proves that day has come already," said Albertine; and, her brows almost knitted, as though she missed, by living with me, the joys of the fine weather, "Spring has begun, if the pigeons have returned." The resemblance between their cooing and the crow of the cock was as profound and as obscure as, in Vinteuil's septet, the resemblance between the theme of the adagio and that of the closing piece, which is based upon the same key-theme as the other but so transformed by differences of tonality, of measure, that the profane outsider if he opens a book upon Vinteuil is astonished to find that they are all three based upon the same four notes, four notes which for that matter he may pick out with one finger upon the piano without recapturing anything of the three fragments. So this melancholy fragment performed by the pigeons was a sort of cock-crow in the minor, which did not soar up into the sky, did not rise vertically, but, regular as the braying of a donkey, enveloped in sweetness, went from one pigeon to another along a single horizontal line, and never raised itself, never changed its lateral plaint into that joyous appeal which had been uttered so often in the allegro of the introduction and in the finale.

Presently the nights grew shorter still and before what had been the hour of daybreak, I could see already stealing above my window-curtains the daily increasing whiteness of the dawn. If I resigned myself to allowing Albertine to continue to lead this life, in which, notwithstanding her denials, I felt that she had the impression of being a prisoner, it was only because I was sure that on the morrow I should be able to set myself, at the same time to work and to leave my bed, to go out of doors, to prepare our departure for some property which we should buy and where Albertine would be able to lead more freely and without anxiety on my account, the life of country or seaside, of boating or hunting, which appealed to her. Only, on the morrow, that past which I loved and detested by turns in Albertine, it would so happen that (as, when it is the present, between himself and us, everyone, from calculation, or courtesy, or pity, sets to work to weave a curtain of falsehood which we mistake for the truth), retrospectively, one of the hours which composed it, and even those which I had supposed myself to know, offered me all of a sudden an aspect which some one no longer made any attempt to conceal from me and which was then quite different from that in which it had previously appeared to me. Behind some look in her eyes, in place of the honest thought which I had formerly supposed that I could read in it, was a desire, unsuspected hitherto, which revealed itself, alienating from me a fresh region of Albertine's heart which I had believed to be assimilated to my own. For instance, when Andrée left Balbec in the month of July, Albertine had never told me that she was to see her again shortly, and I supposed that she had seen her even sooner than she expected, since, in view of the great unhappiness that I had felt at Balbec, on that night of the fourteenth of September, she had made me the sacrifice of not remaining there and of returning at once to Paris. When she had arrived there on the fifteenth, I had asked her to go and see Andrée and had said to her: "Was she pleased to see you again?" Now one day Mme. Bontemps had called, bringing something for Albertine; I saw her for a moment and told her that Albertine had gone out with Andrée: "They have gone for a drive in the country." "Yes," replied Mme. Bontemps, "Albertine is always ready to go to the country. Three years ago, for instance, she simply had to go, every day, to the Buttes-Chaumont." At the name Buttes-Chaumont, a place where Albertine had told me that she had never been, my breath stopped for a moment. The truth is the most cunning of enemies. It launches its attacks upon the points of our heart at which we were not expecting them, and have prepared no defence. Had Albertine been lying to her aunt, then, when she said that she went every day to the Buttes-Chaumont, or to myself, more recently, when she told me that she did not know the place? "Fortunately," Mme. Bontemps went on, "that poor Andrée will soon be leaving for a more bracing country, for the real country, she needs it badly, she is not looking at all well. It is true that she did not have an opportunity this summer of getting the fresh air she requires. Just think, she left Balbec at the end of July, expecting to go back there in September, and then her brother put his knee out, and she was unable to go back." So Albertine was expecting her at Balbec and had concealed this from me. It is true that it was all the more kind of her to have offered to return to Paris with me. Unless. . . . "Yes, I remember Albertine's mentioning it to me" (this was untrue). "When did the accident occur, again? I am not very clear about it." "Why, to my mind, it occurred in the very nick of time, for a day later the lease of the villa began, and Andrée's grandmother would have had to pay a month's rent for nothing. He hurt his leg on the fourteenth of September, she was in time to telegraph to Albertine on the morning of the fifteenth that she was not coming and Albertine was in time to warn the agent. A day later, the lease would have run on to the middle of October." And so, no doubt, when Albertine, changing her mind, had said to me: "Let us go this evening," what she saw with her mind's eye was an apartment, that of Andrée's grandmother, where, as soon as we returned, she would be able to see the friend whom, without my suspecting it, she had supposed that she would be seeing in a few days at Balbec. Those kind words which she had used, in offering to return to Paris with me, in contrast to her headstrong refusal a little earlier, I had sought to attribute them to a reawakening of her good nature. They were simply and solely the effect of a change that had occurred in a situation which we do not know, and which is the whole secret of the variation of the conduct of the women who are not in love with us. They obstinately refuse to give us an assignation for the morrow, because they are tired, because their grandfather insists upon their dining with him: "But come later," we insist. "He keeps me very late. He may want to see me home." The whole truth is that they have made an appointment with some man whom they like. Suddenly it happens that he is no longer free. And they come to tell us how sorry they are to have disappointed us, that the grandfather can go and hang himself, that there is nothing in the world to keep them from remaining with us. I ought to have recognised these phrases in Albertine's language to me on the day of my departure from Balbec, but to interpret that language I should have needed to remember at the time two special features in Albertine's character which now recurred to my mind, one to console me, the other to make me wretched, for we find a little of everything in our memory; it is a sort of pharmacy, of chemical laboratory, in which our groping hand comes to rest now upon a sedative drug, now upon a dangerous poison. The first, the consoling feature was that habit of making a single action serve the pleasure of several persons, that multiple utilisation of whatever she did, which was typical of Albertine. It was quite in keeping with her character, when she returned to Paris (the fact that Andrée was not coming back might make it inconvenient for her to remain at Balbec, without any implication that she could not exist apart from Andrée), to derive from that single journey an opportunity of touching two people each of whom she genuinely loved, myself, by making me believe that she was coming in order not to let me be alone, so that I should not be unhappy, out of devotion to me, Andrée by persuading her that, as soon as there was no longer any question of her coming to Balbec, she herself did not wish to remain there a moment longer, that she had prolonged her stay there only in the hope of seeing Andrée and was now hurrying back to join her. Now, Albertine's departure with myself was such an immediate sequel, on the one hand to my grief, my desire to return to Paris, on the other hand to Andrée's telegram, that it was quite natural that Andrée and I, unaware, respectively, she of my grief, I of her telegram, should have supposed that Albertine's departure from Balbec was the effect of the one cause that each of us knew, which indeed it followed at so short an interval and so unexpectedly. And in this case, I might still believe that the thought of keeping me company had been Albertine's real object, while she had not chosen to overlook an opportunity of thereby establishing a claim to Andrée's gratitude. But unfortunately I remembered almost at once another of Albertine's characteristics, which was the vivacity with which she was gripped by the irresistible temptation of a pleasure. And so I recalled how, when she had decided to leave, she had been so impatient to get to the tram, how she had pushed past the Manager who, as he tried to detain us, might have made us miss the omnibus, the shrug of connivance that she had given me, by which I had been so touched, when, on the crawler, M. de Cambremer had asked us whether we could not 'postpone it by a week.' Yes, what she saw before her eyes at that moment, what made her so feverishly anxious to leave, what she was so impatient to see again was that emptied apartment which I had once visited, the home of Andrée's grandmother, left in charge of an old footman, a luxurious apartment, facing south, but so empty, so silent, that the sun appeared to have spread dust-sheets over the sofa, the armchairs of the room in which Albertine and Andrée would ask the respectful caretaker, perhaps unsuspecting, perhaps an accomplice, to allow them to rest for a while. I could always see it now, empty, with a bed or a sofa, that room, to which, whenever Albertine seemed pressed for time and serious, she set off to meet her friend, who had doubtless arrived there before her since her time was more her own. I had never before given a thought to that apartment which now possessed for me a horrible beauty. The unknown element in the lives of other people is like that in nature, which each fresh scientific discovery merely reduces, but does not abolish. A jealous lover exasperates the woman with whom he is in love by depriving her of a thousand unimportant pleasures, but those pleasures which are the keystone of her life she conceals in a place where, in the moments in which he thinks that he is shewing the most intelligent perspicacity and third parties are keeping him most closely informed, he never dreams of looking. Anyhow, Andrée was at least going to leave Paris. But I did not wish that Albertine should be in a position to despise me as having been the dupe of herself and Andrée. One of these days, I would tell her. And thus I should force her perhaps to speak to me more frankly, by shewing her that I was informed, all the same, of the things that she concealed from me. But I did not wish to mention it to her for the moment, first of all because, so soon after her aunt's visit, she would guess from where my information came, would block that source and would not dread other, unknown sources. Also because I did not wish to risk, so long as I was not absolutely certain of keeping Albertine for as long as I chose, arousing in her too frequent irritations which might have the effect of making her decide to leave me. It is true that if I reasoned, sought the truth, prognosticated the future on the basis of her speech, which always approved of all my plans, assuring me how much she loved this life, of how little her seclusion deprived her, I had no doubt that she would remain with me always. I was indeed greatly annoyed by the thought, I felt that I was missing life, the universe, which I had never enjoyed, bartered for a woman in whom I could no longer find anything novel. I could not even go to Venice, where, while I lay in bed, I should be too keenly tormented by the fear of the advances that might be made to her by the gondolier, the people in the hotel, the Venetian women. But if I reasoned, on the other hand, upon the other hypothesis, that which rested not upon Albertine's speech, but upon silences, looks, blushes, sulks, and indeed bursts of anger, which I could quite easily have shewn her to be unfounded and which I preferred to appear not to notice, then I said to myself that she was finding this life insupportable, that all the time she found herself deprived of what she loved, and that inevitably she must one day leave me. All that I wished, if she did so, was that I might choose the moment in which it would not be too painful to me, and also that it might be in a season when she could not go to any of the places in which I imagined her debaucheries, either at Amsterdam, or with Andrée whom she would see again, it was true, a few months later. But in the interval I should have grown calm and their meeting would leave me unmoved. In any case, I must wait before I could think of it until I was cured of the slight relapse that had been caused by my discovery of the reasons by which Albertine, at an interval of a few hours, had been determined not to leave, and then to leave Balbec immediately. I must allow time for the symptoms to disappear which could only go on diminishing if I learned nothing new, but which were still too acute not to render more painful, more difficult, an operation of rupture recognised now as inevitable, but in no sense urgent, and one that would be better performed in 'cold blood.' Of this choice of the right moment I was the master, for if she decided to leave me before I had made up my mind, at the moment when she informed me that she had had enough of this life, there would always be time for me to think of resisting her arguments, to offer her a larger freedom, to promise her some great pleasure in the near future which she herself would be anxious to await, at worst, if I could find no recourse save to her heart, to assure her of my grief. I was therefore quite at my ease from this point of view, without, however, being very logical with myself. For, in the hypotheses in which I left out of account the things which she said and announced, I supposed that, when it was a question of her leaving me, she would give me her reasons beforehand, would allow me to fight and to conquer them. I felt that my life with Albertine was, on the one hand, when I was not jealous, mere boredom, and on the other hand, when I was jealous, constant suffering. Supposing that there was any happiness in it, it could not last. I possessed the same spirit of wisdom which had inspired me at Balbec, when, on the evening when we had been happy together

after Mme. de Cambremer's call, I determined to give her up, because I
knew that by prolonging our intimacy I should gain nothing. Only, even
now, I imagined that the memory which I should preserve of her would be
like a sort of vibration prolonged by a pedal from the last moment of our
parting. And so I intended to choose a pleasant moment, so that it might be
it which continued to vibrate in me. It must not be too difficult, I must not
wait too long, I must be prudent. And yet, having waited so long, it would
be madness not to wait a few days longer, until an acceptable moment
should offer itself, rather than risk seeing her depart with that same sense
of revolt which I had felt in the past when Mamma left my bedside without
bidding me good night, or when she said good-bye to me at the station. At
all costs I multiplied the favours that I was able to bestow upon her. As
for the Fortuny gowns, we had at length decided upon one in blue and
gold lined with pink which was just ready. And I had ordered, at the same
time, the other five which she had relinquished with regret, out of preference
for this last. Yet with the coming of spring, two months after her aunt's
conversation with me, I allowed myself to be carried away by anger one
evening. It was the very evening on which Albertine had put on for the
first time the indoor gown in gold and blue by Fortuny which, by reminding
me of Venice, made me feel all the more strongly what I was sacrificing for
her, who felt no corresponding gratitude towards me. If I had never seen
Venice, I had dreamed of it incessantly since those Easter holidays which,
when still a boy, I had been going to spend there, and earlier still, since the
Titian prints and Giotto photographs which Swann had given me long ago
at Combray. The Fortuny gown which Albertine was wearing that evening
seemed to me the tempting phantom of that invisible Venice. It swarmed
with Arabic ornaments, like the Venetian palaces hidden like sultanas behind a screen of pierced stone, like the bindings in the Ambrosian library,
like the columns from which the Oriental birds that symbolised alter-
natively life and death were repeated in the mirror of the fabric, of an intense blue which, as my gaze extended over it, was changed into a malleable
gold, by those same transmutations which, before the advancing gondolas,
change into flaming metal the azure of the Grand Canal. And the sleeves
were lined with a cherry pink which is so peculiarly Venetian that it is called
Tiepolo pink.

In the course of the day, Françoise had let fall in my hearing that Albertine was satisfied with nothing, that when I sent word to her that I
would be going out with her, or that I would not be going out, that the motor-car would come to fetch her, or would not come, she almost shrugged
her shoulders and would barely give a polite answer. This evening, when I
felt that she was in a bad temper, and when the first heat of summer had
wrought upon my nerves, I could not restrain my anger and reproached
her with her ingratitude. "Yes, you can ask anybody," I shouted at the top
of my voice, quite beyond myself, "you can ask Françoise, it is common
knowledge." But immediately I remembered how Albertine had once told
me how terrifying she found me when I was angry, and had applied to myself the speech of Esther:

Jugez combien ce front irrité contre moi
Dans mon âme troublée a dû jeter d'émoi.
Hélas sans frissonner quel cœur audacieux
Soutiendrait les éclairs qui partent de ses yeux.

I felt ashamed of my violence. And, to make reparation for what I had done, without, however, acknowledging a defeat, so that my peace might be an armed and awe-inspiring peace, while at the same time I thought it as well to shew her once again that I was not afraid of a rupture so that she might not feel any temptation to break with me: "Forgive me, my little Albertine, I am ashamed of my violence, I don't know how to apologise. If we are not able to get on together, if we are to be obliged to part, it must not be in this fashion, it would not be worthy of us. We will part, if part we must, but first of all I wish to beg your pardon most humbly and from the bottom of my heart." I decided that, to atone for my rudeness and also to make certain of her intention to remain with me for some time to come, at any rate until Andrée should have left Paris, which would be in three weeks, it would be as well, next day, to think of some pleasure greater than any that she had yet had and fairly slow in its fulfilment; also, since I was going to wipe out the offence that I had given her, perhaps I should do well to take advantage of this moment to shew her that I knew more about her life than she supposed. The resentment that she would feel would be removed on the morrow by my kindness, but the warning would remain in her mind. "Yes, my little Albertine, forgive me if I was violent. I am not quite as much to blame as you think. There are wicked people in the world who are trying to make us quarrel; I have always refrained from mentioning this, as I did not wish to torment you. But sometimes I am driven out of my mind by certain accusations. For instance," I went on, "they are tormenting me at present, they are persecuting me with reports of your relations, but with Andrée." "With Andrée?" she cried, her face ablaze with anger. And astonishment or the desire to appear astonished made her open her eyes wide. "How charming! And may one know who has been telling you these pretty tales, may I be allowed to speak to these persons, to learn from them upon what they are basing their scandals?" "My little Albertine, I do not know, the letters are anonymous, but from people whom you would perhaps have no difficulty in finding" (this to shew her that I did not believe that she would try) "for they must know you quite well. The last one, I must admit (and I mention it because it deals with a trifle, and there is nothing at all unpleasant in it), made me furious all the same. It informed me that if, on the day when we left Balbec, you first of all wished to remain there and then decided to go, that was because in the interval you had received a letter from Andrée telling you that she was not coming." "I know quite well that Andrée wrote to tell me that she wasn't coming, in fact she telegraphed; I can't shew you the telegram because I didn't keep it, but it wasn't that day; what difference do you suppose it could make to me whether Andrée came or not?" The words "what difference do you suppose it could make to me" were a proof of anger and that 'it did make' some difference, but were not necessarily a proof that Albertine had returned to Paris solely from a desire to see Andrée. Whenever Albertine saw one of the real or alleged motives of one of her actions discovered by a person to whom she had pleaded a different motive, she became angry, even if the person were he for whose sake she had really performed the action. That Albertine believed that this information as to what she had been doing was not furnished me in anonymous letters against my will but was eagerly demanded by myself, could never have been deduced from the words which she next uttered, in which she appeared to accept my story of the anonymous letters, but rather from her air of anger with myself, an anger which appeared to be merely the explosion of her previous ill humour, just as the espionage in which, by this hypothesis, she must suppose that I had been indulging would have been only the culmination of a supervision of all her actions as to which she had felt no doubt for a long time past. Her anger extended even to Andrée herself, and deciding no doubt that from now onwards I should never be calm again even when she went out with Andrée: "Besides, Andrée makes me wild. She is a deadly bore. I never want to go anywhere with her again. You can tell that to the people who informed you that I came back to Paris for her sake. Suppose I were to tell you that after all the years I've known Andrée, I couldn't even describe her face to you, I've hardly ever looked at it!" Now at Balbec, in that first year, she had said to me: "Andrée is lovely." It is true that this did not mean that she had had amorous relations with her, and indeed I had never heard her speak at that time save with indignation of any relations of that sort. But could she not have changed even without being aware that she had changed, never supposing that her amusements with a girl friend were the same thing as the immoral relations, not clearly defined in her own mind, which she condemned in other women? Was it not possible also that this same change, and this same unconsciousness of change, might have occurred in her relations with myself, whose kisses she had repulsed at Balbec with such indignation, kisses which afterwards she was to give me of her own accord every day, which (so, at least, I hoped) she would give me for a long time to come, and which she was going to give me in a moment? "But, my darling, how do you expect me to tell them when I do not know who they are?" This answer was so forceful that it ought to have melted the objections and doubts which I saw crystallised in Albertine's pupils. But it left them intact. I was now silent, and yet she continued to gaze at me with that persistent attention which we give to some one who has not finished speaking. I begged her pardon once more. She replied that she had nothing to forgive me. She had grown very gentle again. But, beneath her sad and troubled features, it seemed to me that a secret had taken shape. I knew quite well that she could not leave me without warning me, besides she could not either wish to leave me (it was in a week's time that she was to try on the new Fortuny gowns), nor decently do so, as my mother was returning to Paris at the end of the week and her aunt also. Why, since it was impossible for her to depart, did I repeat to her several times that we should be going out together next day to look at some Venetian glass which I wished to give her, and why was I comforted when I heard her say that that was settled? When it was time for her to bid me good night and I kissed her, she did not behave as usual, but turned aside —it was barely a minute or two since I had been thinking how pleasant it was that she now gave me every evening what she had refused me at Balbec —she did not return my kiss. One would have said that, having quarrelled with me, she was not prepared to give me a token of affection which might later on have appeared to me a treacherous denial of that quarrel. One would have said that she was attuning her actions to that quarrel, and yet with moderation, whether so as not to announce it, or because, while breaking off her carnal relations with me, she wished still to remain my friend. I embraced her then a second time, pressing to my heart the mirroring and gilded azure of the Grand Canal and the mating birds, symbols of death and resurrection. But for the second time she drew away and, instead of returning my kiss, withdrew with the sort of instinctive and fatal obstinacy of animals that feel the hand of death. This presentiment which she seemed to be expressing overpowered me also, and filled me with so anxious an alarm that when she had reached the door I had not the courage to let her go, and called her back. "Albertine," I said to her, "I am not at all sleepy. If you don't want to go to sleep yourself, you might stay here a little longer, if you like, but I don't really mind, and I don't on any account want to tire you." I felt that if I had been able to make her undress, and to have her there in her white nightgown, in which she seemed more rosy, warmer, in which she excited my senses more keenly, the reconciliation would have been more complete. But I hesitated for an instant, for the blue border of her gown added to her face a beauty, an illumination, a sky without which she would have seemed to me more harsh. She came back slowly and said to me very sweetly, and still with the same downcast, sorrowful expression: "I can stay as long as you like, I am not sleepy." Her reply calmed me, for, so long as she was in the room, I felt that I could take thought for the future and that moreover it implied friendship, obedience, but of a certain sort, which seemed to me to be bounded by that secret which I felt to exist behind her sorrowful gaze, her altered manner, partly in spite of herself, partly no doubt to attune them beforehand to something which I did not know. I felt that, all the same, I needed only to have her all in white, with her throat bare, in front of me, as I had seen her at Balbec in bed, to find the courage which would make her obliged to yield. "Since you are so kind as to stay here a moment to console me, you ought to take off your gown, it is too hot, too stiff, I dare not approach you for fear of crumpling that fine stuff and we have those symbolic birds between us. Undress, my darling." "No, I couldn't possibly take off this dress here. I shall undress in my own room presently." "Then you won't even come and sit down on my bed?" "Why, of course." She remained, however, a little way from me, by my feet. We talked. I know that I then uttered the word death, as though Albertine were about to die. It seems that events are larger than the moment in which they occur and cannot confine themselves in it. Certainly they overflow into the future through the memory that we retain of them, but they demand a place also in the time that precedes them. One may say that we do not then see them as they are to be, but in memory are they not modified also?

When I saw that she deliberately refrained from kissing me, realising that I was merely wasting my time, that it was only after the kiss that the soothing, the genuine minutes would begin, I said to her: "Good night, it is too late," because that would make her kiss me and we could then continue. But after saying: "Good night, see you sleep well," exactly as she had done twice already, she contented herself with letting me kiss her on the cheek. This time I dared not call her back, but my heart beat so violently that I could not lie down again. Like a bird that flies from one end of its cage to the other, without stopping I passed from the anxiety lest Albertine should leave the house to a state of comparative calm. This calm was produced by the argument which I kept on repeating several times every minute: "She cannot go without warning me, she never said anything about going," and I was more or less calmed. But at once I reminded myself: "And yet if to-morrow I find that she has gone. My very anxiety must be founded upon something; why did she not kiss me?" At this my heart ached horribly. Then it was slightly soothed by the argument which I advanced once more, but I ended with a headache, so incessant and monotonous was this movement of my thoughts. There are thus certain mental states, and especially anxiety, which, as they offer us only two alternatives, are in a way as atrociously circumscribed as a merely physical pain. I perpetually repeated the argument which justified my anxiety and that which proved it false and reassured me, within as narrow a space as the sick man who explores without ceasing, by an internal movement, the organ that is causing his suffering, and withdraws for an instant from the painful spot to return to it a moment later. Suddenly, in the silence of the night, I was startled by a sound apparently insignificant which, however, filled me with terror, the sound of Albertine's window being violently opened. When I heard no further sound, I asked myself why this had caused me such alarm. In itself there was nothing so extraordinary; but I probably gave it two interpretations which appalled me equally. In the first place it was one of the conventions of our life in common, since I was afraid of draughts, that nobody must ever open a window at night. This had been explained to Albertine when she came to stay in the house, and albeit she was convinced that this was a mania on my part and thoroughly unhealthy, she had promised me that she would never break the rule. And she was so timorous about everything that she knew to be my wish, even if she blamed me for it, that she would have gone to sleep with the stench of a chimney on fire rather than open her window, just as, however important the circumstances, she would not have had me called in the morning. It was only one of the minor conventions of our life, but from the moment when she violated it without having said anything to me, did not that mean that she no longer needed to take precautions, that she would violate them all just as easily? Besides, the sound had been violent, almost ill-bred, as though she had flung the window open crimson with rage, and saying: "This life is stifling me, so that's that, I must have air!" I did not exactly say all this to myself, but I continued to think, as of a presage more mysterious and

more funereal than the hoot of an owl, of that sound of the window which
Albertine had opened. Filled with an agitation such as I had not felt perhaps since the evening at Combray when Swann had been dining downstairs, I paced the corridor for a long time, hoping, by the noise that I
made, to attract Albertine's attention, hoping that she would take pity
upon me and would call me to her, but I heard no sound come from her
room. Gradually I began to feel that it was too late. She must long have
been asleep. I went back to bed. In the morning, as soon as I awoke,
since no one ever came to my room, whatever might have happened, without a summons, I rang for Françoise. And at the same time I thought: "I
must speak to Albertine about a yacht which I mean to have built for her."
As I took my letters I said to Françoise without looking at her: "Presently
I shall have something to say to Mlle. Albertine; is she out of bed yet?"
"Yes, she got up early." I felt arise in me, as in a sudden gust of wind, a
thousand anxieties, which I was unable to keep in suspense in my bosom.
The tumult there was so great that I was quite out of breath as though
caught in a tempest. "Ah! But where is she just now?" "I expect she's in
her room." "Ah! Good! Very well, I shall see her presently." I breathed
again, she was still in the house, my agitation subsided. Albertine was
there, it was almost immaterial to me whether she was or not. Besides, had
it not been absurd to suppose that she could possibly not be there? I fell
asleep, but, in spite of my certainty that she would not leave me, into a
light sleep and of a lightness relative to her alone. For by the sounds that
could be connected only with work in the courtyard, while I heard them
vaguely in my sleep, I remained unmoved, whereas the slightest rustle
that came from her room, when she left it, or noiselessly returned, pressing
the bell so gently, made me start, ran through my whole body, left me
with a throbbing heart, albeit I had heard it in a profound slumber, just
as my grandmother in the last days before her death, when she was
plunged in an immobility which nothing could disturb and which the doctors called coma, would begin, I was told, to tremble for a moment like a
leaf when she heard the three rings with which I was in the habit of sum-
moning Françoise, and which, even when I made them softer, during that
week, so as not to disturb the silence of the death-chamber, nobody,
Françoise assured me, could mistake, because of a way that I had, and was
quite unconscious of having, of pressing the bell, for the ring of anyone
else. Had I then entered myself into my last agony, was this the approach
of death?

That day and the next we went out together, since Albertine refused to
go out again with Andrée. I never even mentioned the yacht to her. These
excursions had completely restored my peace of mind. But she had continued at night to embrace me in the same novel fashion, which left me
furious. I could interpret it now in no other way than as a method of
shewing me that she was cross with me, which seemed to me perfectly
absurd after my incessant kindness to her. And so, no longer deriving from
her even those carnal satisfactions on which I depended, finding her positively ugly in her ill humour, I felt all the more keenly my deprivation of
all the women and of the travels for which these first warm days re-

awakened my desire. Thanks no doubt to the scattered memory of the forgotten assignations that I had had, while still a schoolboy, with women, beneath trees already in full leaf, this springtime region in which the endless round of our dwelling-place travelling through the seasons had halted for the last three days, beneath a clement sky, and from which all the roads pointed towards picnics in the country, boating parties, pleasure trips, seemed to me to be the land of women just as much as it was the land of trees, and the land in which a pleasure that was everywhere offered became permissible to my convalescent strength. Resigning myself to idleness, resigning myself to chastity, to tasting pleasure only with a woman whom I did not love, resigning myself to remaining shut up in my room, to not travelling, all this was possible in the Old World in which we had been only the day before, in the empty world of winter, but was no longer possible in this new universe bursting with green leaves, in which I had awaked like a young Adam faced for the first time with the problem of existence, of happiness, who is not bowed down beneath the weight of the accumulation of previous negative solutions. Albertine's presence weighed upon me, and so I regarded her sullenly, feeling that it was a pity that we had not had a rupture. I wanted to go to Venice, I wanted in the meantime to go to the Louvre to look at Venetian pictures and to the Luxembourg to see the two Elstirs which, as I had just heard, the Duchesse de Guermantes had recently sold to that gallery, those that I had so greatly admired, the *Pleasures of the Dance* and the *Portrait of the X Family*. But I was afraid that, in the former, certain lascivious poses might give Albertine a desire, a regretful longing for popular rejoicings, making her say to herself that perhaps a certain life which she had never led, a life of fireworks and country taverns, was not so bad. Already, in anticipation, I was afraid lest, on the Fourteenth of July, she would ask me to take her to a popular ball and I dreamed of some impossible event which would cancel the national holiday. And besides, there were also present, in Elstir's pictures, certain nude female figures in the leafy landscapes of the South which might make Albertine think of certain pleasures, albeit Elstir himself (but would she not lower the standard of his work?) had seen in them nothing more than plastic beauty, or rather the beauty of snowy monuments which is assumed by the bodies of women seated among verdure. And so I resigned myself to abandoning that pleasure and made up my mind to go to Versailles. Albertine had remained in her room, reading, in her Fortuny gown. I asked her if she would like to go with me to Versailles. She had the charming quality of being always ready for anything, perhaps because she had been accustomed in the past to spend half her time as the guest of other people, and, just as she had made up her mind to come to Paris, in two minutes, she said to me: "I can come as I am, we shan't be getting out of the car." She hesitated for a moment between two cloaks in which to conceal her indoor dress—as she might have hesitated between two friends in the choice of an escort—chose one of dark blue, an admirable choice, thrust a pin into a hat. In a minute, she was ready, before I had put on my greatcoat, and we went to Versailles. This very promptitude, this absolute docility left me more reassured, as though indeed, without having any special reason for uneasiness, I had been in need of reassurance. "After all I have nothing to fear, she does everything that I ask, in spite of the noise she made with her window the other night. The moment I spoke of going out, she flung that blue cloak over her gown and out she came, that is not what a rebel would have done, a person who was no longer on friendly terms with me," I said to myself as we went to Versailles. We stayed there a long time. The whole sky was formed of that radiant and almost pale blue which the wayfarer lying down in a field sees at times above his head, but so consistent, so intense, that he feels that the blue of which it is composed has been utilised without any alloy and with such an inexhaustible richness that one might delve more and more deeply into its substance without encountering an atom of anything but that same blue. I thought of my grandmother who—in human art as in nature—loved grandeur, and who used to enjoy watching the steeple of Saint-Hilaire soar into the same blue. Suddenly I felt once again a longing for my lost freedom as I heard a sound which I did not at first identify, a sound which my grandmother would have loved as well. It was like the buzz of a wasp. "Why," said Albertine, "there is an aeroplane, it is high up in the sky, so high." I looked in every direction but could see only, unmarred by any black spot, the unbroken pallor of the serene azure. I continued nevertheless to hear the humming of the wings which suddenly came into my field of vision. Up there a pair of tiny wings, dark and flashing, punctured the continuous blue of the unalterable sky. I had at length been able to attach the buzzing to its cause, to that little insect throbbing up there in the sky, probably quite five thousand feet above me; I could see it hum. Perhaps at a time when distances by land had not yet been habitually shortened by speed as they are to-day, the whistle of a passing train a mile off was endowed with that beauty which now and for some time to come will stir our emotions in the hum of an aeroplane five thousand feet up, with the thought that the distances traversed in this vertical journey are the same as those on the ground, and that in this other direction, where the measurements appeared to us different because it had seemed impossible to make the attempt, an aeroplane at five thousand feet is no farther away than a train a mile off, is indeed nearer, the identical trajectory occurring in a purer medium, with no separation of the traveller from his starting point, just as on the sea or across the plains, in calm weather, the wake of a ship that is already far away or the breath of a single zephyr will furrow the ocean of water or of grain.

"After all neither of us is really hungry, we might have looked in at the Verdurins'," Albertine said to me, "this is their day and their hour." "But I thought you were angry with them?" "Oh! There are all sorts of stories about them, but really they're not so bad as all that. Madame Verdurin has always been very nice to me. Besides, one can't keep on quarrelling all the time with everybody. They have their faults, but who hasn't?" "You are not dressed, you would have to go home and dress, that would make us very late." I added that I was hungry. "Yes, you are right, let us eat by ourselves," replied Albertine with that marvellous docility which continued to stupefy me. We stopped at a big pastrycook's, situated almost

outside the town, which at that time enjoyed a certain reputation. A lady
was leaving the place, and asked the girl in charge for her things. And
after the lady had gone, Albertine cast repeated glances at the girl as
though she wished to attract her attention while the other was putting
away cups, plates, cakes, for it was getting late. She came near me only if
I asked for something. And what happened then was that as the girl, who
moreover was extremely tall, was standing up while she waited upon us
and Albertine was seated beside me, each time, Albertine, in an attempt to
attract her attention, raised vertically towards her a sunny gaze which
compelled her to elevate her pupils to an even higher angle since, the girl
being directly in front of us, Albertine had not the remedy of tempering
the angle with the obliquity of her gaze. She was obliged, without raising
her head unduly, to make her eyes ascend to that disproportionate height
at which the girl's eyes were situated. Out of consideration for myself,
Albertine lowered her own at once, and, as the girl had paid her no attention, began again. This led to a series of vain imploring elevations before
an inaccessible deity. Then the girl had nothing left to do but to put
straight a big table, next to ours. Now Albertine's gaze need only be
natural. But never once did the girl's eyes rest upon my mistress. This did
not surprise me, for I knew that the woman, with whom I was slightly
acquainted, had lovers, although she was married, but managed to conceal
her intrigues completely, which astonished me vastly in view of her prodigious stupidity. I studied the woman while we finished eating. Concentrated upon her task, she was almost impolite to Albertine, in the sense
that she had not a glance to spare for her, not that Albertine's attitude was
not perfectly correct. The other arranged things, went on arranging things,
without letting anything distract her. The counting and putting away
of the coffee-spoons, the fruit-knives, might have been entrusted not to
this large and handsome woman, but, by a 'labour-saving' device, to a
mere machine, and you would not have seen so complete an isolation
from Albertine's attention, and yet she did not lower her eyes, did not let
herself become absorbed, allowed her eyes, her charms to shine in an
undivided attention to her work. It is true that if this woman had not been
a particularly foolish person (not only was this her reputation, but I knew
it by experience), this detachment might have been a supreme proof of her
cunning. And I know very well that the stupidest person, if his desire or
his pocket is involved, can, in that sole instance, emerging from the nullity
of his stupid life, adapt himself immediately to the workings of the most
complicated machinery; all the same, this would have been too subtle a
supposition in the case of a woman as idiotic as this. Her idiocy even assumed the improbable form of impoliteness! Never once did she look at
Albertine whom, after all, she could not help seeing. It was not very flattering for my mistress, but, when all was said, I was delighted that Albertine should receive this little lesson and should see that frequently
women paid no attention to her. We left the pastrycook's, got into our
carriage and were already on our way home when I was seized by a sudden
regret that I had not taken the waitress aside and begged her on no account
to tell the lady who had come out of the shop as we were going in my name

and address, which she must know because of the orders I had constantly
left with her. It was indeed undesirable that the lady should be enabled
thus to learn, indirectly, Albertine's address. But I felt that it would be a
waste of time to turn back for so small a matter, and that I should appear
to be attaching too great an importance to it in the eyes of the idiotic and
untruthful waitress. I decided, finally, that I should have to return there,
in a week's time, to make this request, and that it was a great bore, since
one always forgot half the things that one had to say, to have to do even
the simplest things in instalments. In this connexion, I cannot tell you how
densely, now that I come to think of it, Albertine's life was covered in a
network of alternate, fugitive, often contradictory desires. No doubt falsehood complicated this still further, for, as she retained no accurate memory
of our conversations, when she had said to me: "Ah! That's a pretty girl, if
you like, and a good golfer," and I had asked the girl's name, she had answered with that detached, universal, superior air of which no doubt there
is always enough and to spare, for every liar of this category borrows it for
a moment when he does not wish to answer a question, and it never fails
him: "Ah! That I don't know" (with regret at her inability to enlighten
me). "I never knew her name, I used to see her on the golf course, but I
didn't know what she was called";—if, a month later, I said to her: "Albertine, you remember that pretty girl you mentioned to me, who plays
golf so well." "Ah, yes," she would answer without thinking: "Emilie
Daltier, I don't know what has become of her." And the lie, like a line of
earthworks, was carried back from the defence of the name, now captured, to the possibilities of meeting her again. "Oh, I can't tell you, I
never knew her address. I never see anybody who could tell you. Oh, no!
Andrée never knew her. She wasn't one of our little band, now so scattered." At other times the lie took the form of a base admission: "Ah! If I
had three hundred thousand francs a year. . . ." She bit her lip. "Well?
What would you do then?" "I should ask you," she said, kissing me as
she spoke, "to allow me to remain with you always. Where else could I be
so happy?" But, even when one took her lies into account, it was incredible
how spasmodic her life was, how fugitive her strongest desires. She would
be mad about a person whom, three days later, she would refuse to see.
She could not wait for an hour while I sent out for canvas and colours, for
she wished to start painting again. For two whole days she was impatient,
almost shed the tears, quickly dried, of an infant that has just been weaned
from its nurse. And this instability of her feelings with regard to people,
things, occupations, arts, places, was in fact so universal that, if she did
love money, which I do not believe, she cannot have loved it for longer
than anything else. When she said: "Ah! If I had three hundred thousand
francs a year!" or even if she expressed a bad but very transient thought,
she could not have attached herself to it any longer than to the idea of
going to Les Rochers, of which she had seen an engraving in my grandmother's edition of Mme. de Sévigné, of meeting an old friend from the golf
course, of going up in an aeroplane, of going to spend Christmas with her
aunt, or of taking up painting again.

We returned home very late one evening while, here and there, by the roadside, a pair of red breeches pressed against a skirt revealed an amorous couple. Our carriage passed in through the Porte Maillot. For the monuments of Paris had been substituted, pure, linear, without depth, a drawing of the monuments of Paris, as though in an attempt to recall the appearance of a city that had been destroyed. But, round about this picture, there stood out so delicately the pale-blue mounting in which it was framed that one's greedy eyes sought everywhere for a further trace of that delicious shade which was too sparingly measured out to them: the moon was shining. Albertine admired the moonlight. I dared not tell her that I would have admired it more if I had been alone, or in quest of a strange woman. I repeated to her poetry or passages of prose about moonlight, pointing out to her how from 'silvery' which it had been at one time, it had turned 'blue' in Chateaubriand, in the Victor Hugo of *Eviradnus* and *La Fête chez Thérèse,* to become in turn yellow and metallic in Baudelaire and Leconte de Lisle. Then, reminding her of the image that is used for the crescent moon at the end of *Booz endormi,* I repeated the whole of that poem to her. And so we came to the house. The fine weather that night made a leap forwards as the mercury in the thermometer darts upward. In the early-rising mornings of spring that followed, I could hear the tramcars moving, through a cloud of perfumes, in an air with which the prevailing warmth became more and more blended until it reached the solidification and density of noon. When the unctuous air had succeeded in varnishing with it and isolating in it the scent of the wash-stand, the scent of the wardrobe, the scent of the sofa, simply by the sharpness with which, vertical and erect, they stood out in adjacent but distinct slices, in a pearly chiaroscuro which added a softer glaze to the shimmer of the curtains and the blue satin armchairs, I saw myself, not by a mere caprice of my imagination, but because it was physically possible, following in some new quarter of the suburbs, like that in which Bloch's house at Balbec was situated, the streets blinded by the sun, and finding in them not the dull butchers' shops and the white freestone facings, but the country diningroom which I could reach in no time, and the scents that I would find there on my arrival, that of the bowl of cherries and apricots, the scent of cider, that of gruyère cheese, held in suspense in the luminous congelation of shadow which they delicately vein like the heart of an agate, while the knife-rests of prismatic glass scatter rainbows athwart the room or paint the waxcloth here and there with peacock-eyes. Like a wind that swells in a regular progression, I heard with joy a motor-car beneath the window. I smelt its odour of petrol. It may seem regrettable to the over-sensitive (who are always materialists) for whom it spoils the country, and to certain thinkers (materialists after their own fashion also) who, believing in the importance of facts, imagine that man would be happier, capable of higher flights of poetry, if his eyes were able to perceive more colours, his nostrils to distinguish more scents, a philosophical adaptation of the simple thought of those who believe that life was finer when men wore, instead of the black coats of to-day, sumptuous costumes. But to me (just as an aroma, unpleasant perhaps in itself, of naphthaline and flowering grasses would have thrilled me by giving me back the blue purity of the sea on the day of my arrival at Balbec), this smell of petrol which, with the smoke from the exhaust of the car, had so often melted into the pale azure, on those scorching days when I used to drive from Saint-Jean de la Haise to Gourville, as it had accompanied me on my excursions during those summer afternoons when I had left Albertine painting, called into blossom now on either side of me, for all that I was lying in my darkened bedroom, cornflowers, poppies and red clover, intoxicated me like a country scent, not circumscribed and fixed, like that which is spread before the hawthorns and, retained in its unctuous and dense elements, floats with a certain stability before the hedge, but like a scent before which the roads took flight, the sun's face changed, castles came hurrying to meet me, the sky turned pale, force was increased tenfold, a scent which was like a symbol of elastic motion and power, and which revived the desire that I had felt at Balbec, to enter the cage of steel and crystal, but this time not to go any longer on visits to familiar houses with a woman whom I knew too well, but to make love in new places with a woman unknown. A scent that was accompanied at every moment by the horns of passing motors, which I set to words like a military call: "Parisian, get up, get up, come out and picnic in the country, and take a boat on the river, under the trees, with a pretty girl; get up, get up!" And all these musings were so agreeable that I congratulated myself upon the 'stern decree' which prescribed that until I should have rung my bell, no 'timid mortal,' whether Françoise or Albertine, should dream of coming in to disturb me 'within this palace' where

> ". . . a terrible
> Majesty makes me all invisible
> To my subjects."

But all of a sudden the scene changed; it was the memory, no longer of old impressions, but of an old desire, quite recently reawakened by the Fortuny gown in blue and gold, that spread itself before me, another spring, a spring not leafy at all but suddenly stripped, on the contrary, of its trees and flowers by the name that I had just uttered to myself: 'Venice,' a decanted spring, which is reduced to its essential qualities, and expresses the lengthening, the warming, the gradual maturing of its days by the progressive fermentation, not (this time) of an impure soil, but of a blue and virgin water, springlike without bud or blossom, which could answer the call of May only by gleaming facets, carved by that month, harmonising exactly with it in the radiant, unaltering nakedness of its dusky sapphire. And so, no more than the seasons to its unflowering inlets of the sea, do modern years bring any change to the gothic city; I knew it, I could not imagine it, but this was what I longed to contemplate with the same desire which long ago, when I was a boy, in the very ardour of my departure had shattered the strength necessary for the journey; I wished to find myself face to face with my Venetian imaginings, to behold how that divided sea enclosed in its meanderings, like the streams of Ocean, an urbane and refined civilisation, but one that, isolated by their azure belt, had developed by itself, had had its own schools of painting and architecture, to admire that fabulous garden of fruits and birds in coloured stone, flowering in the midst of the sea which kept it refreshed, splashed with its tide against the base of the columns and, on the bold relief of the capitals, like a dark blue eye watching in the shadows, laid patches, which it kept perpetually moving, of light. Yes, I must go, the time had come. Now that Albertine no longer appeared to be cross with me, the possession of her no longer seemed to me a treasure in exchange for which we are prepared to sacrifice every other. For we should have done so only to rid ourselves of a grief, an anxiety which were now appeased. We have succeeded in jumping through the calico hoop through which we thought for a moment that we should never be able to pass. We have lightened the storm, brought back the serenity of the smile. The agonising mystery of a hatred without any known cause, and perhaps without end, is dispelled. Henceforward we find ourselves once more face to face with the problem, momentarily thrust aside, of a happiness which we know to be impossible. Now that life with Albertine had become possible once again, I felt that I could derive nothing from it but misery, since she did not love me; better to part from her in the pleasant moment of her consent which I should prolong in memory. Yes, this was the moment; I must make quite certain of the date on which Andrée was leaving Paris, use all my influence with Mme. Bontemps to make sure that at that moment Albertine should not be able to go either to Holland or to Montjouvain. It would fall to our lot, were we better able to analyse our loves, to see that often women rise in our estimation only because of the dead weight of men with whom we have to compete for them, although we can hardly bear the thought of that competition; the counterpoise removed, the charm of the woman declines. We have a painful and salutary example of this in the predilection that men feel for the women who, before coming to know them, have gone astray, for those women whom they feel to be sinking in perilous quicksands and whom they must spend the whole period of their love in rescuing; a posthumous example, on the other hand, and one that is not at all dramatic, in the man who, conscious of a decline in his affection for the woman whom he loves, spontaneously applies the rules that he has deduced, and, to make sure of his not ceasing to love the woman, places her in a dangerous environment from which he is obliged to protect her daily. (The opposite of the men who insist upon a woman's retiring from the stage even when it was because of her being upon the stage that they fell in love with her.)

When in this way there could be no objection to Albertine's departure, I should have to choose a fine day like this—and there would be plenty of them before long—one on which she would have ceased to matter to me, on which I should be tempted by countless desires, I should have to let her leave the house without my seeing her, then, rising from my bed, making all my preparations in haste, leave a note for her, taking advantage of the fact that as she could not for the time being go to any place the thought of which would upset me, I might be spared, during my travels, from imagining the wicked things that she was perhaps doing—which for that matter seemed to me at the moment to be quite unimportant—and, without seeing her again, might leave for Venice.

I rang for Françoise to ask her to buy me a guide-book and a time-table, as I had done as a boy, when I wished to prepare in advance a journey to Venice, the realisation of a desire as violent as that which I felt at this moment; I forgot that, in the interval, there was a desire which I had attained, without any satisfaction, the desire for Balbec, and that Venice, being also a visible phenomenon, was probably no more able than Balbec to realise an ineffable dream, that of the gothic age, made actual by a springtime sea, and coming at moments to stir my soul with an enchanted, caressing, unseizable, mysterious, confused image. Françoise having heard my ring came into the room, in considerable uneasiness as to how I would receive what she had to say and what she had done. "It has been most awkward," she said to me, "that Monsieur is so late in ringing this morning. I didn't know what I ought to do. This morning at eight o'clock Mademoiselle Albertine asked me for her trunks, I dared not refuse her, I was afraid of Monsieur's scolding me if I came and waked him. It was no use my putting her through her catechism, telling her to wait an hour because I expected all the time that Monsieur would ring; she wouldn't have it, she left this letter with me for Monsieur, and at nine o'clock off she went." Then—so ignorant may we be of what we have within us, since I was convinced of my own indifference to Albertine— my breath was cut short, I gripped my heart in my hands suddenly moistened by a perspiration which I had not known since the revelation that my mistress had made on the little tram with regard to Mlle. Vinteuil's friend, without my being able to say anything else than: "Ah! Very good, you did quite right not to wake me, leave me now for a little, I shall ring for you presently."

MARCEL PROUST (1871–1922) was born and died in Paris.
Educated at the Lycée Condorcet, he did one year's military service and briefly studied law and political science.
Proust's charm and ambition gained him entrance to the
salons of Parisian society—the setting that provides the
background for *A la recherche du temps perdu.* After
his mother's death in 1905 Proust, suffering from asthma,
retreated from active social life and secluded himself in
a cork-lined room in his Paris apartment. From 1910 on
he was at work on *A la recherche du temps perdu,* publishing the first volume at his own expense in 1913. In
1920 the second volume won him the Prix Goncourt.
Until his death in 1922 he continued writing and re-
writing his monumental work.

A free catalogue of VINTAGE BOOKS *will be sent at your request. Write to* Vintage Books, 457 Madison Avenue, New York, New York 10022.

A free catalogue of VINTAGE BOOKS *will be sent at your request. Write to* Vintage Books, 457 Madison Avenue, New York, New York 10022.

VINTAGE BELLES-LETTRES

VINTAGE HISTORY—AMERICAN

A free catalogue of VINTAGE BOOKS *will be sent at your request. Write to* Vintage Books, 457 Madison Avenue, New York, New York 10022.

A free catalogue of VINTAGE BOOKS *will be sent at your request. Write to* Vintage Books, 457 Madison Avenue, New York, New York 10022.